CAPTURED ON KAUAI

R. BARRI FLOWERS

In memory of my beloved mother, Marjah Aljean, a lifelong fan of Mills & Boon romances, who provided me the tools needed to find success in both my professional and personal lives. To Loraine, the one and only love of my life, whose support has been steadfast through the many years together. And to the loyal fans of my romance, mystery, suspense and thriller fiction published over the years. Lastly, a nod goes out to my super editors, Allison Lyons and Denise Zaza, for the opportunity to become a valued part of Mills & Boon Heroes.

CAPTURED ON KAUAI

R. BARRI FLOWERS

COLTON'S ROGUE INVESTIGATION

JENNIFER D. BOKAL

MILLS & BOON

First Published in Great Britain 2022
by Mills & Boon, an imprint of HarperCollins*Publishers* Ltd
1 London Bridge Street, London, SE1 9GF

www.harpercollins.co.uk

HarperCollins*Publishers*
1st Floor, Watermarque Building,
Ringsend Road, Dublin 4, Ireland

Captured on Kauai © 2022 R. Barri Flowers
Colton's Rogue Investigation © 2022 Harlequin Enterprises ULC

Special thanks and acknowledgement are given to Jennifer D. Bokal for her contribution to *The Coltons of Colorado* series.

ISBN: 978-0-263-30359-9

0922

MIX
Paper | Supporting
responsible forestry
FSC™ C007454

This book is produced from independently certified FSC™ paper to ensure responsible forest management.

For more information visit: www.harpercollins.co.uk/green

Printed and Bound in Spain using 100% Renewable electricity at CPI Black Print, Barcelona

Prologue

Her cover had been blown. DEA Agent Roxanne Yamamoto tensed behind the wheel of her Toyota Tacoma
as she drove down Kaumualii Highway in the dark of
night. Was she being followed? Or was it just her overactive imagination after having to flee for her life? She
had a story to tell, one that Roxanne's colleagues in
the United States Drug Enforcement Administration
would definitely want to hear. As an intelligence research specialist, her job was to identify and analyze
the manufacturing, distribution and trafficking of nar-
cotics, wherever it was happening, and start the process
of dismantling the criminal networks. While working
undercover in her latest assignment, it had taken her to
the Hawaiian island of Kauai. Its moniker, the "Garden
Isle," was apropos, with awesome tropical rainforests
and a lush landscape comprising much of the island. If
only she were afforded the time to take it all in, instead
of being on assignment, trying to put the brakes on one
branch of a Western United States drug-trafficking network that marred paradise with its ugliness, turning people into addicts and criminals. Maybe someday.

Roxanne's thoughts turned back to the unsettling moment at hand. She was able to get enough incriminat-

ing information to lead to a full-scale investigation and some arrests. Turned out that the leads they followed proved productive in targeting the operation and some of its operatives. If she survived this, it would no doubt be a feather in her cap and lead to bigger and better assignments. Maybe she would take some time off and work on her love life, which was sorely lacking at the moment, having broken up with her cheating boyfriend six months ago. Or maybe she was better off without all the drama relationships seemed to bring like a daytime soap opera.

Again, she looked up at the rearview mirror to see if anyone was on her tail. No one. Or was this meant to somehow give her a false sense of security now that she had seemingly managed to get away while still in one piece? She reached into the pocket of her flare jeans for her cell phone, needing to let other members of the Drug Task Force assigned to the case know she was in trouble. It wasn't there. Damn. In her haste to get away, she must have left the phone at the cottage she was renting when escaping from her pursuers through the back door. Also left behind was her laptop containing crucial information and incriminating evidence in the investigation.

Only then did Roxanne spot the bright car lights from behind. Someone was following her. And gaining ground. She couldn't make out the driver. Panicked, she increased her own speed, noting that there was virtually no traffic at this time of night to slow her down. She reached down to her waist holster and felt the cold steel of her Glock 17 duty pistol. This gave her some comfort, knowing if push came to shove she might need to use it in self-defense against the enemy.

After she had managed to put some distance between

her and the other vehicle, Roxanne's sense of comfort faded quickly, as the other car rapidly caught up to her. Again, she picked up her speed, hoping to escape to safety. When the pursuer inexplicably slowed down, for a brief moment she wondered if the chase had been entirely in her head. Only upon realizing she was going way too fast to maneuver the car safely, did Roxanne press down on the brakes. Instead of the car decreasing speed, it was just the opposite. She slammed her foot on the brakes again and realized that they weren't working. Had they been tampered with?

I have to get through this, she thought with determination. But before she could attempt to find some way to bring the car to a stop and continue to live her life and build upon her career, Roxanne lost control of the vehicle, crashing into a utility pole with blunt force. There was nothing after that.

Chapter One

DEA special agent Dex Adair prepared to enter the warehouse in Downtown Los Angeles. He and the team of other agents and members of the Los Angeles County Sheriff's Narcotic Bureau, armed with Glocks, Rock River Arms LAR-15 semiautomatic carbines and Remington 870 12-gauge shotguns, stormed the building. They were in search of illegal marijuana, following a months-long investigation of a crime syndicate that had trafficked drugs in California, Nevada and Hawaii. It was a reflection of the flourishing black market in existence for drugs, despite the legality of recreational marijuana in some states and elsewhere.

Dex expected resistance, knowing those operating the lucrative illicit business were unlikely to give up and spend years, if not decades, in prison without a major fight. *Bring it on*, he thought, no stranger to danger and facing perilous predicaments in life. Having grown up in the sometimes mean streets of the Motor City, otherwise known as Detroit, day-to-day survival was anything but a given to young African American males. But survive he did, motivated to do so in picking up his bachelor's and master's degrees in criminal justice from Michigan State University, before building a successful career in law enforcement within the United States Department of Justice. At thirty-three and six feet three inches of solid muscle, he was more than capable of holding his own when duty called. So was his trusty companion, Barnabas, a narcotic detection service dog. The male golden retriever, part of a K-9 unit, was reliable in sniffing out illicit drugs. He didn't take kindly to being attacked and could defend himself, and then some, including coming to the rescue of his fellow law enforcement officers. Still, Dex kept the canine safely outside for the time being as the agents and detectives fanned out, catching the suspects off guard and ill prepared to take on the massive presence and firepower they encountered. When it was over, there were casualties on the side of the bad guys, while the good guys emerged virtually unscathed.

Once arrests were made and the building secured, Dex stepped out and returned with Barnabas. He unleashed the canine in the spacious warehouse and allowed him to do his thing. It paid off big-time. "We've got something," Dex called out excitedly to the team as his hard, coal-gray eyes focused on the pallets attracting the attention of Barnabas.

"Don't keep us in suspense, Adair," Agent Lynda Krause snapped with anticipation. The long-legged, green-eyed forty-year-old had a short, platinum layered bob and an attitude befitting her seventeen years with the DEA. "What do we get for our trouble?"

Dex grinned and scratched his forehead, if only to keep her waiting a little longer, before donning vinyl disposable gloves. He grabbed a crowbar left behind by the perps and ripped open a pallet, causing his eyes to light up. "This treat…" It contained vacuum-sealed cannabis. Opening up another and another revealed much of the same.

"Wow!" Lynda marveled at the haul. "This place is loaded with pallets of the stuff."

"Tell me about it." Dex petted Barnabas behind his ear. "Good job, boy."

"There's cannabis edibles, THC vaping cartridges and psilocybin mushroom bars…" commented Agent Sylvester Ishikawa, his brown eyes wide with disbelief as he opened another pallet. At forty-two, the slender fifteen-year veteran of the DEA was Japanese and had short dark hair worn in an undercut that was slicked backward. "Looks like they made sure there was something for everyone."

"And now no one," quipped Dex, knowing that the illegal drugs would ultimately be destroyed. Barnabas barked, as if happy to take credit for his part.

"Yeah, that's the plan," Ishikawa agreed.

"We're all good with that," Lynda said in support. "The more we can separate the legal from illegal drugs, the better for everyone."

Dex couldn't agree more, having lost his only sister, Rita, years ago to a drug overdose, with heroin the deadly drug of choice. She'd never had a real chance to get cleaned up before being taken away before her time at the tender age of nineteen. He only wished he had been old enough to help her overcome the addiction and related poor choices she'd made in her life. With the better part of their job done, the team turned the cleanup work over to the Los Angeles County Sheriff's Department and its crime scene investigators. The DEA would continue to do its part in overturning every rock where illicit drugs and their facilitators were hiding. Dex intended to give Barnabas the rest of the day off, even while knowing that the job of taking on drug cartels and criminal gangs was never ending. Or so it seemed.

Two hours later, the agents had joined others in a conference room at the DEA's Los Angeles Division, which included within its jurisdiction Santa Ana and Ventura, California, Hawaii, Nevada and Guam. The special agent in charge was Rachel Zavatti, a tall and attractive fifty-year-old with hazel eyes and a chin-length gray shag. She had moved up the ladder in a hurry, thanks in large part to a successful takedown a decade ago of a notorious international cartel that was responsible for an illegal marijuana farm in the Midwest. Dex was admittedly impressed with her dedication to the job, which he shared in the absence of any meaningful relationship since ending things with his unfaithful girlfriend, Suzette, two years ago. Right now, this was it for him and he was grateful for the opportunity to put his skills to good use.

"Job well done," Rachel said of their latest bust. "Apart from arresting a number of drug traffickers, including the reputed leader of the syndicate, Louis Johansson, we ended up confiscating roughly thirty pallets of vacuum-sealed cannabis, nearly four hundred pounds of cannabis edibles, thousands of THC vaping cartridges and over six hundred grams of psilocybin mushroom bars. I'd say that's quite a load for one operation."

"Not to mention the AR-15 semiautomatic assault rifles, .223 caliber assault rifles, some handguns and enough ammo to go to war," Dex pitched in, though doubtful this had slipped her mind, thorough as she was.

"Oh, did I fail to mention that?" she quipped good-naturedly. "Leave it up to Adair to cover all the bases."

"Next he'll be telling us he did it all by himself like a superhero," Lynda tossed out with a straight face.

"Or maybe just an average guy who displayed abilities Adair didn't even know he had," Ishikawa said. "Do we need to applaud him, or what?"

Dex chuckled, cool with being part of a team that learned not to take things too seriously, though at times it couldn't be helped. They all knew that when it came to the illicit drug trade and its negative impact on society, it was definitely no laughing matter. "I'd much rather give credit where credit's due," he offered modestly. "Barnabas found the marijuana without giving it a second thought. The K-9 knows his business and makes my job that much easier. If he were here and could do it, I'm sure he'd happily take a bow."

Rachel smiled. "I'm sure you deserve at least half the credit for his productivity. But Barnabas's half is still crucial to our operation." She smoothed creases on her open-front blazer. "In any event, before we start patting each other on the back, there are more important matters to discuss—" Dex noted a distinct change in her expression. She turned to a large presentation display and, using a remote, turned it on. A face appeared on the screen of an Asian female in her early thirties with short black hair in a wedge bob. "Last month, DEA Agent Roxanne Yamamoto was on an undercover operation on Kauai, Hawaii, when she died in an apparent single vehicle crash. What first seemed like an unfortunate accident has proven to be a deliberate act of murder. After a mechanical inspection of the vehicle, it was discovered that Agent Yamamoto's brake lines were cut, causing her to lose control of the car. Moreover, she was driving past midnight and didn't have her cell phone, which suggests that Roxanne was in a hurry to get away from one or more individuals. Both the phone and her laptop are missing, along with any pertinent information they contained, which we have thus far been unable to retrieve."

Dex winced at the sight of Roxanne Yamamoto on the screen. They were friends, hanging out together once after a drug bust in Las Vegas, in which seventy pounds of methamphetamine was seized, resulting in multiple arrests. Roxanne was a nice person who, like him, loved her work and gave her all. She didn't deserve to die, as it turned out, in the line of duty and at such a young age with her whole life still ahead of her.

Rachel switched to another picture. "This is the Maoli Lodge," she said. "It has long been suspected of being a front for drug trafficking with ties to the same crime organization that we busted wide-open today, but we haven't been able to make anything stick. Agent Yamamoto was working undercover there as a housekeeper, hoping to gather information that she could pass on to other agents in the field, as part of a Drug Task Force on drug-related criminality on Kauai that included members of the FBI and IRS, US Postal Inspectors and Kauai Police Department's vice section." Rachel's brow furrowed. "She was killed before Agent Yamamoto was able to tell us what, if anything, she had discovered with respect to criminal activity at the resort location. Though there is an active investigation by the locals into her death and suspicion that there may have been another vehicle involved in the crash, there are no solid leads at the moment as to any suspects." The special agent in charge sighed. "We need to find out what's going on at that lodge, if it's anything illegal, and who is responsible for the loss of one of our own."

She flipped to another image of a biracial male with brown eyes and a curly raven faux-hawk haircut. "Joseph Sizemore, age thirty-six, was the co-owner of the Maoli Lodge. He was being investigated as possibly being involved in the trafficking of drugs. Unfortunately, he died in a mysterious kayaking accident six months ago off the Nāpali Coast, effectively taking him out of the equation, though the probe of Sizemore's potential involvement is still ongoing." Rachel switched to another picture of an adult white female. "Katrina Sizemore is his thirty-two-year-old widow, who co-owned the lodge. Upon Sizemore's death, she took over as the sole owner. She's definitely a person of interest as someone who may be part of the illegal drug-trafficking operation."

Dex took in the image of the striking widow. She had big, bold, blue eyes and a square face with a dimpled chin. Long red hair was parted in the middle with voluminous curls. He imagined what a catch she was for her late husband. But was she also a drug trafficker, using her lodge as a legitimate means to funnel illegal profits?

"How's your piano playing talent these days, Adair?" Rachel got his attention.

Dex looked at her. He had learned to play the piano as a boy, taking lessons from his mother, who was an excellent pianist till the day she passed away five years ago. Though he hardly considered himself a great talent in that regard, Dex did feel he could more than hold his own when called upon to perform in a nonprofessional capacity. Indeed, he had played a few jazz numbers at the retirement party last year of fellow agent Bradley Lancaster. "I play every now and then," Dex said tentatively.

"Perfect." That seemed to be enough for her to consider him to be something akin to a concert pianist. "I need you to familiarize yourself with a few classic Hawaiian tunes."

"Uh, okay…" He cocked a brow, wondering where she was going with this.

"You'll be working undercover as a piano player at the Maoli Lodge," Rachel directed him. "They happen to be looking for a replacement for their pianist who is currently on maternity leave. Operating from the inside can give you a better opportunity to gather intelligence."

Undercover? Dex hesitated. Seriously? He had gone down this road before a time or two, and pulled it off masterfully. But not where it concerned using music in a covert operation. And what about Barnabas? Rachel clearly read his mind as she continued, "You'll be taking your K-9 with you. Fortunately, it's a pet friendly lodge, the perfect cover for Barnabas to see what shows up under his trusty radar. You need to pick up where Agent Yamamoto left off. Is that going to be a problem?"

"Not at all," Dex answered predictably. He could hardly turn down an assignment that apparently cost Roxanne her life. And it would give him the opportunity to take stock of Katrina Sizemore up close and personal. "I'm sure Barnabas will welcome a trip to Hawaii and probably want to stay, once the dust settles."

"Not happening." The special agent in charge put her foot down. "He's much too valuable for us to give up anytime soon."

"Figured as much," he cracked. Not that he would ever even truly consider leaving his best friend behind. Unless, of course, they were able to retire to the island together, which also seemed very unlikely.

"You'll be Dex Matheson for the time being," she informed him, knowing that the cover would only work if it was difficult to prove otherwise. "With Agent Ya-mamoto's death, we need to be extra diligent in protecting your identity till we get what we need to complete the mission."

"Understood." Dex knew that she had borrowed the surname from Sally Matheson, her sister, who was a federal attorney.

"Good." Rachel turned her attention elsewhere. "Krause and Ishikawa, you'll be checking into the Maoli Lodge as Mr. and Mrs. Sylvester Hayashi to dig around for evidence of drug trafficking, while providing backup for Adair should all hell break loose."

"I always wanted to marry Ishikawa—or should I say, Hayashi—and have our honeymoon in Hawaii," Lynda joked.

"Your wish is my command, Mrs. Hayashi." Ishikawa played his part in earnest. "Of course, the job comes first."

"Absolutely!" she insisted in all seriousness.

"Glad we're clear on that." Rachel spoke in a commanding tone. "You'll be working with the Task Force investigating drug trafficking on the island and its connection to the lodge as well as to the crime syndicate right here in LA." She paused. "Any questions?" Dex decided that anything he had a problem with could be brought up later. Apparently, his colleagues felt the same way, prompting the special agent in charge to unceremoniously conclude, "So go pack your bags and let's get this done for Agent Yamamoto."

It was something Dex agreed wholeheartedly with. The worst thing would be for her death to be in vain. Especially if they could give Roxanne the ability to rest in peace. Half an hour later, fresh with the assignments handed out, Dex headed to his Huston Street Moorish style home in the Valley Village part of LA to prep Barnabas and brush up on his skills on the piano… Katrina Sizemore and her role, if any, in the trafficking of drugs and possibly the death of Agent Yamamoto squarely in his thoughts.

KATRINA SIZEMORE STOOD in slip-on espadrille flats at her ergonomic adjustable desk in the small office of the Maoli Lodge. It still blew her mind that she had fallen into the role of lodge owner all by her lonesome, following the untimely death six months ago of her husband, Joseph. Three years earlier, which seemed like a lifetime ago, they had relocated to Kauai from Salem, Oregon, with the dream of opening their own lodging accommodations on the amazing Hawaiian island where they had honeymooned four years prior to their move. They found the perfect place up for sale: a forty-room and four suites plantation-style oceanfront property on Poipu Road, with a swimming pool, its own tropical gardens, swaying coconut palm trees, mature monkeypod trees and spectacular mountain views. It was located in the neighborhood of Poipu, which in Hawaiian meant "crashing waves," on the south shore, a popular destination for tourists and locals. Neither of them realized just how much money it would take and how much work they would have to put in to run such a business successfully. Or the strain it would place on their marriage, which had begun to falter even before Joseph died in an accident while kayaking.

Katrina shuddered to think of what might have happened to them had he lived. Could things have continued to go the way they were without it costing them

their marriage? Or the love they promised to hold on
to forever, as if a bond that couldn't be broken? Were
that the case, what would have happened to the lodge?
Would either of them have been willing to give up what
belonged to both of them with no hard feelings? She
couldn't imagine remaining in business together while
no longer husband and wife.

She ran thin fingers through her lengthy and loose
crimson locks, feeling saddened and guilty that she had
been left to make it work alone, thanks in part to a payout on Joseph's life insurance that helped keep the lodge
afloat. But somehow she was determined to do just that,
both in Joseph's memory and that of a housekeeper, Roxanne Kitaoka, who passed away last month in a car accident. Katrina still couldn't believe she was gone. Just
like that. It still wasn't clear to her how this could happen. What was Roxanne doing out on the road past midnight? From what little Katrina knew of her life outside
the lodge, in Roxanne's free time she seemed pretty
much a homebody, similar to herself when not working,
which for Katrina had proven to be a 24/7 job. When she
did find the time, she ran, a favorite activity to keep in
shape and take in as much of the wondrous landscape
as possible. The authorities had been sketchy at best in
telling her anything, but indicated that Roxanne's death
had been the result of foul play. Who would have wanted
her dead? And why?

As she pondered these disturbing thoughts, Katrina
did miss her employee, who even if they weren't friends,
was like family as part of the staff, and could only hope
that Roxanne didn't suffer too much at the end, while
praying the same as well for Joseph. When she heard her
name called, it startled Katrina. Looking up from her

musing, she saw Alyson Tennison, her assistant manager, standing there. Six years Katrina's senior, at thirty-
eight, Alyson was just as slender and maybe an inch
shorter than Katrina's five feet eight inches height. An
attractive blue-eyed divorcée, she came with lots of experience in hotel management and seemed a perfect fit
for the position.

"Aloha." Katrina spoke routinely.

"Didn't mean to wake you up," Alyson quipped,
sporting a mid-length brunette blunt lob.

"I'm wide-awake. My mind was just wandering." Katrina colored. "What's up?"

"There's a gentleman here to see you."

"Oh…?" Katrina wondered if it was the new land-
scaper checking in. Or someone else hoping to sell her
on this or that for the lodge, now that this role had fallen
entirely on her shoulders as the sole proprietor.

"He's applying for the pianist opening," Alyson said.
"I figured the best way to check him out was to audi-
tion. You'll find him waiting in the lounge at the piano."

"Good idea." Katrina smiled. With her rather hec-
tic life these days, she had practically forgotten about
needing a piano player. Since her current pianist, Gina
Oxenberg, was on maternity leave, they had substituted
her impressive skills with taped music, mostly Hawaiian, along with some jazz and easy listening. Maybe
they could get by without hiring someone for the job.
Might as well at least see what he brings to the table,
Katrina told herself. She glanced at her casual attire of
a gold scoop-neck top and black straight-leg trousers.
Deciding they were acceptable for greeting a prospec-
tive employee, she followed Alyson out of the office.

They split up in the lobby that had pearl mosaic tiles

for the flooring and Hawaiian-style furnishings and tropical plants. Katrina could hear the baby grand piano as she stepped inside the Kahiko Lounge, which was decorated in 1940s retro élan. She spied the handsome man seated at the piano. African American and in his early thirties, she guessed; he was tall, muscled, with short jet-black hair in a line up haircut and a five-o'clock shadow beard. He wore a floral print shirt and brown slacks. She noticed that a gorgeous golden retriever was seated by his side on the floor, seemingly just as enchanted by the piano sounds of the Hawaiian song, "King's Serenade," as she was.

When he noticed her standing there, the piano player stopped on a dime and faced her. Katrina could see that he was even better looking upon gazing into incredibly deep sable-gray eyes. Trying to find words in that moment, she managed to utter, "That was lovely."

He flashed a brilliant smile, making her weak in the knees. "Thanks."

"I take it you're here for the job…?" Katrina gave him a knowing look.

"Yeah, if it's still available." A long arm stretched out and his large hand reached for a shake. "I'm Dex Matheson."

She cupped hands with him, feeling as though her own were engulfed within his. "Aloha. Katrina Sizemore. And, yes, it's still available," she admitted, finding herself wanting to hear more of his piano playing. She wondered where he learned the craft and was even more curious about other aspects of his life that made the man before her.

"Cool." Dex grinned again, displaying white teeth,

straight as an arrow. He gazed down at the dog that now stood on its four legs. "This is Barnabas."

"Hi, Barnabas." She petted him on the base of his neck. The dog licked her hand, seeming to take to her instantly. Good sign? Looking back at its owner, Katrina remembered there was still a process to go through before she could hire him. She had been burned before in bringing on someone who couldn't or refused to measure up to the job. Something told her Dex would measure up just fine. But still… "Why don't we head to my office and get your basic information and I'll tell you what we're looking for in a piano player."

Dex gave her an agreeable and confident nod. "Works for me."

Katrina smiled and led the way.

Chapter Two

Dex was admittedly transfixed by the red-haired beauty of Katrina Sizemore. The screen image of the lodge owner, nice as it was, did no justice when compared to the real person. The face, taut and squared, was flawless and he loved that cute little cleft on her chin. And could those enticing eyes be any bluer, as if taken straight from the ocean itself on a good day? He was also taken by her slender physique and just the right height in relation to his own size. Under other circumstances, Dex imagined they would be a good—and maybe perfect—fit. But at the moment, he feared that beneath the very appealing facade could well be someone involved in the world of illegal drugs. Worse yet was that the widow may have also played a role in the murder of his fellow DEA agent Roxanne Yamamoto.

But Dex took a proverbial step back, even as he sat in the cranberry tub chair, not wanting to get ahead of himself just yet as he did what he needed to do to convince Katrina Sizemore to hire him as a piano player. Having left Barnabas by the piano with his leash attached to it, Dex quickly scanned the office, with a picture window looking out onto an impressive botanical garden and sand-colored vinyl flooring. There were two desks with laptops, a two-drawer white lateral file cabinet, a printer on a folding table and a ceiling fan. A closed door presumably was a storage closet. Or could it lead to another room?

Turning back to the proprietor as she took a seat in the chair angled toward his, Dex gave her a believable friendly grin. "This is a really nice place you have here."

"Mahalo." She clasped her hands thoughtfully and he noted the wedding band on her finger. It indicated to him that she was having trouble letting go, as he would have, had he lost the love of his life prematurely.

This gave Dex an opening. "How long have you and your husband owned it?" He played the innocent.

"Three years." She eyed the ring self-consciously, then unclasped her hands. "I lost my husband six months ago," she murmured.

"I'm sorry to hear that," Dex told her sincerely, even though already privy to this information.

"He died in a kayaking accident." Her shoulders slumped. "So, I'm afraid it's just me now."

"You must have your hands full going it alone?" He wondered if that sounded more coldhearted than he'd intended. Worse would be if it came across as a come-on. Even if the appeal was there, and it was, he had no interest in going after the widow like a lovestruck teenager. She was likely still in love with her late husband. "What I meant was that I could only imagine the burden of running a lodge in Poipu, where tourists flock, with its various attractions," Dex sought to clarify.

"It's fine," she said evenly, not appearing to pick up on his probing. "You're right, it has been overwhelming at times. But I'm hanging in there, thanks in large part

to the support of my staff and being fortunate enough
to own a lodge in the heart of Poipu, keeping me busy."

If she was guilty of anything criminal, Dex was not
picking up on it at present. He wondered if his attraction
to the beautiful widow might have something to do with
that. Or could she really be blameless in the suspected
drug activity at the lodge that had apparently cost Roxanne her life?

"So, tell me a little about yourself, Mr. Matheson,"
Dex heard the soft voice, breaking away from his reverie as he locked eyes with the proprietor.

Don't blow this, he thought, as if she could somehow see right through him. "For starters, please call
me Dex," he insisted, if for no other reason than it was
easier to keep from slipping up if he kept the moniker
to himself. But, better still, he preferred the more personal first name communication for building trust and
getting information.

She smiled. "Dex it is. And please call me Katrina."

"Okay." He nodded agreeably. "Well, Katrina, I just
moved here after living the last few years in the Los
Angeles area."

"Why Hawaii?" came the expected question. "And
Kauai, in particular, if you don't mind my asking?"

"Not at all," Dex said smoothly. Especially when he
had his own questions for her, when the time was right.
"I was at a time in my life when I felt I needed a change.
I'd visited the Islands while in college and found Kauai
the most to my liking. When an opportunity presented
itself, I decided to go give island life a try."

She raised a thin brow curiously. "You mean an opportunity other than playing piano at a lodge?"

He chuckled. "Yeah, you could say that. A friend of

mine has a local private investigation agency and asked if I'd be willing to work there part-time as a PI. Nothing too heavy," Dex stressed, "missing spouses, cheating spouses, rescuing cats from trees. Stuff like that. Since I worked as a private detective in LA before I got injured and decided I'd saved enough to go into an early semi-retirement, I figured, why not?" *Hope she buys this without needing to embellish the story too much more*, he thought.

"Makes sense to me." She laughed a little, then regarded him keenly. "Must have been a serious injury?"

"I hurt my back while chasing a stalker." This much was true. At least hurting the back part. Only it happened during a major drug bust in Santa Ana two years ago. Though he recovered fully, he still felt a twinge in his lower back every now and then. "Not a big deal. Good excuse to move to paradise, anyhow," he kidded.

"If you say so." She studied him. "Did you move here with family or…"

"Just me," he told her without preface. He wondered if her interest was purely out of curiosity. Or her way of asking if he was single and available? Did it matter? She was off-limits, romantically speaking, as a suspect while on an undercover mission.

"I see." Katrina brushed her dainty little nose. "How long have you been playing the piano, Dex?"

"Since I was knee-high. Learned from my mother, who wanted to make sure she passed the talent along to me and my sister, Rita."

"That's nice. Your mother was obviously successful in her efforts."

Dex grinned. "Yeah, I'm happy about that." He only wished Rita hadn't blown it in losing sight of everything she had to offer to the world before it was too late to turn things around.

Katrina leaned forward, making Dex fight the urge to stretch out his long arm and touch her attractive face. "Well, the job doesn't pay particularly well, but does require a couple of hours of your time five evenings a week and two afternoons. Moreover, as my regular piano player may or may not return once her maternity leave ends, it might only be a temporary gig." She paused. "Does this still sound like something you would be interested in?"

She was giving him a way out of this, as if to undercut her own need for a pianist. Was this an attempt to play it safe as a drug trafficker who had second thoughts about having someone new around? He waited a long beat, pretending to be reconsidering whether he wanted to take the position, before eyeing her directly and responding coolly, "Yes, definitely. As I alluded to, I'm in pretty good shape financially, so pay whatever you like. I enjoy playing the piano and entertaining folks with a blend of Hawaiian, contemporary, easy listening and soul music. I'll gladly work whatever hours and days you need me until your regular piano player returns."

"Hard to argue with that." Katrina's full lips curved upward at the corners. "I guess that settles it. You're hired."

Dex flashed his teeth. "Great."

"I'll just need to verify you're with the private investigation agency you indicated you'll be working for on Kauai…"

Smart of you to ask, Dex mused. "Of course." He gave her the cell phone number of the agency and the contact there, Glenn Nakao, who had worked with the DEA in the past and been briefed in advance, agreeing to play along. Being a real detective firm that could easily be looked up on the internet would solidify Dex's cover that much more.

Katrina seemed satisfied with the ease of his cooperation. "When can you start?" she asked eagerly.

Not wishing to appear overeager himself, while at the same time needing to ingratiate himself into her world as soon as possible to get some answers, he replied evenly, "Whenever you like."

"Tomorrow at noon would be great," Katrina said promptly. "We tend to get many of our guests around that time on a Wednesday. It would be wonderful to welcome them with a drink and some entertaining piano music."

"Tomorrow it is." Dex kept his tone relaxed and sure. It would give him some extra time to acclimate himself to the surroundings and size up the lady herself.

"Perfect." She offered him a pleased smile and got to her feet. "Why don't I give you a quick tour and introduce you to the staff."

"Sounds good to me." The more people he met, the better the chances to get a read on them and assess if any or all could be involved in illicit drug activity and murder.

"ALOHA AND WELCOME to the Maoli Lodge," Katrina greeted the new arrivals, who had been introduced to her as Sylvester and Lynda Hayashi and were wearing floral leis.

"Aloha," they returned in unison. "Happy to be able to spend some quality time at your fabulous lodge," Lynda voiced enthusiastically.

Katrina smiled. "If you need anything, just let me or a member of the staff know," she told them.

"We will," Sylvester promised, and gave a friendly nod to Dex, before the couple went on their way.

"Looks like the guests are already feeling right at home," Dex remarked.

"That's the whole idea," Katrina uttered, knowing it was what she and Joseph had envisioned from the start. Even if he was no longer there to share the experience, she knew it was all about providing a welcoming atmosphere for visitors, who would hopefully come back again and again.

"It's working," he declared, making her wonder if Dex was referring to himself as well.

Katrina continued to show her new hire around, surprising herself in already starting to feel somewhat close to him, if that was possible. She sensed she could trust Dex, though she had yet to even check out his reference. With his ID seemingly legit, this was likely only a mere formality and nothing to worry about. She admitted that there was something mysteriously enticing about the piano player that attracted her, even beyond his handsome features. Would she get to know him more? Or was that asking for trouble, considering she wasn't in the market right now for romance. Was he?

She introduced him to Alyson, her assistant manager. "Nice to meet you formally," Alyson said, after they had exchanged words earlier.

"You too," Dex said.

"Can't wait to hear more of your piano playing."

He grinned. "I'll try not to disappoint."

For whatever reason, Katrina felt a spasm of jealousy, which she had no right to. Alyson was a natural flirt and

Dex had admitted, essentially, to being a single man and was presumably available to the right woman. Maybe that was her assistant manager, who was divorced and looking for love again. She generally didn't encourage workplace romance. But Dex was a part-time employee and would likely move on once Gina returned, and Katrina had no desire to try and dictate his or anyone else's love life. Especially when her own love life was non-existent these days and had already hit the skids in her marriage before Joseph's death, whether she wanted to face up to it or not.

They finished the tour back where they'd started in the Kahiko Lounge. Katrina introduced Dex to her bartender, Gordon Guerrero. The thickly built, forty-year-old half Hawaiian had a black-blond Caesar crop top short hairstyle, a short black boxed beard and large brown eyes. "Aloha," Gordon said tonelessly, as they shook hands.

"Aloha," Dex said back, not seeming at all intimidated by the bulkier bartender. Not that he had reason to be, as Katrina felt Gordon was actually a teddy bear in spite of his hardened demeanor.

"Dex is our new pianist," Katrina told him.

"What about Gina?" Gordon threw out worriedly. Their piano player was married to his cousin, Marciel.

"When she's ready to return, she has a job waiting for her," Katrina promised.

This seemed to ease his concerns and Gordon said, "I'd best get back to work now."

"Is he always that friendly?" Dex asked as they walked away from him and toward the piano.

"Yes, pretty much." Katrina chuckled. "Seriously, Gordon's a good guy, if a little rough around the edges."

He had never given them any trouble and had actually become friends with Joseph, even doing things away from the lodge, such as deep sea fishing together.

"I'll take your word for that." Dex's voice was laced with sarcasm, but he seemed able to adjust easily enough to each different personality he encountered amongst the staff.

Dex's dog, Barnabas, sat quietly beside the piano. Katrina loved domesticated animals and would have one or more of her own, had the demands of running a lodge not been too much to properly care for a pet.

"Have you been a good boy?" Dex asked, untangling the leash from the piano leg. He petted the dog, who reacted favorably, clearly smitten with his owner. "Yeah, I think you have."

Katrina imagined that the two were inseparable, other than when Dex was doing private investigation work. Barnabas stood and sniffed her hand playfully. She giggled. "I like you too."

Dex seemed glad to hear that by his agreeable expression. "I better take him home and get out of your hair."

"Okay." She almost hated to see them leave, as though Katrina would never lay eyes on the man and his dog again. Which was silly, of course. After all, Dex was the new piano player. Meaning that Barnabas would also likely make a return visit. "See you tomorrow at noon."

"On the nose," he assured her, and their shoulders brushed, sending electricity throughout Katrina's body. Had Dex noticed too? Or could the whole thing have been her overactive imagination?

Katrina watched as they headed for the door and the humidity and sunshine that awaited them outside, before she went on her merry way. Even then, for whatever reason, she had the feeling she was being observed. Which was odd, considering that she was inside and saw only a few people wandering about seemingly caught up in their own worlds. That included the new guests, Sylvester and Lynda Hayashi, who were busy studying a brochure as if it held the secrets to the universe. Was she really being surveilled? If so, by whom? And for what reason? Or was that, too, only in her head?

Katrina chewed on those uneasy thoughts as she headed back to her office to verify the identity and work reference of Dex Matheson.

DEX STILL HAD Katrina Sizemore very much on his mind as he loaded Barnabas into his rented dark gray Ford Expedition XLT, then hopped behind the wheel. Her striking features notwithstanding, was the lodge owner hiding something relevant to their investigation? It was up to him to find out, whatever it took, with the help of undercover agents Krause and Ishikawa. Along with, of course, his trusty companion who was making himself comfortable beside Dex. He started up the vehicle and drove around the property, looking for entrances and exits that might be employed by traffickers, along with angles and out-of-the-way places and spaces that could provide cover or hideaways for drug activity. There was a black Ford Transit full-size cargo van parked out back that could possibly be used for transporting illicit drugs. What had Roxanne uncovered that likely cost the DEA agent her life?

Knowing he had time to make some determinations with his new piano gig, Dex left the lodge grounds and headed down Poipu Road en route to the rented cottage he would be calling home during his stay on Kauai.

It was the same place Roxanne had operated from before she was killed. He soon reached his destination on Nakoa Street in the nearby unincorporated community of Koloa, but far enough away so as not to draw attention from the locals. Leaving the car, he let Barnabas out and they headed to their new temporary home away from home.

The one-story, two-bedroom farmhouse-style residence had merbau hardwood flooring and vaulted ceilings, with large picture windows covered by fabric blinds. A spacious kitchen had slate countertops and stainless steel appliances as part of an open concept architecture, with modest contemporary furnishings. As Barnabas sized up the place, Dex walked through while imagining Roxanne being made and having to make a hasty escape for her life. It had been scoured for DNA, fingerprints and other evidence, but nothing had stuck with respect to clues as to her killer. Dex couldn't help but think they may have missed something crucial toward getting some answers.

He peeked through the blinds and saw a covered lanai that overlooked a fully fenced backyard with fruit trees and plenty of room for Barnabas to play and get some exercise. Dex let the dog out the back door. "Stay out of trouble," he teased him. After unloading his things from the car, Dex went back inside and plotted his strategy for learning more from and about Katrina, even while the better part of him was just as interested in getting to know the lady herself. Or was that a dumb idea? Maybe not, as he sensed her assessing him with more than a passing glance. If she had no dirty laundry in the closet, who knew if something could be there waiting for them both to explore.

Just as he contemplated that tantalizing thought, Dex heard the sound of a vehicle pulling up to the cottage. He looked out the front window and saw a blue Hyundai Elantra GT in the driveway. Lynda and Ishikawa got out and approached the house. Dex opened the door and greeted them teasingly, "I was beginning to think that you were too caught up in your honeymoon, Mr. and Mrs. Hayashi, to break away from the Maoli Lodge."

"Yeah, right." Lynda rolled her green eyes. "This coming from the man who couldn't seem to take his eyes off the lovely widow."

Dex didn't deny it, but countered with a more defensive tone than he'd intended. "If I'm not mistaken, it's what I've been tasked with."

"Such a grueling task, Adair," she quipped, "but someone's got to do it, right?"

"That's why I get the big bucks." He went along with the ribbing, while knowing that in reality being a DEA special agent was anything but a get rich scheme. But it did give him a general sense of satisfaction that could never be measured in dollars and cents. Something he was sure motivated his colleagues as well.

"We've all got a job to do," Ishikawa said forthrightly, moving past him and into the cottage. Dex allowed Lynda to follow and he went in afterward. "I take it you were hired?"

Dex nodded. "I start in earnest tomorrow at noon."

"Good. Hope you can pull it off with your piano skills without arousing suspicion."

"I'm sure I'll be able to hold my own," Dex assured him, "while seeing what I can dig up."

"Never had a doubt." Ishikawa patted him on the shoulder and looked around. "So, where's your sidekick?"

"Out back. There's lots of space for Barnabas to run around without getting lost, till he's called upon in the line of duty."

"Good for him."

Dex eyed Lynda, who had taken out her cell phone to check for messages. "Come up with anything yet on your end?"

"Still in the honeymoon phase," Ishikawa replied, metaphorically speaking. "We'll be scoping out the lodge in the coming days and seeing what we can learn about its possible ties to drug trafficking."

"I studied the grounds and can see some possibilities for trafficking drugs in and out," Dex said. "Barnabas and I will look into it."

"Good. Maybe we can nip this thing in the bud sooner than later."

Dex gazed at Lynda, who was still glued to her phone. "Care to let us in on who or what's got your attention?"

"Sorry." She cut the phone off. "That was Martin," she said apologetically. Lynda was currently dating Martin O'Sullivan, an investigator for LA County Sheriff's Narcotic Bureau, who was part of the downtown drug bust. "According to him, drug kingpin Louis Johansson is already starting to talk."

"Didn't take much to get him to look out for number one," Dex stated, sure that Johansson was trying to cut a deal to save his own neck. He was also certain that the trafficker couldn't be trusted as far as you could throw him. Dex was confident this would be a factor in seeing what they could get from him and what it was worth, if anything.

"Never does when the screws start to tighten," Ishikawa remarked flippantly, scratching his jaw.

"Martin believes that the ties between the trafficking of drugs in Southern California and Hawaii—Kauai, in particular—may run deeper than we think. So it's even more important that we make the case with the Maoli Lodge as a possible vector for illegal drugs and the related murder of Agent Yamamoto."

Dex furrowed his brow. "I hear you," he muttered. "We'll do what we need to and find out if there's a case to be made. And, if so, how deep it runs." He considered that Katrina could be nothing more than an innocent pawn in a complicated scheme. Or deceptively attractive on the outside, but inside guilty as sin of one or more serious offenses, including responsibility for the death of a federal agent.

"So, this is where Agent Yamamoto laid her head when away from the lodge?" Lynda peeked into the master bedroom. "It's almost as though she's speaking to us from the grave."

"You mean like a ghost?" Ishikawa's mouth hung open.

"Like someone who had unfinished business and can't rest till it's done."

Dex put more weight on one leg than the other. "Can't say I believe in the supernatural," he had to admit. "But I do believe in justice being served when crimes are committed. And since Roxanne was my friend, I'm definitely keen on doing right by her. If that means speaking back to Agent Yamamoto, as such, while caught in spiritual unrest, so be it." To be successful in this endeavor, he sensed that they would need Katrina's cooperation, voluntary or not.

Chapter Three

The following day, Katrina was still rattled by a feeling of being spied upon as she sipped passion fruit tea in the loft suite she called home and her safety net. Claiming the largest of the four suites when she and Joseph bought the lodge, it had three bedrooms, tigerwood exotic flooring and bamboo ceiling fans throughout, and a tropical-style kitchen with smoky quartz countertops, a distressed oak kitchen island and farmhouse apron front sink. The floor-to-ceiling windows in the great room offered plenty of natural light, with plantation shutters. She marveled at the carefully selected custom-made furnishings, an eclectic mixture of woven seagrass and rattan pieces, accented with areca palm and bird-of-paradise plants. While it created a warm and cozy atmosphere, Katrina knew this could not compensate for the loneliness that had started to set in. But when did it truly began? Was it after she had lost her husband? Or before? Would that all-important sense of completion and being loved ever return? Or had it ever been there in the first place during her marriage?

Exactly what am I trying to say? she questioned, while standing barefoot and still in her short satin chemise nightgown. That Joseph never truly loved her? She rejected this, believing that he did in his own way. And her love for him was real too. She just wasn't sure that what they had together was everything she'd signed up for when marrying him and relocating to Kauai. Whether that was widow's remorse or something more, Katrina tried to put it out of her mind as she watched a gecko crawl up the wall before she headed into the master bedroom. It was spacious with wicker furniture, a private lanai and an en suite bath that included a jetted tub.

She got dressed, tied her hair into a side ponytail, and was ready to begin her morning chores and responsibilities. Afterward, she looked forward to listening to Dex work his magic at the piano, believing he was more than capable of delivering for their guests for as long as Gina was away.

When Katrina stepped inside her office, with plans to go over the budget, work schedules and other items that commanded her attention as owner of the lodge, she couldn't help but notice the folded piece of paper sitting on her desk. She picked it up curiously and unfolded it, reading the message. It was sloppily written, as though the writer was in a hurry, but still legible.

Don't believe what you've been told about your husband's death. No accident. He was murdered. Watch your back.

Katrina dropped the note on the desk as though it were on fire, and put a hand to her mouth in shock. She looked about the office as if expecting to find whoever left the note. But it was empty aside from her. Gazing back at the piece of paper, she felt compelled to read it again, as though her eyes had played a cruel trick on her. Picking it up, she read it again and saw the same disturbing words. Who would play such a cruel joke on her? And why? Was it possible that Joseph's death was not from the kayaking accident after all, but had only been masked by it? If so, why would anyone wish to harm her husband, much less kill him?

A hand on her shoulder nearly made Katrina jump out of her skin. She jerked around in a defensive manner, sure that she was about to be attacked, but saw that it was Alyson standing there. "Hey, are you okay?" she asked innocuously enough.

"Yes. You startled me, that's all," Katrina responded honestly.

"Sorry. I saw you standing there, looking as though you'd been spooked by something." Alyson twisted her lips regretfully. "Guess I only made things worse."

"You didn't." Katrina sighed and looked at the paper she was still holding. "But you're right, I was spooked... by this—" She passed the note to her.

Alyson stared at it, her face coloring almost instantly. "Where did you get this?"

"It was on my desk when I came in." Katrina gazed at her. "Did you see anyone in here?"

"No. Not when I was last in the office, about fifteen minutes ago."

"So someone must have dropped it off between then and now?" Katrina surmised disconcertingly, believing that she would likely have noticed since Alyson had to pass by her desk to get to her own.

"I'll ask the staff if anyone saw someone come this way," she said. "Or leave."

Katrina nodded, all types of thoughts running through her head. It was difficult enough just trying to come to terms with Joseph dying in a kayaking accident. Now someone was indicating otherwise. What was she to believe? "What do you make of this?" Katrina asked, valuing her opinion.

For once, Alyson seemed at a loss for words. "Maybe someone's idea of a sick joke?" she finally suggested.

It was Katrina's first reaction too. But it didn't make sense. "What would anyone have to gain by joking about my husband's death?" she questioned. "To watch me become unglued just for the sake of it?"

"You're right." Alyson handed the note back to her. "There's got to be more to it." She paused. "Do you think Joseph really could have been murdered…?"

Katrina considered this for a long beat, trying to picture that horrifying possibility and what implications arose from it, before answering candidly, "I don't know." She placed the note inside the pocket of her knit pants and said determinedly, "But I need to find out."

DEX MADE HIMSELF comfortable at the piano as Barnabas sat beside him, curiously observing those who were present in the Kahiko Lounge drinking, talking or waiting to hear music. *I've got this*, Dex thought, confident in his ability to draw on his musical roots and skills to perform in an undercover role. He noted that Katrina was standing near the entrance, her gaze fixed on him. Was it his imagination or did she seem troubled? Maybe she was suspicious with his hastily arranged reference. Worse, perhaps she was having second thoughts about his ability to hold the attention of his audience as part of their experience at the lodge.

Guess I'll find out soon enough, he told himself. He started off with a classic Hawaiian song, "Ke Kali Nei

Au." That was followed by a string of country, soul, easy listening, and more Hawaiian songs he had learned to play. The audience seemed receptive enough. All, that was, but Katrina, who looked as though she would rather be somewhere else. He couldn't help but wonder if there were other things on her mind. Such as drug trafficking and laundering of money through a legitimate business. Instinctively, Dex pushed back from the latter thoughts, sensing something else was weighing heavily based on her facial expressions.

During a break, he walked up to the lodge owner, unsure what to expect, and said, "Everything okay?"

"I'd like to hire you," Katrina responded straight-forwardly.

Dex cocked a brow. "I thought you already had employed my services?"

"As a private investigator," she made clear.

Admittedly, he hadn't seen that coming. Dex tried to imagine what she would need investigated. Actually, he could think of a few things. Perhaps she was trying to get ahead of whatever may be coming down with the probe into possible illegal activity at the lodge. Beginning to feel the heat from living a double life and looking for a way out? Or was there more going on with her than met the eye?

"Why do you want a PI?" he asked, curious while keeping an open mind.

Katrina looked around nervously and back, before responding ambiguously, "Can we talk in my office?"

"Sure." Dex attached Barnabas's leash to the piano leg wanting him to stay put, then followed her out of the lounge, through the lobby and into the office where he'd been hired. Only this time things seemed much more tense. "What's going on?" he asked, peering into her lovely but clearly disturbed face.

Katrina took a piece of paper out of her pocket and handed it to him. "This was waiting for me on my desk this morning," she uttered.

He read it.

Don't believe what you've been told about your husband's death. No accident. He was murdered. Watch your back.

Dex recalled that Rachel Zavatti, the special agent in charge, had noted that Joseph Sizemore was killed when his kayak capsized. It was thought to be an accidental drowning, but remained suspicious, considering that he had been under investigation for using the lodge to traffic illicit drugs. Did someone have solid information to prove foul play was involved? Dex eyed Sizemore's widow, who seemed genuine in her belief that his death was an accident. "Do you know who left the note?"

"I have no idea," Katrina insisted. "Alyson is asking around to see if any of the staff saw someone heading to or away from my office this morning."

"What do you know about your husband's death?" Dex asked, making sure his tone wasn't accusatory.

"Only what I was told—that it was an accident." She sucked in a steadying breath. "Joseph loved to go kayaking. He and a friend went out that day and apparently got caught in a shore break wave before they got very far, causing the kayak to overturn. Joseph went under and didn't survive. It was investigated and concluded that his death was, in fact, accidental. I accepted that.

But now I get this cryptic message signifying otherwise and I'm just not sure what to believe."

Dex shared her concern with the note and wanted to dig deeper to see if it was a hoax. Or if someone knew something worth pursuing about the nature of Sizemore's death. If he was murdered, was it in relation to the Drug Task Force and DEA's investigation of drug trafficking on the island? And what, if anything, might Katrina know about it? Dex zeroed in on the "Watch your back" part of the message. Was this a veiled threat against her?

"I'd be happy to look into this," Dex told Katrina, in keeping with his undercover role as a private investigator. "There may be nothing to it. Or it could be that your husband's death was no accident, as reported. Did he have any enemies that you know of?"

She shook her head adamantly. "No. Joseph wasn't the type to make enemies. Quite the opposite. It's just that…" Her eyes shifted uncomfortably. "Last month, one of my housekeepers, Roxanne Kitaoka, was killed in a car accident on Kaumualii Highway. The police say she was murdered, but have never explained the circumstances. Now I'm wondering if somehow there could be a link between her death and Joseph's."

Dex had been wondering the same ever since being given the assignment, in spite of the official cause of Sizemore's death being listed as accidental. Now there was even more reason to be suspicious, especially considering Roxanne's own undercover investigation at the Maoli Lodge. Dex kept his cool while resisting the desire to come clean with Katrina, who was still technically a suspect in the drug-trafficking probe, even if he was beginning to believe her hands were clean. "That is something worth looking into," he told her levelly. "You just need to be prepared for whatever I may find…"

She nodded, ill at ease. "I just need to know, one way or the other."

So do I, Dex mused, especially where it concerned her. The last thing he wanted was for the alluring lodge owner to be up to her neck in criminal activities. His gut told him this wasn't the case and he could usually trust his instincts. But could the same be said for her late husband? Was Joseph Sizemore running a drug-trafficking operation right under his wife's pretty nose? Either way, Dex intended to use this new opening to further his investigation at the lodge. "Okay, I'll do some digging, starting with who may have left the note. Mind if I hang on to it?"

"Please do, if it can help you track down whoever wrote it."

Dex deposited it in the pocket of his chino pants. He doubted that whoever had left it would also leave fingerprints or DNA that hadn't already been corrupted, but it was worth a shot. "What's the friend's name who was with your husband on the kayaking trip?"

"Larry Nakanishi. He runs a water sports and gear shop in Lihue."

Dex took out his cell phone and entered the information. "I'll need to speak with your staff to see if anyone knows anything about the message." He left off for now any possibility that someone she was employing could be involved in her husband's death.

"I understand." Katrina met his eyes. "Do I need to pay for your services in advance or…?"

"That won't be necessary," he explained. "Just poking around a bit won't cost you anything. If I learn something useful, we can discuss payment then." Truthfully, he wasn't interested in taking her money for something he needed to do for his own investigation. But he wasn't exactly at liberty to reveal his mission to her just yet.

"Mahalo." Somehow, she managed a smile through the worry lines that sat softly on her forehead. "There's one other thing…" Her voice shook. "Lately, I've had a strange feeling that someone has been watching me."

"Really?" Dex jutted his chin thoughtfully. "I take it this feeling started before you found the note?"

"Yes. I've wanted to believe it was all in my head," Katrina confessed. "But now I'm not so sure. Especially after that unsettling message…and the warning to watch my back. I don't know if I should be scared or not."

Dex wanted to say *not*, but when piecing together what he knew and still needed to uncover, giving her a false sense of security would not be a smart move, all things considered. But having her afraid of her own shadow at this point was not the way to go either. "My advice is for you to not read too much into the feeling of being watched. At least not until you have a bit more to go on in that regard. Could be that between your husband's death and the housekeeper's, it's found a way to play on your psyche."

"You're probably right," she relented, her voice elevating. "I'll try not to get spooked by what's been an invisible presence, more or less."

"Good idea." Dex still didn't want to leave it at that. "Nevertheless, keep your eyes open," he warned, "and don't let your guard down as it relates to being aware of your surroundings, even at the lodge."

Katrina smiled. "I'll try not to."

Her smile accentuated her good looks, and he returned it, welcoming seeing her like that. "In the meantime, I'll try to track down whoever sent the note and go from there. In the meantime, if you receive any more messages, let me know."

She nodded. "I will."

"Well, I better get back to the lounge," he said reluctantly. "I have one more set on the piano."

"Go," she told him. "I can see that everyone is enjoying you playing, myself included. I'll be fine."

"Okay." Dex found himself wanting to spend more time with her outside of an official capacity. But blowing his cover might not be a smart idea. Certainly not if they wanted to continue unimpeded in completing an investigation Roxanne began. He was about to leave when he noticed that a ringlet of hair had managed to escape Katrina's long ponytail and fall across her brow. Without giving it a thought, Dex raised his hand and touched her soft skin, feeling a jolt in return. Had she felt it, too, as he tucked the errant strand behind her ear? "There, that's better," he said equably.

She blushed. "Thanks for noticing."

"My pleasure." He grinned and their eyes locked for a long moment of a connection, before Dex did the only sensible thing he could at that point. He walked away while he was still able to.

Chapter Four

Dex showed Lynda Krause and Sylvester Ishikawa the note someone had left for Katrina, as he huddled with the undercover DEA agents in their room at the lodge that was furnished with two queen beds. Having placed the piece of paper in a plastic bag to try and preserve evidence, should it come to that, Dex said troublingly, "Sizemore's death may not have been accidental…"

Lynda studied the note. "Hmm… Could this have come from someone who's simply venting because he or she doesn't agree with the medical examiner's findings?"

"Maybe," he had to allow, knowing that the note was hardly proof of a homicide in and of itself. "But were that the case, why not simply tell Katrina face-to-face that you believe someone murdered her late husband? Why the scare tactics and anonymity?"

"Point taken. It would also tie into the theory that Sizemore may have been involved in drug trafficking and bit off more than he could chew."

"Yeah, he could easily have gotten in way over his head," Ishikawa pitched in, "and was put out to pasture when he wanted out. Or his usefulness to those calling the shots was up."

"Both those angles are realistic possibilities." Dex

didn't discount the ways traffickers could take out someone they wanted dead. "We have to see if this mystery messenger knows what he or she is talking about. I'd like to get the note dusted for any usable prints, analyzed for DNA, etc."

"Can't hurt to try," Ishikawa contended, grabbing the bag. "Even if it's probably a long shot."

"Yeah," Dex agreed. "It's a start anyway. Whoever left the message obviously wanted to get Katrina's attention. We need to know why and if this is connected to our overall investigation in any way."

"It is now," Lynda declared. "And maybe that was the point, to help her to connect the dots—assuming she wasn't already in on the blueprint."

"Katrina hired me as a private investigator," Dex informed them.

"Is that right?" Ishikawa's eyes widened.

"That note freaked her out. She wants to know who sent it and if there's any merit to the claim that her husband was murdered."

"Smart move on her part," Lynda said. "I'd want to know too, considering."

"Looks like having that second undercover PI role was the right move," Ishikawa stated. "It will allow you to operate more in plain view without fear of blowing your other cover."

"Yeah, I was thinking the same thing." Dex leaned against the wall. He would still work with Barnabas, too, when he could and it was necessary. As for Katrina, she may or may not have legitimate concerns. She deserved to know the truth about her husband, regardless of whatever he may have been up to. "I'm going to nose around and see what I can find out. If Sizemore was murdered, to go along with Roxanne's death, that could very well put Katrina in danger too."

"I don't disagree." Lynda wrinkled her nose. "Everything is still on the table at this point."

"We'll stay on the drug-trafficking angle," Ishikawa said, "and see if we can come up with whatever Agent Yamamoto had latched on to."

"Good." Dex pushed off the wall and patted him on the back. "I'll let you two lovebirds get back to having fun in your honeymoon suite," he teased them.

"Yeah, right," Lynda voiced tonelessly. "It's great being undercover with Ishikawa, but I'm already spoken for, thank you."

"Me too," Ishikawa said, which was news to Dex. Last he knew, the man had sworn off relationships following two failed marriages. Had he been holding out on them? "My horse, Isabella, is the love of my life these days," he explained. "Between her and this job, there's not much room for romance outside of pretend."

"Got it." Dex tried to resist grinning, but failed miserably. He turned his thoughts to the mission at hand. "I'll show myself out."

Half an hour later, Dex met up with Katrina's assistant manager, with whom she shared an office.

"You're a man of many talents," Alyson said from her desk. "Katrina told me she'd asked you to look into the mysterious note."

Dex acknowledged this. "I understand that you were out of the office for approximately fifteen minutes when the note was discovered?"

"Yes, that's right."

"And where were you during that time frame?" he questioned, sitting on a corner of the desk.

"At the front desk," she answered surely. "Like Katrina, working at the lodge requires wearing multiple hats at once."

He didn't doubt that, and tried to imagine what it took to run a successful business in a resort setting. Would outside lures tempt one looking for added sources of revenue? "Other than you and Katrina, who else would have valid reasons to go into the office?"

Alyson sat back thoughtfully. "Someone from housekeeping, maintenance or landscaping," she suggested. "As well as other staff who may have needed to talk to Katrina or me about a problem. Could have been anyone, really. We've always made ourselves accessible in the Hawaiian spirit of family."

Was this a familial thing? Dex wondered. Or something far more nefarious? "Did Joseph Sizemore ever receive any threats that you're aware of?"

Her curly lashes fluttered. "Not that I can think of. He never seemed to me to be under any strain, other than the usual in running a business."

Dex leaned forward. "Do you buy the notion that his death was no accident?"

"It's not for me to say," she spoke pithily. "I can only go by what the authorities are saying. If someone else believes differently, I hope you can find out why."

"So do I," he said, deciding now was not the time as an undercover PI to delve into any possible connections between his death and the trafficking of drugs at the establishment.

Dex left the office and walked around the lodge a couple of times, accompanied by Barnabas, while observing other staff surreptitiously, some of whom he intended to question. It wasn't a stretch to believe that whoever left the note worked there and, as such, could have slipped in and out of Katrina's office without being noticed. On the other hand, there was an open concept to the layout, where a guest or outsider would likely not have much difficulty whizzing in and out of the office with no one being the wiser, in the absence of surveillance cameras. Dex considered that someone knowledgeable about Joseph Sizemore's circumstances had real information to push back against the official read on his death. So, was this person a friend or foe who meant Katrina harm if she didn't go along with the program, whatever that might be?

"I DON'T TRUST the piano player!" Gordon set his jaw as he got Katrina's attention when she stepped inside the Kahiko Lounge.

"Why not?" She favored the bartender with a curious look.

"I caught him snooping around with that dog of his."

Katrina smiled thinly. "He wasn't snooping around. Dex is working for me," she said evasively.

"He wasn't on the piano," Gordon said curtly.

"I know." She debated whether or not to let him in on Dex's new mission. As Joseph's friend, surely he would understand her need to know exactly how her husband died? Katrina peered at the bartender. Was he the one who left the mysterious message? "I hired Dex as a private investigator," she confessed, "his main profession."

Gordon's thick brows knitted. "Why would you do that?"

"Someone left a note in my office claiming that Joseph's death was no accident—but murder."

"What?" His jaw dropped. "And you believe that?"

"I don't know." Her voice weakened. "I need to find out who left the note." She paused, gazing at him. "It wasn't you, was it?"

"No." Gordon shook his head swiftly. "If I felt that someone had killed Joseph, I would have had the courage to tell you to your face."

"Thought so." Katrina nodded. "But someone did leave it and may know something the authorities missed."

"Why would someone want to harm Joseph?" he questioned, scratching the hair on his chin.

It was a question she'd asked herself more than once. As far as she knew, her husband was not on someone's radar to kill. But then, she might have thought the same thing about Roxanne before the police said that someone had murdered her. Maybe the same person or persons had gone after Joseph as well. Which made Katrina wonder if it was possible that he was into something she wasn't privy to. Could he have kept a secret from her so powerful that it got him killed?

"I have no idea," she told Gordon. "Maybe the note was a hoax. As Joseph's friend, I'll keep you informed if Dex learns anything."

"Mahalo." He sighed thoughtfully. "Still not sure I trust Dex. There's something about the man that just doesn't seem quite right."

"I'm sure it's just your imagination." Katrina smiled at him, even as she wondered if her new employee was everything he appeared to be. He had given her no reason to believe otherwise, in spite of Gordon's uncomfortableness with him. That included the fact that Dex's employment with the private detective agency checked out. And there was no denying his skills on the piano. Or, for that matter, his ability to charm her through his good looks, smooth style and even physical touch, if she were honest about it, remembering how she'd tingled when he'd removed the loose hair from her face earlier. Katrina felt her face turning red, while keeping this to herself. "I'll let you get back to it. Catch you later."

After checking in with housekeeping and the landscaping workers, Katrina headed outside to run a few errands. In her private parking space, she hopped into a white Nissan Sentra, started it and drove off. Still occupying her thoughts was the eerie note someone left her. Would Dex be able to track down the sender? Or was this task above his pay grade? Especially if it was a onetime thing and destined to be forever a mystery. As she pondered this, Katrina moved onto Maluhia Road, en route to Lihue, the island's commercial hub and home to Nawiliwili Harbor. No sooner had she begun the drive and turned her thoughts elsewhere, when she spotted a vehicle in her rearview mirror that seemed to be too close for comfort. Peering, she couldn't make out the driver, but saw that the car was black. A Jeep Grand Cherokee, she believed.

"What's your problem?" she spoke out loud, as if the driver could hear her. Katrina sped up, more than she was comfortable with. She recalled that another car was said to have been involved in Roxanne's fatal crash. Was this the same vehicle? Did the driver intend to rear-end her and force her into crashing? Her heart skipped a beat as Katrina fully expected the vehicle to come right up to her again and try to kill her. But then she risked a dangerous maneuver in swiveling her neck around to get a better look at her potential assailant and was surprised to see that the person had dropped back, making it clear that he or she was no longer a threat. Had that been the case all along? Had her imagination run away with itself?

Since when had she become so paranoid? Probably when her husband and housekeeper died less than six months apart. It didn't help matters any when someone left the chilling note claiming that Joseph had been murdered and intimating that she might be next. How was she supposed to respond to that? Maybe by waiting to see if Dex came up with anything before jumping to conclusions. Katrina pressed down on the brake, slowing her momentum to the speed limit. She glanced up at the rearview mirror again. The other car had apparently vanished, as though it had never been on her bumper in the first place.

After stopping off at a shopping center on Rice Street, Katrina casually walked through the mall with her bags. Without warning, once again she had a feeling of being watched. Looking over her shoulder, she spotted a dark-haired, white-skinned, tall, well-built man, maybe in his early forties, wearing a moss-colored Henley T-shirt, jeans and high-top black sneakers. He seemed to be keeping pace, but made no effort to close the distance between them. And yet she sensed that he was still following her. Wearing sling-back heel clogs, she picked up the pace and headed for the exit, at which point she planned a mad dash for her car, while hoping he didn't get to her first.

As she glanced back once more, heart pounding, Katrina saw that the man was still in pursuit. Or appeared to be. She considered ducking into a shop and asking the clerk to call the police, but quickly realized that there was no law against walking in a mall. So she decided to take her chances outside, praying he wasn't armed and prepared to use the weapon against her. Walking as fast as she was, Katrina managed to get her feet tangled and lost her balance. She felt herself start to fall, realizing it was all the man needed to catch up to her.

But instead of going down, perhaps flat on her face, Katrina found herself in the sturdy arms of none other than Dex, who seemed just as surprised and unsettled as she was.

IF THIS WERE any other time or situation, Dex might have found Katrina the perfect fit in his arms and would never want to let her go. But it was the here and now and, from the looks of things, she was in a hurry to vacate the mall just as he was entering it. "Going somewhere?" he joked, though suspecting she was anything but in a playful mood.

Managing to regain her footing while holding on to her bags, her long hair straddling her shoulders loosely, Katrina stammered, "A man was following me."

"What man?"

"That one…" she uttered, darting her eyes as if expecting someone to approach them at any second.

Dex gazed in the direction from which she had come and saw only an elderly woman walking slowly but surely. "There is no man," he told her.

Katrina colored. "He was there," she insisted. "He must have gone into one of the stores when he saw you."

"Hmm…" Dex studied the various shops nearby and considered looking in each and every one, but suspected that it would likely be a wasted effort. "Well, he's gone now."

She frowned at him. "You don't believe me, do you?"

"I believe you believe it," he responded flatly. "That

counts in my book, especially coming after the enigmatic note you found." Dex gazed again over her shoulder, hoping to catch someone trying to run away. "What did the man look like?"

"He was a white male, tall and fit, with dark hair," she described him in generic terms, "late thirties or early forties, I'm guessing." She made a face. "Sorry, but I wasn't exactly in a position to get a read on his physical characteristics."

"Don't apologize," Dex said understandingly. "Did he say anything to you?"

"No," Katrina admitted, as though he should have. "He just followed me practically the length of the mall, but seemed in no hurry to bridge the gap between us. I didn't give him time to change that reckoning. Especially after I thought a black Jeep Grand Cherokee had been following me on the way to the mall, before seeming to fall back in with other traffic…" She sighed. "That's when I ran into you…"

"Good thing I showed up when I did." Dex hoped that didn't come across as flippant, knowing that she perceived herself in real danger and he had no reason to dismiss this out of hand. Especially considering that Roxanne Yamamoto had been murdered in the midst of a drug-trafficking related investigation at the Maoli Lodge. With Joseph Sizemore a potential homicide victim too, why couldn't his widow also be targeted?

Katrina regarded him with suspicion. "What are you doing here anyway?"

"I thought I'd pay Larry Nakanishi a visit at his shop in the mall," Dex responded by way of explaining his presence. Her features instantly relaxed as she understood he wasn't following her too. "After making little headway with the staff members I've spoken with, I was hoping that, as the last person to see your husband alive, Nakanishi might know something about the note. Since you're here, care to tag along?" Dex also felt that was a good idea, so he could keep an eye on her in case the man who was following her should resurface while she was away from the lodge.

"Yes, I'd like that," she spoke eagerly, and he suspected it was as much about feeling safe in his company as needing some answers from the one person who may be in a position to provide them.

"Let me help you with those bags," he said, grabbing two of the three before she could turn him down.

"Thanks." She forced a smile, then said pensively, "Larry's store is down this way."

KATRINA WAS ADMITTEDLY comforted in having Dex by her side as they headed toward Larry's Aquatic Shop. Had he not arrived at just the right time, things could have gone terribly wrong. And yet, if she were being truthful about it, the whole thing regarding the stalker and car following her could have been a big nothing burger. Or, only her imagination. After all, in spite of the scary note and her sense of unrest, in reality no one had actually tried to harm her. Had they? One little message, no matter how unsettling, needn't upend her entire life. Still, she was grateful to have her private eye and pianist as a sort of devilishly handsome protector. At least for the time being. Also, if Larry was responsible for leaving the note, he owed her—and Joseph's memory—some type of explanation.

They walked into the shop where Joseph had first met and struck up a friendship with Larry Nakanishi, based on their love for going out in the water. It was Larry's suggestion, Katrina recalled, that they go kayaking that fateful day. Could he have been responsible for Joseph's death? She studied the man as he stood behind the counter seemingly deep in thoughts of his own. In his midthirties, Larry was slender and of medium height. He had a dark brown mohawk haircut and a fisherman's anchor black goatee.

"That him?" Dex asked her.

"Yes, that's Larry," Katrina confirmed, as he turned their way.

"Katrina…" His voice wavered. "Aloha."

"Hi, Larry." She kept her own tone measured. "This is Dex. He's a private investigator," she added, hoping to leverage it in pressuring him to speak up if the store owner was holding back on anything.

"Hey," Larry muttered, eyeing him warily. "What's up?"

"Do you have a sec?" she asked in a friendly tone.

"Sure." He folded his arms guardedly. "Everything okay?"

"Not really. Someone left me a message saying that Joseph's death was not an accident."

Larry unfolded his arms. "Not sure I understand…"

"The note said that he was murdered," Dex said bluntly. "And also warned Katrina to watch her back." He peered at Larry. "You wouldn't know anything about this, would you?"

"Why would I?" Larry's lips pursed. "It's bogus that Joseph was murdered. I was there. The shore break wave knocked him out of the kayak and he struggled to get back in. I tried to help, but he went under and drifted out to sea. By the time his body was found, it was too late." Larry eyed Katrina. "Someone's messing with you, but it's not me. Joseph was my friend. I thought you were too."

Katrina thought so too. Maybe they were barking up the wrong tree in suspecting him of leaving the note. "Sorry," she apologized. "Since you were with Joseph before he died, I was hoping you might know something about this."

"Wish I did," he said. "I have no idea why someone would leave you such a note."

Dex moved closer to the counter. "Do you know if anyone had a beef with Sizemore?"

Larry hedged. "Not enough to want to kill him," he argued.

"What about maybe to send a message that may have gone too far?"

He shrugged. "The Joseph I knew could rub some people the wrong way because of his competitive nature. But he never came to blows with anyone in my presence. I can't imagine someone wanting him dead."

Katrina was of the same mind here. Yet someone wanted her to believe that was the case. If not Larry, then who? "Someone has been following me," she told him. At least she believed this was true. "In this very mall, a man pursued me… You might know him," she said, admittedly grasping at straws, and described the man.

Larry scratched his goatee musingly. "Doesn't ring a bell. But the description is pretty vague. Sorry I can't be of more help."

"Me too." She frowned and again wondered if the entire note thing was someone's idea of entertainment to watch her squirm.

"Well, I have a customer over there I need to take care of," he said.

Katrina followed his gaze, thinking that it might be the person who had followed her in the mall. Instead, it was a much older Hawaiian man. She wrinkled her nose and faced Larry. "If anything comes to mind…"

"I'll let you know," he promised.

When they'd stepped outside, Dex asked Katrina pointedly, "Do you think Nakanishi was on the level?"

"Yes, I think so," she told him. "I don't see what he would gain by alleging that Joseph was murdered and then denying he left the note. Especially when he wasn't the man who was following me…and possibly the same person who wrote the message."

"Good point, but Nakanishi did look a bit uncomfortable, as if hiding something," he hinted. "Could be that I'm simply misreading him in looking for something that isn't there."

"Hmm… So, what now?"

Dex was still holding two of her bags as he said succinctly, "Guess that puts us back to square one."

"Meaning…?" She looked up at him, hopeful that a dead end wasn't the same as giving up what he may have seen as nothing more than a wild-goose chase.

"Meaning I won't stop until you have some answers, good or bad."

Katrina breathed a sigh of relief that at least he wasn't ready to write her off. They reached her car and she popped the trunk so they could put the bags in. She thanked Dex again for coming to her rescue. "With any luck, I'll make it back to the lodge without someone trailing me—"

"Actually, there will be someone trailing you," he said

firmly. "Me. Luck aside, I'll make sure you get back safe and sound and then be on my way."

She nodded, finding herself wishing he was around all the time for her safety and his sheer physical presence that was starting to work on her, whether he knew it or not. Was this a good thing? Or was she only setting herself up for a big fall as a lonely but still alive widow who might not be ready for a serious romance. Particularly with a man who hadn't given her any real indication that he was interested in anything more than working for her. Maybe it was better that way, as she tried to juggle her busy life as a lodge owner with the mysteries that had suddenly emerged about her late husband's untimely passing.

Chapter Five

After seeing to it that Katrina got back to the lodge without someone stalking her, Dex walked her to her suite and helped bring the bags inside. While he probably should have checked himself at the door, he couldn't resist the opportunity to catch a glimpse of the personal space she occupied at the lodge. "Nice," he said, and imagined her living there alone and possibly lonely, as he set the bags down.

"Mahalo. Took a while to completely furnish, but I like it." Katrina looked comfortable in her element, though Dex could still tell that she was troubled by the recent events that had her on edge. As was he, unable to shake the feeling that what she was going through was somehow connected to his undercover investigation, which increased the stakes even more. "Can I get you something to drink?"

They were standing close enough that Dex could actually kiss Katrina if he had a mind to. While the man in him, clearly attracted to her in ways he struggled to control, wanted nothing more than to throw the playbook out the window when it came to suspects, his more sensible side told him to resist making a move that could undermine the investigation into Roxanne's death. Not to mention the possibility that the Maoli Lodge was a front for drug trafficking on the island. "I need to get back to my place and feed Barnabas," Dex said, declining the invite, as he took a step away from her. He may have read disappointment in her face, prompting him to ask, out of curiosity, "So, how were things between you and your husband?"

Her lips twitched thoughtfully. "If you're asking did I love Joseph when he died?—the answer is yes, I did love him." She paused. "Not sure, though, that I was still in love with him. Does that make sense?"

"Yeah, it does," he told her sincerely.

"Does that make me a bad wife or widow?"

"Not at all." Dex met her eyes. "Some relationships can start to lose steam over time."

She held his gaze. "I suppose."

"Part of life." He gave her a tender smile. "Can I take a rain check on that drink?"

"Of course." Her eyes lit up. "Anytime."

Dex nodded at the thought and found himself wondering what it would be like to get her into bed. Something told him he wouldn't be any more disappointed than she would be, were the opportunity to ever present itself. Dropping his temperature down a notch, Dex said in a professional manner, "If you happen to see the man who was following you again, let me know."

She nodded uneasily. "I will."

"Probably not a bad idea to avoid traveling away from the lodge by yourself for the time being," he strongly suggested, "till we can get a better handle on the note and the person who may be tracking you."

"I hear you and agree," she told him, running a hand

through her hair. "I promise not to go venturing out alone until the coast is clear."

Dex grinned with satisfaction. "I'll see you tomorrow, boss," he said lightheartedly, and left.

BARNABAS ZIGZAGGED IN the backyard, as though on an obstacle course around avocado, lemon, lychee and papaya trees, which the K-9 operative dog handled masterfully in the absence of his real duties, as he went after the ball Dex threw for exercise. "Good boy," he applauded his canine and loyal friend, as Barnabas mouthed the ball and brought it back to him; whereby Dex threw it again for him to fetch. Once they had gotten this out of their systems, they headed back inside the cottage. There, Barnabas was fed, while Dex had a couple of slices of pepperoni, sausage and pineapple pizza and a beer. He updated Lynda and Ishikawa on his progress, or lack thereof, in locating the note writer. He also gave them a description of the man who Katrina said was following her, along with the dark Jeep Grand Cherokee she believed was tracking her, presumably driven by the same man. Finding out both their identities, if not the same person, was key to perhaps linking Joseph Sizemore's death to that of Agent Yamamoto in relation to trafficking of drugs at the lodge.

Dex gave the case a rest as he hopped into the shower. He wondered about Katrina and how good they could be together. Whether or not they ever got to put that to the test remained to be seen. He preferred not to look too far ahead, with things as they were in both their lives. Still, a man could dream a little. Couldn't he?

In the morning, after a mostly sleepless night, Dex went for a brisk walk with Barnabas before meeting

Agents Krause and Ishikawa at the Kauai Police Department on Kaana Street in Lihue for the Drug Task Force briefing. It was held in a conference room and Dex ran into some familiar faces between other DEA agents, FBI, IRS and US Postal inspectors represented; he met members of the PD's vice section for the second time since arriving on Kauai. The fact that everyone seemed on the same page meant a lot to him, as Dex understood that complex multiagency, multistate operations such as this one involving the trafficking of illicit drugs required cooperation, along with patience.

Admittedly, he was short on the latter, as bringing to justice those responsible for the death of Roxanne Yamamoto was front and center with Dex. Along with whether or not Joseph Sizemore's death truly was a homicide, and if someone was after Katrina as well. The idea of the lovely lodge owner falling prey to a killer was something Dex had started to take personally. He would be damned if he let that happen. Even if her own innocence in drug trafficking had yet to be established, in getting to know her so far, he sensed she had no involvement in the criminal activity. Could the same be said of Sizemore before his demise? If so, was the connection there?

As if reading Dex's mind, Ishikawa whispered from the seat beside him, "By the way, we came up with nothing in the way of fingerprints from the note. Pulling DNA from it will take a little longer, but I wouldn't hold my breath on anything coming from it either."

"What a shock," Dex said wryly. "Maybe whoever left the note will do us a favor the next time around and give us something to help identify them. Obviously, I'm really hoping it's the last Katrina will hear from the person," he made clear.

"Don't count on it." Lynda threw cold water on that, sitting on the other side of Dex. "If this unsub truly believes what he or she says and is not tossing garbage at the lady just to push her buttons, then Katrina is likely to hear from them again."

That's what I'm afraid of, Dex told himself, as he considered the impact of such on the investigation. He homed in on Kauai PD Vice's veteran detective Clayton Pietz, who was the lead local investigator of the case with a proven record of drug-trafficking interdiction. Thirtysomething, tall and slender, he had a dark buzz-cut fade hairstyle and horseshoe mustache.

Pietz stood by a large touch screen monitor and updated them on the investigation. "I don't think I need to tell any of you here that West Coast and international drug-trafficking gangs and organizations, attracted to the year-round great weather and drug use among tourists, are flocking to Hawaii, pedaling everything, including lethal fentanyl-laced meth, heroin and opioids." He switched from a picturesque image to that of various drugs with a Hawaiian backdrop. "Here on Kauai, we're being hit just as hard as the other islands, with illicit drugs being smuggled in and out at a premium, moved around in an effort to avoid detection and apprehension of the traffickers, and often controlled by well-armed thugs. Our job is to break up these highly profitable operations whenever possible and, when not, put a serious dent in them so they think twice about doing business on Kauai."

Pietz touched the screen and showed various locations on the island, while he said, "We believe that traffickers have chosen different sites to hold, display and distribute illegal drugs, including the Maoli Lodge, which the owners may or may not have been aware of." He put a photograph of Roxanne on the screen. "As you know, a member of our Task Force, DEA Agent Roxanne Yamamoto, was killed last month during an undercover assignment in apparent retaliation by traffickers for doing her job in trying to build a case against them. We're doing everything we can to bring her killer or killers to justice. Assisting in this regard is DEA special agent Dex Adair and agents Lynda Krause and Sylvester Ishikawa. On behalf of Agent Yamamoto, you've got our full support."

That was just what Dex needed to hear, as he was determined to get to the bottom of Roxanne's death and how it fit with the other dynamics of the investigation. He watched as US Postal Inspector Pauline Taomoto took Pietz's place. Fortysomething and slim, with an ash-blond shag, she connected the dots between the drug bust in Downtown Los Angeles and trafficking on Kauai.

"As part of this wide-ranging drug operation, some of the same players have been involved in the attempted shipping of packages of crystal meth from LA to the island," Pauline was saying, "which we were able to intercept with the assistance of a no-nonsense drug detection K-9 named Kimiko. To make a long story shorter, with the illicit goods in our possession, along with damaging calls and text messages between suspects, we're building a case against them that will likely result in lengthy prison sentences."

This was music to everyone's ears, including Dex's. After the briefing wrapped up, he sent Lynda and Ishikawa to get more from Pauline on the case being made against the traffickers in Southern California and Kauai and linking it to their own investigation. Dex met with Detective Pietz in his spacious office with a picture window for some follow-up questions.

"Have a seat," he said casually, blue-gray eyes upon Dex while sitting in a brown high-backed chair at an oak desk.

Dex sat across from him on a beige task chair, noting a framed photograph on the wall of Pietz with his wife and a young son. Another framed pic held a commendation he received for his work with drug-related investigations and organized crime. Without any small talk, Dex went right at it in seeking any new leads in the probe into Roxanne's death. "Where are we in the investigation?"

"We're following some paths that should soon result in one or more arrests," Pietz said, leaning back with his large hands pressed together.

"Can you be more specific?" Dex asked, narrowing his gaze.

"Yeah, specifically, we're homing in on an ex-con who we think may've cut the brake lines of the car Agent Yamamoto was driving that night. I can't tell you much more right now, other than that we're attempting to establish who he may have been working for and how far up the chain this goes…"

"Where does the Maoli Lodge fit into this?"

Pietz ran a hand across his mustache. "As of now, we believe it may be a drop-off point for drugs and drug money that is quickly moved to other more secure locations for handling and distribution. It's still being investigated."

"And also got Agent Yamamoto killed," Dex pointed

out hotly, not wanting her death to be undermined in any way.

"I understand that and we're not cutting any corners to nail the unsub," Pietz insisted calmly. "We're all on the same page here, Adair."

"Good to know." Dex realized he may have overreacted. He had no beef with the detective and wanted to work with him for the common good. "Have you been able to tie Joseph Sizemore to drug trafficking?"

Pietz jutted his chin. "Not in so many words."

"What does that mean?" Dex pressed.

"It means that, as of now, we have no solid evidence that Sizemore was trafficking in drugs before his kayaking accident. But we are aware that he was having money problems in running the lodge. Whether he financed it with dirty money has yet to be determined."

Money troubles? Dex wondered if Katrina was aware of this. And if the lodge could still be under water and under pressure from drug traffickers or other criminals. "What about Sizemore's widow?"

"We haven't been able to make a case for her being involved in any illicit activities or Agent Yamamoto's death," Pietz told him frankly, which allowed Dex to breathe a sigh of relief. Clearing Katrina of any wrongdoing would make it easier to be around her without having to wonder if there was something sinister below the attractive surface to her.

"Someone's been following Katrina Sizemore," he told the detective thoughtfully.

Pietz lifted a brow. "What, you mean like stalking her?"

"Yeah, you could say that." Dex took a breath. "This comes after she was left a note saying that Sizemore's death wasn't an accident, but murder, with the implication that Katrina could be next."

"That's news to me," Pietz contended.

"You mean that Sizemore's death may not have been accidental or the note?" Dex pressed his shoes against the brown carpet tile.

"Both. The autopsy report indicated that the man drowned as a result of his kayak capsizing. I have no reason to believe otherwise." Pietz glanced out the window and back. "As for the stalker and note, neither came from this office, I can promise you. If someone is after Katrina Sizemore, it's not related to our investigation."

Dex wasn't sure he bought that, given the correlation between one thing and another. But in the absence of anything to push back, he thought it best to leave it alone right now. At least insofar as pressing for answers the detective apparently didn't have. Instead, Dex would channel his focus toward Katrina and her safety, having been given a whole new reason to cozy up to her now that she was off the radar as a suspect in Roxanne's murder.

"ALOHA AND WELCOME to the Maoli Lodge," Katrina greeted her newest guests. They were an attractive family of four, having ventured to the island all the way from Dublin, Ireland, for vacation. Someday, she hoped to return the favor, welcoming the opportunity to visit Ireland and elsewhere in Europe as well as Australia and New Zealand. She and Joseph had talked about it as something to do down the line once they were established on Kauai. But then the dreams had been shattered and any such plans for herself were put on hold.

After checking the Byrnes family in, Katrina used a pause in the action to check her cell phone. For what-

ever reason, she had hoped to hear from Dex. Why?
Maybe because they had come so close to kissing yesterday after he'd walked her back to her suite. And what
if he had? How might that have changed the dynamic of
their, up to this point, strictly working relationship? She
wasn't sure, but wouldn't run away from the fact that
the pianist and private investigator did stir something
in her and maybe it wouldn't be such a bad thing to see
where it could lead.

Her mind pivoted to the man who she believed was
following her the day before. Who was he? Had he stayed
at the lodge and somehow become fixated on her? Or
did it have something—or everything—to do with the
note she received? When another guest showed up to
check in, Katrina dropped that train of thought and put
on her hospitable smile as she laid eyes on the tall and
thin Hawaiian girl who looked to be in her teens with
long, straight raven hair. "Are you Katrina Sizemore?"
she asked nervously.

"Yes, that's me," Katrina said, looking at her curiously.

"I was told to give this to you…" She handed her a
folded piece of paper.

A chill ran through Katrina. "Who told you?"

The teenager tensed. "Just a man. He gave me ten
bucks to give that to you…told me not to open it."

"What did he look like?" Katrina demanded, narrowing her eyes.

"I don't know," she shrugged. "Tall, muscular, I
guess. Had dark hair and was wearing shades."

That had to be the same man who was following me,
Katrina thought with dread. Had he been inside the
lodge, watching her as she had sensed someone doing?

Where was he now? She glared at the teen. "Can you show him to me?"

"Nope, sorry. He got in a Jeep afterward and drove off."

Had to be the same Jeep Grand Cherokee that trailed me to the mall, Katrina told herself undoubtedly. "Was he with anyone in the Jeep?"

"Don't know. Couldn't see inside." The girl looked jittery. "I have to go."

Katrina nodded understandingly, realizing that she was merely a messenger who this mysterious man used to further conceal his identity. She watched as the teen walked outside and then started to run, as though she couldn't get away fast enough. Only then did Katrina look down at the still folded note in her hands, almost afraid to open it. But she was more afraid not to see what he had to say next about Joseph and her. Unfolding the note with shaky fingers, she read.

> *Joseph Sizemore died as the result of an intentional drug overdose, whether you choose to believe it or not. Drowning only masked the truth about his murder. Speaking of truth, trust no one. That includes your pianist and so-called protector. He's not who you think he is.*

Katrina dropped the note on the counter, as if it were a hot coal, while trying to come to grips with its portentous message. Drug overdose homicide? Trust no one? Could Dex actually be involved in the murder of Joseph, while pretending to be someone she could count on for support?

"Hey," she was given a start when hearing the familiar deep voice. Katrina raised her head and stared into the handsome face of Dex Matheson, whom she was seeing in a whole new and disturbing light. He was standing there beside his dog, Barnabas. "Is everything all right?" Dex asked, his tone seemingly picking up on her combination of vexation and worry.

"Just who the hell are you?" Katrina demanded, her own inflection making it clear that nothing less than the truth would suffice. And even that, she sensed, would alter the essence of whatever existed between them.

Chapter Six

Dex was admittedly speechless for a long moment as he took in the exacting question, feeling as though he had been caught red-handed. Or worse, that she could suddenly see through his facade. It was obvious to him that something—or someone—had exposed him, to one degree or another. Who? He noted the piece of paper on the counter that separated them, seemingly into a deep divide. No doubt, it was another cryptic message. Dex decided for the time being to play the innocent and pretend he was befuddled by the question. "Not sure I follow you," he said coolly, while holding on to Barnabas's leash. "I'm the same guy you hired—twice—to work for you…"

"And who are you beyond that, Dex?" Katrina peered at him through narrowed eyes. "Is that even your real name?" Before he could respond, she pushed the note toward him. "You might want to read that first."

Eager to do just that, Dex grabbed the note and read the distressing words. They threw him for a loop on more than one front. Asserting that Sizemore had been murdered, as if an authority on this rather than pure speculation, told him that someone was determined to spin a narrative contrary to the official cause of death.

Equally troubling to Dex was that this same mystery writer had fingered him as an imposter, for all intents and purposes. Who could know this, apart from someone in law enforcement? Was a cop or even another DEA agent behind the notes? If so, to what end?

Dex met Katrina's hard gaze. "Where did you get this?" He held the note on a corner, in case evidence could be removed from it.

"A teenage girl gave it to me," she responded coldly. "The girl said a man, who matched the description of the one who was following me yesterday, handed it to her, along with ten dollars, and asked her to deliver it to me by name. He then got into a vehicle that sounded a lot like the Jeep Grand Cherokee that trailed me to the mall, and drove away." Katrina's mouth tightened as she planted a hand on her hip atop the green tiered maxi skirt she wore. "So, are you going to tell me who you are and why you've come to my lodge? Or do I fire you right now and ask you and your dog to vacate the premises immediately?"

Wow, she doesn't pull any punches, Dex thought, knowing that his options were slim to none at this point. Now that this can of worms had been opened, trying to come up with something plausible might only put him in a deeper hole. He needed to keep working there to further conduct his investigation. Then there was the matter of Joseph Sizemore's death that was starting to look more and more suspicious, in spite of the beliefs to the contrary. If that wasn't enough, Dex hated the thought of being kicked off the premises by someone with whom his vested interest had only grown over this short span of time. He couldn't walk away from her. At least not before trying to convince her that he was one of the good guys and one she could trust, in spite of his necessary deception.

He took a breath and asked in earnest, "Can we go somewhere and talk? Preferably in private…"

KATRINA HAD RESERVATIONS about inviting Dex to her suite. The mysterious note left her with more questions than answers. But even if she was wary of who he might be and what he was up to, something told her instinctively that Dex would not hurt her. At least not physically. Still, she owed it to herself, and maybe him too, to hear him out. He sat on one side of the rattan wicker cream-colored sectional in the great room, while she sat on the other, as if needing to keep some distance between them for the time being. Barnabas lay on the floor obediently beside his owner.

"Well, I'm listening…" Katrina gazed at Dex, trying to imagine what he had to say and how it might affect things between them.

He waited a beat and then said forthrightly, "All right, first of all, my name's not Dex Matheson." He reached into his pocket and pulled out his identification, which included a badge, and slid it her way. "Actually, I'm DEA special agent Dex Adair. I'm here on an undercover assignment…"

Katrina's eyes popped wide as she studied his ID and found herself momentarily speechless. She had to admit, she hadn't seen that one coming. With the Drug Enforcement Administration? A special agent? Why would he need to be at her lodge? And was the dog undercover too? "You're not a private investigator?" she asked, though the answer was obvious.

"Afraid not." His voice lowered an octave. "But the piano playing is a real pastime of mine."

Under other circumstances, she might have found that amusing. But in this instance, her thoughts were less about his skills on her baby grand, good as they were, and more on the fact that he might have only been stringing her along in supposedly helping her as a PI. "I don't quite understand," she confessed, while withholding judgment. "Care to explain the ruse?"

Dex leaned forward, stretched out his long arm and retrieved the ID. He put it away and sat back thoughtfully, rubbing his chin. "I'm investigating drug trafficking on the island."

"Drug trafficking?" She frowned. "What does that have to do with my lodge?"

"We believe that traffickers may be using your lodge to distribute, disperse or hide illicit drugs," he spoke candidly.

"That's not possible," she uttered defensively. If it were true, wouldn't she have known? Or at least suspected such activity in her midst?

"A Task Force on drug trafficking on Kauai disagrees," Dex said sharply. His face darkened. "Last month, one of our agents, Roxanne Yamamoto, was murdered. You knew her as Roxanne Kitaoka—"

"Roxanne…" Katrina cringed as the implications registered as to the fate of her former housekeeper. "Are you saying…?"

"She was undercover while in your employ," Dex said bleakly. "Before Agent Yamamoto could issue her findings, she was killed."

"So, you're here to investigate her death?" Katrina asked, as the sadness of Roxanne's death took on even greater meaning and the truth of his presence began to fall into place.

"Yes." He pinched his nose. "And to continue the investigation into drug trafficking."

As he regarded her keenly, it dawned on Katrina that if Dex believed the Maoli Lodge was a site for trafficking drugs, then as its proprietor she must be suspected of participating. "Wait…" she gasped, "you don't think I'm a drug dealer or whatever, do you?" The notion that she could be involved in criminal activity didn't sit well with her.

"No, I don't," Dex answered firmly, allowing Katrina to breathe again. At least on that score. The other inferences of the lodge being a front for drug trafficking were no less disturbing. "I admit that initially, in doing my job, I needed to check you out, as part of the broader probe underway on the island. You're no longer a target of the investigation, Katrina," he claimed.

"I suppose I should be thanking you for that," she said sardonically, but was quite relieved, in fact, if true. Being targeted for something she was totally innocent of would have distressed anyone. Especially coming from someone she had actually begun to feel something for.

"Unfortunately, the probe into your lodge is still ongoing," Dex pointed out. "Now that the cat's out of the bag as to my identity, I would like us to work together."

Katrina glared at him. "You're joking, right?"

"Can you think of a better way to put this behind you and continue operations with a clean slate?" He locked eyes with her, illustrating his seriousness and forcing her to reassess her initial resistance. "If we determine that we're way off base, the investigation will move elsewhere. No questions asked. But if there is something to this, and I believe Agent Yamamoto's death adds credence to that, we both owe it to her to see this through. So, are you game?"

Katrina's resolve weakened in support of her friend Roxanne, even if she had been working undercover. "When you put it that way, yes, I'm in."

"Cool." Dex grinned and Katrina remembered her attraction to him before the big reveal. So what did that mean for them beyond his investigation? Were the strong vibes between them only an act on his part in the course of an undercover assignment? "I'd like you to keep my real identity and mission to yourself," he stressed. "The less people who know what's going on, the better. If there is anyone on your staff or otherwise involved with the lodge who's trafficking drugs or committing related crimes, we wouldn't want to tip them off and compromise the investigation."

"I understand," she said, knowing that cooperating while not jeopardizing the case was in her best interest as well as the lodge's. "Your secret is safe with me," Katrina promised, and cast her gaze upon the dog, who hadn't moved and was obviously well trained. "So, I suppose that Barnabas is more than just a good companion to you?"

Dex smiled. "Yes, Barnabas is part of a DEA K-9 unit, trained in narcotic and drug detection." He spoke proudly of the canine.

Katrina swallowed. "And has he detected any illegal drugs on the property?" She hesitated to ask, but needed to know.

"Not yet. But then, I haven't really had a chance to let him loose to do his thing," Dex said honestly. "Could be that Barnabas comes up with nothing. But that wouldn't necessarily mean you've gotten over the hump at this point with respect to the lodge being a front for drug trafficking. Let's just hope for the best."

She picked up the sincerity in his tone in not wanting her lodge to be a party to drug criminality. Was this a natural reaction on his part? Or an indication that he did care for her as a person beyond his undercover work? Did it make a difference at this point, considering she had only established a rapport with him under false pretenses? Katrina considered that it was likely there were other undercover DEA agents at or around the lodge. She wouldn't ask Dex to confirm or deny, figuring it was on a need-to-know basis and, as such, he wouldn't want to blow their covers. Even for her. She wouldn't hold that against him, knowing that this was what he did for a living, whether she was entirely comfortable with it or not.

It brought Katrina back to the last note she'd been given. Or, more specifically, the insinuations about Joseph's death. Did Dex know more than he was letting on? Was there a connection to Roxanne's death and the drug-trafficking investigation? She peered at the DEA special agent. "Do you believe Joseph was murdered for being involved in drug trafficking?" she asked point-blank, the idea that he was killed by someone nauseating to her. Worse was the thought that her husband could have been dealing in drugs. Had that been the case, wouldn't she have known? If she had been privy to this, of course she would have, done her very best to put a stop to it?

Dex ran a hand along his jawline. "Someone sure

as hell seems to think so," he responded ambivalently. "As you know, the official word is that your husband died in a kayaking accident with no apparent foul play involved. That being said, the timing in relation to the ongoing drug-trafficking investigation on Kauai is more than a little suspicious. It will need to be further investigated. Particularly, in light of the allegations made in the note you were given." He paused, running his hand along the top of Barnabas's head. The dog was receptive. "Was Joseph using any drugs at the time of his death?"

Katrina stared at the thought. "Two years ago, he hurt his back while scuba diving. Joseph was prescribed fentanyl to deal with the pain. As far as I was aware, he overcame it and was no longer taking anything."

"We'll go on that assumption till I have a chat with the medical examiner," Dex said matter-of-factly. "Until then, let's not jump to any conclusions based on an anonymous note, in spite of its insinuations."

"I'm trying not to," she told him. "But between the notes and discovering that we've been under investigation for drug trafficking, it's hard not to think that someone may have murdered Joseph, even if it was for all the wrong reasons." Katrina extended her chin sadly. "Same person or persons who murdered Roxanne."

"If that proves to be the case, we'll work through it together," he offered gently.

"Okay." She looked at him and Katrina knew that it was a sympathetic gesture on his part. Whatever happened, she needed to believe that someone was still looking out for her. Maybe that person was Dex, even if not the man she first thought him to be. Something inside her hoped she could still get to know the *real* him.

Dex stood up. "Barnabas and I will get out of here and give you some time to process things."

Katrina rose as well and flashed her eyes. "I don't really have any choice, do I?"

He moved toward her and ran a hand along her cheek. "I'm sorry you had to be caught up in this."

"So am I." She closed her eyes for a moment and soaked in the tenderness of his touch, before opening them again. "But for the sake of everything I've worked so hard for, I am committed to doing everything I can to protect the lodge and my place on Kauai. That includes cooperating with your investigation."

"Fair enough." Dex removed his hand from her face. "I'll have the note analyzed for any prints or DNA the man may have left. Other than that, if you see him again or he tries to contact you, stay away from him and let me know about it."

She nodded. "I will."

"I still have a date with the piano this evening," he reminded her, in keeping up appearances. "So, I'll see you then."

"Aloha," she said dryly, walking him and Barnabas to the door.

Only after she was left alone did Katrina wonder where this would all end. Would the lodge, and Joseph by extension, be exonerated of any wrongdoing? Or were people she thought she could trust committing crimes behind her back and right under her nose? And what would become of any possibilities between her and Dex, now that she knew he was a DEA agent who would in all likelihood be heading back to wherever he was from once the case had ended? Would he put behind him any feelings that seemed to exist between them?

"MY COVER'S BEEN BLOWN," Dex informed Lynda and Ishikawa at the cottage, as each stood with beer bottles in their hands and Barnabas looked on, appearing disinterested.

Lynda gazed at him in shock. "How?"

"Damn if I know." Dex was still trying to figure it out, short of pointing fingers. "Katrina received another note…" He slipped the plastic evidence bag out of his pocket and read the message out loud. "This was left for her by the man who's been following her. Whoever he is, he's on to me."

Ishikawa grabbed the note, reading it again. "Who the hell is this person?"

"That's what we need to find out." Dex took a sip of beer pensively. "He's obviously going out of his way to maintain a low profile."

"Think he's one of us?" Lynda questioned.

"Doesn't seem likely, if we're talking about the DEA. As for the locals or someone else on the Task Force, it's anyone's guess."

Ishikawa narrowed his eyes. "But why would any of them want to push the homicide narrative for Sizemore's death in direct contrast to the official findings?"

"Maybe because the person disagrees with the assertion that Sizemore's death was accidental, but is not in a position to say so," Dex suggested, and thought about how this had adversely weighed on Katrina. He wanted to do whatever he could to get to the truth for her as well as himself regarding any association between the deaths of Sizemore and Roxanne.

"On the other hand," Lynda put out, tilting her beer bottle, "it could be that the note came from the person responsible for Sizemore's death and they don't want to see the truth swept under the rug."

"You mean he wants to take credit for murdering him," Ishikawa contended, "and is also sending a signal to whoever else may be involved in the drug-trafficking scheme that he means business?"

"Exactly," she said flatly.

"Any of those theories is plausible," Dex told them. "Maybe this time we'll get lucky and get some evidence off the note."

"How are things with the widow after the latest note?" Ishikawa asked.

"Not very good, I'm afraid." Dex took another gulp of his beer. "She's pretty shaken up about it, quite naturally."

"And what's the status of your undercover identity?" Lynda eyed him sidelong.

"She knows I'm a DEA special agent," he responded without batting an eye. "Once the thought that I wasn't being straight with her had been planted, I had no choice but to come clean. Or be fired. Since it was already pretty clear that Katrina was not involved in any wrongdoing, I figured she could be an asset if I revealed my real identity and mission."

"I think you're right about that," Ishikawa said, and swallowed beer. "Having someone on the inside who can be trusted is a good thing at this point."

"Does she know about us too?" Lynda faced Dex intently.

"No," he emphasized. "That's the good news. The mystery man doesn't appear to be privy to your undercover assignments. I saw no reason to divulge this to Katrina," Dex said, holding the line on a need-to-know basis. "As such, you'll be able to carry on with what you're doing while keeping an eye out for anyone suspicious lurking around."

"That works for me." Ishikawa leaned over to rub one of Barnabas's ears.

"Same here," Lynda agreed and finished off the beer.

"I'll bring Rachel up to date on where thing's stand," Dex told them, knowing the SAC would have his back in continuing the investigation, even with his cover exposed. In this instance, he welcomed being able to be up-front with Katrina, wanting her to get to know him for who he truly was and hoping to take the opportunity to get to know her better as well beyond their professional lives and tenuous circumstances.

Chapter Seven

After a mostly restless sleep, Katrina welcomed the morning sunshine and an opportunity to stretch her legs with a walk along the south shore of Poipu Beach. Considered as one of the top beaches in the country, its string of sandy crescents, cool trade winds and spectacular ocean view made the beach a favorite place for her to spend time outside the Maoli Lodge. Mindful of Dex's warning not to leave the lodge on her own as long as someone was stalking her, she was accompanied by Alyson, who routinely took advantage of the setting with daily walks to stay in shape.

I refuse to be a prisoner in my own home, Katrina thought defiantly, as her bare feet stepped across the soft sand. While heeding Dex's advice, she felt a need to be out and about relishing the setting Kauai afforded her. Honestly, she hoped the DEA special agent and his cronies were able to prove that the lodge was not a place for drug trafficking. Neither she nor Joseph, when he was alive, would have tolerated such activity. But what if traffickers were operating outside their knowledge and this had somehow cost Joseph his life? The pain at the thought was enough for Katrina to shift her focus. She gazed at the tombola splitting the two coves. Called Nukumoi Point, it was a resting place for Hawaiian monk seals, an endangered species. She admired the earless seals, while hoping they would stay protected, just as she wanted to be from anyone who may wish her harm.

"So, any more news on that weird note somebody left you?" Alyson broke into her thoughts.

Katrina, who kept in stride with her fast-walking assistant manager, smiled at her, while responding evenly, "Not yet. But Dex is still looking into it." She had refrained from mentioning the second alarming and revealing note she'd received yesterday, if only to protect Dex's cover as promised. Though she trusted Alyson, Katrina would hate for the talkative assistant manager to accidentally say something to someone that might impede the investigation. Or endanger Dex. "I don't intend to let it occupy my every waking moment," she lied.

"Good for you," Alyson told her while keeping up the brisk pace. "Joseph was a good man. If someone had truly wanted to harm him, I'm sure the authorities would be on top of it. Just as they were in deciding that Roxanne's death was the result of foul play, even if there's no reason to believe it had anything to do with her employment at the Maoli Lodge."

I'm afraid it may have had everything to do with that, Katrina mused bleakly in thinking about Roxanne being an undercover DEA agent, like Dex, at the lodge. Had she discovered something nefarious that made her a target? Or could her death have been a random act of violence? "Let's hope not," she muttered. "We'll just have to wait and see when the investigation is completed."

"True." Alyson frowned. "Let's not freak out about it till then. Agreed?"

Katrina grinned. "Agreed." She took a breath and was

able to stay in lockstep with her. Then, all of a sudden, a strange yet familiar feeling came over Katrina. As before, it seemed as though she was being watched. Her eyes darted around, expecting to see the stalker trailing them. Or ready to pounce like a leopard. She saw no one, but her heart continued to race nonetheless. Perspiration dripped beneath her armpits. Was it her imagination this time, making her go crazy?

Alyson noticed. "Hey, are you all right?"

"Yes, I'm fine," Katrina pretended. "It's just that… I thought…"

"Thought what?"

"Never mind." Katrina decided not to overreact. "It was nothing." Still, she was concerned enough to look around again. If the man who left the notes was out there lurking in the shadows, she didn't want to get caught blindsided. But there was no one there. She turned to Alyson, who had taken her cue and scanned the beach.

"Looking for someone?" she asked, inquisitiveness flickering in her eyes.

"Not really," Katrina claimed. "Just checking out who else is up and at it this morning." Rather than belabor the point and feel foolish in the process, she said the most practical thing to be on the safe side, "Anyway, we better get back to the lodge before they start to miss us."

Alyson smiled. "Whatever you say."

As they reversed course, Katrina once more looked over her shoulder for someone who wasn't there. She could only assume that Dex would come up with some answers, even if no longer working for her as a private investigator. At least, she mused, he truly was a gifted pianist, giving her this much to look forward to for as long as he cared to keep this undercover role going.

Dex stepped into the Kauai County Medical Examiner and Coroner's office on Kuhio Highway in Lihue, where he was greeted by the ME herself. Francesca Espanto was in her early forties and petite, with medium-length champagne blond hair in a feathered cut. She wore oval eyeglasses over brown eyes.

"Aloha," she said routinely. "I'm Dr. Espanto."

"Aloha." He was starting to catch on with some of the common Hawaiian lingo. "DEA Special Agent Adair," he said, flashing his ID for effect, after speaking with her briefly over the phone.

"You wanted to know about Joseph Sizemore's death?"

"Yes, a little more clarity on how he died." Dex mused that anything other than an accidental drowning would not only raise red flags, but be that much more difficult for Katrina to stomach. He realized, though, that the unanswered questions about foul play would be even tougher for her.

"Follow me…"

They went down a corridor and entered a nice-sized office with modern furnishings and white cement tile flooring. Francesca offered him a seat on one of two vanilla leather chairs with flip arms. She sat in an oversize red ergonomic chair at an L-shaped espresso computer desk, and pulled up the file on Sizemore on her laptop. After a moment or two, she said matter-of-factly, "Officially, Mr. Sizemore's death came as the result of drowning. As I understand it, his kayak got hit with a shore break wave, causing him to take a tumble, whereby he drowned. By all appearances, it was an accidental tragedy."

"Were there any drugs in Sizemore's system?" Dex asked, sensing there was more to the story.

"Yes." Francesca furrowed her brow as she pulled up more information. "The toxicology report revealed that Mr. Sizemore had nonlethal concentrations of fentanyl and methamphetamine in his body at the time of death."

"Hmm…" Dex recalled the mysterious note indicating with certainty that Sizemore's death was due to an OD, the drowning notwithstanding. Which was in stark contrast to Katrina's belief that he was not using any medications or drugs at the time of his death. "Could someone have deliberately administered the fentanyl or meth to Sizemore with the intention of killing him or knocking him out—had the shore break wave not beaten them to the punch—with the water finishing him off?"

Francesca stared at the question. "Without getting into the head of someone with such an intent, I suppose it's possible that someone tried to kill the victim with the fentanyl and meth," she surmised. "But had that been the case, the levels of the drugs in Joseph Sizemore's system were simply not strong enough in and of themselves to deal the decedent a fatal blow. On the other hand, it is possible that the drug combo could have been enough to render Mr. Sizemore unconscious when or after he hit the water, which then led to his drowning…"

Dex mulled that over as another thought entered his head. "Is it possible that Sizemore took the meth and fentanyl together with the intention of committing suicide? Or to help himself along while anticipating the wave, making drowning more palatable?" He recalled Detective Clayton Pietz indicating that Sizemore had run into financial difficulties. Could taking his own life been his ticket out, while ensuring that Katrina would have the money from insurance to keep the Maoli Lodge running?

"Anything's possible," the medical examiner allowed. "But again, my job is not to interpret the precise mindset of the dead, per se, rather to determine the actual cause of death and any contributory factors, while leaving a question of intent and conjecture to other professionals such as yourself, Agent Adair."

"I understand." He gave a little self-conscious grin respectfully and then stood. "Thanks for your time."

"Mahalo." She smiled back. "I'm here to help in any way I can."

Dex felt the same way. He only hoped that Katrina would accept his help in the spirit intended, even if in the process she was likely to experience more pain before things got better.

"I'VE GOT NEWS…" Dex said in a tone that told Katrina it wasn't good. Though she wanted to run away from anything that might further shake her world, she knew it wasn't a realistic option. She needed to know whatever he was willing to share, for the sake of the lodge and the memory of her late husband.

"Why don't we go out into the garden," she suggested, knowing there was a quiet place where they could talk. She led him through an assortment of flowering, spice and tropical fruit trees, and past a fish-filled pond surrounded by exotic Hawaiian plants, until reaching a wooden octagonal gazebo. They sat near each other on a cedar bench, before Katrina asked hesitantly, "What did you find out?"

Dex waited a beat and said evenly, "I spoke with the medical examiner and she's sticking with the belief that

Joseph's death was due to drowning, and most likely an unfortunate accident." He waited another beat, telling Katrina that there was more to the story. "The toxicology report showed that there was fentanyl and methamphetamine in his system at the time of death, which may or may not have contributed to it…"

"Fentanyl and methamphetamine?" she uttered, as though foreign words. Had Joseph continued to use painkillers even after he had told her he had quit? Why wouldn't he have confided in her? Tried to get through his pain without overmedicating himself?

"I'm sorry," she heard the gentle words come from Dex's mouth. "I know you thought he was off the fentanyl and maybe the meth is news to you…"

Katrina reacted. "Yes, I never knew he was using meth," she admitted with frustration. "And I'd really hoped the fentanyl was behind him." She paused. "Obviously, I didn't know my husband as well as I thought I did," she muttered sadly.

"By keeping you in the dark, he was probably trying to protect you the only way he knew how," Dex suggested.

She thought about the stalker and his role in creating suspicion about how Joseph died. "What about the notes insisting there was foul play involved in Joseph's death?"

Dex angled his head and had a thoughtful look. "I'm guessing that whoever has been leaving you the notes has some knowledge of Joseph using the drugs—maybe his supplier or even another user—and may have been acting out of guilt or some misplaced sense of duty in believing the drugs had truly killed him."

"Perhaps," she allowed, still trying to make sense of Joseph using fentanyl again, along with meth, when he seemed to be doing so well. How could she have not known this wasn't the case? Something about this entire scenario still wasn't sitting well with her. Why was the man stalking her so adamant in his position? What did he hope to gain from this harassment? Katrina turned toward Dex, who also seemed to be wrestling with the conclusions from the medical examiner. "What if the man stalking me knows more than he's said so far about Joseph's death and something is still being missed in the official findings?" She couldn't help but think about the feeling she had this morning of being watched, even if there was no proof of that to make it worth mentioning to Dex. But that didn't mean her instincts weren't correct.

"That's possible," Dex said with a ragged sigh. "The one other person who may be in a position to know about the drug use and any intentions to commit murder would be Larry Nakanishi, the last one to see your husband alive. Maybe the fact that the stalker followed you to the very mall where he works could be more than just coincidence. They could be in this together…"

"You think?" Katrina quivered at the consideration that Larry could have aligned himself with someone stalking her. If so, to what end?

"There's only one way to find out." Dex's warm breath fell onto her cheek. "Do you have your phone?" When she nodded, he said, "Let's give Nakanishi a call right now—and let's do a video chat."

Katrina took the cell phone out of the pocket of her wide leg pants, pulled up Larry's name from her contact list and tapped the video camera icon. After a couple of rings, he accepted the video chat request.

"Aloha, Katrina." His voice was cagy. "What's going on?"

"You tell me," she said tersely. "Did you know that Joseph was using meth and fentanyl on the day he died?"

Larry's chin sagged. "Knew about the meth—we both just wanted a little buzz before going out on the kayaks—but not the fentanyl," he claimed. "I don't know anything about that."

"How long had Joseph being using meth?" Katrina questioned, not sure she believed his lack of knowledge about the fentanyl.

"As long as I've known him. Said he needed it to deal with some back pain and just to get high."

Katrina cringed at the thought that her husband had chosen to keep this from her, knowing she would have done everything in her power to get him off and away from drugs and their destructive nature. "Well, the drugs may have contributed to his death," she alleged.

A brow shot up and Larry scratched his neck. "If it's true, I'm sorry to hear it, but it's not my fault. Joseph did what he wanted."

She couldn't argue with that as the realities of the life they had and the secrets he kept with his drug use dawned on her. Gazing at Dex, who indicated with his fierce eyes that he wanted in on the conversation, Katrina turned back to Larry and said firmly, "The private investigator I'm working with would like to have a word with you—"

Before Larry could object, Dex took the phone and asked commandingly, "Where did Sizemore get the meth he used that day?" Katrina knew that, by extension, Dex was assuming the supplier could have also given Joseph synthetic fentanyl—possibly her stalker.

"Just a dude," Larry muttered shakily.

"That's not good enough, Nakanishi." Dex furrowed his forehead. "I need a name!" When Larry hesitated, Dex added while maintaining his cover, "I have friends with the DEA. I'd be happy to give them a call and have them show up at your door to see just what they might find inside. I suspect it might not go well for you or your aquatic shop…"

"All right, all right," he relented. "His name is Julio."

"Julio what?"

"He only goes by Julio," Larry contended.

"What does he look like?" Dex asked.

Katrina listened as the drug dealer named Julio was described as an olive-skinned, brown-haired male in his early thirties. She exchanged glances with Dex, as they both realized this was not the same man who had been stalking her.

"Where can I find this Julio?" Dex demanded.

"You can't." Larry colored. "Heard he left the island in a hurry a few months back. Maybe to Oahu. As for me, after what happened to Joseph, I've been off meth for a while now, trying to clean up my act."

"For your sake, I hope you're leveling with me," Dex said in a threatening tone; then he pivoted to a more friendly voice. "While we have you, we're still looking for the man who's been stalking Katrina and seems to believe Joseph was murdered. Are you sure he's not someone you know?" Dex repeated his description, which Katrina believed was spot-on. Larry didn't buckle, insisting that he didn't recognize the man, which meant they were no closer to identifying him than before. It indicated that the stalking and messages might not be over. The thought gave her a chill.

After the conversation with Larry ended, Dex peered at Katrina and asked point-blank, "Do you think it's possible that Joseph may have taken his own life?"

Her head jerked as if she'd been hit. "You mean suicide?" she asked, though the answer was obvious.

"It's the one angle we haven't tackled," Dex said honestly. "That might explain taking fentanyl and meth at the same time he was going on a kayaking trip."

"No, Joseph would not have killed himself," Katrina said with certainty, putting aside the accidental or deliberate act of murder possibilities. At least she was trying to convince herself that, no matter what, taking such an extreme measure was not in the cards for him. "Though he may have been using drugs willingly, he still had too much to live for to simply throw it all away just like that."

Dex turned away and back, his eyes pinning on her face. "In the course of the drug-trafficking investigation, it's been discovered that Joseph was having some money issues. Do you know anything about that?"

Katrina didn't like the implication. But she couldn't allow it to throw her off-balance, even if this wasn't necessarily Dex's aim. Was it? "I'm not quite sure what you're getting at," she told him, while reading between the lines. "Yes, we've had our struggles making ends meet, like other small business owners. But through it all, we were able to balance the budget and keep things going just fine. When Joseph died, his insurance allowed me to use the payment to cover any outstanding debts and complete a few overdue repairs to the lodge with a bit left over for my savings." Her brows lowered. "If there's something else on your mind, just say it."

"All right." He drew a breath and held her steady gaze. "With the investigation still ongoing, it's possible that your husband could have engaged in drug trafficking to make enough money to help with the bills without you ever being the wiser." Dex let that settle in before continuing. "If that's true, he could have put himself in danger and lost control of the situation, resulting in his murder. Or he could have simply gotten in over his head in dealing with some bad people, or even just being overwhelmed with the finances or lack thereof in running the lodge, and decided to check out, sparing you to the extent possible, while seeing to it that his insurance would kick in to ease your burden. If you think I'm way off base here, feel free to say so."

Everything in Katrina wanted to totally disagree with all of Dex's theories: the assertion that her dead husband had taken his own life due to financial pressures or to provide her operating money from insurance upon his death; or to escape the physical pain he'd apparently still been enduring; or even aligning himself with drug traffickers in some ill-advised scheme of helping them keep their heads above water in operating the lodge. But the truth was she wasn't sure what to think at this point. Joseph had already shaken her confidence in discovering that he was using drugs illegally. What else did she not know? What other secrets would she discover about her husband of seven years that would further shake her foundation?

She took a breath and met Dex's eyes. "Maybe you're not off base," she conceded. "I simply don't know. In my heart and soul, I can't bring myself to believe the man I once loved would rather kill himself than face whatever demons he had together. But we were struggling somewhat in making ends meet and…it's possible that he could have resorted to drastic measures behind my back to do what he thought was necessary to stem the tide—" Her voice shook. "If that's true, I won't shirk from my responsibilities as a law-abiding citizen and loyal resident of Kauai to make things right in any way I can."

"You already have by cooperating with me," Dex said, placing a hand upon hers, causing Katrina to react favorably as she found her other hand overlapping his. She felt the connection throughout her entire body and maybe right into her soul.

"I can do more," she insisted, releasing his hand reluctantly. He continued to caress her other hand, which was torturously appealing. "If Joseph was dealing in drugs to bring in more money, the one person who may know about it is Gordon, whom he seemed to confide in."

Dex nodded, taking his hand back and standing. "Why don't we pay the bartender a little visit and see what he can tell us…"

Katrina agreed as she got up, while at the same time fearful of what Gordon might have to say about the man she once believed she would spend the rest of her life with. Instead, he was gone and she had to deal with the aftermath alone. For better or worse. Or might she be able to somehow come out of this on the right side of the track with the help of a DEA agent who seemed as much dedicated to her health and well-being as his job and getting to the truth?

Chapter Eight

There was no getting around it as they headed out of the tropical gardens and its impressive offerings. Dex liked touching Katrina. She had such soft hands and he could only imagine the softness of the rest of her body. Not to mention, she clearly had a heart of gold. Any man would be lucky to have her as the love of his life. Joseph Sizemore had her in the palm of his hand and allowed her to slip away. Or had it been outside of his control? Did the man purposely end his life through drugs and drowning? Or, as contended in the notes left for Katrina, had someone murdered Sizemore? If so, was it because he no longer wanted to play ball with traffickers? Or had he gotten on someone else's bad side?

Dex was eager to get this resolved. He knew that was even more important to Katrina. She deserved some closure. Whether that put Sizemore in a positive or negative light, at least she could move on with her life knowing the truth. Then maybe she would be more open to starting over and having a new relationship to work on. Dex would love to be on the receiving end of that affection. But could it work when his career as a DEA special agent had him crisscrossing the states within his jurisdiction, leaving not nearly enough time to put his all into a romance with a beautiful woman who merited no less in a man?

When they entered the Kahiko Lounge, Gordon Guerrero was busy unboxing liquor on the other side of the bar. It was obvious to Dex that the bartender didn't particularly care for him, based on their exchanges. He didn't sense that the man was interested in pursuing Katrina romantically. But maybe as a friend to her and Sizemore, Gordon hoped to protect Katrina from getting hurt. Or was it more about wanting to make sure his cousin's wife had a place to return to after her maternity leave was up? As it was, Dex had run a criminal background check on Guerrero in relation to their drug-trafficking probe. Other than a DUI five years ago, he saw no red flags that suggested he was dealing in drugs on the side while bartending.

"Hey," Katrina said, walking up to the counter.

"Hey." Gordon stopped doing what he was doing. He regarded Dex uneasily.

"Can we talk to you for a moment?" she asked.

"Yeah." He leaned against the counter. "What do you need?"

"Information," she put out solidly.

"What kind of information?"

"Did Joseph ever mention anything to you about money problems?"

Gordon shrugged. "Yeah, I suppose, from time to time. Comes with the territory. Why do you ask?"

"Because I need to know if he was in any kind of trouble," Katrina answered bluntly.

"Trouble?" The bartender grabbed a clean glass and a cloth to dry it, which Dex interpreted as a sign of nervousness. Or was it guilt by association?

She peered at Gordon. "Do you know if Joseph was selling drugs at the lodge—or somewhere else?"

"No, not that I know of." His brows descended. "Why would you think that?"

"Because he had drugs in his system at the time of death," she replied, "according to the medical examiner. Joseph was also quite worried about our finances. If this resulted in his trafficking drugs, I need to know. So does Dex here…" Dex cringed when he thought she might blow his cover. Instead, Katrina merely said truthfully, "Someone has been stalking me. I believe it's the same person who's been leaving me notes, indicating that Joseph was the victim of foul play. As a PI, Dex has learned that the authorities are looking into drug trafficking on the island. Maybe even taking place at the Maoli Lodge. If you know anything about this and Joseph's involvement, you need to tell me, Gordon."

"If it's true, it's only a matter of time before the police piece it together—" Dex decided to up the ante "—and bring down anyone who is an accomplice to the trafficking of drugs on Kauai soil…"

"Joseph never indicated to me that he was dealing drugs," Gordon maintained, sneering at him. "Whether he was using or not to get through the day, he wouldn't have disrespected the land or you, Katrina," he emphasized, "by going down that path." The bartender drew a sharp breath. "But Joseph did confide in me that he was short on funds and needed to buy some time till business picked up, since he wasn't able to get anything more from the bank. I suggested he try calling a local moneylender I know…"

Dex's mouth turned down. "You mean a loan shark?"

Gordon's chin jutted. "Yeah, I guess."

"Did Joseph get in touch with him?" Katrina demanded.

"I believe so."

"We need the person's name and address," Dex told the bartender, making it clear it wasn't a casual request. Gordon wasted no time in giving them what they needed.

After leaving the lounge, Dex told Katrina, "I'll go talk to the loan shark and see if Joseph borrowed money from him with a high interest rate." Though far from advisable, if true, it would at least make it less likely that Sizemore turned to trafficking drugs for profit to fund his business or drug habit.

"I'm coming with you," she said firmly.

"Not sure that's such a good idea." As a DEA agent in an official capacity, Dex was hesitant to bring a civilian into the case. Especially Sizemore's widow.

"I have to beg to differ there." Katrina gave him a hard look that indicated she meant business. "Joseph was my husband. I need to find this out for myself—with or without you." She sighed. "I'm sure you understand."

As it became clear to him that she was as stubborn as he was, perhaps more so, Dex didn't fight it. "Yes, I think I do. Just be prepared for whatever may come out of this," he warned in the nicest manner possible.

"I could say the same to you, Agent Adair." She steeled herself for any pushback. "Let's just get this over with."

Dex grinned, liking this unflappable side of her. He imagined that would come in handy under other more intimate circumstances. But for now, they were on a mission to either clear her late husband of any wrongdoing relative to the drug-trafficking probe or discover that Sizemore had dug himself an even deeper hole that could well have cost Roxanne her life.

KATRINA HAD VOLUNTEERED to drive, seeing that she knew the island better than Dex, to get to the loan shark's office more quickly. He surprised her by agreeing to ride along. Now she was on pins and needles, wondering if Joseph had leveraged the lodge itself in borrowing against it, potentially defaulting and putting her livelihood at risk. Though in her mind the books were balancing each month, what if Joseph had hidden his loans from her and had a separate set of books that had her well under water, even with the insurance payout that had seemingly given her the necessary breathing room to continue operating the lodge effectively with enough left over for savings.

I can't freak out about this, Katrina mused, willing herself to keep her thoughts in check as she drove down Maluhia Road. At least not until they spoke with the moneylender and determined whether or not Joseph had followed through in contacting him. And assessed what he might have done had his house of cards come crashing down upon him. Along with her.

"How are you holding up?" she heard Dex's deep voice ask with concern.

"I'll reserve comment on that for now, if you don't mind," Katrina told him, figuring there was no need to sugarcoat some of the emotions she was feeling at the moment in speculating whether or not the man she was married to had gone too far in making poor decisions. Better to wait and see just what she might be up against, as though the allegation of drug trafficking at the lodge wasn't bad enough.

"I don't mind at all," Dex assured her from the passenger seat. "But just so you know, however this goes, you're in the clear and I won't let the investigation impede your ability to run the Maoli Lodge and look ahead."

"Mahalo." Katrina appreciated his kind words and couldn't help but wonder what was in the cards for him in looking ahead. Did he ever plan to settle down? Or was his world of going undercover and tracking down drug offenders never to change? Was there anyone special in his life who he'd failed to mention in their mutual flirtation now that his true identity was out in the open? She glanced his way and decided to just ask boldly what was on her mind. "So, in your real world, Dex, do have a wife or girlfriend waiting back home for you to finish your latest assignment? Or is that confidential information?"

"Not confidential." He grinned at her. "There's neither a wife nor girlfriend waiting for me anywhere," he responded succinctly. "There was someone special once in my life, but it never came even close to us walking down the aisle."

"Oh…?" She wondered whether or not he got cold feet. Maybe Dex wasn't the type to commit.

"She cheated on me and seemed to think it was no big deal." He shook his head with a look of betrayal. "In any event, that was the name of that tune."

"Sorry about that," Katrina said sincerely. Though things were less than perfect between her and Joseph, she had always been faithful to him and believed the same was true from his side. Or could she be way off base here too about the man she was wed to?

"It happens," Dex muttered. "Lessons learned and all that."

"I'm sure there's someone out there for you." Did she really just say that? Katrina had always worn her heart on her sleeve. But was she telling him that she was ready, able and willing to take up with him—at least while he was around? If so, would she be able to put the past behind her as he seemed to be willing to do?

"You too," he countered surely, as though reading her thoughts, and added tellingly, "All you have to do is be willing to go the extra mile…once you're ready for that—"

Katrina allowed that to sink in, knowing her first step in that direction was to find out if Joseph had poisoned the well in destroying what was once their dream together. Only then could she truly turn the corner in regrouping. "I've gone a few extra miles for the time being," she quipped, while driving onto Kipuni Way in Kapaa, a town on the island's east side that was known for its Sleeping Giant Trail for hikers and the 151-foot Ho'olalaea Waterfall.

He chuckled. "Yeah, I can see that."

Four blocks later, Katrina pulled into the parking lot of a place called Cash to Give, wondering if she was about to encounter another disappointment in her marriage and roadblock in her business.

"You ready for this?" Dex asked in earnest.

"I have to be," she replied squarely, wanting to get it over with. Or was that even possible at this stage?

"Then let's go," he said without further ado.

They stepped inside the small, cluttered office with a dirty picture window. A sixtysomething, thickset, deeply tanned man with short thin gray hair in a brushed back style and a salt-and-pepper beard fade was seated at a computer desk that included file drawers. When he saw them, he leaned back in his black leather chair and said, "Aloha. How can I help you?"

"Are you Philip Shepherd?" Dex asked.

"Yeah, that's me. Who are you?"

"DEA Special Agent Adair," he said, flashing his ID. This surprised Katrina, but she instinctively understood that it was meant to intimidate him into cooperating. "This is Katrina Sizemore. We need to know if her late husband, Joseph Sizemore, contacted you for a loan."

Shepherd rubbed his stomach. "Afraid I'm not at liberty to give out confidential information between me and my clients, assuming he ever was one."

"I'd rethink that if I were you." Dex leaned over the desk menacingly. "I'm investigating drug trafficking on Kauai. If any loaned money turned out to be used to buy or distribute illicit drugs, that makes you an accessory. That means the feds will rain down on this place and if you have any skeletons in the closet, trust me, we'll find them…"

"Okay, okay—no need for this to go that far." Shepherd sucked in a deep breath. "The man's name doesn't actually pop out at me. Give me a moment to look him up." He started typing on his laptop. "Spell that for me?"

Katrina volunteered in doing so, adding, "He would have gotten in touch with you within the past year or so," she assumed." She hated to think that Joseph had reached such a stage of desperation to seek money from a loan shark.

"Hmm…" Shepherd muttered. "Nothing's showing up. You have a picture of your husband?"

"Yes." She took out her cell phone from a shoulder baguette bag and pulled up what was probably the last picture of Joseph. It was taken at the lodge, in the lobby, where he actually posed for her. How could she have known that he was hiding things from her even then?

Katrina held the small screen up to the moneylender. "That's him," she uttered.

Shepherd needed only a moment, before saying, "Right, I remember him now… He never took out a loan."

"Why not?" Dex asked dubiously.

"Said he needed fifty grand. I told him no problem, but after I explained what I expected in return in terms of interest and date of payback in full, the man balked."

Katrina wrinkled her brow. "Are you saying Joseph never took out a loan from you?" she questioned to be sure.

"Yeah, that's what I'm saying," he reiterated and eyed her musingly. "Your husband had second thoughts, said instead he would cash in some stocks that you weren't aware he had to cover his debts. Then he left. Never saw him again."

Back in the car, Dex said, "If what Shepherd said was true, it should be easy enough to verify the sale of secret stocks to help cover debts."

Katrina was a mixture of emotions. She felt relief that her husband had apparently not followed through on taking money from a loan shark. Better still, it suggested that Joseph had not gotten himself involved in drug trafficking to make money. But the fact that he had invested in the stock market without bothering to tell her was frustrating in its own right. "How could he have not told me about the stocks?" she griped aloud.

"Maybe he wanted to wait and see how they did first before letting you in," Dex indicated, which Katrina knew was his way of trying to ease her sense of betrayal.

"Nice try, but it won't fly." She tightened her grip on the steering wheel. "If Joseph had that much of our money invested in stocks, I had every right to know about it."

"I couldn't agree more," he made clear. "That's not the way a marriage should work. On the other hand, if the return was enough to help keep the lodge running, this would seem to exonerate Joseph of trafficking drugs for capital."

"You're right." Katrina loosened her fingers on the steering wheel. "I suppose I should be thanking him for not committing crimes to prevent us from going under," she said sarcastically.

Dex faced her profile. "You should be pissed. No excuses for what he did. He screwed up. Having never run a lodge such as yours, I can't begin to know the pressures one must be under to succeed in the competitive hospitality business in a resort setting. Apparently, though, selling stocks does seem to take suicide off the table. And, as of now, the murder angle is not holding water either, as the notes maintained, the drug use notwithstanding."

"I feel relieved about that," she had to admit, in spite of her disappointment in Joseph on so many other levels. Not the least of which was his uncanny ability to pull the wool over her eyes in some of his actions and inactions. But that didn't mean she would ever want to see him be the victim of foul play. "I just want to put this behind me. Hopefully, the stalker will leave well enough alone and not continue to harass me with unfounded allegations." She considered her earlier sense of being watched. What did this person hope to gain, other than fill her with doubts about Joseph and what he may or may not have been up to, placing her in danger? Or was there some other angle to this yet to unfold?

"I hope that too," Dex said, his tone suggesting he wasn't entirely convinced that would be the case. "I'll continue to try and find out who this man is and what he wants from you. My guess is that he's merely looking for attention and singled you out as a young widow who's vulnerable for obvious reasons. So far, he seems to be stopping just short of crossing the line. Let me know if this changes or if you are otherwise contacted by him."

Katrina nodded and turned to him with a soft smile. She wondered what she would do without the handsome DEA agent and piano player. The fact that she had to ask told her how much she had grown to depend on his presence in her life, limited as it was. It scared her to think that this would likely end as soon as his investigation was completed. Yet expecting any more from him afterward would be asking too much. Wouldn't it?

Chapter Nine

"The pool maintenance tech is here," Alyson informed Katrina that afternoon as she stood at her adjustable desk. Katrina had been going over the books with a fine-tooth comb, looking for any discrepancies in the numbers that she might have missed before learning of Joseph's questionable business practices. There were no red flags, giving her some sense of solace. Later, she intended to see if there might be more stock investments made by him, other than their joint investments, that needed to be accessed. She hoped that Dex wouldn't find any illegal financial transactions along the way that could impact her livelihood. As for Joseph's drug use, the medical examiner did not believe it led to his death and this was something for Katrina to hold on to, though she would forever be left feeling disappointed that her husband had not tried harder to deal with pain management through legitimate means and allow her to help him through it.

"Katrina… Did you hear me?" Alyson said, and repeated her information. "You wanted to know when the new guy arrived so you could make sure we were on the same page with him in terms of his work ethic and keeping the pool up and running."

"Yes, I did want to talk with him," Katrina said, snapping out of her daydreaming. "Thanks."

"Is everything okay?" the assistant manager asked. "You've seemed a bit off ever since we were on the beach this morning."

"I'm fine, Alyson." Katrina needed to keep up appearances, not wanting to bring her problems to her employees. Even one she considered a friend. At least where it concerned matters that were more of a personal nature and, thus, best kept to herself. Along with Dex, though still trying to decide if his involvement was more on the side of law enforcement or as someone who had taken it upon himself to be just as invested in her welfare. "It's been one of those days," she stated, leaving it at that.

"Tell me about it." Alyson gave her a knowing look. "Honestly, sometimes I can't tell whether I'm coming or going."

"Welcome to the club." Katrina managed a chuckle. "What's the pool guy's name?"

"Marc Neeson."

"Got it!" Katrina told her, as she headed to see him, hoping he would be as good as the previous swimming pool service technician, Wendy Holokai, who retired and relocated to the Big Island of Hawaii to live with her daughter.

When she got to the swimming pool, the man had his back turned to Katrina, as he was studying the pool. Only after she called out to him, "Mr. Neeson," did he turn around. Her pulse raced in that moment as, at first glance, all Katrina could see was her stalker. Only instead of being clad in a moss-colored Henley T-shirt, denim jeans and high-top black sneakers, he was wearing a chocolate brown uniform. His thick sable hair was in a quiff cut and he had rock and roll–type sideburns. "You—" she stammered.

He cocked a thick brow above solid blue eyes. "Excuse me..."

"What do you want with me?" Katrina demanded, taking a step backward and wondering if she should scream, assuming he meant her harm.

He looked taken aback. "Only to make sure your swimming pool is up to standards for safe and fun use," he insisted. Then, studying her, he asked questioningly, "Is that what you meant?"

Just as she was about to hightail it out of the pool area, Katrina took a second hard look at Marc Neeson. She realized that though he bore some resemblance, her stalker was actually a little taller, more muscular and wore his hair a different way. *It's not the same guy*, she told herself, red-faced. She regretted jumping the gun.

"Yes, of course," she pivoted, and forced a smile. "I'm Katrina Sizemore."

"Marc Neeson, at your service." He stuck out a friendly narrow hand and she shook it. "Great place you have here."

"Mahalo."

"I can just go over the pool maintenance procedures and if you have any questions, I'm happy to answer."

"Sounds like a plan." Katrina wondered how she could have mistaken him for her stalker. Maybe the idea of him still lurking out there somewhere, as if waiting to catch her at her weakest moment, was getting to her more than she cared to admit. Surely, he wasn't so brazen as to try and confront her at the lodge? Or was he no longer a threat now that his allegations about Joseph's death had been debunked by and large? She turned her attention back to the pool tech and his responsibilities in keeping the pool up to snuff for guests.

"HIS NAME IS JULIO," Dex told Agent Lynda Krause as she played with Barnabas in the backyard of the rented cottage. "He may or may not still be on the island. As the one who supplied Joseph Sizemore with illegal drugs, this Julio could have intended to deal Sizemore a lethal dose. Or been working with other drug traffickers that may have wanted him dead for one reason or another, possibly related to using the Maoli Lodge as one of the points around the island for distributing drugs."

"Looks like we need to find Julio," Lynda agreed, holding a red ball that Barnabas tried to bite as she kept it just out of his reach. "We'll put the first name and physical description through the DEA Intelligence Division's database and see if we can come up with a full name in the system and where he might be holed up."

"Good. The sooner we find Julio, the sooner we can see where he fits into the puzzle in our overall investigation." It was just as important to Dex to give Katrina some peace of mind, once and for all, that Sizemore's death was neither murder nor suicide, but actually due to an accidental drowning.

"So, what else have you come up with from the widow?" Lynda looked at him. "Any new leads?"

"Only in reaffirming that she has played no part in any drug trafficking at the lodge," Dex asserted. "Moreover, Joseph Sizemore appears off the hook as well on that front." He explained how Sizemore sold stocks, which had been verified, to put the money into the lodge, with no indication that he used drug money for that purpose. "If he was caught up in anything else, we'll find out. For now, our focus needs to be on the connections between known drug dealers on the island and use of the lodge, if any."

"I'm down with that." She tossed the ball and they watched as Barnabas scurried after it. "We're making progress," she stated. "Even as we speak, Ishikawa is checking out a storage facility near the property that could be used for drug storage and distribution and even stockpiling of illegal weapons as part of the criminal activities."

Dex nodded with interest as the dog came up to him, dropping the ball at his feet. "Barnabas is ready whenever called upon, aren't you, boy?" He barked in agreement.

Lynda laughed. "Someone's getting antsy being cooped up in this cottage and yard."

"Actually, I think he's enjoying this little vacation." Dex picked up the ball, flung it toward the trees and watched Barnabas go after it. "I don't suppose you were able to come up with any DNA or prints from the second note left by Katrina's stalker?"

"Sorry." Lynda shook her head. "Whoever the man is, he's too clever to make it easy to identify him. Has she seen him again? Or been left any more notes?"

"Not that I'm aware of." Dex assumed Katrina wasn't holding back on him. Now that she knew his true identity, he hoped she knew she could trust him to be on her side. As it was, they both needed to try and get out in front of whoever had left the messages. Though he had downplayed the threat, Dex was still concerned that the man might not be through with the cryptic notes and surveillance. The question was why? What was his end game?

"Maybe the unsub is doing this with ulterior motives," Lynda posed, reading his mind.

"Such as?" Dex wondered.

"To help further along the investigation, while remaining incognito to the degree possible."

"You mean an undercover agent who doesn't want to blow his cover?" Dex rolled his eyes skeptically. "But had no problem throwing me under the bus by exposing me?"

"Yeah, there is that," she conceded. "Maybe he's a drug trafficker who's gone rogue, but still has connections in law enforcement."

"Well, whoever he is, your cover and Ishikawa's still seem to be intact."

"For now." Lynda flexed her hands. "Maybe not forever."

"We all need to remain vigilant," Dex told her. "If he tries anything that can jeopardize this investigation, we have to be ready to act at a moment's notice."

"I hear you," she agreed.

As he contemplated this and keeping Katrina safe and sound, Dex's cell phone rang. He slipped it out of the pocket of his slim fit jeans and saw that the caller was Agent Ishikawa. "Hey," he answered.

"There's been a break in the investigation," Ishikawa said keenly. "A suspect's been taken into custody for the murder of Agent Roxanne Yamamoto."

DEX STARED THROUGH the one-way window into the interrogation room. Detective Clayton Pietz was grilling the suspect, Kenneth Monaghan, thirtysomething and husky, with long blond hair in a rope ponytail and dark eyes. He was dressed in black jeans and a faded gray jersey T-shirt.

"You're in some deep trouble, Monaghan," Pietz blasted him on the other side of a square metal table. "We know you cut the brake lines on the Toyota Tacoma that DEA Agent Roxanne Yamamoto was driving the night of Saturday, January 7, which led to the vehicle crashing and Agent Yamamoto's death. How do we know this? Because you left behind just enough of a fingerprint on a brake line that we were able to run it through an FBI database and match it with a fingerprint that was already in the system for your prior criminality."

Monaghan squirmed. "That don't prove I killed her," he snapped defiantly.

"Think again!" Pietz knitted his brows. "We have an eyewitness who can place you hovering around the victim's vehicle prior to her entering it for the fatal drive. If that isn't enough, we confiscated a pair of scissors from your house that you foolishly never bothered to throw away and we were able to link them to the cut brake lines. There's no escaping this, Monaghan," the detective said forcefully. "The first-degree murder of a federal law enforcement officer is serious business with serious consequences. Obviously, you didn't decide to do this all on your own. Your best bet, if you know what's good for you, is to come clean and tell us who put you up to it. Your call…"

Dex groaned within, wondering if the suspect would realize that the hole he'd dug for himself was one he couldn't possibly hope to climb out of. Or was he more frightened by the drug traffickers involved and therefore wouldn't crack? It pained Dex to think that he was looking at the perp responsible for taking away Roxanne's life. He deserved no less. Putting him away for the rest of his miserable life would be anything but a picnic while behind bars, nevertheless. Assuming he didn't cut a deal that gave him some daylight at the end of the tunnel.

"Yeah, I cut the brake lines," Monaghan admitted, head down. "A clean cut."

Pietz leaned forward. "Who hired you to kill her?"

"I don't know. Not exactly." Monaghan drew a long breath. "I was offered twenty grand to slice the brake lines. I only spoke to the guy over the phone," he insisted.

"How did you get the money?" Pietz asked, his voice soaked with skepticism.

"It was left for me in a garbage can in the park," Monaghan claimed.

"What park?"

"Hā'ena State Park." Monaghan's shoulders slumped. "I went right where I was told, found the cash in a brown paper bag and took it. Never heard from the guy again."

Dex couldn't decide if the perp was telling the truth or not. His instincts told him that someone else was calling the shots. But who? When had Roxanne's cover been blown and who ordered the hit on her? Could Katrina's stalker be involved in her murder? Was there any way for the DEA agent to convey what damning information she had come up with from the grave?

He had been so caught up in his thoughts that Dex failed to notice Katrina had come into the room. How long had she been standing there? He had requested that she come in and take a good look at the suspect and see if he had any connection whatsoever to the lodge or any of its employees. Or would being there and observing someone who had confessed to cutting the brake lines of Roxanne's car only unnerve Katrina that much more, given the women's workplace association and Katrina's fragility in coming to terms with her husband's untimely death?

WHEN DEX HAD given her the news that someone had been arrested for Roxanne's murder, Katrina was elated. The fact that she had been an undercover DEA agent did not take away from the friendship they developed during the short time Katrina knew her as Roxanne Kitaoka. Roxanne's heart was in the right place in trying to do her part to rid the island of illicit drugs and those who profited from the trafficking of them. Now Katrina was at the Kauai Police Department, at Dex's request, to see if she recognized the suspect. She jumped at the opportunity that included a squad car to take her there, temporarily leaving the lodge in the more than capable hands of her second in command, Alyson Tennison, to run the ship, in her absence.

Truthfully, Katrina welcomed the chance to shift her attention away from the embarrassing case of mistaken identity she had with the pool service technician. Turned out he wasn't her stalker after all. Maybe he was gone from her life for good, along with his disturbing notes, his pathetic attempt to play with her head. It was up to her to not allow him to get to her, especially in the face of the evidence that proved Joseph's death an unfortunate accident, notwithstanding his use of meth and fentanyl at the time, ill-fated as it was.

But Roxanne's accident had been ruled a homicide and Katrina gazed through the one-way window at the man suspected of cutting her brake lines—the same man who commanded Dex's attention in that moment, in mourning the death of his DEA colleague. So absorbed was Dex, that he'd failed to look her way when she entered the viewing room. Not that she could blame him, as she understood that whatever feelings he may have developed for her, his priority had to be seeking justice for Agent Yamamoto and tying her death to the drug-trafficking investigation underway on Kauai. Along with the possibilities that its reach could extend to Maoli Lodge.

Running her fingers the length of her long and low ponytail, Katrina cleared her throat to get Dex's attention. He gave her an apologetic crooked grin and said, "Hey. Thanks for coming…"

"Happy to help." She flashed him a thin smile and turned to the window, where she saw Detective Pietz—who had interviewed her shortly after Roxanne's death—interrogating the male suspect. "That him?" she asked.

"Yeah," Dex confirmed. "Name's Kenneth Monaghan. Do you recognize him?"

Katrina zeroed in again on the suspect, studying his face to be sure, before turning back to Dex. "Yes, I do. Two months ago, Kenneth Monaghan was employed by me as a maintenance worker." She paused. "I was forced to fire him after a guest claimed she caught him in the act of stealing items from her room. He tried to deny it, but the jewelry was found among his belongings."

"Did you or the guest press charges?"

"I wanted to," Katrina stressed, "but the guest, content to get back all that was stolen, declined the offer to report it to the police. Apparently, she felt it would take too much time and effort away from making the most of the rest of her vacation."

Dex nodded understandingly and peered at the suspect. "Interesting connection between Monaghan and the Maoli Lodge, nonetheless."

"Do you think he was holding a grudge for being fired," she said with a gasp, "and went after Roxanne in retaliation?" The thought that she might have been responsible for her death unnerved Katrina.

"I seriously doubt one thing had anything to do with the other." Dex set his jaw. "This wasn't about you, Katrina. Without getting into it too deeply, Monaghan was hired to cut the brake lines of Agent Yamamoto's vehicle by someone who wanted to stop her investigation into drug trafficking. Instead, it only emboldened us to work harder to stop the flow of illicit drugs on the island and bring those responsible to justice."

Katrina gulped musingly, putting aside her relief that her actions in firing Kenneth had not cost Roxanne her life. "Do you think whoever was responsible for Roxanne's death was in any way connected to the lodge?" She dreaded to ask.

Dex hunched a shoulder. "No way to know for sure at this point," he said. "My guess is that the drug kingpin has a long reach that spans the island and crosses over to the mainland." He rested a hand on her shoulder, which seemed to penetrate to her very bones. "Whatever the case, Katrina, I'm confident that if anyone associated with the lodge is involved in this, we'll flush out without any of it coming back on you."

"Mahalo, Dex." She took solace with that reassurance, even as Katrina felt a tenseness that told her this still needed to play out like a theater production. Until then, she had to be patient and allow the investigation to run its course. And allow Dex the access he needed in her world until such time, if not beyond.

She gazed into the one-way window and saw the suspect being led out of the room in handcuffs; followed by Detective Pietz, who came inside the viewing room alone. "We've got him," he declared, eyeing Dex.

"Looks that way." Dex met his gaze. "Good work in tracking down Monaghan."

"It was a team effort, Adair." Pietz made a modest expression. "We all wanted to get the person who took out Agent Yamamoto. And we won't stop till the mastermind is brought to justice and anyone else involved in her murder and the drug-trafficking ring."

"Good." Dex stiffened and turned to Katrina.

But before he could say something, Pietz stepped toward her and said evenly, "Mrs. Sizemore, I appreciate your continued cooperation in the investigation."

Katrina smiled. "You can count on me to do whatever I can to further it along in relation to my lodge."

He nodded. "I'll keep that in mind."

Dex informed him that Kenneth Monaghan had once worked at the Maoli Lodge before being terminated. Though Pietz seemed mildly intrigued, he gave that information little weight in the case being built against Monaghan. The murder suspect was to be turned over to the feds for further interrogation and prosecution for the murder of DEA agent Roxanne Yamamoto.

Chapter Ten

"Have you eaten yet?" Dex asked Katrina after they got into his car to take her back to the lodge. He wasn't sure if he was asking her out on a date spontaneously or because he was hungry himself and preferred not to eat alone. Either way, he welcomed a respite from the grind of a DEA investigation.

"No," she said swiftly, adding, "in fact, I'm starving."

"Me too." He grinned at her coolly. "Can I buy you dinner?"

"Yes, I'd love that. But as an island resident, I think it's more appropriate and hospitable that I spring for the meal since you're a visitor—even if you're here on official business…"

Dex wasn't sure whether to be flattered or hold out on paying for the dinner as the right thing to do. Particularly considering that he had invited her. Not the other way around. On the other hand, he was in her neck of the woods, and as such, he wasn't about to argue when all he truly wanted was the chance to spend some personal time with her. What difference did it make who foot the bill? "You're on," he said with genuine enthusiasm.

"Perfect." Her teeth shone. "Where did you have in mind?"

"Anywhere you like," he told her. "I'm game to try anything."

"All right. In that case, I know a great little steak house with a Hawaiian flare on Kiahuna Plantation Drive in the Poipu Shopping Village."

Dex smiled. "Sounds good to me." He followed her directions in getting there and they went inside, taking a seat in a booth. They were handed menus.

"See anything you like?" Katrina asked curiously.

Looking over the menu, from where he sat, Dex couldn't imagine anything more appetizing than the woman across from him. Forcing himself to study the food choices, he saw any number of things that sounded tasty. In the end, he decided to live dangerously insofar as taking a chance on food choices he may not be used to. "Why don't you surprise me with something that tickles your own taste buds," he challenged her.

"I can do that." She curved her nice lips upward in accepting the challenge. "Let's see…"

Katrina ordered them both the filet mignon with red wine sauce, steamed white rice, creamed spinach and Hawaiian herbal tea. She suggested they could try the coconut cheesecake for dessert and Dex was all in.

"So, Dex, you know a lot about me, but I actually know very little about you," Katrina said twenty minutes later, digging her fork into the steamed rice.

He couldn't deny that he had not delved too much into his life for obvious reasons. But now he wanted to share and share alike with the lodge owner. "What would you like to know?" he asked, slicing into the tender filet mignon.

"Well, aside from being a DEA agent with a cover backstory, never married and currently single, I don't suppose you have any children from that onetime special relationship you mentioned, or any other?" She flushed diffidently. "It happens—"

"That it does," he allowed. "But not to me. No kids."

"Would you like to have a family someday?" she asked. "Or is that not in the cards for you and the type of life you lead?"

She's really putting me on the spot with this, Dex told himself, feeling slightly uncomfortable with it. But not in the way she might think. "Yes, I would love to have a family one day—wife, kids, the whole thing," he stressed freely. "It's definitely in the cards and, if anything, the type of life I lead makes me want the stability family brings all the more."

"I see," she murmured, eating her food musingly. He wondered just how much her vision was able to see the full landscape. Being a federal law enforcement officer certainly had its perks and was more than worth his while, but it hardly defined what he truly wanted in life.

Dex gazed at her and asked, curious as well, "What about you? When Joseph was still alive, had you talked about having children?" Dex had little doubt that Katrina would make a great mother, even if she wasn't as sure.

"We talked about it," she said with a maudlin slant to her tone. "The plan was to get established with the lodge and then start a family." Katrina stared down at her plate and back up. "Sometimes plans have a way of blowing up in your face. Or at least thrown entirely off track by fate."

"I understand where you're coming from." Dex sat back, taking a breath. "When I was young, I used to hang out a lot with my older sister, Rita. I thought the world of her and imagined being a doting uncle to her kids when she found someone to love and be loved by. But that didn't happen," he bemoaned. "The man she ended up with was a drug dealer. He got her hooked on heroin. Rita overdosed on the drug... She never lived to reach the age of twenty."

Katrina reacted, reaching a hand across the table to touch his. "I'm so sorry, Dex."

"Yeah, I am too." Their skin connecting did wonders to lessen the sad memories, if not take away the pain altogether. "As you said, sometimes fate steps in the way of what you thought would happen and you just have to deal with it."

She met his eyes. "Was it your sister's death that motivated you to become a DEA agent?"

"That was certainly a factor," he acknowledged. "Along with growing up in Detroit and wanting to do my part to help rid the country of drug addiction and the people who profited from this as drug dealers and the like."

"Which brought you to Kauai and into my life," Katrina pointed out with a sensitive look.

"Yeah." He saw the irony in that, considering this was likely the only way they would have ever crossed paths. And given the fact that this meant something to him, he wouldn't have changed a thing. Other than to have not wanted to see her and the Maoli Lodge dragged into the investigation, causing Katrina burdens she did not need. Dex was glad, nevertheless, that she had been cleared of involvement in any drug-related crimes and he could see her in the right light as someone who captured his attention. Over and beyond being duty bound as a DEA agent.

"Are you up for that coconut cheesecake for dessert?" Katrina broke his reverie, having removed her hand from his.

"Absolutely," he answered smilingly.

As they ate, Katrina leaned toward Dex and asked, "Do you have any plans to settle down anytime soon? Or is your calling as a DEA agent such that you don't see that happening for the foreseeable future?"

If he didn't know better, Dex might almost think that she was interviewing him to become her husband at some point. Or was he misinterpreting because the idea appealed to him in more ways than he had come to terms with? "I haven't really thought that far ahead," he spoke truthfully. "If I had, I would like to believe that for the right person I would love to settle down to a life together." He allowed that to hang there before continuing. "Regarding my job, I don't really see it as a calling, but rather a privilege to use my education and skills in a productive manner. That said, it doesn't mean I couldn't find other ways to make a meaningful contribution to society…and that special someone who would become the most important reason for waking up every morning."

Katrina's eyes lit with admiration. "Well said."

"Mahalo." Dex thought the Hawaiian word was apropos. He also hoped she took his words for what they were worth, knowing she was just the type of woman he could fall for in a big way and have that kind of life in paradise with. He thought about her earlier confession of no longer being in love with her husband at the time of his death. Dex wondered where things stood between himself and Katrina and if she might be willing to open her heart to someone else. Him. "So, just how bad were things between you and Joseph toward the end?"

Katrina dabbed a napkin at the corner of her generous mouth as she mulled over the question that obviously required some careful thought. "Bad enough to have me questioning if we were truly ever meant to be together," she stated sadly.

"What did you come up with…?" he pressed.

"The reality that the romance in our lives had stalled. Whether it was from the daily grind of running a lodge, or Joseph being consumed with work, play and apparently illicit drug use, we weren't clicking at that point and I think he knew that as much as I did." She sighed plaintively and made a face. "So, if you're asking if I am able to move past my marriage to Joseph if someone new were to enter my life, the answer is yes."

"Good to know." Dex grinned. Her words were music to his ears, and he felt an irregular patter of his heart and its potential for falling in love thereafter. She was clearly of the same mind, even if he was still presently caught up in a drug-trafficking investigation that commanded his attention, whether he preferred that to be the case or not. "Do you want to get out of here?"

Katrina smiled readily. "Yes, I believe I would."

"WOULD YOU LIKE to come in?" she asked as he walked her to her door a little while later. *Please say yes*, Katrina thought, not wanting to appear too eager. But they had waited long enough to act on the sexual vibes that had sizzled between them since practically the very beginning. If Dex should turn her down, Katrina wasn't quite sure how she would take it. Unless she was reading him wrong during the dinner conversation, he was as open to the possibilities for romance as she was. The fact that he was still investigating drug trafficking on the island and even within the boundaries of her property did not preclude them from testing the waters and seeing if there was anything there worth fighting for.

"I'd love to come in," Dex told her, showing his teeth in a handsome smile, warming her heart in the process.

Katrina smiled back, ignoring the butterflies in her stomach as she led him inside. It was the first time since Joseph's death that she had been so inclined to want another man's company. But she believed the timing was right. Or, if not perfect, certainly lent itself to the moment at hand and whatever came of it. "Can I get you something to drink?" she asked, thinking that some wine might be nice about now.

"Sure, whatever you're having," he said, seemingly unable to take his eyes off her.

"Two glasses of wine coming up. Be right back." Katrina left him standing in the great room as she stepped inside the kitchen. She glanced at the wedding band still on her finger since it was first put there by her late husband, and Katrina realized it was time to remove it. The ring that had once been a symbol of love was now merely a piece of jewelry that was no longer apropos for who she was today and the future she wanted to move toward. She twisted it off her finger and quietly put the ring in a drawer. Removing two goblets from the distressed oak cabinet, Katrina set them on the quartz countertop. From the fridge, she took out an opened bottle of tropical guava wine and half-filled each wineglass. Only when she felt his warm breath on the back of her neck did Katrina realize Dex had come into the kitchen. She faced him, her heart suddenly beating wildly, and handed him a goblet. "For you."

He tasted, allowing the liquid to roll through his mouth. "Excellent."

"You think?" She sipped her own wine, feeling jittery and excited at the same time.

"Yeah." He set his glass on the counter and hers as well. Wrapping his arms around her slender waist and pulling her closer, Dex uttered in a sexy voice, "There's something else I have a taste for even more…"

"Oh really?" Her lashes fluttered with anticipation. "And what might that be?"

"This…" He cupped her face, tilted his head and moved in for a kiss. She reciprocated in kind, feeling its potency from head to toe. They stood there tasting each other's mouths for what seemed like an eternity of unbearable desire, before Dex pried their lips apart. "I don't think I'm telling you anything you don't already know, but I find you to be incredibly attractive, Katrina," he voiced gutturally.

"I could say the same about you, Dex," she uttered with swollen lips, and meant every word. She could only imagine what a specimen he was with his clothes off. "Maybe we should head to the bedroom…"

He gave her another mouthwatering kiss, then looked her in the eye. "You sure you're ready for that?"

If she was any surer, Katrina imagined she would burst. "Yes, I'm sure." Then she held his gaze with uncertainty. "Are you?" she asked.

"Never been more ready," he declared lustfully.

"Neither have I." Katrina couldn't argue with what her body was telling her loud and clear. She wanted him in the worst way. Make that the best way between a man and woman. That was more than enough for her without overthinking it, as she took one more sip of wine and he did the same, before she led him by the hand to her bedroom.

There, Katrina took her hair out of the ponytail, allowing it to hang free and loose. "I love your hair that way," Dex told her and ran a hand through it before cupping her chin and putting their lips together.

"Nice to know," she said, enjoying the feel of his mouth on hers as they kissed passionately, before separating and removing their clothes like they were on fire. As she stood naked, Katrina was surprised at just how relaxed and confident she felt being naked with a man for the first time since Joseph's death. Was she truly ready to make love again? Give away her heart and body? Or was it more who she was about to go to bed with, as she stared at the physical specimen Dex represented. She couldn't remember a time when she was so enamored with and desirous of someone. Whether this was wrong or so very right, her instincts were in overdrive in making this happen.

Forcing her eyes away from Dex, who seemed just as taken by what he saw, she stepped over to a rattan nightstand and took a condom package out of the drawer. "This is for you," she said, handing it to him.

He accepted it without preface and, in practically a blink of an eye, was ready to pick up where they left off. And so much more. Effortlessly. Dex lifted Katrina off her feet and carried her to the driftwood queen low bed, where he pulled down the quilted ivory bedspread and laid her on the soft pomegranate-colored sateen sheets. Sliding next to her, he wasted little time in using his big hands and nimble fingers to caress Katrina's breasts and body expertly, sending waves of delight throughout her. By the time he kissed her again, she was more than ready to move to the next stage of lovemaking. "Take me, Dex," she murmured, reaching out and pulling him toward her. "Please. Now!"

"Believe me, it would be my pleasure," he voiced thickly. "Make that *our* pleasure, by the time we're through!" He made his way between her legs and she urgently guided him inside. As though a tidal wave of unbridled desire were unleashed, their bodies came together wildly, and Katrina found herself unable to hold back from climaxing almost immediately. How did it happen so soon? She tried to recall when this had ever occurred during her marriage. Sadly, no memories surfaced. Was it simply not as good previously? Her focus returned to the moment at hand with her legs wrapped securely around Dex's firm back, holding on for dear life as the powerful sensations paralyzed her with pleasure.

Only when she came back down from the incredible high, did Katrina know that it was but the opening salvo of an experience that she embraced wholeheartedly. She wanted to feel the joy of their mutual orgasm and suspected it would be even more earth-shattering. "Your turn," she murmured selflessly to her lover.

"Our turn together," Dex countered urgently, as he kissed her and picked up the pace. With staying power that amazed Katrina, she arched her back and met him halfway every time, their hunger-driven gazes locked on to one another unblinkingly. The primeval urges took over Katrina like never before and she didn't question her need. Or his, as the fan overhead did nothing to lessen the soaring temperatures in the bedroom while they made love. She felt Dex's trembling body and ragged breaths, as the level of intensity soared higher and higher and their rhythmical heartbeats fell in total sync.

By the time it was over, Katrina breathlessly rode the wave of pure sexual delight for as long as it carried her lithe, moist body, while clinging to Dex in the aftermath. Only then did she wonder where they would go from there. Or had this incredible journey in the face of a drug-trafficking and murder investigation already run its course?

"This doesn't have to mean anything," Katrina found herself saying, feeling the need to not put any pressure or expectations on the man she had just made love to. No matter her own thoughts on the subject, which based on the ardent way she'd reacted to him, pretty much spoke for itself. Didn't it?

Chapter Eleven

"But it does mean something," Dex said with more than a little assurance, his voice unwavering and his arms holding Katrina up against his body. He had just engaged in mind-blowing sex with arguably the most beautiful woman he'd ever seen. Or, at the very least, had the pleasure of getting to know in the biblical sense. To suggest it meant nothing would indicate that the last hour of all-consuming intimacy was merely a flash in the pan. A simple sexual release void of any emotional attachment. He wasn't wired that way. Not in the slightest. Not with her. And the incredibly seductive sounds she made and her sensual body movements during their lovemaking told him that it was much more than just casual sex for her too. Dex suspected that her statement was more of a defense mechanism than anything, to avoid getting hurt. This was something he would never do to her willfully. Especially not after their succumbing to a mutual attraction, leaving him wanting so much more.

"And just what is that something?" Katrina challenged him, with a silky-smooth leg draped invitingly over his. "Or do you even know?"

Dex touched her flushed cheek. "I know that what we just did was amazing," he spoke sincerely. More than he could ever have imagined when handed this assignment. "We're good together, Katrina. There's no denying that."

"I'm not denying it," she promised him. "But that's the problem, isn't it? I'm a widow, operating a lodge on Kauai. You have an entirely different life going on. With the demands of your profession as a DEA agent, I'm not sure I'm cut out for a 'whenever we can get together but are otherwise apart' type relationship."

"Neither am I," he confessed, never expecting to meet someone who could be the woman of his dreams. But he had and he didn't want to see her slip away. How could he prevent it and maintain the unpredictable life on the go that he had become accustomed to in combatting drug-related criminality in the United States and beyond? "I care for you," Dex told her, locking eyes with Katrina so she knew how serious he was.

"I care for you too, Dex." She rested her head on his shoulder. "But is that enough for either of us?"

It was certainly a good place to start, Dex believed. That was enough to give him hope of a future with Katrina. "We'll figure it out," he promised.

She nodded, seemingly content in that thought. But for how long? Dex knew it was on him to make it work and he fully intended to. He lifted her chin and kissed Katrina on the mouth. The kiss lingered for a while, with both of them into it, before he reluctantly pulled back. "Hate to kiss and run, but I need to check on Barnabas."

"Of course." She licked her lips. "He's probably wondering where you've been."

Dex chuckled. "Yeah, he does tend to get a bit antsy when we're apart too long."

"I can only imagine," she uttered teasingly.

"Me too." He hadn't even left and Dex was already

starting to miss her company. The thought of them being apart too long was excruciating. But duty called. He kissed Katrina's soft shoulder and rolled off the bed, enjoying the view of her lying there naked tantalizingly. "Stay there," he said. "I can see myself out."

Dex quickly dressed and pushed aside his hesitancy to leave, knowing he had no choice. "Catch you later," he told Katrina and gave her a goodbye kiss, as she remained in bed, covered up but smiling to let him know the door was open. All he had to do was be willing to meet her halfway. It seemed more than reasonable to him, once he got past the current investigation that included keeping her safe.

THE MOMENT HE stepped inside the cottage, Dex knew something was wrong. The place had been ransacked as if it had been hit by a tornado. His first thought was Barnabas. Was he hurt? Was the intruder, or intruders, still there? Immediately, Dex removed his DEA-issued and loaded 40 caliber Glock 27 pistol from a concealed carry holster. He had taken the liberty of arming himself routinely, after leaving the firearm locked in his glove compartment while visiting Katrina. Moving cautiously through the cottage, he checked each room, nook and cranny, and saw no sign of anyone. What the hell were they looking for? He considered that this was where Roxanne was staying. Did the break-in have anything to do with her undercover assignment, which he had inherited?

Dex kept the gun in a ready-to-use position as he went to the back door. His heart was racing in fear of what he might find in the backyard, where he had left Barnabas for some exercise. The thought that someone had harmed—or perhaps killed—his canine best friend nearly broke Dex. He opened the door, expecting either the worst or to come face-to-face with an armed assailant, instead there was only Barnabas standing there on all four feet with seemingly not a care in the world, while showing no signs of being injured. Dex nearly jumped for joy and, after determining that there was no one hiding amongst the fruit trees, embraced the K-9 dog. "Good to see you're safe and sound, boy!" Barnabas demonstrated mutual affection by licking his hands and face. "You wait out here and I'll get you something to eat and finish checking out the place."

The K-9 cop seemed reluctant to remain in the backyard, but obeyed, as Dex wanted to get a forensic team in there to see what they could come up with, if anything. The fact that someone was willing to boldly encroach on his space told him that they must be closing in on the drug traffickers and others with a stake in the game. And they were willing to do whatever they needed to get what they wanted. No matter who got in their way. Well, as far as Dex was concerned, this was hardly going to deter the Task Force from going after those who were committing offenses on Kauai soil, including murder. He left Barnabas to himself, while Dex went back inside and got on the cell phone, first calling Lynda and Ishikawa, then Clayton Pietz and some other members of the Task Force, to inform them of the break-in.

Thirty minutes later, Dex was being interviewed by Detective Sergeant Vera Tolentino of the Kauai PD's Property Crimes Unit. In her early thirties, she was of medium height and build, with brunette hair in an A-line cut, and light brown eyes. "Is there anything missing that you know of, Agent Adair?"

Dex considered the mess left behind, but couldn't actually say anything of note was missing. "Doesn't look like they took anything of value," he admitted, while knowing that as a precautionary measure—given the disappearance of key items from Roxanne's belongings upon her death—he had taken the liberty of keeping his cell phone, laptop and two firearms on his person or locked inside the car whenever away from the cottage.

"Lucky you," Vera remarked, as they stood in the main room. "Lately, there's been a number of burglaries in the Koloa area. Mostly teenagers looking to grab anything they can steal to pay for drugs or just to pass the time out of plain boredom. Apparently, from what you're telling me, they came away from here empty-handed."

"Not sure this was a simple case of burglary." Dex almost hated to tell her, even if she made a good argument on that front.

She flashed him a suspicious stare. "What aren't you telling me?"

Sticking to the need-to-know basis for information, he responded evasively, "Let's just say that with a major drug-trafficking operation underway on the island, there are more than burglars who may have wanted to hit the place in a bad way."

"I see." She made a note of this. "Well, our crime scene investigators will be here shortly to collect any evidence they can find. We'll be sure to coordinate our efforts with the vice section and you guys and go from there."

"Sounds good." Dex smiled at her and watched briefly as she got on her cell phone. Ten minutes later, he was conferring with Lynda, Ishikawa and Clayton Pietz on the mysteries of the break-in. None of them were quite certain what—or who—was behind it. They all seemed to rule out the burglary angle on the whole.

Detective Pietz drew his brows together. "Your cottage being ransacked so soon after we nailed Kenneth Monaghan does appear to be more than coincidence."

"Yeah, I was thinking the same thing." Dex concurred in connecting the dots between their investigation and his role in the scheme of things. Including working with Katrina to weed out potential perpetrators and unsubs. Could her firing Monaghan just before he cut the brake lines of Roxanne's car be a factor in her onetime cottage being burglarized? Was that something that could still put Katrina in jeopardy?

"So, you think this is something akin to a warning shot to say we're on to you and the probe into drug trafficking?" Ishikawa questioned.

"It's possible," Dex conceded, thinking about Katrina's still unidentified stalker, whose motivation and insinuations remained a mystery. "It's just as likely that whoever killed Roxanne had figured out our connection and were still looking for something she left behind. Or at least they believed that to be the case."

"I think that's a bit of a stretch," Lynda chimed in, standing flat-footed. "If they didn't find it after she was killed, there's no reason to believe she would have passed the torch to you, so to speak, and you would be dumb enough to leave it hanging around for them to find."

"Good point as well," Dex said, thoughtful. "But here's the thing. My cover has been blown...and likely my trusty and thankfully unharmed K-9 companion's as well. At least in the eyes of someone. And I'm staying at the same place where Agent Yamamoto had ample time to collect and hide evidence. Maybe it's still here somewhere and can bring down the entire illicit drug operation, if found. We need to keep all options on the table as we try to get to the root of it."

"I agree," Pietz said. "The people we're dealing with mean business. They'll stop at nothing to keep their profitable trafficking of drugs going. That includes sending a message to any of us involved in the criminal investigation, whether it's a warning shot, as Ishikawa put it, or an all-out war. We need to be ready for whatever comes next and come back twice as hard."

"We're with you, Pietz," Lynda declared, and Dex didn't argue against it. They did need to remain united as a Task Force in fighting a common enemy. One that he feared still potentially placed Katrina and her lodge in the line of fire.

KATRINA WAS STILL riding high on the explosive sex with Dex, if not the uncertainty of where this might carry them for the future. *We'll figure it out*, she replayed in her head what he'd said in that respect. Would they? Or were they really just fooling themselves that it could work? Yes, they were great in bed and had hit it off. But could they truly bridge the gap between a mainlander who worked on dangerous missions for the Drug Enforcement Administration and a widowed owner of a lodge on a relatively peaceful Hawaiian island?

I can't allow myself to get too carried away after one night in bed, incredible as it was, Katrina thought, having put her clothes back on and made herself a cup of coconut coffee. What would be, would be. She needed to keep a proper perspective and refrain from putting too much pressure on Dex or herself in wanting to make this work between them. Perhaps once he had put his current investigation into drug trafficking in the case closed category, they could sit down and talk about what they envisioned in a real relationship and see if the two measured up. In the meantime, as a single, healthy woman with needs like everyone else, there was no harm in enjoying Dex's company for as long as they both saw eye to eye regarding spending time together, and go from there.

Her ruminations were halted as Katrina became aware of the knock on her door. Though she was technically off duty, the dictates of operating a lodge successfully required her to be on call at all times for anything that came up. What was it this time? A leaking sink? Overflowing tub? A belligerent or inebriated guest? Katrina prepared herself for any possibility as she padded in her bare feet across the floor to the door and opened it. To her joyous surprise, standing there was Dex. Along with Barnabas.

"Hey," she said demurely, eyeing the DEA agent curiously. "Didn't expect to see you again so soon."

"Barnabas and I need a place to crash for the night," Dex said tonelessly, adding, "he's perfectly housetrained."

"Of course, you're welcome to stay for as long as you like." Katrina smiled and welcomed them inside. She didn't feel at all as though her offer was being too generous, because she had plenty of room. She doubted Dex would ever take her up on it, so long as they hadn't made a firm commitment to each other. Only then did she gaze at him and ask nervously, "What happened?"

Dex grimaced. "My cottage was vandalized," he voiced angrily.

"What?" Her eyes popped wide. "By who?"

"We're still trying to determine that. The police department seems to think it was just some locals looking for money to buy drugs. Or to wreck the place just for the hell of it."

"But you don't believe that," she deduced.

He gazed down at his dark loafers and back up. "If I had to hazard a guess, I'd say someone broke in looking for something connected to the drug-trafficking case."

She glanced at Barnabas, who had moved quietly into a corner and seemed totally disinterested in the conversation. "That would mean whoever was behind it had to know you're a DEA agent."

"Or that Roxanne was and had stayed there before me. Either way, it's definitely suspicious in nature."

Katrina's heart dropped. "Are we talking about maybe the stalker who warned me about not trusting you?" she asked with dread.

Dex's jaw tensed. "Not necessarily," he said. "He would certainly be a suspect. But the people trafficking drugs in and around the island have more than one way to come at you. Whoever got Kenneth Monaghan to do their dirty work in killing Agent Roxanne Yamamoto could've easily figured out that she might have a replacement and made it their business to determine who it was."

Katrina knew he was also trying to tell her it had nothing to do with their involvement, per se. Or even her own association with both Roxanne and, of course, Joseph, as his widow. Yet Katrina still got a chill in believing that the danger was all around them and the perpetrators would not stop as long as whoever was calling the shots felt confidently above the law.

Before she knew it, Dex had wrapped his arms around her. "It'll be all right." He spoke with a mixture of softness and sureness. "For both of us. I promise."

"You think?" She lifted her chin at him.

"Yeah, I do." He took a breath and held her a little tighter.

Katrina leaned against his hard body, taking in his words and what she took as a dual meaning that they would both get past the current dangerous environment and also be okay in their own future. She embraced both concepts, while still being concerned about what it all meant.

Chapter Twelve

Katrina was restless as she slept through the rainy night, despite being held snugly for much of it by Dex. She had a frightening dream about coming face-to-face with her stalker, only to have him lunge at her with a long-bladed supersharp knife. The type one could imagine Jack the Ripper used to carve up his victims. Just as she screamed, Katrina snapped open her eyes and heard only a low hum coming from her mouth. It was only a nightmare. The first she could remember that involved the mystery man who had left her notes and followed her around at least once.

As she regained her bearings, Katrina turned around, expecting to find Dex sound asleep. Instead, his side of the bed was empty. Feeling slightly disappointed, she dragged herself up, wondering if he had made breakfast or at least coffee. Slipping into a short kimono robe, she left the room and went into the kitchen. No Dex. Or even Barnabas. Did she drive them away? After not finding a note, Katrina checked her cell phone for messages. There was a text from Dex that told her he had gotten up early to give Barnabas some exercise and then both would need to get back to work. He asked that she keep him informed if she ran into any problems. That was code to Katrina for possibly whoever ransacked his cottage. Or perhaps if she spotted the man who had stalked her.

Dex ended the text message with the words, Miss you. Katrina missed him too. Maybe more than she was willing to admit to him, if not herself. Wherever this was going, she still needed to remain grounded and remember that the lodge needed to be her first priority at the moment. Just as Dex had an ongoing investigation that he had to focus on if they were ever to get past it. Asking him to push that aside, or to the back burner and instead explore their budding romance, wouldn't be fair to either of them. Especially not when drug-related criminals were still within their midst and apparently as dangerous as ever.

Twenty minutes later, Katrina was in her office, working. In fact, business had been brisk of late, with bookings going through the roof for this time of year and few empty rooms for the foreseeable future. It looked as though they were finally beginning to turn the corner in becoming profitable, in spite of Joseph's mismanagement before he died. *I certainly can't take anything for granted*, she told herself, knowing that you got what you put into it. Beyond that, to keep the lodge running smoothly, it needed to continue to be a go-to resort location in the ever-competitive town of Poipu on the island's south shore. Katrina understood that for her long-term survival in the hospitality business, the Maoli Lodge had to get past the drug-trafficking probe once and for all.

"Hey, I've been looking for you," Alyson said, stepping inside the room and snapping Katrina from her musings.

"You found me." She smiled at the assistant manager. "What's up?"

"Just a scheduling conflict with a housekeeper. Apparently, Sophie had a little too much to drink last night and overslept."

"Oh dear." Katrina made a face. Sophie Fernandez was one of their recent hires. What she lacked in experience, she more than made up for with hard work. Till now.

"Fear not, I took care of it," Alyson stated proudly. "Did a little rearranging of schedules so she could come in later without a single room needing to be delayed for cleaning."

Katrina's eyes lit with gratitude. "What would I ever do without you?"

"You'd manage just fine," she insisted, downplaying her role in keeping things running as smoothly as possible. "I'm happy to be your right hand in making sure things don't fall apart."

"And I'm just as happy to have you around, believe me." Katrina couldn't help but think about someone who was no longer around, Roxanne Yamamoto. Though she'd been only using her position with housekeeping to investigate the lodge, Katrina sincerely believed the DEA agent was a good person and obviously good at her job. She would have loved to have gotten to know Roxanne better. But she would never have that chance, as fate had intervened in the cruelest way. At least the man responsible for her brakes failing had been brought to justice and would pay the price. Katrina could only wonder how many more heads would roll before this was fully over.

"So, I noticed you've been spending time lately with the piano man." Alyson again cut into her thoughts.

Katrina blushed. "You're right," she admitted. She

saw no reason to deny it, even if she had to maintain Dex's cover for as long as he needed her to. "We sort of hit it off."

"Figured as much." Alyson flashed her teeth. "Good for you. I know you loved Joseph, but you're allowed to move on at some point. Now seems to be as good a time as any."

"I agree." Katrina welcomed her support. Getting past Joseph's passing was not going to be easy. But she had a right to meet someone else with whom she could find a rapport and fall in love. *Did I just say fall in love?* Katrina asked herself in shock at the suddenness of the emotion toward a man she had not known for very long. But then again, she had known Joseph for a while before they became an item. As it turned out, in many ways she had not known him at all. And if the truth be told, may never have really been in love, so much as liking the idea of love. Not the way she was beginning to feel about Dex. Could he feel the same way about her? Or did he need more time—and even distance—to come to terms with what she meant to him? "We'll see how it goes," she tossed out, as if what they had was strictly casual. It wasn't to her anyway.

"At least he has some musical talent to keep you going," Alyson said with a chuckle. "Wish I could say that about the men I've been dating lately."

Katrina laughed. "Well, there is that." She was amazed Dex found the time to keep up with the piano playing, given his day job. Admittedly, having such a skill was a great cover for someone working undercover.

"Being a private investigator to boot probably doesn't hurt the cause either," Alyson joked, moving over to her desk. "Never know when you might need someone to do a little digging for you."

"That's true too." Katrina thought it wise to move away from this conversation, knowing that Dex was doing digging that went well beyond her needs. "Anyway, let's talk about the hula dancers we have coming in to perform in the Kahiko Lounge this weekend…"

WITH BARNABAS ON a leash and behaving himself, Dex walked around the lodge, allowing the dog to stretch his legs and see if he picked up any signs of drugs. Though Katrina wasn't a suspect any longer, there was still the possibility that the lodge was being used by traffickers to facilitate their agenda. Particularly considering that someone had the gall to break into his rented cottage, suggesting that the connection was there. It irked him that this was putting Katrina at risk, especially as he was trying his best to lessen the threat to her health and well-being. Now that they had moved their relationship up a notch—make that a few notches—he wasn't about to let the bad guys rain on their parade and prevent more sunshine between him and Katrina on Kauai. Or anywhere else they could get closer.

Dex went outside to allow Barnabas to do his thing in a cluster of bushes, while barely noticing a bakery delivery truck parked out front. He didn't have much of a sweet tooth, though he was definitely becoming sweet on Katrina, who was much more to his liking as a delicacy. Besides his delight in spending the night together, getting little sleep in the process, she was everything he'd ever wanted in a woman and partner to build a life with. And, yes, to fall in love with. What was not to love in the beautiful, intelligent and successful businesswoman? Dex wasn't about to shy away from the type of life he could have with Katrina. She seemed amenable to the possibilities, which thrilled him even more. Once the investigation was over, he looked forward to having a conversation with her about a future and, hopefully, find a way to make this work between them. No matter the obstacles that might present themselves, given their different lots in life.

Back inside, Dex was sure Katrina was up and at it, meaning no chance for any morning delight. What about the afternoon to have a repeat performance of last night? He found himself inside the Kahiko Lounge, which was mostly empty at this time of day. Dex didn't spot Gordon, but the head bartender was never far away, and seemed to have his eye on one of the daytime waitresses. Dex drifted toward the piano. He wasn't scheduled to play today, but felt the spirit move him in doing a song or two as a freebie and for practice. Sitting on the bench, he freed Barnabas from the leash, which the dog clearly welcomed as he curled up silently beside Dex, seemingly ready to snooze.

Dex started playing "Hawaiian Lullaby," and was about halfway through the popular song, when Barnabas stood up and shot across the lounge. He wound up near the bar and seemed attracted to something atop it. The dog had been trained to react this way in the presence of drugs. Dex's own radar activated. *What have you latched upon, boy?* He took his fingers off the piano keys and headed over to see for himself.

Approaching the bar, Dex spotted the sheet cake on the counter. Jumping up at it, but just out of his reach, Barnabas only settled down when Dex reached the dog and kept him at bay. "What do we have here?" Dex asked out loud as he studied the rectangular cake in a baking pan with a see-through plastic lid. Grabbing a napkin off the counter, he carefully lifted a corner of the lid until it gave and came off in its entirety. Setting it aside, he saw a layer of coffee grounds. He dug into and lifted up a cellophane wrapped package. Putting it up to his nose, Dex smelled a mixture of a flowery and chemical scent that he recognized. There were several other packages hidden as well. The coffee sheet cake was a clever front for what Dex knew to be several pounds of cocaine. What the hell was it doing there?

"Good job, Barnabas," he praised the dog, while continuing to study the illicit finding. "I'll take it from here." The drug-sniffing canine seemed content at that point to wait for further instructions.

When Gordon Guerrero came from the back room carrying a case of wine, he saw Dex and said nonchalantly, "Hey."

"Where did this come from?" Dex glanced at the disguised cake and back at the bartender with a hard gaze.

"Why do you ask?" He set the wine down and took note of Barnabas suddenly growling at him as though the enemy. "And what's with your dog?"

Dex realized now was the time to end the charade and come clean. Either Gordon Guerrero would prove to be an asset. Or a drug trafficker. What came next would determine whether to solicit his help. Or place him under arrest. Removing his badge, Dex flashed it in the face of the potential suspect. "DEA Special Agent Adair," he announced firmly. "And this is Barnabas, my narcotic detection K-9."

Gordon's mouth dropped. He looked ill at ease. "Does Katrina know…?"

"Yes, she knows." Dex didn't beat around the bush. He was glad that Katrina had kept his cover under wraps. But the moment had come when everything was about to be out on the table. "Let's get back to the cake," he said sharply. "Who brought it here?"

"A woman from the bakery delivered it," Gordon claimed. "Said it was for a guest's birthday. We have birthdays, graduations, weddings, you-name-it events at the lodge all the time."

Dex recollected the bakery delivery truck outside. He must have just missed getting a look at the driver. "I need to know everything you can tell me about the delivery woman."

Gordon peered at him inquisitively. "You wanna tell me what this is all about, Agent Adair?"

Dex held his gaze. "The cake is actually made of cocaine."

"Seriously?"

"Do you see me laughing?" Dex's mouth was decidedly downturned at the corners. "Who is the cake of cocaine for?"

"The woman said his name was Julio," Gordon responded succinctly.

Julio. The name immediately rang a bell in Dex's head like a fire alarm, as he recalled that a Julio was the drug dealer Larry Nakanishi said gave Joseph Sizemore the meth. Dex was all but certain that the unsub also supplied Katrina's late husband with synthetic fentanyl and that he and the man slated to receive the cocaine cake was, in fact, one and the same. "When is Julio supposed to pick up the birthday cake?" Dex asked.

Gordon glanced at his watch. "She said he would come and get it at noon."

Dex got out his cell phone and noted that was more than an hour away. Not much time to operate, but enough. He regarded the bartender and stated in earnest, "I'm giving you the benefit of the doubt, for Katrina's sake, that you're not caught up in this, Guerrero."

"I'm not," he insisted with a strained look of innocence. "If someone is dealing drugs at the lodge, I want to help bring 'em down."

Dex's instincts told him the man was on the level. "You can start by describing the delivery woman," he told him. "Then we'll need your cooperation as we set up a sting to go after the dealers…"

"You've got it." Gordon said convincingly, as Barnabas kept his eyes glued to him. "The woman was Hawaiian, I think, maybe in her late twenties, slim, and had long dark hair that was tied up in the back." He sighed. "I wasn't exactly checking her out, so can't give you much more than that."

"It's enough," Dex assured him. The description would give them something to work with.

He stepped away from the bartender and called Ishikawa and Lynda with the latest and unexpected turn of events in their investigation. Then he got Pietz on the line to help set things in motion for what they hoped would be an all-important step in taking down a drug-trafficking organization on Kauai.

Then came the hard part for Dex. He needed to inform Katrina that the Maoli Lodge was being used to camouflage and transport cocaine in the form of a sheet cake. And worse, one of the suspects they hoped to nab was very likely the same person who gave illegal drugs to Joseph Sizemore. Which may well have contributed to his death.

Chapter Thirteen

To say she was shocked to learn that four to five pounds of cocaine had been brought to the lodge disguised as a cake would be an understatement. Katrina was sickened when Dex delivered the news, having pulled her to the side just when she had gone looking for him and Barnabas after they had left her suite this morning without waking her to say goodbye. Their investigation involving the Maoli Lodge had brought them to this point and she would have to deal with it. Including the fact that the cocaine had reportedly been left for a man named Julio, possibly the same drug dealer Joseph used to get meth and perhaps fentanyl as well. Then there was the reintroduction of Dex's fellow DEA agents, Sylvester Ishikawa and Lynda Krause, whom Katrina knew as lodge guests, Mr. and Mrs. Sylvester Hayashi. According to Dex, the urgency of the situation demanded that the team work out in the open with full disclosure, as it related to her in giving them full cooperation. Katrina welcomed this and completely understood the need for secrecy for as long as was necessary to keep from jeopardizing the investigation. She had to admit that Agents Ishikawa and Krause were convincing as a loving couple, enjoying what was supposed to be a second honeymoon on Kauai. Katrina couldn't help but wonder just how much of the chemistry was the real deal. She considered the strength of the chemistry between her and Dex that had actually strengthened once his own cover had been exposed and she got to know the true man behind the mask.

"We believe the cocaine came from a bakery that may be used as a front for receiving and distributing the stuff," Dex informed her as they stood near a fountain and in between tropical plants. "We're trying to locate the delivery woman, along with the source of the illegal drug operation."

"How long do you think this has been going on?" Katrina dreaded to ask. If she were held liable for being a party to drug trafficking, it would be equally devastating to her business and to her personally.

"Can't say for sure, but my belief is that the traffickers are adept at moving from one location to another in their efforts to minimize risk and maximize profits." Dex lowered his voice a heartening octave. "There is no evidence that this has been a regular occurrence at the lodge. Gordon felt certain that he had never before seen the woman who delivered the cocaine. And I asked the front desk and there's no indication that a Julio ever checked in today or yesterday."

"Maybe he used a fake name." Katrina creased her nose. "Or his real one."

"More likely that he wouldn't have wanted to leave a trail of DNA and fingerprints behind by taking a room," Dex said confidently. "I'm guessing that he only intends to pick up his cocaine and get the hell out of the lodge as quickly and inconspicuously as possible."

Katrina sucked in a deep breath. "So, when is this

going to go down?" she asked, having been briefed on the sting he had put into gear.

"Anytime now." Dex put his hands on her shoulders. "We aren't expecting any trouble, but to be on the safe side, I think it's best if you stay in your suite until the operation is complete."

She gazed up at him uneasily. "You really think that's necessary?" He had told her that the plan was to allow Julio to pick up the cocaine cake and leave unscathed, while hoping he would lead them to bigger fish, other players and more evidence of criminal activity in the illicit trade.

"Better safe than sorry." Dex met her eyes warmly. "I've really grown to care for you, Katrina. If anything were to happen to you because of this, I'd never forgive myself."

"I feel the same way about you," she said boldly. "On both counts. You need to be safe too, Dex. Promise me that you won't put yourself in harm's way beyond what's necessary to achieve your objectives."

"You have my word." He grinned. "I have too much to live for to take any foolish risks," he insisted. "I'm looking at the best example of that that I know."

Katrina blushed. He seemed to always be able to charm his way out of any worry on her part. She supposed that played a big part in making her feel as she did about him. "Mahalo," she murmured. "I'll go to my suite and catch up on some chores till you tell me the danger has passed."

Dex nodded, satisfied. "Good."

Katrina walked away, glancing over her shoulder as he got on his cell phone and conferred with others on their plan of action. The entire thing made her nervous, quite frankly. She hoped it would be over quickly with no bloodshed at the lodge and the drug trafficker who fed Joseph's habit brought to justice.

DEX SAT CASUALLY at the Kahiko Lounge table alongside Lynda and Ishikawa, since their true identities had been revealed to Katrina. She had taken it well and intimated to Dex that it didn't come as a total shock, as she had suspected that he wasn't working alone in investigating drug trafficking at the lodge and on the island. *Good insight on her part*, Dex thought, resisting a smile, and feeling it was but one reason why he was so taken with her. The other reasons, such as personality, courage and vision, were just as important to him in the attraction. Not to mention being great in bed.

His thoughts returned to the present as he engaged in faux small talk with his colleagues, all pretending to be nursing cocktails, which were actually nonalcoholic tropical drinks. Other undercover law enforcement was in various degrees of pretending to be vacationers or staff throughout the Maoli Lodge. The hope was that this would all go peacefully. The suspect would pick up his cocaine dessert and exit with no fanfare and no one getting hurt. But Dex had been around long enough to know that the best laid plans could fall apart quickly. It was in that regard contingency tactics were in place to apprehend the suspect before he ever had a chance to grab his weapon, assuming he was armed. And Dex always assumed that where it concerned offenders in the drug trade.

Whatever went down, Dex's first priority was to see to it that not a hair on Katrina's precious head was harmed. Much less, the rest of her body. He was happy that she had cooperated with him without much fuss about staying put in her loft suite until this was over and her lodge was clear of the threat. While he knew the investigation was far from over, Dex needed to know for his own peace of mind that Katrina was safe and sound. He cared for her too much to wish for anything less. Quite the contrary, he was beginning to believe that there really could be light at the end of the tunnel when it came to getting the woman of his dreams and having a life that didn't revolve around battling drug dealers and the like. Maybe he had done enough, in memory of Rita, toward getting drugs off the streets and preventing some other young people from falling prey to addiction and dying. Maybe it was time he looked in a different direction in living life to the fullest. One that included Katrina.

But for now, he was still Special Agent Dex Adair and he had a job to do. At ten o'clock sharp, he watched as a tall and fit Hawaiian male entered the Kahiko Lounge. He had thick black hair in a messy hairstyle and a full goatee. The suspect wore a blue muscle tank T-shirt, athletic fit jeans and gray-black running sneakers.

"It's showtime," Dex said to the team as the suspect approached the bar's counter, where the cake sat.

"With a front row seat, all that's missing is the popcorn," Ishikawa quipped.

"Or ice cream to go with the cake," Lynda did him one better, before getting serious. "Let's get this done."

"We'll follow his lead," Dex said, "and go from there." He sent off a text to notify other law enforcement to stand down, but be on alert.

The suspect known only as Julio chatted in a friendly manner with Gordon briefly, who kept up his end of the bargain in not arousing suspicion. After the suspect looked around cautiously, he lifted the sheet cake and headed out of the lounge.

"He's on the move." Dex alerted Pietz on his cell phone. "Don't apprehend!" he emphasized.

"We'll let him go," the detective assured Dex, "see where he takes the cocaine."

Once the wheels were in motion, Dex, Lynda and Ishikawa left the table and followed the suspect without giving him a clue that they were on to him. Julio headed outside, where undercover agents did nothing to stop him from entering a black Jeep Grand Cherokee. It occurred to Dex that Katrina had believed that someone driving a vehicle of that color, make and model, had followed her that day. Could Julio have been her stalker? He didn't seem to fit with her description of the stalker as a white male, Dex considered. This led him to believe that the person who left Katrina the warning messages could have been working in tandem with Julio. If so, what did he get out of surveilling her? Could it have been a power play to undermine Julio or others in the drug organization?

Dex and the team rode together in his car in pursuit of the suspect, leading the way at a safe distance. All were armed and wearing bulletproof vests in preparation for a possible shoot-out. Dex kept in mind his promise to Katrina to not do anything foolish in the line of duty. He fully intended to honor that, but also knew that going after violent and seasoned drug offenders did not come without risk. This time was no different. Still, Dex was confident that with the heavily armed law enforcement in on the operation, his own chances for survival were pretty good.

"Where do you think he's taking his drug stash?" Lynda asked from the passenger seat.

"Could be anywhere," Dex responded honestly. "Most likely, it's somewhere nearby, where he can unload the cocaine quickly and distribute it accordingly."

"That's my way of thinking," Ishikawa agreed from the back seat, where he was keeping Barnabas company. "His cake is too hot to handle for very long."

"Not without getting burned," Dex said humorlessly. But just as he let out the words, he noted that the Jeep Grand Cherokee had suddenly picked up speed. The suspect was clearly attempting to flee. "Damn, we've been made." Dex made a face, wondering if he should have held back a bit more.

"So it seems," Lynda groaned, and then used her cell phone to notify the others in pursuit.

Dex pressed down on the accelerator to keep pace. "You can run, but you can't hide," he snapped.

"Not as long as he's on this island!" Ishikawa roared. "And I'm pretty sure the perp hasn't developed wings like a bird."

"If so, they've been clipped," Dex said. He found himself darting through traffic as the suspect drove at a high speed through the streets of Poipu as if he could somehow lose them. With an attempt by members of the police department to cut him off ahead, Dex was more concerned about innocent people being hit by the drug trafficker's vehicle.

When it appeared as though they had him boxed in, the suspect somehow managed to elude capture and doubled back toward the Maoli Lodge. Dex's pulse raced as he imagined in his worst fears that Katrina might still be in danger should they fail to stop him. Then the suspect veered away from the lodge and sped off in another direction.

"Looks like the perp's headed for the storage unit I surveilled," Ishikawa called out. "Something told me there was more going on inside than keeping some old books and antiques in boxes."

"Could be you've hit the mark," Dex offered, preferring that to the lodge, as the lineup of official vehicles were in hot pursuit.

The fleeing suspect drove the Jeep into the parking lot of the storage facility on Koloa Road in Kalaheo, a quaint town not far from Poipu. With the cocaine coffee cake in hand, he darted inside the unit.

Dex parked away from the Jeep, fearing it could be booby-trapped. Exiting with Lynda and Ishikawa, they removed their weapons and used the car as cover, while waiting for the arrival of other law enforcement.

"Wonder who else is in there with him?" Ishikawa questioned.

"I'm betting he's not alone," Lynda warned.

Dex peered at the door of the facility. "And apparently has no intention of surrendering."

"That will be entirely up to him," Pietz declared bluntly from behind them. "We sure as hell won't wait around while he thinks about it. Not on my watch."

"I feel the same," Dex affirmed, not wanting to see the suspect find any way to climb out of the hole he'd dug for himself.

After coordinating with members of the Task Force on hand, the team, equipped with Glock pistols, Remington 870 shotguns, Smith & Wesson double-action semiautos, and Rock River Arms LAR-15 carbines, surrounded the facility. Without the element of surprise on their side and no desire to give anyone inside more of an opportunity to flush the evidence down the drain, Dex watched as Pietz nodded it was time to go in and do their business as officers of the law.

They used a battering ram to break open the door and entered the spacious storage unit in a flurry of actions, commands, chaos and exchange of gunfire with the two male individuals inside. They included the suspect in question and a stocky Asian man in his midthirties with short bleached blond hair worn in a Samurai bun. Both were armed with high-powered weapons and refused to surrender without a fight. They got just that. When it was over, both were mortally wounded before either could be interrogated about the drug-trafficking enterprise and other participants still at large. Not to mention, Dex had hoped to grill the suspect known only as Julio about both his assumed role in giving drugs to Joseph Sizemore and his possible connection to Katrina's stalker.

On the plus side, the dead suspects left behind a treasure trove of evidence of illegal activity that Dex figured might take a while to go through, but yield important information in the fight against drug trafficking. He brought in his K-9 pal to help sniff out more illicit drugs, which he did. Apart from finding the approximately four pounds of cocaine as a sheet cake, still largely intact, Barnabas helped them to locate yet more cocaine, along with a fair amount of hydrocodone, oxycodone, methamphetamine and fentanyl. The thought of the drugs making their way to users and turning them into addicts and criminals sickened Dex, thinking about his sister. He took solace in the fact that these illegal drugs would never harm a soul.

"Look what else they gave us," Lynda practically

gushed, as she held in a nitrile-gloved hand a 9mm "ghost gun"—a self-assembled firearm without a commercial serial number.

Dex acknowledged the find. "I take it there's more of them?"

"You bet. Along with a cache of illegal weapons, I spotted a couple of Bushmaster .223 5.56mm-caliber AR-15 rifles and a HS Produkt .45-caliber handgun, among other firearms, along with rounds and magazines of ammo."

"There's also a boatload of cash as drug profits and for buying more weapons," Ishikawa said, walking up to the two.

"Quite a haul," Dex said, pleased. "Too bad they'll never get to use it."

Pietz joined them. "True, but this is just a drop in the bucket for these guys. Or those still amongst the living. They'll take the hit, lament over their losses and regroup. But not before we deal them more pain," he said intently. "We're still trying to track down the woman who delivered the bogus cake and any other associates."

"Once word spreads about what just went down, she's likely going to try to go underground," Lynda speculated.

Dex pursed his lips. "We can't allow that to happen," he insisted. "We need to beat the traffickers to the punch by disrupting their plans for escape and business as usual." In his way of thinking, that meant tracking down the ringleaders. Dex had a feeling that the two men killed were just foot soldiers, with someone else calling the shots. Until such person or persons were identified and apprehended, this case couldn't be put to rest. Nor would he feel Katrina was out of the woods, as long as the stalker was still out there, as if waiting for the right time and place to resurface.

Chapter Fourteen

Dex had texted Katrina to tell her that the coast was clear, insofar as her freedom of movement at the Maoli Lodge. Apparently, the suspect and a second person had been trapped and taken down at a storage facility. Thankfully, she had been spared the details. She relished being able to go about her business in the face of a tense situation between a suspected drug dealer and the authorities. But it still bothered her that this continued to hang over her and the lodge like a dark cumulus cloud. Dex had assured her that she had nothing to worry about and that they were on the verge of breaking the back of the drug cartel. But seeing was believing.

Until then, Katrina vowed to keep things as normal as possible as she entered the Kahiko Lounge. A few guests were seated with no drama to speak of. As she understood it, the operation inside the lounge went off without a hitch. Meaning few, if any, tourists were none the wiser in enjoying their stay and the amenities provided. Katrina greeted each of them as the owner and made her way to the bar, where Gordon was flirting with a pretty African American waitress named Rosalee Du-Bois, who was clearly eating up his words.

"Hey, Katrina." Rosalee flashed a big smile, with a brunette Afro blowout hairstyle shimmering.

"Aloha, Rosalee." She smiled back at her.

The slender waitress lifted a tray full of mai tais and walked away.

Katrina turned to Gordon, who asked with concern, "Are you okay?"

"Yes, I'm fine," she responded, glancing at the piano and picturing Dex sitting there and filling the lounge with sweet music. He really had been a good fit in that capacity. But there was no turning back, was there? In this case, she believed it was for the better, as Katrina had warmed up in a big way to the man as she saw him now.

"So, how long have you known Dex was an undercover DEA agent?" Gordon asked, as if reading her thoughts.

Katrina faced the bartender. "Long enough," she admitted. "I was sworn to secrecy while he did his job."

"Figured as much."

She tucked some strands of hair behind an ear. "Mahalo for going along with the operation. I'm sure it helped keep things from getting out of hand."

Gordon shrugged. "Did what I needed to." He used a cloth towel to wipe off the counter. "If I'd suspected the cake was cocaine, I never would have allowed her to leave it."

"I know." Katrina offered him a grateful smile. "Guess we all need to be more on guard against these types of things in the future." How desperate were drug dealers that they needed to be so creative in order to hide and distribute their product?

"You're right. My bad." He eyed her sorrowfully. "In any event, I heard they nailed the dude."

"I heard that too." She gulped, wishing it hadn't come down to a violent confrontation. "Maybe something good can come out of this if more and more people can educate themselves about the horrors of drug use and addiction." She couldn't help but think about Dex's sister. Having her die that way and not being able to do anything about it must have been devastating. Just as it was for her to discover that Joseph had been using drugs, which may have led to his falling out of the kayak and drowning.

"Yeah, I'm with you there," Gordon told her. "Better get back to it."

"You and me both," Katrina said, waving goodbye and greeting other guests as she left the lounge. She played host in the lobby before heading back to her office.

When she felt a hand on her shoulder before entering the office, she jumped and turned to see Alyson standing there with a frown on her face. "Mind telling me what just happened at the lodge?"

Katrina batted her eyes innocently. "Excuse me?"

"There was some commotion," she voiced. "One of the guests said that the authorities raided the place—is that true?"

"No. Not exactly."

Alyson looked nonplussed. "What does that mean?"

Katrina ushered her into the office so they could speak in private. She decided there was no reason to withhold what others already knew or apparently figured out, in spite of the surreptitious nature of the stakeout. "Someone left cocaine disguised as a sheet cake at the lodge," she told her. "When a man came to pick it up, the feds and members of the Kauai PD watched and allowed him to leave, but followed. Apparently, there was a wild car chase and things came to a head at a storage facility, where the suspect and another drug trafficker were holed up. It ended there with them being killed…" She shuddered at the thought that Dex could have lost his own life in the gun battle, but had managed to come away unharmed, thankfully.

"You should have given me a heads-up on this operation," Alyson griped. "It would have been nice to have had some sort of advance warning so I wouldn't have freaked out wondering what was going on."

"It wasn't my place to spill the beans prematurely, without jeopardizing the mission," Katrina countered, though sympathetic to her assistant manager's point of view. "I'm sorry you were left out of the loop."

Alyson sighed. "I'm the one who should be apologizing," she insisted abruptly. "Didn't mean to overstep. You had every right to follow the lead of the authorities in this matter."

"No harm." Katrina offered her a friendly smile. "We've all been a bit on edge of late. Hopefully, we can turn the page now and get back to the business of running a lodge without the threat of drug trafficking in our midst." At least that was the plan, as far as she was concerned. But in the back of her mind, Katrina feared that this wasn't over yet, in spite of her wishes to the contrary.

"I can't argue with you there," Alyson agreed. "Anything of that sort is obviously bad for business. I'm glad the police put a stop to it before the situation could get any worse."

"That, they did." Katrina couldn't help but wonder

if whatever secrets Julio held regarding Joseph's final hours would now be buried forever, along with the two men.

They went to their respective desks and Alyson quickly moved on to discussing upcoming work on the landscaping.

"WE RAN THEIR PRINTS," Lynda told Dex a couple of hours later regarding the two men killed at the storage facility shootout. "And, not too surprisingly, considering their chosen profession, we got a hit."

"I'm listening," Dex said anxiously, as they conferred at the Kauai PD headquarters to get some details on the criminal suspects.

She glanced at a laptop on the table. "The Asian male is identified as Freddie Bautista. Age thirty-six and Filipino American. Using the FBI's Advanced Fingerprint Identification Technology, we learned that Bautista has priors in Hawaii and New York for drug-related offenses, such as possession with the intent to distribute meth and selling counterfeit oxycodone pills containing fentanyl."

"Sounds like a real piece of work." Dex's forehead creased, looking at his mug shot. "What about the one who took off with the cocaine cake?" he asked interestedly.

"Full name's Eduardo Julio Nihei," she said, putting his info on the screen. "Age thirty-two. Has a long rap sheet with everything from drug-related to weapons-related offenses. Nihei was wanted in Arizona on distribution of fentanyl and possessing ecstasy and meth for distribution."

Dex had used his cell phone to take a picture of the dead perp, with the information virtually cinching the connection between Nihei and Joseph Sizemore. So, Julio spoon-fed Sizemore the meth and fentanyl? Was the intent to commit murder? Or to keep the late lodge co-owner hooked and unable to know what was possibly happening all around him in plain view? "They say the dead can't speak, but Nihei seems to be saying plenty from the morgue," Dex commented tongue in cheek, "about his role as a trafficker of drugs in Poipu, Kalaheo and elsewhere on the island."

"He and Bautista definitely weren't acting alone," Lynda informed him. "I've done a little digging and see that Nihei has an older brother named Rafael Carlos Nihei. He, too, has a history of drug-involved criminality, violence and racketeering." She put his mug shot on the screen and Dex saw that he resembled Julio, only his face was fuller and he had a French crop haircut and was clean-shaven. "The elder Nihei is thought to be trafficking drugs between the Hawaiian Islands and the mainland, while operating out of Kauai."

"Which means Julio was working for his brother," Dex stated, "and not the other way around."

"That's the way I'm reading it," she said.

Dex was thoughtful. "And the same is likely true for the unsub who's been stalking Katrina. He obviously has more insight into me and our operation than I'm comfortable with."

Lynda nodded. "Whoever he is, the walls are beginning to close in on the entire drug-trafficking operation. And he'll be another casualty, one way or another."

"We'll see about that," Dex muttered, still having an uneasy feeling in that regard while Katrina's safety was on the line.

Ishikawa entered the room, his eyes shifting back and

forth. "Just spoke with forensics about the Jeep Grand Cherokee Eduardo Nihei was driving. So far, the only legible prints they've come up with belonged to Nihei and Freddie Bautista."

Dex frowned. "I was afraid you'd say that." He was sure it was the same vehicle as the one driven by Katrina's stalker. "What about DNA?"

"They're still looking into that."

Dex sighed. "What about the cake delivery woman?"

Ishikawa plopped into a chair. "According to Clayton Pietz, they should have a name and location anytime now."

"Good." Dex hoped to interrogate her sooner than later to see what light she could shed on the organization and its participants. At the same time, he feared that the unsub was expendable, as Rafael Nihei started to feel the heat with the death of his brother. Along with the screws tightening at every turn of his crumbling world of illicit drug distribution.

WHILE IN LIHUE, Dex popped over to Larry's Aquatic Shop, where he tracked down Larry Nakanishi, who was stocking a shelf. No longer needing to remain undercover, Dex flashed his identification and said, pulling no punches, "DEA Special Agent Dex Adair."

"Why am I not surprised?" Larry flinched. "Are you here to arrest me for using meth at one time?"

Dex gave a humorless chuckle. "Lucky you, I'm not interested in your previous or even current drug use, if you had a relapse," he told him truthfully.

Larry exhaled. "Well, if you're still investigating Joseph's death, I've already told you everything I know."

"Maybe not everything." Dex took out his cell phone

and pulled up the picture he'd taken of Eduardo Julio Nihei's mug shot. "Is this Julio, the man you say sold Joseph Sizemore the meth the day he died after the kayaking accident?" Dex waited a beat. "Take a good look."

Apparently, Larry needed no time to ponder, as he responded with certitude the moment he saw the mug shot. "Yeah, that's definitely Julio." Dex figured as much, but needed to hear it from the person who was with Sizemore that fateful day. Larry looked at him. "Is he back on the island?"

"Maybe he never left," Dex suggested, scrutinizing him. "Why? You thinking about hooking up with him again for some meth?"

Larry scowled. "No way. I'm done with the stuff," he maintained. "Just wondering, that's all."

"Julio's dead," Dex almost hated to inform him. On second thought, lessons learned, he hoped. "His days of dealing drugs are over." He watched Larry lean awkwardly on one foot in perturbed silence, before Dex said, "I'll let you get back to stocking shelves." He left the shop on that note, armed with further information in making a solid connection between Nihei and Katrina's late husband as part of the broader picture of trafficking drugs on the island.

BACK AT THE LODGE, Dex acknowledged Lynda and Ishikawa, who, in spite of their identities as DEA agents being revealed to Katrina, continued to keep up their facade as married tourists while maintaining a watchful eye for any signs of trouble that might have arisen after the takedown of Eduardo Julio Nihei. By all appearances, things looked peaceful as Dex walked around with Barnabas on a leash. Yet there was an uneasy feel-

ing in the pit of his stomach that Nihei's brother, or perhaps the stalker, might try to retaliate for the two drug
dealers' deaths or the financial losses incurred from the
drug bust.

Not spotting her, Dex sent Katrina a text asking if
they could talk in her suite. She replied yes and said she
would meet him there in five minutes. He waited by her
door with Barnabas as fresh memories ran through Dex's
head of the blazing intimacy between him and Katrina.
She was special and he would do everything in his power
to keep her alive and well. That started with keeping
her abreast of where things stood in the investigation.

"Hey," Dex heard the tender sound of Katrina's voice.

"Hey." He grinned as she approached. "Hope you
weren't too busy?"

"Not too busy." Katrina's eyes twinkled. "Some
things are more important than others."

"I agree." In his book, she was one of those things.
Dex was starting to realize that more and more with
each passing day.

Inside, he commanded Barnabas to sit and, as always,
the dog was obedient and eager to please. They sat side
by side on the sectional, where Dex recalled first coming clean about being a DEA agent and investigating
drug trafficking and the death of Roxanne. The fact that
Katrina had initially been a suspect was something Dex
wished he could take back, given what he knew now.
But she had apparently never held that against him, for
which he was beyond appreciative. He wanted to be a
part of her life now and maybe much more.

"I'm glad you're here in one piece after your confrontation," she said, soft worry lines creasing her forehead.

"So am I." He chewed on his lower lip. "As for the

way things went down, if there had been any other way, I would've preferred to take them in alive."

"I believe you." Katrina put her hand on the knee of his linen pants. "You have to do your job. No one could fault that."

Dex nodded to that effect and said evenly, "The dead drug dealer who picked up the cake is the same one who supplied Joseph with meth and fentanyl. His full name is Eduardo Julio Nihei. Larry Nakanishi confirmed his identity." Dex removed the cell phone from his back pocket and showed her Nihei's mug shot. "Have you seen him before?"

"I don't think so." Katrina shook her head, grimacing. "I just can't believe Joseph got mixed up with the likes of him."

"I know." Dex sympathized with her. "When it comes to drug use and addiction, many have a tendency to get involved with the wrong people." His sister came to mind, as was often the case.

"Yeah, I guess," she groaned, contemplative.

He showed her the mug shots of Julio's brother, Rafael Carlos Nihei, and Freddie Bautista, identifying the latter as the other fatality in the storage unit. "Have you seen either of these men before?"

Katrina sat back. "Neither rings a bell," she indicated and gazed at Dex. "Should I have?"

"Not really." He rubbed his jawline. "I wondered if the man who's been stalking you could have been one or the other?" Dex asked doubtfully.

Her lashes danced above wide eyes. "Uh, not unless he's a chameleon with his complexion. Other than that, the person who was stalking me is someone else."

"I suspected as much." Dex didn't mean to question

her judgment. "Had to be sure," he stressed, as they continued to try and connect the mystery man to the drug-trafficking probe.

"I understand," she said, her features brightening. "I haven't gotten any more notes or been shadowed by him. Could be that whatever his intentions, he's turned his attention elsewhere."

"I'd like to believe that," Dex told her, stretching an arm across the top of the sofa.

"But you don't…?" Her voice cracked with unease.

She could read him well, so he wasn't going to downplay the threat the man still posed to her safety. "Let's just say that until the unsub is eliminated as a person of interest and you no longer have to look over your shoulder at every turn, I'll keep him in the crosshairs."

Katrina beamed and ran a hand along the side of his face. "Mahalo."

"Just keeping it real," Dex claimed, knowing it went much further than that. She had become someone he couldn't get out of his mind. And didn't want to. Whatever their future, he was bound to protecting her in the present.

"Yes, let's keep it real, Dex." She inched closer to him, tilted his chin and planted a firm kiss on his mouth before pulling back. "Is that real enough for you?"

He grinned, tasting the sweetness of the kiss. "Yeah, about as real as it gets. In fact, maybe we need to try that again."

"Good idea," Katrina murmured, and leaned into him, whereby this time Dex was more than happy to take the lead. With a hand behind her neck, he brought them together and their mouths opened onto each other's for a searing kiss that turned his heart and soul upside down.

If he hadn't known it before, he did now. He had fallen in love with her and would need to process it in relation to the cards on the table, that defined their lives at this time.

Just as his introspection gave way to the passions and sounds of their lips locked, Dex's cell phone buzzed. He wanted to simply ignore it, hoping it might go away, but given the serious nature of his current assignment, that wasn't an option. Taking his mouth off Katrina's, Dex said apologetically, "I need to get that."

She touched her slightly open lips dazedly. "Please do."

He grabbed the phone off the sectional and saw that the caller was Detective Pietz. "Hey," Dex said coolly, standing and turning his back toward Katrina.

"We've got a bead on the woman who delivered the cocaine sheet cake," Pietz informed him. "Laurie Hoapili. Age twenty-seven. She runs a bakery called Laurie's Baked Treats in Hanapepe. We believe she was working for Rafael Carlos Nihei, along with his brother, Eduardo. I'm sending you a photo of her now…" Dex received it and studied the face. A pretty woman, she had bold brown eyes and long raven hair in a beach waves style. "We're headed to the bakery now with a warrant for Ms. Hoapili's arrest and a narcotics-related felony search warrant, if you and your team want in on this."

"We'll meet you there," Dex told him.

"And bring along your K-9 buddy, Barnabas," the detective said. "We may need him."

"Will do. See you soon." Dex disconnected and turned to Katrina, reading the curious expression on her face.

"What was that all about?" she asked, getting to her feet.

"The police have identified the woman who delivered the cocaine cake to the lodge this morning." He showed her the photograph on his cell phone. "Name's Laurie Hoapili. I don't suppose you've seen her before?"

Katrina peered at the image and said forlornly, "I'm afraid not. Looks like I'm striking out in placing faces…"

"Actually, that's a good thing," Dex countered. "Means that none of these people have been regulars at the Maoli Lodge, disassociating it primarily with illicit drug activity."

"Yes, that is good to know," she said. "I'd never want the lodge to be thought of as some sort of drug haven for traffickers. Even if it was beyond my knowledge."

"Didn't think so." He smiled thinly. "Anyway, a raid is about to go down at the delivery woman's bakery. I need to be there."

She nodded, touching his chest. "Be careful."

"I will." Dex took her hand off him and kissed the back of it. He called Barnabas and the dog ran over to them. "We'll be back soon," he promised, even while wondering how long it would be and where they could take their relationship.

Without saying a word, Katrina gave him a going away present with a big kiss on the mouth, making sure Dex wouldn't go very far without thinking of being with her in every way possible.

Chapter Fifteen

Dex arrived at Laurie's Baked Treats on Hanapepe Road, accompanied by Lynda and Ishikawa. The area was swarming with members of armed law enforcement, which had evacuated nearby shops and residences out of an abundance of caution. With a heightened sense of urgency and uneasiness all around, following the gunfight that took place at the storage facility earlier, no one was taking any chances on innocent lives being lost. Or, for that matter, the safety of those tasked with serving the warrants and ending this peacefully.

Barnabas was kept in the car until proven safe for him to go into action, as Dex joined Pietz and others wearing bulletproof vests and carrying firearms in approaching the bakery. Though there was no outward indication that whoever was inside would rather fight to the death than give up, Dex wasn't sure which way this would go. All he knew for certain was that Katrina had given him a new reason for wanting to come out ahead in any potentially dangerous mission. Yes, he wanted to rid the world—or at least the United States—of the scourge of drug abuse and trafficking. But one person could only do so much. He wanted more to make his life worthwhile. With Katrina, Dex believed he just might have that more than he could have ever imagined.

"Listen up," Pietz said. "A delivery truck and a white Dodge Charger, both registered to the suspect, are parked in the back, suggesting she's inside the building."

Dex thought about seeing the delivery truck at the lodge before realizing just what the woman was up to. If he could do it over again, maybe he could have caught her prior to reaching this point. "She might not be alone," he said, with the possibility that other unsubs or employees and customers could be inside. Any of whom could be used as hostages or shields.

"We've got a hostage negotiator ready and able to step in if needed," Pietz told him. "So far, there's no indication there are any customers inside."

"That's good," Dex said, not wanting to risk a bloodbath.

"Which is why we need to be quick and decisive," the detective warned. "Can't allow her to try and hide behind others. Or slip through our grasp."

"Don't see the latter happening," Ishikawa insisted, holding his weapon toward the ground. "She's someone who may be able to lead us to Rafael Carlos Nihei."

"That's the plan. Okay," Pietz told those leading the brigade, "let's do this."

Dex was onboard, bracing himself as they approached the bakery's front door. It was locked. Even in the apparent absence of customers, the whereabouts of the suspect was still in question, giving him reason to be concerned.

The door was forced open with a Halligan bar before Dex and Pietz rushed inside, their firearms ready to use, if necessary. The bakery was dimly lit with guava malasadas, cookies, doughnuts, cream puffs and other tasty treats on display. But no sign of the owner. They believed she might be hiding in the kitchen. Or in the company of other drug traffickers, perhaps waiting to ambush them.

When Pietz nodded at him, Dex shouted ahead as they approached cautiously, "Laurie Hoapili, this is DEA Special Agent Adair. We have a warrant for your arrest. Come out with your hands up and this can end without anyone getting hurt."

There was no response. And no indication that she wasn't alone. It seemed reasonable to Dex that the suspect may have already fled on foot or in a different vehicle, anticipating the raid. Or been tipped off by someone, perhaps from the inside. The idea that one of their own could have been in cahoots with the drug cartel bothered Dex. But he couldn't dismiss the possibility altogether, in spite of hoping otherwise.

They burst into the kitchen and there was no gunfire aimed at them. A quick scan showed Dex just the usual trappings of a bakery, with its baked goods and equipment. It was only as he made his way around a rectangle stainless steel table, that he spotted the body sprawled on the floor. The slender female's head was lying in a pool of blood. Beside it was a handgun that looked to be a Luger 9mm pistol. Turning back to the unmoving victim, he recognized her as the woman suspected of delivering the cocaine coffee sheet cake to the Maoli Lodge. Laurie Hoapili.

To Dex, it appeared to be a suicide, but he was taking nothing for granted. Once the bakery was deemed clear of any other victims or possible assailants, and potential evidence of the killing preserved, he employed his K-9 cop to search for any drugs on the premises. As expected, the canine delivered in discovering hidden in the refrigerator and a back storage room, countless vape cartridges containing more than 80 percent tetrahydrocannabinol or THC, as labeled, many grams of psilocybin mushrooms, pounds of marijuana and fentanyl, and medicated edibles.

"Looks like this place was offering a lot more than glazed doughnuts and guava malasadas," Pietz said humorously.

"Yeah, mix and match, according to your tastes," Dex said dryly, holding Barnabas on a leash.

"A perfect front for manufacturing, collecting and distributing illicit drugs," Lynda reasoned.

"Tell me about it," Ishikawa tsked. "Then they pass it out like candy across the island, the other Hawaiian Islands and the mainland, getting filthy rich in the process."

Dex grimaced, while weighing the items confiscated, including nearly a dozen firearms, such as semiautomatic rifles and other weapons. "I think the traffickers' luck is just about ready to run its course." At least this was his fervent wish. But he knew there were still more hoops to climb through before any of them could take a bow.

Twenty minutes later, Dex's fears on the cause of death were confirmed by the medical examiner, Francesca Espanto, who examined the victim at the scene. "Once the autopsy has been completed, I'll be able to give you my final report, but in my preliminary exam of the decedent, based on the angle and size of the wound to the side of the head and proximity of the firearm on the floor, I'd say in all likelihood Ms. Hoapili's fatal injuries were self-inflicted by a gunshot."

"I'd already come to that conclusion," he told her sadly, preferring that they would have had a chance to interrogate the bakery owner.

"Hoapili obviously felt the pressure of the drug-trafficking operation about to blow up in their faces," Pietz surmised, "and decided to check out before she could be arrested and sent to prison."

Dex did not disagree, but added, "With another box checked in dismantling the drug-trafficking ring on Kauai, we still need to track down the ringleader, Rafael Carlos Nihei. As well as his associates…"

"We will." The detective sounded confident. "We've just turned up the heat a few notches. Something tells me that Nihei knows we're coming for him and is looking for a way out—but won't find it."

"I'll second that." Dex wanted to see the drug trafficker, who undoubtedly ordered the hit on Roxanne Yamamoto and caused Katrina more stress and strain than she deserved, brought to his knees. Along with any others in his orbit, such as Katrina's stalker, who may have been vying for control of the organization and saw her as a convenient means to an end as the proprietor of the Maoli Lodge while under investigation. As such, Dex felt the man was still unpredictable, in spite of no further attempts to contact or surveil her of late. That made him dangerous. Possibly to Katrina, giving Dex cause for concern.

KATRINA WAS STILL trying to come to terms with Joseph's involvement with drug dealer Eduardo Julio Nihei, who may or may not have been introduced to him by Larry Nakanishi. Just how long had Joseph been using? And would he have ever sought help had he lived? Then there were some of the other players in the drug business, Julio's brother, Rafael Carlos Nihei, and Freddie Bautista. Not to mention Laurie Hoapili, the woman who brought a sheet cake of cocaine to the lodge. Katrina hoped that once she had been arrested, she might be able to shed more light on the ins and outs of the business. Or was there a code of silence among drug dealers?

As Katrina resumed her duties as host to new arrivals, her head was spinning as she thought about the life she once had with Joseph that was left behind with his death. *I just need to forgive him and move on,* she told herself, feeling there was no other choice. It was time for her to focus more on what she wanted for the rest of her life. Quite simply, it was to find love and be loved by someone who wouldn't betray her trust when the chips were down. Maybe someone to start a family with. Was that asking too much? Or not enough? Did Dex have what it took to make her feelings for him stand the test of time?

While pondering those conflicting thoughts, she headed across the lobby, surprised when her cell phone chimed. She reached for it in the pocket of her one-button charcoal blazer. She saw that Dex was requesting a video chat and quickly accepted it, eager to know that he and his K-9 companion were all right and they had located the delivery woman. "Hey," she said, gazing at his handsome face filling the small screen as she moved away from others toward a collection of areca palms.

"Hey. Wanted to let you know we were able to find Laurie Hoapili." His features darkened. "I'm afraid she's dead. The medical examiner believes it was suicide. I have no reason to dispute that."

"Oh dear." Katrina's heart lurched as she pondered the finality of it. Taking one's own life was never the answer, no matter what issues they faced. "I wish she'd given herself a chance to turn her life around."

"So do I. Unfortunately, casualties are par for the course in the illegal drug trade," Dex asserted.

"I guess," she said, still troubled by it coming so soon after Roxanne's death.

"She left behind more evidence that we hope will lead to arrests and putting the drug traffickers out of commission on and around Kauai."

"Yes, that would be a blessing." Katrina took a breath as she wondered what would become of them when that happened. Had he thought about it in a serious way? Or should she just let it play out…whatever was meant to be?

"Well, I have to go," Dex told her, and abruptly turned the cell phone to show Barnabas. "Like me, he can't wait to spend more time with you."

She smiled. "I feel the same way about both of you."

"Cool." Dex favored her with a boyish grin. "What do you like on your pizza?"

"Hmm…" She thought about it, in spite of not being a big pizza lover. "How about fresh basil and black olives?"

"Sure, I can work with that." He laughed. "Along with maybe some sausage and extra cheese."

"Sounds good," she told him.

"Same here. See you soon."

After they disconnected, Katrina smiled, relishing another opportunity to have a meal with him. She wondered naughtily what they might want to do for dessert. And even beyond, she considered, because it appeared as though the investigation into drug trafficking was nearing its conclusion. Their future was something they would definitely need to talk about.

Her cell phone chimed while she was still holding it, indicating she had a text message. Her pulse raced as she read it,

This isn't over. Don't let down your guard. Still a target, like your late husband. Be smart. Adair can't always protect. No one can. I'm watching you.

Nearly dropping the phone out of trepidation, Katrina's knees buckled as she looked around, expecting to find the man who was stalking her and apparently threatening again with this text after the earlier messages. She saw no sign of him. At least not one that was recognizable. Could he be wearing a disguise? She examined faces of those milling about or passing through. Could be any one of the younger and fit men, she supposed. *Am I a sitting duck right now?* Katrina asked herself with dread, as she moved quickly away from the lobby.

She nearly ran smack-dab into Alyson, who asked perceptively, "What is it?"

Katrina was tongue-tied with anxiety. "The stalker just sent me a text," she stammered, and showed it to her.

"Seriously?" Alyson's lips pursed with anger.

"I think he's inside the lodge," Katrina said, shuddering.

The assistant manager scanned the area. "I don't see anyone acting suspicious. Maybe this creep is just toying with you for who knows what sick reason."

Though she almost found that preferable, Katrina sensed that he was trying to tell her something. But what exactly? That Joseph had, in fact, been a murder victim? And that someone was trying to kill her too? If so, why? Was she powerless to protect herself, even with

Dex in her corner and seemingly on the verge of bringing down the drug cartel? Or was this even about that?

"I'm going to my room," she told Alyson anxiously,
believing she would be safe there until Dex returned.
"Can you handle things for now?"

Alyson frowned. "Yes, but—"

"Mahalo," Katrina said, cutting her off, feeling very
vulnerable at the moment and wanting only to keep an
apparent enemy at a somewhat safe distance.

"WE'VE GOT AN interesting hit on DNA pulled off the
dashboard of the Jeep Grand Cherokee that Eduardo
Julio Nihei was driving," Lynda informed Dex from the
passenger side of his vehicle.

"Go on…" He glanced away from the road and at her
as she studied a laptop. Ishikawa had volunteered to dog-
sit Barnabas, who needed some fresh air.

"It belongs to Zachary Lawrence, according to the
FBI's CODIS DNA database and DNA Casework Unit."

"Why does that name ring a bell?" Dex asked, searching his memory.

"Because he's one of us," she pointed out. "At least he
used to be. Two years ago, the then forty-year-old Lawrence was a DEA special agent with the Phoenix division. After his wife and daughter were killed during a
botched robbery, he went rogue. Was initially suspended
for allegedly pocketing drug money from raids on drug
traffickers. Though no charges were ever filed, he was
fired and basically went off the map. Till now."

"Hmm…" Dex was thoughtful. He had never met the
man but was familiar with the case. Being a dirty DEA
agent was debatably even worse than the standard scum-
bags who trafficked in drugs for profit. Had Lawrence

really fallen this low as a bitter and greedy ex agent? "Can you pull up his picture?"

"Got it right here." Lynda turned the laptop around and Dex took a quick look at the image of Zachary Lawrence. His face was diamond-shaped and he had blue eyes and thick black hair in a slicked back style with a taper fade. "You think he's the mystery man who's been stalking Katrina and sending her messages?"

"Seems to fit her general description of him," Dex said, crossing an intersection on Ala Kalanikaumaka Street, "and someone who was in a position to know I was a DEA agent he could expose and cause other trouble for Katrina. Only one way to know for sure."

"What would be his motivation?" Lynda wondered verbally. "Let me guess, to seize the perfect opportunity to cause confusion during our investigation, sowing seeds of doubt here and there—including the cause of Sizemore's death?"

"Maybe. Or because he has relevant information to share, but not at the expense of—or in spite of—his greater goal to be in control of the highly profitable drug operation by eliminating the competition." Dex mulled over the possibilities as he pulled into the pizza restaurant lot. "Whatever the case, something tells me that wherever Nihei is holed up, Lawrence is probably by his side and plotting to undermine him."

When his cell phone hummed as they stepped out of the car, Dex grabbed it and saw that it was Katrina. "Are you okay?" he asked, sensing otherwise.

"Just got a chilling text message from the stalker." Her voice shook. "I think he may be at the lodge."

"Where are you now?" Dex wondered if Lawrence would be so bold as to make a move in plain view.

"In my suite," Katrina responded.

"Stay put," he ordered. "I'm on my way."

"Was that Katrina?" Lynda gazed at him.

He nodded. "Someone, presumably Zachary Lawrence, just sent her a text. We better get back there now."

"Let's go," Lynda agreed gamely.

The pizza would have to wait, Dex felt, not willing to take any chances that Lawrence might try to harm Katrina if the opening was there, along with intent.

Chapter Sixteen

Once Katrina confirmed it was Dex on the other side of the door, she opened it and wrapped her arms around him, as if needing the reassurance of their bodies close together. "Thanks for coming," she uttered.

"Couldn't keep me away," he insisted, pulling them apart and going inside the suite.

"Where's the pizza?" Katrina asked, noting he was empty-handed and feeling guilty about that.

"We can have it delivered." Dex gave her a serious look. "Can I see the text message?"

"Have it right here." She had kept the cell phone on in her pocket, and removed it to show him.

Dex took the cell phone and read the words silently.

"They probably used a burner phone." Dex's brow furrowed, handing the phone back to her. "You never saw him?"

"Not to my knowledge." Her lips pursed. "He could have been hiding, but still able to watch me." She sighed. "What do you make of this?"

His chin tautened. "I think I know who's behind it."

"Really?" She looked up at him tensely. "Who?"

He took out his own cell phone and showed her a photo. "Does this look like the man who followed you?"

Katrina studied the image and flashed back to that day at the shopping center when she was trying to get away from him. "Yes, I'm pretty sure that's him." She met Dex's eyes. "Who is he?"

"His name is Zachary Lawrence. He's a former DEA agent."

Shock registered across her face. "What?"

"Lawrence's DNA was found in the Jeep Grand Cherokee that Julio was driving," Dex informed her. "We believe it was likely the same Jeep that was following you."

Katrina tried to wrap her head around this. Why would an ex-DEA agent be sending her text messages and stalking her? "Do you know why he's chosen me to obsess on?" she queried.

Dex drew a breath. "Apparently, Lawrence jumped ship from good to bad following the deaths of his wife and daughter. And ended up stealing illicit drug money and evidently graduated into hard-core drug trafficking. How he got involved with the Nihei brothers and their operation on Kauai is anyone's guess."

She frowned. "I'm still not sure what any of that has to do with me? He says I'm a target and intimated that Joseph was too. What does any of this mean?"

Dex held her shoulders. "It means that we've now identified Zachary Lawrence, taking away his one and only advantage in terrorizing you. Until we find him, I won't let anything happen to you."

"Promise?" She gazed into his eyes, unblinking. Even then, Katrina understood that if this man was determined to get to her, Dex couldn't guarantee that it wouldn't happen. But hearing the words from him to that effect still gave her comfort.

"Count on it," he reaffirmed in a convincing tone.

Right now, what she needed most from him was the feel of his lips upon hers. This prompted Katrina to raise her chin so he could read her mind. Before she could give him a hint, Dex pulled her close and laid a ravenous kiss on her mouth, which she received wholeheartedly. If nothing else, it took them away from more pressing concerns for some intimate time. To Katrina, this was a welcome interlude and, she hoped, a harbinger for things to come in their lives together. They went to bed and made love with the same sense of urgency and sexual chemistry as before—only this time it was with even more energy and compatibility in satisfying their needs.

Instead of ordering pizza afterward, they slept and had leftovers, before more sex and sleeping through the night. Katrina was certain that, at some point, the word *love* passed through Dex's lips. Or was it her own in speaking from the heart? When morning came, neither broached the subject, and she wondered if it was all in her imagination. Or were they both merely waiting for the right time to delve into those feelings and what they meant in moving forward?

They were enjoying a hearty breakfast she'd made of taro pancakes, bacon and Ulu Fiti breadfruit, with coffee, when Dex asked casually, "Just to be on the safe side, would it be okay if I put a GPS tracker on your cell phone? Probably won't need to access it, but until we can fully neutralize the threat to your safety, I'd feel a lot better knowing where you are when we're apart."

Holding her mug, Katrina eyed him. "I'm fine with that." She welcomed giving him the ability to track her whereabouts right now. Especially with an ex-DEA agent seemingly unwilling to leave her alone. And his behavior could escalate to something more dangerous.

"Good." Dex grinned and grabbed a piece of bacon from the plate. "If it were up to me, I wouldn't let you out of my sight."

"And I wouldn't let you out of mine," Katrina teased, but meant every single word. Waking up to his good-looking face and getting to enjoy him all day long, every day, was something she relished the fantasy of as a reality.

"Nice to hear." He showed his teeth. "Be that as it may, with duty calling, I've asked Lynda to shadow you today, if that's all right."

"Yes," she agreed, having felt comfortable around the DEA agent when chatting with her as a vacationer, even if Katrina preferred his company to anyone else's.

"After that, we'll see…"

She wondered if he was weighing where things stood between them and if sleeping in the same bed could turn into a more permanent arrangement. "You can stay here for the remainder of your time on the island, Dex," she volunteered, in case he had any doubt of her comfort level with him. "So can Barnabas."

"I appreciate the offer." He dug his fork into some taro pancakes musingly. "I'll let you know."

At least he's considering it, Katrina told herself, lifting the breadfruit, while wondering just how long this remarkable ride with an amazing man would last once his assignment was over.

DEX WAITED FOR Lynda to show up before leaving Katrina's loft suite. He really did wish he never had to leave her side, which was indicative of the strong feelings he was developing for the lodge owner. It wasn't lost on him that the *L*-word slipped from his mouth—and maybe hers too—during the night. This gave him hope that they were working toward something he never wanted to let go of. But right now, he needed to finish up the investigation and keep her safe, not necessarily in that order.

After picking up Barnabas from his overnight stay in Lynda and Ishikawa's room, Dex headed back to the cottage, where Ishikawa would join him later to compare notes. Once there, the cranky canine was let loose in the yard, after being sedentary too long inside. Dex looked around, not missing the place a bit since spending the past two nights at Katrina's. Before leaving the other day, he had put things back in order somewhat. Presumably, it had been ransacked by someone intending to send him a message. Was it Zachary Lawrence? Rafael Carlos Nihei? Or both, as partners in drug trafficking?

Whatever the case, Dex was not intimidated in the least. It was what he'd signed up for with the DEA. Still, it was all beginning to wear just a bit thin. He wanted more than this out of life. He had decided to take Katrina up on her offer to house him and Barnabas for the rest of their visit to Kauai, if for no other reason than to be able to stay close to her and ward off any threats to her life and security. Of course, there were other important reasons too for wanting to be in her presence. Not the least of which was that she made him happy, and feel as if there was a greater purpose to his life and a real ability and opportunity to share it with someone he considered an equal in all the ways that counted.

As Dex tossed his clothes into a leather duffel bag, he heard Barnabas barking. *What's he up to?* Dex wondered. Maybe chasing a gecko? Or perhaps a feral chicken, with thousands of them roaming around the island like they owned the place. He stopped packing and went into the backyard. The K-9 was jumping at a low hanging branch of a fig tree that managed to stay just out of his reach. Walking over to the dog, Dex checked out what was so captivating to him. There appeared to be something tied to the branch. What was that? He realized it was a small cotton pouch with a drawstring.

Using his height and long arm, Dex had no trouble reaching and grabbing it. Opening the pouch, while keeping it away from Barnabas, he sniffed and smelled the distinctive pungent odor of marijuana, but only saw a flash drive. What was it doing up in the tree? Had it been hidden there with important information by Roxanne as insurance should she run into trouble? How could he have missed that before?

Back inside, Dex sat down on a tufted leather wingback chair with his laptop and put in the flash drive. He saw two files. One was labeled "Special Agent Zachary Lawrence." His interest piqued, Dex opened it and watched anxiously as a video of the disgraced DEA agent materialized.

Lawrence, who sported a three-day stubble beard, was calm and collected as he said, "If you're watching this, Adair, it means your K-9 pooch did his drug-detection job and you're finally starting to figure things out. What took you so long? Or maybe you need a little help, which I'm here to provide. I'm DEA Special Agent Zachary Lawrence. I'm sure you've done your homework and drawn the wrong conclusions. No, I'm not a dirty agent. Just the opposite. I've been deep undercover for more than a year now, bouncing from one assignment to another, infiltrating illegal drug-trafficking operations and helping to bring the perps to justice. Your boss, Rachel

Zavatti, whom I've been reporting to as well for the last six months, will vouch for me.

"Anyway, to make a long story short, yes, I'm the one who's been leaving Katrina Sizemore the cryptic notes and following her—not as some psycho stalker, but to try and protect her and get you to step up in that role without blowing my own cover. Looks like it's worked. Regarding Katrina and the Maoli Lodge, it was never supposed to be a location to traffic drugs. But then Joseph Sizemore had the misfortune to get involved with Eduardo Julio Nihei as his dealer. It got Sizemore killed and made his widow a target. Julio's crazed brother, Rafael Carlos Nihei, has a fortified compound in Waimea Canyon on Kauai's west side. But with his drug empire disintegrating before his very eyes, he's getting sloppy and even more unstable than usual ever since Julio was killed."

Lawrence sucked in a long breath. "Working as Nihei's right hand, I've gathered enough evidence, along with the Task Force, to put him away for a very long time. Agent Roxanne Yamamoto—who was a friend of mine before I lost my wife and child, when I was doing standard DEA work—added to that pertinent info with her undercover assignment at the lodge. I was able to retrieve that from her laptop before Rafael's thugs could destroy it. I suggest you take a look at the file, which should be very telling and instrumental in bringing a close to the investigation.

"Well, I better get out of here now, unless I want Nihei to catch me in the act. Not a good idea." He furrowed his brow. "We're not likely to speak face-to-face, Adair, till this thing is over. Either that, or I'll already be dead from overplaying my hand. In which case, guess this would be goodbye and sorry we couldn't meet under better circumstances."

Dex watched him give a mock salute and the video ended as he stared at the empty screen in unadulterated disbelief. Had his assumptions about Lawrence just been turned upside down? Was he actually trying, like himself, to keep Katrina from being harmed rather than the other way around? While pondering this unexpected twist in the investigation, Dex placed a video call to Rachel on the laptop.

"Hey," she said routinely, from her office.

"Is it true that Special Agent Zachary Lawrence is deep undercover as a drug trafficker on Kauai?"

Rachel blinked as she exhaled. "Yes, it's true."

Dex frowned. "Would've appreciated a heads-up about this while conducting our investigation."

"That wasn't possible," she insisted. "You know how it works. We never expose operatives at work, jeopardizing their lives and missions. It was up to Lawrence to decide if and when he was ready to break his cover, which has proven to be invaluable in infiltrating criminal organizations and drug cartels as a credible DEA agent gone bad. Apparently, that time is now."

Dex waited a beat, before conceding that Lawrence did everything the right way. Even if the current investigation had become much more personal to carry out, with the strong feelings Dex had for Katrina. But he was still loyal to the DEA and its objectives. As a result, he needed to see this through to completion. "Is there anything else I need to know?" he asked respectfully.

"Only that I want you and Lawrence, along with Krause and Ishikawa, to work together in your respective capacities to bring down the drug-trafficking ring

on Kauai, on behalf of our fallen agent Roxanne Yamamoto, and others affected by this thing in Hawaii and
the mainland." The special agent in charge peered at
him. "Are we clear?"

"Yeah, we're clear." Dex knew when to quit while he
was ahead, knowing there were other issues on the table
that needed his focus. Including seeing what information Roxanne had gathered and left behind for them to
make use of in breaking up the crime syndicate. "I'll be
in touch," he said evenly.

"I'll be waiting." Rachel nodded as if expecting no
less of him. "See you soon."

Dex opened the file labeled "DEA Agent Roxanne
Yamamoto." It contained a video and a Word document.
He held his breath while clicking on the video, wondering what his friend had to say from the grave that, in
the words of Agent Lawrence, "should be very telling
and instrumental" to the case.

"LOVE YOUR FURNISHINGS," Lynda said, after Katrina welcomed her into the loft and made them Japanese green
tea. "I could use some similar pieces to spruce up my
condo in LA."

"Thanks." She smiled at her, while wondering if the
attractive DEA agent was merely being polite. After
all, Katrina was pretty sure that essentially acting as a
babysitter for a grown woman, whom her fellow agent
Dex was romantically involved with, probably wasn't in
her job description. Still, Katrina was grateful to have
her there to help safeguard against any possible attack
by Zachary Lawrence. "If you're serious, I'd be happy
to show you where I purchased them."

Lynda ran a hand through her short hair and responded, "Yeah, definitely. It would be a good way to impress my real significant other, Martin O'Sullivan, who works for the LA County Sheriff's Department."

Katrina chuckled. "And to think, you and Agent Ishikawa seemed like such an item," she teased her.

"We do make a good team." Lynda laughed and sipped her tea as she stood next to the kitchen island. "Maybe in another universe, but not this one. Besides, after going down the aisle twice unsuccessfully, Ishikawa isn't exactly every girl's dream for a guy to bring home to mommy, sweet as he may be when not on the job. Never mind that my own mother has been dead for more than a decade now."

"Do you think that Dex is a good catch to bring home?" Katrina tossed out from the other side of the island and almost immediately wished she could take it back. If only because she wasn't sure just how much his colleagues knew, or wanted to know, about Dex's personal life. On the other hand, maybe this was a good gauge to see where things stood between them from someone in his inner circle.

"Actually, I think Dex is a great catch for someone," Lynda said straightforwardly. "He's been burned once, but is a stand-up guy and knows what he wants in a mate."

"Does he?" Katrina gave her a curious look, as she tasted the tea. *Do I fit the bill?* she asked herself.

"You hit the spot perfectly in that vein," Lynda pointed out. "I can see that Dex is crazy about you."

"Is he?" She couldn't help but blush because the words were melodious to Katrina's ears.

"Yes." The agent didn't back down.

"I feel the same about him." Katrina figured she

might as well put it out there. "But I do worry about whether he'll stick around long enough to give it a go," she admitted in all honestly.

Lynda leaned forward. "Whatever happens between you two once our investigation is over, I'm guessing Dex won't be foolish enough to let you get away."

Katrina beamed with that belief. But she knew she needed to hear it from Dex to know for sure that having a future together was real and not a mirage.

When there was a knock on the door, Katrina reacted with nervousness. So did Lynda, who was immediately alert and asked, "Are you expecting anyone?"

"Not really," she replied cautiously, "but I do run a lodge, so an employee may need me for one thing or another." Would ex-agent Lawrence, her stalker, be so bold as to try something with a former associate on hand and ready to make an arrest?

As if to make sure it was there, Lynda put a hand on the firearm inside the waistband holster tucked beneath her two-button black blazer. "Why don't you take a look at who's there through the peephole."

Katrina nodded and walked to the door. Her heart raced as she looked out, and then leveled off when she saw Alyson standing there. "It's my assistant manager," she told Lynda.

The strain on her face eased and the agent said, "Let her in."

Katrina opened the door and managed a smile. "Hey, Alyson."

Alyson smiled back. "Just dropped by to make sure you were all right."

"I'm good. You want to come in?"

Alyson shook her head. "Actually, there is a small

problem…" she started. "Someone had an accident in the pool. Hit her head…"

"Is it serious?" Katrina swallowed a lump in her throat while considering the possibilities.

"She seems fine now, but I thought you should know." Alyson paused. "I'll just double-check—"

When she began to walk away, Katrina impulsively went after her to discuss it further. She felt Lynda hot on her heels. It was only after they both had left the suite that Katrina noticed someone came up behind the DEA agent and whacked her on the back of the head with the butt of a gun. Lynda went down in a heap, knocked unconscious. Only then did Katrina lock eyes with the assailant. She recognized him from his picture as Rafael Carlos Nihei. Aiming the gun directly at her, he said in a no-nonsense, cold tone of voice, "Nice to finally meet you face-to-face, Katrina."

Chapter Seventeen

It was admittedly painful to Dex to see Agent Roxanne Yamamoto spring back to life via video, in what amounted to her final contribution to the DEA and a dedication that proved to be fatal. But if he had anything to say about it, he would see that her great sacrifice was not all for naught. Homing in on the laptop screen, Dex listened to his late friend and former colleague.

"I'm Agent Roxanne Yamamoto," she started, fear in her voice. "If you're watching this, it probably means my cover has been blown and I'm likely dead. I won't bore you with the mundane details of my assignment in posing as a housekeeper at the Maoli Lodge in Poipu on Kauai, investigating possible drug trafficking. These can be found in the other file, along with what I've been able to uncover thus far. Here, I mainly want to say that while working for the lodge, I have seen no evidence whatsoever that its proprietor, Katrina Sizemore, is involved in any way in the trafficking of drugs in and out of her property."

Dex was happy to see that they had reached the same conclusions about Katrina, as Roxanne sucked in a deep breath and continued, "But unfortunately, I have been able to find a secondary connection between the lodge and drug traffickers. Turns out that Katrina's late husband, Joseph Sizemore, was using drugs when he hooked up with drug dealer Eduardo Julio Nihei. Seems like Nihei, along with his brother, Rafael Carlos Nihei, a local drug kingpin, sought to leverage this to use the Maoli Lodge for distributing drugs. It appears as though Sizemore balked and paid for it with his life."

Roxanne ran a finger across a thin brow. "The story doesn't end there," she said contemplatively. "Not even Sizemore's death stopped the Nihei brothers from targeting the lodge as a portal for their illicit drug business. Rafael managed to find someone on the inside to charm into working for his interests. That would be Katrina's assistant manager Alyson Tennison, who, by all accounts, seemed to have fallen head over heels for the drug dealer, based on my surveillance. I haven't been able to warn Katrina yet, without putting her life and mine in danger, but that's my top priority. More later..."

As the video ended, Dex was left with his mouth agape, shocked to learn that someone Katrina obviously trusted was stabbing her in the back. Instead of Zachary Lawrence, it was actually Alyson, hidden in clear view, who posed the real threat to Katrina's safety. Along with the drug trafficker Alyson was romantically involved with, Rafael Carlos Nihei.

I've got to warn Katrina and Lynda, Dex thought anxiously, as he took out his cell phone. Before he could make a move, the phone rang. It was Lynda. He put her on video chat. "Katrina's been kidnapped!" she spoke frantically, with Ishikawa by her side.

Dex's heart pounded loudly in his ears with those frightening words. "What?"

"Her assistant, Alyson, came to the suite," Lynda explained. "Gave her some song and dance about a swimming pool incident. When Katrina stepped out of the room, I followed and someone hit me from behind. I think it might have been Lawrence."

"It wasn't," Dex told her confidently, getting to his feet. "Special Agent Zachary Lawrence is clean. He's been working in a deep uncover capacity."

Lynda gasped with surprise. "If it wasn't him, then I must have been clocked by—"

Dex frowned. "Rafael Carlos Nihei."

"Nihei must have been the one I saw shove Katrina into the back of a pearl beige metallic GMC Yukon Denali," Ishikawa pointed out. "They drove off before I could stop them. I reported the kidnapping and gave the make and model of the vehicle to Detective Pietz, then came back inside to check on Krause and found her unconscious in Katrina's suite."

"I'm fine," Lynda assured him, before Dex could ask, as she put on a brave face. "I always did have a hard head. Guess it came in handy."

"I'm just glad you're okay." Dex wondered if the same could be said for Katrina. The thought of losing her was something he didn't even want to seriously consider. All he knew was that he wasn't about to count on Pietz and the Kauai PD to bring Katrina back to him alive. Dex let Barnabas inside.

"What's the connection between Alyson and Nihei?" Ishikawa asked interestedly.

"Turns out, the two apparently are romantically involved," Dex responded sourly, wondering if Katrina had suspected anything about her double-dealing assistant.

"Alyson sure fooled me," Lynda grumbled. "I should've seen this coming."

"It's no one's fault." He wasn't about to blame her for the assistant manager's conniving and putting on a good act. The important thing was that they find Katrina before it was too late. "I put a GPS tracker on Katrina's phone," Dex told them. Looking at his cell phone, he activated the device, hoping she had left her cell phone on and that the kidnappers hadn't taken or destroyed it. His stomach churned with satisfaction when Dex saw that Katrina's phone was turned on and he could see her location. "They're on the move," he announced, heading out the door. He gave the agents the current location and Dex went after the woman he loved.

"ALYSON'S MY GIRLFRIEND, in case you haven't already put it together," Rafael Carlos Nihei all but bragged to Katrina from where he sat in the front passenger seat of the SUV that she had been forced into the back of at gunpoint. The driver was her stalker, crooked former DEA agent Zachary Lawrence, who had remained mute during the drive, while occasionally making his presence known by glancing in the rearview mirror. Sitting beside Katrina was the woman Rafael was referencing and who had betrayed her: Alyson Tennison. Katrina glared at her assistant manager. Alyson was now holding the gun and pointed it at her somewhat precariously. Katrina found it hard to fathom that the Alyson she thought she knew would have allowed herself to get attached to the wanted and dangerous drug trafficker. Rafael laughed, as though reading her thoughts. "Even you must admit that Alyson played her part well as the devoted employee who never quite got the respect she deserved from you."

"That's not true." Katrina pushed back on that premise. "I always respected you and your role with the Maoli Lodge."

"Yeah, right." Alyson rolled her eyes with a disdain Katrina had never seen before. "Neither you nor Joseph ever gave me the credit I was due for keeping the lodge running smoothly for the most part. You were far too busy sniping at one another or otherwise taking me for granted. I couldn't take it anymore."

"And so, what? This is payback—getting in bed with a drug trafficker and kidnapping me? That doesn't make any sense," Katrina declared, not holding back in giving her a piece of her mind. She only hoped that Lynda hadn't been seriously hurt when Rafael hit her on the back of the head during the abduction.

"Shut up!" Alyson snapped, her eyes slits. "Whatever you may think of Rafael, he's not a bad person, unless provoked. He provides a needed service that people like your dead husband asked for. If only Joseph hadn't played on his worst instincts, he might be alive today. Think about that!"

Does she really believe that? Katrina drew a disbelieving breath as she considered the toxic words, while conceding that there was a ring of truth to them. But that hardly justified the actions apparently taken in fueling his drug habit. Anger filled her eyes. "Was Joseph murdered?" She needed to know, even as Katrina took note of where they were headed. It seemed to be toward the north shore. Dex had put the tracker on her phone, which she kept on in the back pocket of her high-waist skinny pants. He must surely know by now that she'd been abducted and had some sense of her whereabouts.

When Alyson suddenly went speechless, Rafael said in a callous voice, "He left us no choice but to take him out. When your husband refused to play ball in letting us use the lodge for business, he had to go, to send a message to others who were uncooperative. Joseph's plan to go kayaking was the perfect means. Giving him just enough fentanyl-laced meth to make sure he never survived the outing, meant no more interfering with our agenda."

Katrina put hands to her mouth as the truth settled in. The idea that Joseph had been the victim of foul play hit her like a ton of bricks. The fact that Alyson played a role made it all the more devastating. And what were their plans for her? Did she truly want to know? *Keep a cool head*, Katrina told herself, realizing it might be her only chance for surviving this ordeal. "I suppose it was you who ordered the hit on my housekeeper, Roxanne?" she addressed the question to the drug trafficker, pretending not to know Roxanne was a DEA agent, while hoping to buy time and that somehow Dex would manage to come to her rescue. Or other law enforcement.

Rafael never wavered in his response, admitting flat out, "Agent Yamamoto got what was coming to her. Once Alyson discovered what she was up to as an undercover investigator for the DEA, overhearing on the phone, we needed to know what she knew, before soliciting the services of a greedy ex-con to tamper with her brake lines."

Katrina shot Alyson an icy stare, knowing she bore the blame for Roxanne's murder. And perhaps for her own as well, if the traffickers had their way. "Don't look at me like that," Alyson blared, putting the gun up to her face. "I never asked Roxanne to stick her nose where it didn't belong. That's the price she had to pay."

Katrina withdrew her gaze, not willing to put the battle of wills to the test. Alyson pulled the gun back. Still, she couldn't help but ask the trio, "Whose idea was it to bring cocaine disguised as a cake to my lodge?"

Alyson snarled at her. "I thought it was worth trying to see if we could make this a regular thing," she hissed. "I didn't count on Dex coming in the lounge to play the piano on what was supposed to be his off day. Or that damned dog of his with an uncanny ability to pick up the scent of the cocaine. That's when we knew Dex had to be part of a DEA K-9 unit, along with his supposed pet Barnabas."

Katrina didn't deny it. Nor did she wish to push their buttons any more by praising what Dex and other law enforcement had done in thwarting the drug traffickers' plans.

"Cost my brother, Julio, his life!" Rafael bristled, angling his face at her. "And a valued soldier in Laurie Hoapili. For that, they'll pay…"

The ambiguity of the comment shook Katrina to the core. Was he planning to go after Dex in particular? The DEA? Or the entire Task Force? "Where are you taking me?" she decided to ask, for more stalling, as they drove down Kuhio Highway, believing they would have already killed her by now if Rafael and Zachary Lawrence had wanted to.

"To the airport, if you must know," Zachary spoke for the first time. "With the feds and locals breathing down our necks, we're getting out of Dodge—or off the island—and merely taking you along as an insurance policy in case your DEA pals try to stop us."

"And what then?" Katrina shuddered to think of anything but the worst-case scenario.

"Once we're onboard and there's no trouble, we'll

let you go unharmed," he said convincingly. Only she wasn't convinced in the slightest that Rafael—or even Alyson, for that matter—had any intentions of letting her go free. Given that she saw their faces and knew their names, Katrina sensed that she was a dead woman if Dex and company could not reach her in time. Scariest yet was the thought of never getting to tell Dex in straightforward terms how much she loved him and wanted to build a life together.

"JUST GOT A TEXT message from Lawrence, confirming that they have Katrina and are heading to the Princeville Airport," Dex said on his cell speakerphone, the information corresponding with the GPS tracking of Katrina's cell phone. He was passing the information to Lynda and Ishikawa, as Dex roared down Kuhio Highway or Route 560. Beside him was Barnabas, strapped in a dog car seat. "According to the undercover agent, Nihei has at least one airport official on his payroll." Dex guessed that the drug traffickers were planning to escape on a private jet, possibly to Honolulu, where they would try to get lost and rebuild their operation there. And where would this leave Katrina? Dex was certain that she was being kept alive as an abducted hostage, in case one was needed. Afterward, he had no doubt they planned to kill her, leaving behind no living witnesses. *I can't let that happen*, Dex thought, more determined than he had ever been for anything in his life. He would never get over it if Katrina didn't come out of this alive and before things between them truly had a chance to jell. She needed to know how he felt about her, leaving no doubt. And what he wanted to build with her for the future.

"We'll notify the airport authorities and police to

be on the lookout for the vehicle," Ishikawa told him, "which we now know is actually registered to Rafael Carlos Nihei."

"Okay," Dex said anxiously. "With any luck, this can end with no blood being shed." *Certainly not that of Katrina*, he mused, but knew he had to prepare for the real possibility that Nihei would use her as a bargaining chip. Should that fail, it wouldn't take much for him to take his frustrations out on Katrina. Without knowing just how many people the drug trafficker had in his pocket and were equipped to do battle, Dex could only hope that Agent Zachary Lawrence was ready to step up in evening the playing field. Even if it meant compromising his cover in order to protect Katrina. Or anyone else at risk.

"A SWAT team is on its way," Lynda informed him.

"Good." Dex was pleased to hear that, but feared it could be too late to save Katrina. "I'll get there first," he told them assuredly, and disconnected.

Pressing down on the accelerator to close the distance between him and the vehicle carrying Katrina, Dex ignored the speed limit and dared anyone to try and stop him. Within minutes, he had reached the private airport, some three nautical miles from Hanalei. Having cleared some hurdles with the help of Clayton Pietz and Rachel Zavatti, Dex was able to go straight through to near the single airstrip, where he spotted the Yukon Denali. The doors were open and Dex could see no one inside. Where the hell were they?

Then he saw a group of five people—including Katrina, who was being held by Rafael Carlos Nihei, followed by Agent Lawrence, Alyson Tennison, and a tall and thickset bald Hawaiian male—headed toward a light jet. Dex recognized it as a Hawker 400XP. He got out of his own car, along with Barnabas, determined to stop them from boarding the aircraft at all costs. Taking out his Glock 27 pistol, Dex approached the group and yelled at Nihei, "Let her go!"

The drug kingpin turned toward Dex and immediately grabbed Katrina around the neck from behind while whipping out his own firearm and holding it to her head. "I don't think so, Agent Adair. Your girlfriend's coming with us. Back off!"

"It's over, Nihei." Dex's voice was commanding. "I suggest you and your cronies do yourselves a favor and give up the fight. This place will be swarming with law enforcement any moment now. You're never going to get off the island."

"We'll see about that!" Nihei pressed the gun to Katrina's temple. "Try and stop us and she dies, right before your very eyes."

Dex sized up the situation. He knew there were three actual perpetrators against two good guys—him and, he believed, Lawrence. With backup about to join them. He wasn't willing to wait that long, at risk to Katrina's life. But making the wrong move could backfire and leave his beloved dead. In a split second, Dex watched as Katrina took matters into her own hands. She grabbed her kidnapper's wrist and moved the gun away from her face and into the air as a shot went off. She then slammed her foot as hard as she could into Nihei's ankle.

He let out a loud scream and tried to regain control as Katrina squatted. Dex wasn't about to give him that chance. Using the clear view of his face, he fired a single shot that hit Nihei squarely in the temple, dropping him like a stone and putting his lights out for good. When the bald-headed man, who had removed a firearm, took aim at Dex and fired, it was Lawrence who grabbed his arm just in time to miss by a mile. The agent then landed a roundhouse punch straight to the jaw of the drug trafficker. Though staggered, he managed to get off another shot, hitting Lawrence in the chest, sending him down.

Before the bald assailant could take a second shot at Dex, Barnabas, acting in his dual role as a handler protector, went after him, jumping on him before the unsub could respond, holding him prisoner. Dex moved quickly toward Katrina, who was engaged in battle with Nihei's lover, Alyson. Just when Dex thought he might have to lend her a helping hand, Katrina downed her former assistant manager with a solid punch to the nose, knocking Alyson out cold.

The SWAT team and other law enforcement converged upon the scene, placing Alyson and the bald-headed man under arrest. They surrounded the private jet, preventing the pilot from departing, before taking her into custody.

En route to Katrina, who seemed to have things well under control for the moment, Dex checked on Agent Lawrence, still down. "You okay?"

"Been better, to tell you the truth." Zachary sat up and rubbed the Hawaiian shirt with plumerias covering his chest. "Fortunately, I always wear a bulletproof vest, as I'm sure you do, when on the job."

"Always." Dex gave him a nod of respect. "Have to admit, Lawrence, you had me going for a while there."

"Had the situations been reversed, I would've had my own doubts about you." Zachary winced. "But we both chose this life and have to go with the flow."

"Yeah." Dex was thoughtful.

"Better go see about Katrina. She needs you right now more than I do."

Dex nodded and headed toward her. Katrina ran into Dex's arms, both clinging to each other for a long moment. "Did they hurt you?" he asked.

"No, but I have a feeling they planned to kill me had this thing gone south," she said honestly.

"I wouldn't have let that happen." Dex cupped her dimpled chin and kissed her lips. "Not in this lifetime."

Katrina glanced over at Zachary, who was now on his feet and conversing with Pietz and Ishikawa. "I saw you talking to Zachary Lawrence," she noted.

Dex smiled. "Turns out, he wasn't one of the bad guys after all."

"Yes, he kind of intimated that to me when we had a moment," she stated musingly, "and he apologized about the messages and stalking. I started to really believe him when he stepped in to prevent Nihei's henchman from shooting you. Before Barnabas took over from there."

"Yeah, there was that," Dex acknowledged, knowing he owed Lawrence one. Even if the agent had put them through the paces with his undercover assignment. Just then, Barnabas came running up to them, the golden retriever wagging his tale triumphantly for a job well done in picking up where Lawrence left off in protecting Dex, as intended. He stroked the K-9 cop's neck and said, "Really good job, boy!"

"I second that!" Katrina sang, petting the dog under his chin. "You really did save the day, along with your handler." Barnabas reacted favorably by barking his approval and lapping up the attention.

"You did good, too," he praised her. "Frustrating

Nihei and giving me just the space I needed to take him out."

She chuckled. "Figured I needed to do something to come out of this in one piece."

Dex laughed, loving the camaraderie between them as a trio and wanting to keep it going for as long as possible. He became serious again as he cast his eyes upon Katrina, musing about the way things turned out with her assistant manager. "I'm sorry that Alyson betrayed your trust."

"Me too." Katrina winced. "She'll likely have a pretty sore, if not broken, nose for a while, and plenty of time to think about all the problems she's brought upon herself."

"You're right." He was glad that Katrina knew how to handle herself in a pinch. "Shouldn't be too hard to find a new and reliable assistant manager," he imagined.

"I suppose." She held his hands. "Apart from that, you and I make a great team, Dex, even when danger was swirling all around us like a vortex."

"Agreed." He grinned, and decided now was as good a time as any to make his pitch. "I'd like to make our teamwork even better," he told her. "I'm in love with you, Katrina. I have some money saved up and would love to go into early retirement and become your partner in running the Maoli Lodge. And eventually make a go of it as husband and wife. I know that's a lot to take in. If you need time to think about it, that's perfectly understandable."

"I don't need to think about it," she professed. "Yes and yes, Dex! I'd love to go into partnership with you as co-owners of the Maoli Lodge. And it would be my honor to marry the man I've fallen in love with and have him as my future husband." Katrina paused, gazing into his eyes doubtfully. "Are you sure you're ready to give up working as a DEA special agent?"

"More than I've ever been about anything in my life—" Dex spoke from the heart "—with the exception of the deep love I feel for you."

"Good answer." She grinned. "In that case, shall we seal the deal with another kiss?"

"Absolutely," he laughed. Dex was more than happy to take the lead on this one, before giving way to a lifetime of equality in matters of love and the successful operation of a lodge in the Poipu resort on the island of Kauai, Hawaii.

Epilogue

The raid on Rafael Carlos Nihei's compound in Waimea Canyon, netted the DEA large quantities of crystal methamphetamine and fentanyl, drug paraphernalia, illegal firearms and cash. Several members of the slain leader's drug network were arrested as a result, putting a serious dent into the illicit drug-trafficking operation between the island, other parts of Hawaii and the mainland. This was eight months ago and Dex's last assignment as a DEA special agent, before entering into voluntary retirement, along with his trusted canine companion, Barnabas. After selling his Los Angeles home, they resettled in Poipu. Joining forces with his gorgeous wife, Katrina, in operating the Maoli Lodge—where he also shared piano duties with new mom, Gina Oxenberg— was the smartest move Dex believed he'd ever made. Next to marrying the crimson-haired beauty.

To say he didn't miss being a federal law enforcement agent in the slightest would be dishonoring the men and women he worked with in going after drug traffickers, crime syndicates and related wrongdoers. On the contrary, Dex had no problem going through the withdrawal pains of absence from the DEA as part of the natural process. But that was easily overcome by being in the daily company of the love of his life in Katrina. He was already looking forward to the day when their attempt to get pregnant would be successful and they could welcome a girl or boy into the world to love as much as they did one another.

THE KAUAI MARATHON and Half Marathon was held in September and Katrina was proud to be a participant, along with her husband, Dex. With her love for running and adventure, she considered it a great way to do both, while tapping into his desire to stay in shape in the post DEA era for him. At the same time, Katrina was doing her best to help as he made the transition from special agent to a married man, leaving behind his LA life to make a new one with her in paradise on Kauai. Luckily, Dex was all in, embracing the challenge of stepping out of his comfort zone and into the Hawaiian experience of running in the spirit of community, passing by Taiko drum troupes and exotic hula dancers along the way.

"I think running could become a regular part of my routine," Dex told her, grinning, "as long as I can continue to keep up with you."

Katrina chuckled, gazing at him in his T-shirt and sweat shorts, muscles bulging in his arms and legs. "Something tells me you'll have no problem in that department." She warmed to the thought of their lovemaking and the ability to keep up with each other. Wearing a sports bra and running shorts, with her red hair in a high ponytail, Katrina winked and ran ahead of Dex. She fought hard to wait until they got back to their suite in the lodge, before she sprang on Dex what she had just discovered herself. "Just so you know, you're going to be a dad."

His eyes lit with delight. "Are you saying what I think you are?"

She broke into a huge smile, knowing he wanted this as much as she did. "Yes, Dex, we're having a baby!"

Katrina's husband cried as he wrapped her in his arms and swirled her around. "You've just made me the happiest man in the world."

"And you've made me the happiest woman on the planet," she proclaimed, "so there."

They kissed on that treasured emotion and were already starting to pick out names for the new addition to the Adair family.

* * * * *

COLTON'S ROGUE INVESTIGATION

JENNIFER D. BOKAL

To John – now, always, forever.

Prologue

Thursday night
Outside Blue Larkspur, Colorado
11:37 p.m.

The fog of cigarette smoke filled the front room of the small house. The acrid scent mingled with body odor and the smell of stale beer. Henry Rollins looked again at the cards he held and fought to keep the smile from his lips. "Read 'em and weep, boys. Read 'em and weep." He set his hand on the table in front of him. "Straight flush. Four to eight."

Everyone around the table groaned.

Henry didn't care—tonight, he'd been the big winner. And the $750 pot would go a long way to paying off that loan shark, Silas Dunn. As he reached for his haul, he stood. "And with that, I'm outta here."

"Come on, man," said Frank, the host for tonight's card game. "Ain't you going to let us win back our money?"

Henry hesitated. The need to stay longer—and maybe win more—was like a thirst. It wouldn't be like last time when he was ahead and then lost everything, would it?

No. He had to leave while he could.

Stacking the bills, Henry said, "Can't tonight. I got an early meeting in the morning."

Everyone around the table knew it was a lie. Henry had been out of a job for more than four months. Not a lot of work for a cowboy these days. He folded the wad and tucked it into the front pocket of his shirt. "See you next week."

His departure was met with a round of booing—some good-natured, some not. It didn't matter. Henry had done it. He'd won and left the table with cash in hand. Like he'd just climbed a mountain, his heartbeat raced, and his breath came in short and ragged gasps.

Like he did every Thursday, Henry met with the guys in his neighborhood for a game of poker. It wasn't the only place he gambled—and that was part of the problem. He'd lost more than once. He owed too many people too much money.

That was when someone had suggested that Henry visit Silas Dunn. Dunn had promised easy money—and Henry had accepted. But the short-term loan was now due, and Henry was nowhere close to having the money needed to pay.

Moving down the sidewalk at a good clip, Henry promised himself that this was the last time he'd let himself get this far into debt. His house was only two blocks away. The night air held a bite of cold—a reminder that soon winter would come to Western Colorado. Three houses up, a car sat at the curb. It was a luxury sedan, at odds with the run-down pickup trucks and small cars that most of his neighbors drove.

He walked quicker.

As Henry approached, the headlights came on, leaving him blind.

The door opened, and a shadowy figure emerged. "Rollins?"

Henry stumbled to a stop. "Yeah."

"Mr. Dunn would like a word. Get in the car."

His gut turned to water, and Henry worried that he might actually crap his pants. "I got some money." He pulled the cash from his pocket. Sure, he owed $2,000 but this money made a real dent in the loan. "It's seven hundred and fifty dollars. That should go to show that I'm good for my loan."

The goon took the money from Henry's hand. He could see the guy clearly now. He was tall with broad shoulders and bulging biceps. "Get in the car."

"But you took my money. You can give it to Mr. Dunn." His tone was close to pleading. In the moment, Henry didn't care. "I'll get more."

A second thug got out of the passenger seat, holding a pipe. He was like the first guy in build. Yet, he said nothing, just hit Henry on the back of the knees. A shock wave of pain knocked him forward. He hit the sidewalk and his vision turned fuzzy. Enough of his faculties were left for him to know that he was being dragged to the car and thrown into the back seat.

As the car pulled to a stop next to a black SUV in front of the abandoned warehouse that he could glimpse through the window, Henry began to pray. *Dear God, I know You haven't heard from me recently. But please, let me survive and I'll do the right thing.*

"Get out," the driver ordered.

"I'm not ready to die," said Henry, his words becoming a mantra. "I'm not ready to die."

"Out." Behind the driver stood the second goon with his pipe.

Henry stumbled from the car. With each step agony radiated from the back of his knees to his feet.

The door of the SUV opened, and the loan shark himself stepped onto the cracked pavement. The headlights from the vehicles cut through the darkness as Dunn walked into one of the beams, which threw a long shadow.

Henry took another step forward, his heartbeat racing. "Silas," he began. "Listen, I gave that guy seven hundred and fifty bucks. It's not everything I owe, but it's a beginning…"

The goon drove his pipe into Henry's middle. Bending double, he retched on the broken asphalt. A fist to the chin. To the nose. Another blow from the pipe—this one on his back. Henry could do nothing other than curl on the ground and try to protect himself from the assault. He was certain that despite his prayers, this was when and how he would die.

All three men surrounded him. The two thugs seemed to enjoy their violent job too much to be anything other than sadists, psychopaths—or both.

Yet, it was the other guy who was truly dangerous. Silas Dunn was a mean little man with a gold ring on his pinky and a thick accent from the East Coast. New

York? New Jersey? Henry didn't know. What he did know was that Silas was the one giving the orders.

One of Henry's eyes was swollen shut. His nose bled. Two of his teeth were loose. His head pounded. Through the haze of anguish and dread, a plan came to him with a clarity that was startling, and for a moment the pounding in his head abated. Holding up a bruised arm to fend off a blow, he said, "I know how you can make back all the money I owe you."

Silas said, "You don't seem to understand our arrangement. I don't need to make back the money you owe—you gotta do that. And if you can't? Well, then someone has to be an example, am I right?"

One of the thugs kicked Henry in the side, which drove the air from his lungs. He wheezed. "I know how you can make back all the money and more. Lots more."

The boss stood near the grille of the luxury sedan. He lifted his hand, the gesture cutting through the beam of a headlight. "What d'you mean by 'lots more'?"

"There are horses. Wild horses. People pay money for the mustangs, but they're only rounded up and sold every few years." Henry had been a cowboy on the last roundup. Most of the horses were sold for $125, but a few prime mustangs were auctioned off for more. Hell, he'd seen one horse sell for damn near $600. "I know where they graze. I know how to find them and bring them in safely."

"You still haven't put a number on 'lots more.' What is it?"

Through his swollen lips, he said, "If you get the right kind of horse and train it, only a couple would pay off my loan." In fact, it would be more than what he owed Silas, including interest.

"How many horses are in this herd?"

"Dozens." He guessed, "Maybe thirty-five or thirty-six head."

Silas rubbed his chin. Henry could tell that the loan shark was interested. Thank goodness. Now the pain—both physical and emotional—could stop. Bracing his hands on the ground, he rolled to his knees and drew in a deep breath. A pain shot through his side. Was a rib busted? He wouldn't be surprised if it was. "Tell me how you know about this herd of gold."

Henry explained that to prevent overgrazing, every four years horses were rounded up. He also told Silas that the last roundup in Blue Larkspur took place two years back.

"So, nobody from the government's paying attention right now, is that what you're telling me?" Silas asked.

"They're monitoring the situation, but not too closely." Henry wasn't sure if he was telling the truth—or not. Still, it seemed like something that Silas wanted to hear.

"You know who would buy these horses?"

"I met a few of the brokers." One of them seemed less than honest. "I can give you a name."

"If you give me the name of a broker, what do I need you for?" Silas asked.

It was a good question, and one for which Henry didn't have a ready answer. "I haven't told you anything yet," he began.

Silas nodded. "Fair enough." He paused a beat. "But

you can't just give me a name and expect that you and I are done."

That was the exact scenario he had hoped for. "What, then?"

"Me, I'm not going to hire a new crew. And who in the hell is really a cowboy—except for you, that is?" Silas twisted the big ring around his pinky finger.

Henry should've guessed that this was the turn that events would take. "What does that make us? Partners?"

Silas laughed. The goons laughed. Henry chuckled, though everything on his body hurt like hell.

"Partners?" Silas echoed. "That's funny. No, me and you ain't partners. I'm the boss and you work for me."

Henry could do it. He could pull a few mustangs out of the herd and turn them over to a broker. It meant that the animal would lead a nice life in captivity. "After I get you a couple of horses then, we're done."

"We'll be done, all right," Silas began. "But you misunderstood our negotiations."

Maybe he'd taken too many hits to the head. What was Silas getting at? "Oh?"

"You won't be getting me a few mustangs."

"I won't?"

"No." Silas shook his head. "Four or five aren't enough. You want to pay back your debt to me—I want them all."

"All of them?"

Henry was pulled to his feet and shoved into the back seat of the car. As the goons drove him back to his house, Henry knew two things to be certain. He couldn't cross Silas Dunn, not if he wanted to live. He also couldn't let the herd of wild mustangs get taken off the range. It meant he had to make a call—and hope that the woman who'd been in charge at the roundup last time would know what to do.

Chapter One

The Bureau of Land Management's Denver office was located in the newly built Federal Plaza. The campus of more than a dozen buildings was the footprint of the federal government for not only Colorado, but much of the sparsely populated Mountain West.

As a wildlife biologist, Jacqui Reyes helped conservation efforts in Colorado. But what she wanted was a promotion that gave her even more responsibility. There was so much she could do to fight climate change and protect endangered species. What's more, she'd led a team that had worked on water-saving efforts for the Blue Larkspur area. It had been a rousing success—even if she had to work with her ex-boyfriend to make it happen. In the end, they'd been able to put aside their enmity. He'd even done the report's final edits.

As she strode through the conference-room door, her blood buzzed with excited energy. The big boss, Jeremy Michaels, the acting director for the Bureau of

Land Management in Colorado, had called this morning's meeting. Certainly, he was here to offer Jacqui the promotion.

For the big day, she'd taken extra time with her appearance. She'd applied a little makeup—mascara, blush and lipstick—and wore her dark hair loose around her shoulders. She'd donned a pair of blue slacks, a silk T-shirt, a plaid blazer and a pair of loafers. The outfit accentuated her petite and curvy frame perfectly—while also projecting professionalism and efficiency.

Mr. Michaels looked up as Jacqui entered the room. Her ex, Zeke Shaw, already sat at the acting director's side. The fact that a prime position had been taken dampened her enthusiasm, but only a little.

Her best friend, a meteorologist named Steffanie, sat halfway down the conference table. A seat next to her was open and Jacqui slid into the chair.

"Looks like Zeke has made himself chummy with Mr. Michaels," Jacqui said with a good dose of sarcasm. She set her phone, notepad and pen on the table.

Steffanie rolled her eyes. "Looks like it."

Before she could say anything else, Mr. Michaels rose from his seat. He was a tall man in a dark suit and yellow tie, and he held Jacqui's report in his hand. "I'm here today to discuss the water conservation project in Blue Larkspur. Thanks to Mr. Shaw and his team—this was so successful that I'd like to replicate it in other communities along the Colorado River."

"Mr. Shaw's team." Jacqui was on her feet, before she even knew that she'd stood. "What a load of garbage. It's not Mr. Shaw's team. It's mine."

"Excuse me?" The man's tone was steely.

Drawing in a long breath, Jacqui understood the mistake she'd made in interrupting a bigwig. Still, she'd done it and there was no going back. "It's not Mr. Shaw's team," she said again. "I was in charge of the team. And that report you're holding says as much."

Mr. Michaels made a big show of flipping through the pages. "I'm looking at this report, and it clearly states that the team was led by Zeke Shaw. You, Ms. Reyes, are listed as part of the team…"

"It doesn't make sense that this project would belong to Zeke," she began. The shrill ringing of a phone stopped Jacqui midsentence. Her cell shimmied on the tabletop. The caller ID read: Contact Unknown. Jacqui quickly sent the call to voice mail and picked up where she left off. "Conservation for the Colorado River is part of my job description—not Zeke's…" Her phone began to ring again. Contact Unknown. An ember of frustration was lodged in her throat. She put her phone on mute.

"Do you want to take that call, Ms. Reyes? Because I'd like to get back to this report."

Her entire life, Jacqui had fought to be taken seriously. As the daughter of Cuban immigrants, she'd faced discrimination. Was this one of those moments? Or had Jacqui been foolish to trust Zeke?

In reality, it didn't matter. She wasn't going to argue with Michaels—at least not right now.

"Yes, sir." Jacqui dropped into her seat, defeated, confused and exhausted.

The next hour passed in agony as Zeke stared daggers at Jacqui. For her part, Jacqui pretended that he wasn't even in the room. The meeting ended and people began to collect notepads and tablets.

"If I could have a moment with both Mr. Shaw and Ms. Reyes," said Michaels.

Since Zeke was already at the head of the table, he stayed where he sat. It was Jacqui who had to walk forward. After collecting her notepad, phone and pen, she walked to the end of the room, feeling very much like she'd been called to the principal's office.

Steffanie gave a quick smile of encouragement as she exited the conference room.

"Are there problems between you two?" Mr. Michaels asked, once the conference room had cleared out.

"No problems," she lied.

Michaels grunted. "Why would you interrupt with your claims that you were in charge of the team, then?"

Jacqui refused to be cowed. "Because I was."

Zeke said, "Western Colorado is my area. I was the one who submitted the final report—something that the team leader should do."

"You only submitted that final report because you offered to help." Although she clearly saw the game that Zeke was playing. He had tricked Jacqui into letting him do more than his job—and now he was trying to take credit for it all. She turned her attention to Mr. Michaels. "With all due respect, talk to our superiors. You'll see that I was assigned as the team leader."

"But you'll also see that she failed to meet the mandates of that position," Zeke said.

Michaels held up his hands. "I work in DC. I leave

the Beltway to get away from squabbling and politics." He sighed. "I'm sure you're both aware that there's a promotion to be had. Both of your names have been mentioned, but I'm not making any decisions now. I'd like to congratulate you both on a job well done. The water conservation effort was truly remarkable. Teamwork is what I like to see from my leaders. I have another meeting but will be in touch. And Ms. Reyes?"

"Yes, sir?"

"Remember to mute your phone before meetings begin."

Her face burned with embarrassment. Would the acting director speak to Zeke that way? Or was it Jacqui's gender and race that made him think he could use a condescending tone?

She tightened her jaw and reminded herself of one simple truth. If Jacqui wanted to get ahead, she had to be the best. That—and to never trust Zeke again.

"Yes, sir."

After collecting his belongings, Michaels left.

Without a word, Zeke followed.

It was probably just as well. Whatever Jacqui might have said to her ex-boyfriend wouldn't have been professional—and would probably cause her more trouble than it was worth. She stalked back to her cubicle. Her mood was darker than a rain cloud.

Steffanie leaned on a partition between their desks and waited. "So, what'd Michaels say?"

"Zeke isn't getting the promotion—at least not today." Jacqui dropped into her desk chair. "But neither am I."

"Damn." Steffanie chewed on her fingernail. "Your ex is a snake."

"That's an insult to snakes."

"Too bad your phone kept ringing. I think Michaels would've heard you out on the spot."

"Yeah," Jacqui agreed. "Too bad."

"Who called, anyway?"

"No idea." She looked at the call log. "They aren't in my contacts, and a number didn't even show up." The voice mail icon appeared. After turning on the speaker function, Jacqui played the message.

The first few seconds were filled with silence. Then, an unnaturally deep voice emanated from the phone's tiny speaker. "Ms. Reyes. You don't know me, but I know that you're someone who wants to help the wild horses of Colorado." The voice was more than deep but muffled. It was almost like a kid's prank of changing their voice and speaking through a towel. "The herd outside of Blue Larkspur has been targeted by thieves. By the end of the month, there won't be any left. You have to help—without you, the wild mustangs won't have a champion."

"What the hell?" Steffanie whispered.

"Hell is about right." Jacqui's blood turned cold. "Someone's stealing horses from the range?"

"What're you going to do?" Steffanie asked before answering her own question. "You have to tell Zeke."

"Tell Zeke?" she echoed. How had she ever let herself get involved with him in the first place? Maybe now was time for Jacqui to admit—at least to herself—that she had lousy taste in men. Before Zeke, there was the bartender who borrowed $200 when his credit card was supposedly stolen. The same night she lent him the cash, he took an Instagram model out for a pricey dinner. His date posted twice before the appetizers were served. Before him was the guy from the Air National Guard who wasn't as divorced as he claimed.

Before him… Well, she didn't need to think of every lousy boyfriend to know that the list was long. Maybe this was the time for Jacqui to swear off dating…

Steffanie was still talking. "But that herd is near Blue Larkspur. And that's Zeke's territory."

"And managing the herd is my job." Jacqui saved the message to her phone before checking the time. It was almost 10:00 a.m. "If I left now, I'd be in Blue Larkspur by four this afternoon. There'd be plenty of daylight left to check on the herd and at least see if this message is true."

"And if someone is trying to steal the horses, then what?" Steffanie asked.

That was the real question, wasn't it? Well, Jacqui didn't have the answer—not yet. But once she got to Blue Larkspur, she'd figure it out.

GAVIN COLTON SAT in his makeshift studio. In reality, it was a desk that sat in front of a window and overlooked a lake and the mountain peaks beyond. He'd brought everything he needed with him from his places in Manhattan and Chicago to this rented cabin—two laptops, a high-quality mic and one to spare. A set of noise-canceling headphones hung around his neck, and he stared at the script.

The morning was already warm, and he wore a T-shirt, shorts and no shoes. Whenever he made a public appearance, he dressed in sleek suits by European design houses. After all these years, Gavin was still a Colorado boy through and through.

After setting the headphones into place, he leaned into the mic and began recording. "Benjamin Colton was a celebrated judge with a wife who loved him. Children who admired him. And a community that trusted him to do the right thing.

"Then one day, he did the unthinkable and handed down a harsh sentence for cash. And it wasn't just once that Ben betrayed his office. For years, he sold verdicts. When a man has a nearly perfect life, one must ask a single question. Why risk it all for money?

"That question is especially important to me because Ben Colton was my father. The decisions he made when I was young have forever shaped my family—and my life. This is Gavin Colton with a new episode of *Crime Time*. I'll be exploring the many fraudulent sentences handed down by my father and the ramifications of those verdicts."

He stopped the recording and listened to his words. Not bad for an introduction. He read over the next part of his script as his smartwatch vibrated with an incoming text.

He glanced at the small screen. It was a text from his eldest brother, Caleb.

We need to talk.

Was Caleb sore that he hadn't attended his wedding? It's not that Gavin wanted to miss the affair—well, okay, he did. But coming to Colorado for the wedding would have been impossible with his production schedule. And, he had to admit to himself, he hadn't been thrilled at the idea of his siblings piling on him with criticisms and nagging.

Gavin had been renting this cabin outside Blue Larkspur for nearly three weeks. In all that time, he'd avoided talking to anyone from his family. Sure, he'd been poking around town and doing research for his podcast. Then again, recently he'd brought up doing a podcast on their father with his siblings. Everyone in the family hated the idea. But Gavin, forever the black sheep of the family, had moved forward with the project.

It didn't bother him that nobody liked his ideas—it had been like that from the beginning. With so many twins and triplets in the family, many of his siblings had built-in allies. Even if they weren't part of multiple births, each had found a sibling upon whom they relied. All of them, it seemed, except Gavin.

If he had to guess, he'd say that those siblings he hadn't told had finally heard about his plans. He'd also guess that Caleb's call was meant to talk Gavin out of using Ben Colton as a subject.

Gavin didn't need that kind of pressure. He deleted the message.

His phone began to ring a second later, and he checked the caller ID on his watch. It was Caleb.

He considered sending the call to voice mail, but what if it really was an emergency?

He swiped the call open and spoke into his wrist. "Hey."

"Baby brother. It's good to hear your voice."

"It's good to be heard—even though you insist on calling me 'baby brother.'"

Caleb ignored the reprimand. "I was talking to one of my clients the other day, and she mentioned that you met with her." His older sibling paused—waiting for Gavin to say something. He didn't. Caleb added, "You were asking about Dad and such."

"Yeah. So."

"Well, when we spoke recently, I thought we all decided that you wouldn't do a podcast about him."

"No," Gavin interrupted. His temper flared and he clenched his teeth together. Yeah, this was exactly why he hadn't come for the wedding. After working his jaw back and forth, he spoke. "When we talked, you all told me what you thought. I took your opinions into consideration and moved on with the project anyway."

"What about our conversations?"

"What about them?" Gavin felt the heat of his temper beginning to climb. He rose from the chair and paced across the small bedroom.

"I didn't call to start a fight," Caleb said, his tone less than conciliatory.

"What is it that you want, then?"

"We've all discussed this podcast, Gavin. You can't do it."

Gavin gaped. "You're kidding me, right?"

"Just listen," Caleb told him.

His temper flared and he began to sweat. "What gives you—or any of our other siblings—the right to dictate what I do for my job? You, especially. Hell, you've made a career out of righting all of Dad's wrongs." He paused a beat, knowing full well what he was about to say. "Or maybe that *is* the issue. Are you bent on being the hero? If I do a podcast, would that refocus the spotlight from you?"

"That's not fair." Caleb's voice had risen. "I work for the Truth Foundation—we help people wrongfully imprisoned."

"By Dad." How was it that hearing Caleb's voice turned Gavin into a pissed-off fifteen-year-old kid once again? Maybe he'd been wrong to come back home and do a story.

"Not always."

"But a lot of the time, right."

Caleb said nothing and the silence stretched out. "A lot of the time," he said, finally agreeing.

Gavin walked out of the small bedroom and down a short hallway to a set of stairs that led to the main level of the cabin. From there, he opened a set of sliding glass doors and stood on a large deck that overlooked the lake. He drew in a deep breath. He felt the heat of his anger cool.

"What Dad did all those years ago affected each and every one of us kids. You became a lawyer and started your foundation. Dom became an FBI agent. Alexa's with the US Marshals. Hell, Rachel's even a DA, although I don't know how anyone in Blue Larkspur ever voted for a Colton. And me, I do podcasts. I try to find out the truth. But here's the thing." He paused. Was he willing to share his reasons with his brother? "I don't

know *my* truth. I don't know how I feel about him because I've never examined what he did. Do you get it?"

"Actually, I do get it." He sighed. "But you still can't
do the podcast."

Gavin cursed. "What's your problem, man? How's
this. I'll donate every cent I make to your foundation.
Is that good enough?" The truth was, Gavin could well
afford to make the donation. *Crime Time* was one of
the most popular shows on most podcast platforms. The
money he made from advertising was enough to pay
for a fancy sports car, a closet full of designer suits and
apartments in both Manhattan and Chicago.

"I don't want your money. It's Ronald Spence."

"Who is he again?"

"Spence is a guy who Dad sent to jail for drug smug-
gling years ago. I thought that Spence was wrongfully
convicted. Hell, I worked for months to get him out of
jail." Caleb sighed. "As it turns out, I might've let a
criminal go free."

Now that would make a killer episode. "What does
this have to do with me?"

"You asking questions is getting people spooked. It's
making it harder to track Spence."

Damn. Was Gavin being selfish for doing the story?
"I'm not making any promises, but I'll think about
changing my topic." But to what? He'd already spent
three weeks doing research on his father's old cases.
What's more, his sponsors expected a new episode by
the beginning of November—only six weeks away. It
didn't give Gavin a lot of time.

Caleb said, "Thanks, man. I appreciate it."

For a moment, Gavin didn't know what to say. "Well, I guess congratulations are in order. I heard you tied the knot."

"Yeah, we missed you at the wedding."

"Sorry I couldn't make it." And maybe he was the littlest bit sorry that he hadn't been able to share in Caleb's big day. All the same, every time Gavin visited his family, it ended with an argument. It's why he lived across the country, even though he could record his podcast anywhere. "Work is busy."

"You know, we're all real proud of your success. Not everyone is related to the number one podcaster in the country. Or is it the world now?" Caleb paused a beat. Gavin didn't bother to fill the silence, mostly because he didn't know how to respond. His big brother continued, "Since you're in town, you'll have to come over to our new house. You can meet Nadine. She's an artist. You'll like her."

"Yeah. Maybe. Sounds great."

"How about tomorrow evening," Caleb suggested. "I've got some steaks that need grilling."

"Tomorrow?" The last thing Gavin wanted was to get rooked into a family dinner. Rubbing the back of his neck, he gave the first excuse that came to mind. "You know, if I change the focus of this next episode, then I'm really going to have to scramble." At least it wasn't a lie.

"Who better to help you find a new crime to investigate than a lawyer? I'll invite Rachel. Maybe she'll have some local leads."

Crap. Now there was no way to get out of a visit. "Okay, man. See you tomorrow evening."

"I'll text you the address," Caleb promised. Then, he ended the call.

Gavin's watch buzzed with the promised text. He walked down to the lake and let the water wash over his bare feet as he asked himself a single question. What now?

Actually, he did know what he should do—at least for the rest of the day. He returned to the cabin. There, he changed into a Henley and jeans. Then, he started to collect his gear. For the next few hours, he planned to find a nice spot on the river—one without any cell service or calls from his large family—and fish.

Chapter Two

Traffic leaving Denver had been horrible. Jacqui's plans to make it to Blue Larkspur by late afternoon had been abandoned hours earlier. At 5:15 p.m., she'd checked into her hotel and changed from her slacks, blazer and loafers into a pair of jeans, long sleeved T-shirt and hiking boots. Now, it was 6:00 p.m.; she stood on a bluff outside the town. A late September wind carried a whisper of cold that told of the winter that was to come. Looking through a pair of binoculars, she scanned the small valley below. The setting sun reflected off a small stream—another feat made possible by conservation efforts. A herd of wild mustangs grazed on late summer grasses, oblivious to her as she watched.

Her gaze traveled over each animal. The power in the flanks. The gleam of waning sunlight on their coats. The twitch of their ears in the breeze. For Jacqui, the wild mustang was nearly a magical creature. And being tasked with their safety was as near to a fairy tale as she'd ever come.

Continuing to scan the herd, her heart skipped a beat. She blinked hard. Had she really seen it?

Looking back at an ebony-colored stallion, she refocused the ocular to get a better look. A red welt ringed the horse's neck. From where she stood, the burn was consistent with a lasso mark.

Letting the binoculars hang from a strap around her neck, Jacqui pulled her phone from her pocket. Was now the time to let the authorities know about the tip and the injury?

Yet, who would she call? The local police? The FBI? In a case like this, was Jacqui the authority in charge? She glanced at the screen and swallowed down a curse. "No bars."

It didn't mean that she couldn't collect some evidence. She snapped several pictures of the black stallion. She checked her pictures. Even with the aspect fully zoomed, the horse was little more than a midnight-colored dot. With a sigh, she opened her recording app. "This is Jacqui Reyes, a wildlife biologist from the Denver office of the Bureau of Land Management." She then gave the date and time. "I'm outside of Blue Larkspur, Colorado, and following up on a tip that horses are being taken from a herd of wild mustangs. The herd has thirty-seven horses. Thirteen males and two dozen females. A male horse presents with injuries consistent with a rope burn to his neck."

Using her thumb, she stopped the recording. Sure, there was no reason for the mustang to have a rope wound on his neck—other than someone tried to lasso the animal. That fact alone would go a long way to prove that the tip Jacqui received was true.

The skin on the nape of her neck stood on end. It

felt as if someone—somewhere—was watching her. Jacqui glanced quickly over her shoulder. There was nobody. The rocky landscape stretched on for miles. Long shadows stretched over the ground, yet the sky overhead was still bright blue. She had a little time before heading back to town.

She hit play and listened to the message she received that morning.

The first few seconds were filled with silence. Then, an unnaturally deep voice boomed from the phone's tiny speaker. "Ms. Reyes. You don't know me, but I know that you're someone who wants to help the wild horses of Colorado. The herd outside of Blue Larkspur has been targeted by thieves. By the end of the month, there won't be any left. You have to help—without you, the wild mustangs won't have a champion." The line went dead, and the recording ended.

Stuffing the phone back into her pocket, she shivered—and it wasn't entirely from the cold. The caller, whoever he or she was, had been right. That left Jacqui with a bigger mystery—who wanted to steal the wild mustangs, and why?

She walked to the edge of the bluff and looked back at the horses. There had to be a clue out there, somewhere. The binoculars still hung around her neck, and she lifted them to her eyes once more. This time, she searched the terrain.

She had no idea what to look for—other than when she found it, she'd know. There, halfway down the hill, was a flash of red. She focused on the object. It was a bag of some kind. Was it really a clue?

Jacqui sidestepped toward the spot where she'd seen the red object. The ground underfoot crumbled, and she began to slide. Grabbing at a rock, she halted her descent. Tangled in the low branches of a juniper was a cellophane bag. She pulled it free and read the label. In golden script were the words "Royal Moravian Tobacco. The finest tobacco known to man. Product of Spain." The bag was half-full of black tobacco. If Jacqui had to guess—and really, she did—she'd say that the garbage hadn't been out here long.

Yet was this a link to whoever tried to lasso the black stallion?

A breeze blew from the ridge, carrying with it the faintly nutty scent of cigarette smoke. Jacqui froze, yet her heart began to race. Was someone else out here?

For the first time, she realized that she was a woman alone and had no way to reach the outside world. For now, her investigation was done.

Turning her eyes to the top of the hill, she trudged upward without another look. Sweat snaked down her back, and her breath came in short gasps. When she reached her car, she slid behind the wheel and locked the door.

From this vantage point, she could see the whole valley. The horses still grazed, oblivious to everything and everyone. She looked at the surrounding hills— there was nothing, not even the wink of glass or metal in the rapidly setting sun. In short, nobody was around. Which meant what? That Jacqui had imagined the scent of smoke? Had she spooked herself into thinking that she was being watched? Was it all because of her favorite podcast—*Crime Time* with Gavin Colton? She knew he was from Blue Larkspur, too.

Gavin had a way of weaving the story that drew in the listener until they were a part of the tale. Had Jacqui gotten carried away? Yet, she still held the bag of tobacco—so it wasn't all her imagination. She tossed the tobacco onto the passenger seat and started the ignition.

The in-car audio came on automatically. Gavin's voice emanated from the speakers. "The police allowed me to review the case file," he said, the episode picking up where Jacqui had left off. "If there were any clues as to who abducted Marjorie, they were going to be here." His voice was rich and deep, like dark chocolate or red wine, and she consumed the sound.

Putting the car into reverse, Jacqui swung her vehicle around and headed down the gravel lane. It was three miles to the paved road, and by the time she eased onto asphalt, the sun had dropped below the horizon.

The car was on her bumper before Jacqui even realized that she was no longer alone. Driving without headlights, the dark sedan was nothing more than a shape that loomed in her rearview mirror. She dropped her foot onto the accelerator, hoping to create space. The other driver kept pace.

"What a jerk," she muttered, pushing her foot on the gas a little harder.

The narrow road wound down the mountainside and Jacqui squeezed the steering wheel, her palms becoming sweaty. The podcast, once so alluring, became background noise and a distraction.

The turn ahead was tighter than Jacqui expected.

She moved her foot to the brake and her tires slid off the road, spinning on the gravel. The car at her rear smashed into her.

Her car careened off the side of the road. She braced her arms on the steering wheel, as her stomach dropped to her shoes. Surrounded by a cloud of dust, she came to rest on the side of the hill. Her heart slammed into her ribs. Her hands shook, and sweat dotted her upper lip.

As the dust cleared, she watched the other car disappear around the bend.

"Are you serious?" she asked out loud. "You clip my bumper and then drive away? Jeez, you really are a jerk."

She checked her phone for a signal. Still, there were no bars.

"Dammit," she cursed. She tossed her phone onto the passenger seat.

After slipping the gearshift into reverse, she pressed her foot on the gas. The tires kicked up a cloud of dust, and she slid farther down the hill. Her stomach lurched. She let off the accelerator and slipped the gearshift into park. The undercarriage groaned as the vehicle shifted another foot.

What was she supposed to do now?

The car was unstable and unsafe.

Blue Larkspur was over twenty miles away.

It was dark.

The road was abandoned.

Her heart slammed against her chest. The metallic taste of panic coated her tongue.

Jacqui swallowed. Inhaled fully. Exhaled fully. Her

intentional breathing calmed her racing heart. Yet, it didn't make any of her bad options better.

The car shifted again, slipping forward a foot or two. She made up her mind.

Unbuckling her seat belt, Jacqui turned off the engine. She grabbed her phone, the tobacco and her jacket. Carefully, she opened the door. After crawling from the car, she scrambled up the hill to the pavement. At the road, she placed her phone and the tobacco into the pockets of her jacket. Thank goodness this jacket had reflective trim.

Because Jacqui knew that she had only one option. She had to start walking toward town. Eventually, she'd get a cell signal—right?

GAVIN DROVE DOWN the winding mountain road. He'd spent hours fishing and had nothing to show for his efforts other than a sunburned nose. He was no closer to deciding what to do about his next series. In truth, there was no easy answer. If he gave in to his siblings' demands—and quit exploring their father's dubious legacy—he'd lose more than several weeks of work. He'd also lose his ability to make sense of what his father had done and—more important to Gavin—*why.* Then, there was the fact that he didn't have another suitable replacement case.

All of that was juxtaposed to the question he kept asking himself: What was Gavin willing to do to keep the peace with his brothers and sisters?

Too bad hours on the river hadn't brought him closer to any answers.

His headlights cut through the gathering darkness and caught the glint of glass and metal. He let off the gas and looked out the windshield. A car was tilted precariously on the side of a downhill slope. "That's not good," he said out loud. He also knew that talking to himself wasn't exactly a great habit either. It's just that Gavin spent so much of his time alone that it had become an impossible habit to break.

Pulling to the side of the road, he turned on his hazard lights and stepped from his own automobile. "Hello," he called out, raising his voice to be heard above the purr of his car's engine. "Anyone here? Everyone okay?"

He waited a moment. There was no answer.

He sidestepped to the car and peered inside. It was empty.

At least nobody was injured or trapped inside.

But that brought up another question—how long had the car been here? Hours? Days? Gavin placed his hand on the hood. The metal was still warm. So not hours or days—but only minutes. Maybe it was years of producing his own true crime podcast, but Gavin had a hard time leaving any mystery alone.

Where was the driver?

Who were they?

Did they need help?

He returned to his own car and slid behind the steering wheel. Turning off the car's hazard lights, he pulled back onto the road. The pavement followed the terrain and crested a hill. The headlights caught a thin line of reflectors and then, a female figure materialized out of the gloom.

She was maybe five foot six. A tumble of dark hair fell over her shoulders.

As Gavin drove closer, he flashed his high beams to catch her attention. Shading her eyes, the woman turned. His breath caught in his chest. She was more than pretty, she was alluring.

Slowing as he approached, he rolled down the passenger window. "Hey," he called out. "Is that your car back there?"

She bent toward the opened window and Gavin got a good look at the woman. She had dark brown eyes, dark lashes and full lips. A lock of hair fell forward, and she tucked it behind her ear. "It is."

"You okay?"

She rocked her hand from side to side. "I'm not hurt, but some jerk tapped my bumper from behind. Then they had the nerve to drive off when I ended up off the road."

"*Some jerk* is right," he echoed.

"You wouldn't happen to have any cell coverage?" she asked.

This bit of road wasn't far from his family's home. Gavin grew up driving these roads as a kid. "The tower's signal doesn't reach all the way over here. You've got to get on the other side of the mountain. It's another four miles." He paused. "I can give you a ride back to Blue Larkspur if you want."

The woman took a step back. And honestly, he didn't blame her for hesitating. He was a stranger. They were on a dark and abandoned road. Her car was disabled. There was no cellular coverage.

He exhaled. "I can call Theo Lawson—the chief of police—when I get a signal and ask him to come back and find you. But honestly, I hate leaving you on the side of the road." Gavin gave a small shrug. "It doesn't seem right."

The woman stepped closer to the car and regarded him with narrowed eyes. "You seem familiar. Do I know you?"

Great, so this lady was a local. She probably knew all about the Colton family history. Worse than Gavin being berated about how awful his dad had been, would be if she knew one of his siblings and gushed. "I dunno, maybe. Who do I look like to you?"

"It's not your face." She paused and pressed her lips together. "But there's something about you... I'm Jacqui Reyes, by the way. I work for the Bureau of Land Management."

"Gavin," he said, introducing himself. "Gavin Colton."

Her large eyes got even wider. "No way. You're *the* Gavin Colton. I knew I recognized you. It's your voice. I love, love, love your podcast."

His chest warmed with her praise. "Thanks."

"I've got to be one of your biggest fans." She pulled her phone from the pocket of her jacket and held it up so he could see. On the lock screen was the cover image for his latest episode. "See."

Gavin laughed. "You really are one of my biggest

fans. Now, I can't leave you on the side of the road. Let me at least drive you to where we can make a call."

This time, she opened the door of his car and slipped into the passenger seat. She slammed the door shut. "Thanks a ton. Just wait till I tell my friend that I actually met you." She paused a beat. "I can tell her that we met, right?"

Sure, Gavin's podcast was popular. It's just that his voice was what people knew. It gave him a certain level of anonymity. Still, he couldn't help but smile. He eased onto the pavement and drove. "Sure, you can tell your friend."

A few minutes passed and he shifted in his seat. Usually, Gavin appreciated the quiet—a rarity growing up with eleven siblings. But right now, the silence was uncomfortable—like an ill-fitting coat.

"Soooo." He stretched out the one word. He glanced at Jacqui. Her profile was a shadow against the opposite window. Even without being able to see her features, she was still exquisite. He swallowed. "What were you doing all the way out here?"

"I got a tip that something was happening to the local herd of wild mustangs. I came from Denver to check it out."

Something was happening to the local herd of wild mustangs? The hair at the nape of his neck stood on end. Gavin's interest was piqued. *"Something...like what?"*

"Something like official federal business," she said. Her tone was terse and clearly meant to stop any further discussion.

And really, any normal person would leave well

enough alone. It's just that Gavin's job was far from ordinary. Over the years, he'd developed a sense of story. To him, the woman who sat beside him was the key to a larger mystery. That question was—what was it?

Chapter Three

Gavin drove a luxury two-seater. The sleek dashboard looked like something out of a space shuttle or a fighter jet—that was if mahogany was used in either. Jacqui tried to relax into the leather passenger seat, but her shoulders were tight and her neck was sore. Maybe her aches were injuries from her accident. Or maybe it was stress. This morning started off bad—and the day had only gotten worse.

Her luck today had *all* been bad. Had her fortunes changed when Gavin stopped to help her?

Sure, she knew that getting into a car with a stranger went against every prudent bone in her body. All the same, sitting on the side of the road and waiting for someone else to come by wasn't exactly a smart idea either.

A fluttering filled her middle—and it wasn't exactly her nerves. Gavin Colton had more than a nice voice—he was a handsome man. Medium brown hair. Blue eyes. Thick lashes and a chiseled jaw. Jacqui realized that she was staring and dropped her gaze to the phone she held in her lap. Still no bars.

"We get coverage just over this ridge." Gavin pointed to the road ahead. "It'll just be a minute and you can call the police. Then, I'll take you back to your car. Hopefully, the tow truck will be able to meet us soon."

Just then, the coupe crested the hill. As Gavin promised, a single bar appeared on Jacqui's phone—enough to place a call.

She glanced at Gavin. His features were illuminated by the silvery lights from the dashboard. The effect was ethereal. Maybe he was her guardian angel. "Do I call nine-one-one?" she asked. "Is this an emergency? Or do you think there's a different number for accidents like mine?"

Gavin eased the car onto the shoulder of the road. "I'll do you one better." His phone was tucked into a drink holder between the two front seats. "I'll call the chief of police myself, like I promised." The call automatically went through the car's audio system. It rang twice before being answered.

"Gavin? That you? Everything okay? How's your mom?"

"Hi—it's me. And as far as I know, she's okay."

The man on the other end exhaled. "What can I do you for, then?"

"Listen, I found a stranded motorist. She's fine, but her car is stuck. Any chance a tow truck can meet us and get her out of the ditch?"

Theo exhaled again. "I can dispatch a tow truck, but it'll take some time. There was a fender bender on North Avenue. To top it off, a big high school football game started. Now, there's traffic backed up all over town. You remember how those games can get. Or maybe not. The players were always in the locker rooms before kickoff."

The mention that Gavin might have played football in high school gave Jacqui a little thrill. It was like peeking through the gap between curtains and getting a glimpse of what someone kept hidden. What else might she discover about Gavin Colton?

Sitting back hard, she sucked in a breath. She didn't even know this man—not really. Just his body of work.

"I can imagine." He paused. "How long before you can get a truck out here?"

"An hour and a half. Maybe a little less."

Her heart dropped to her shoes. What was she supposed to do in the middle of nowhere for ninety minutes? Then again, it'd give her a chance to ask him about his podcast. An excited shiver ran down her spine. Was she really going to get time alone with Gavin Colton?

Gavin grimaced, and she imagined he was thinking that ninety minutes was too long to wait. "I was...um... hoping to meet someone here in the next few minutes."

"No can do, buddy." Theo's voice filled the small car. "I got everyone—including the tow truck operators—working on the accident in town. It'll be a while. That's the best I can do."

"I understand," said Gavin. Then he asked, "Can you have the car brought into town? That way we don't have to wait on the side of the road."

Theo paused. "I suppose we can. Where should we bring the car?"

"I'm at the Stay-A-While Inn. It's by the airport,"

Jacqui said. She paused a beat before continuing. "I'm Jacqui Reyes, by the way, stranded motorist."

"Reyes," the police chief repeated. In the background, Jacqui could hear the scratching of pen on paper. "R-E-Y-E-S. Stay-A-While Inn."

She gave him her cell phone number before adding, "I'm in room two-fifteen."

"You'll get a call when your car is delivered," Theo added.

She sighed and a cord of tension loosened in her neck. "Thanks. You're both lifesavers."

"You're welcome, Ms. Reyes," said the police chief. Then to Gavin, he said, "Give your mom my best."

"Will do." Gavin used the controls on his steering wheel to end the call. He pulled back on the pavement and drove for a mile. "Don't worry. I'll get you back to your hotel. The police chief will get you the car soon."

"Thanks," she said, her voice barely above a whisper. Her elbow sat on the armrest. His wrist was so close that she could feel the heat from his skin. She let her arm drop to her lap. Using the sleeve of her jacket to polish the phone's screen, she cleared her throat. "You really are a lifesaver."

"It's the least I can do for a superfan."

Was he teasing?

She glanced in his direction. Sure, she'd been drawn to his voice from the first time she heard his podcast. And yeah, she always imagined he'd be nice-looking. But what she wasn't prepared for was the fact that he was supremely handsome.

His eyes were a shade of bright blue that reminded

her of the ocean waters near her home in Miami. His skin was smooth. His chestnut hair was thick, and she wondered what it would feel like to let the short strands run through her fingers. He wore a Henley, open at the neck. It exposed a sliver of his muscular chest.

He looked at Jacqui and smiled. *Dear Lord, did he actually have a dimple in his cheek?* Her pulse did a stutter step, and she dropped her gaze to her hands. She needed to find something else to say before she started gushing again like a fangirl.

"So, you live in Blue Larkspur. For some reason I always thought you were from New York City. Like, you mention that in your podcast sometimes."

"I'm from Blue Larkspur—key word, *from*. I live in Manhattan now. Sometimes, Chicago."

Sure, it was just small talk—completely inconsequential. Yet, she asked, "You here visiting family, then?"

He snorted. "Sorta."

Jacqui wasn't sure what to make of that answer and tried again. "They must be so proud of you. Not many podcasts have as many listeners as yours."

He snorted again, only this time he didn't bother to add anything else.

Was that strike two for making conversation? Did she dare to try a third time? "Do you miss living here? I mean, Blue Larkspur is about as different from Manhattan as you can get. And I grew up in Miami, so trust me, I know."

He avoided answering her question and instead asked

one of his own. "Miami, huh? How'd you end up in Western Colorado?"

"A master's degree in both wildlife biology and environmental conservation got me a job with the Bureau of Land Management. They sent me to Denver, where I live now."

"What got you interested in wildlife biology and conservation?"

"In middle school, my environmental science teacher showed a news segment about the wild mustangs of Blue Larkspur. The reporter talked about the horses and how their range was disappearing because of climate change and housing developments. They interviewed a guy—a wildlife biologist in charge of the roundup. Then, they showed a bunch of people sitting around a campfire at night. Everyone seemed happy and they had a purpose. In that moment, it's what I wanted to do with my life, so I went and studied it in undergrad and got my master's before working for the Bureau. And so far, no regrets." Jacqui realized that she'd talked too much and let her words fade to nothing.

"That's a great story," said Gavin. "Like you said, people are happiest with a purpose. You're lucky to have your work be your passion."

"What about you and your podcast? Isn't that a passion for you?"

"Sometimes, yeah. It can be." He paused and added nothing more.

Looking back out the window, Jacqui watched the night and tried to find something else to say.

Gavin saved her by asking, "Did you get a good look

at the car that hit you from behind? Or even better—a license plate number?"

Glancing at Gavin, she shook her head. "I definitely didn't see a license plate." She brought back those moments on the winding road. "It was a dark sedan—and drove without any headlights—so I didn't see it until it was tight to my bumper."

"No headlights?" he echoed. "That seem weird to you, at all? All cars manufactured in the past few decades have automatic lights. It's damn near impossible to drive without lights—unless it's intentional."

A chill ran up Jacqui's spine. "I guess that is weird."

"You definitely need to mention that to the police chief."

Was there something in his tone? The memory of the half-full tobacco bag and the scent of cigarette smoke on the breeze was as real as the car in which she now sat. Had there been more to the accident than aggressive driving—as if that wasn't bad enough. Had Jacqui been forced from the road as a warning to stay away from the wild mustangs? Or worse?

Keeping the alarm from her voice, she said, "I'll definitely mention the car to the police chief."

On a frontage road, Gavin turned left and continued to drive parallel to the interstate. She shifted in her seat, suddenly aware that her time with Gavin Colton was ending. Sure, she was still excited to meet her favorite podcaster in person. She just needed to focus on her job. Someone had called Jacqui directly with a chilling warning. What's more, someone had tried to take a wild mustang from public land.

That meant there were horse thieves on the loose in Blue Larkspur. She glanced at Gavin before looking out the side window. What would he, as a true crime podcaster, think of her problem?

What she didn't know was, who was responsible? And what's more, how far would they go to keep her from finding out?

TIGHTENING HIS GRIP on the steering wheel, Gavin turned onto the road that led toward the regional airport. The street was lined on both sides with chain restaurants and chain motels. Streetlights made this section of town bright as day. It was progress, he supposed. Still, he remembered Fridays from his adolescence. Postgame, Gavin and his teammates would pile into a car and come to this part of town.

Back then, they'd park near the runway and pass around a bottle of booze—usually stolen from a parent's liquor cabinet—stare at the stars and hope that a plane would land. They always had a designated driver, but it was never Gavin.

The airport tower was the same as it had always been, white brick against the black night—almost like a lighthouse on a rocky coast. Yet so much had changed in the decade since he left Blue Larkspur. Like the fact there were so many lights that he'd never be able to see the stars.

Funny that he should be annoyed by lights and commotion. After all, he lived in Manhattan—and sincerely, New York City never did sleep.

"So," Jacqui began. "How do you get ideas for your

podcasts?" Even in the darkened car, he could see that her cheeks were bright. Was she blushing? When was the last time Gavin had spoken to a woman who was honest enough to blush? The reaction was completely opposite to the models and actresses he usually dated. He suspected that most of those women only wanted him for clout on social media—or a mention by the press. Not that he hated their company, but the conversation never went beyond the superficial. "I mean, if you don't mind telling me."

It was a question he got often. He had a well-practiced answer ready. Yet, his usual—*I keep an eye on the papers and work with the police*—didn't seem right. It wasn't exactly a lie, but it wasn't exactly the truth.

"I read a lot of local newspapers and work to have relationships with detectives all over the country," he began. "A lot of my ideas come from those places. But to be honest, I'm not sure why I pick a specific case. I hear something or read something, and I don't know." He paused, trying to bring back that feeling when he just knew a topic was right for his show. "My breath catches. My heart skips a beat. I can already imagine the first few lines of the script."

Jacqui gave a short laugh. "Kinda sounds like falling in love. Except for the script part, I mean."

Perceptive and pretty? Not a bad combo. "You know, I've never thought of it that way—but you're right. It is." He turned into the parking lot of the Stay-A-While Inn.

The inn was a two-story structure with rooms accessible by an outdoor walkway. As a kid, he remembered it had been a regular motel, but over the years it had been renovated into suites and rented for long-term stays.

He pulled into a spot directly under room 215 and let the engine idle. His time with Jacqui was almost over. A pang of regret struck him in the chest.

The dashboard clock read 7:47 p.m. Had it really only been half an hour since he spotted Jacqui's car in a ditch? Sure, he didn't know her well—or even at all, really. It's just that for the first time in forever, he hated the idea of being alone. The isolated cabin he'd rented for the month felt less like sanctuary and more like a prison.

If he wanted some company, he could always call any one of his siblings. Hell, most of his old friends from school still lived in the area. But Gavin wasn't in the mood to be judged by his past. What he wanted most of all was a clean slate. It was part of why he wanted—make that *needed*—to do a story on his father's crimes.

"Well, here you are." He put the gearshift into park. "You'll be able to get into your room okay, right? You didn't leave your key in your car or anything."

Jacqui produced a keycard from her pocket. "I'm all set." She smiled and reached for the door handle. "Thanks again."

"And good luck with your official federal business. Sounds important."

She paused. Her fingertips still rested on the handle. "Can I ask for your expert opinion?"

"I'm not sure how being a podcaster makes me an expert on much of anything, but I'll help if I can."

"If you wanted to watch over an area without being seen, how would you do it?"

Gavin sat back in his seat. Whatever he expected Jacqui to ask, that wasn't it. "I'm definitely the wrong Colton to ask about stuff like that. Me, I'm more like a journalist than a cop. But, if you want my opinion, you need to do surveillance. Park your car, try to blend in, and see what happens."

She nodded, as if considering his words. "But what if this isn't really in an area where there are roads and other cars."

"That makes it a little harder to blend in." He paused and gave himself a moment to think. "You can plant cameras and get video."

"Even without a power source?"

For Gavin, every story was a bit like a puzzle. He just needed to figure out how the pieces fit. He was starting to get a picture of what Jacqui needed, but there was one big hole. "I thought you said you work with the Bureau of Land Management. That's part of the federal government. Don't you have your own resources?"

"Let's say that I'm doing some reconnaissance and trying to figure out if I have a problem."

Gavin knew there was more to her story. Did he press her for more information—or not? Before his mind could decide, his mouth moved forward. "What kind of problem?"

She looked out the window and said nothing.

"I can't help if I don't know what you need," he coaxed.

"Horse thieves," she said. "I got a tip that there's a

gang of horse thieves trying to round up a herd of wild mustangs. That's where I was this afternoon—checking it out."

"And?"

"And I think the tip was right." She turned to look at Gavin. Their gazes met and held. His chest tightened. She said, "I need help—and you're just the guy—"

Before she said any more, he held up his hands. "Whoa. I'll agree that horse thieves are interesting. What's not interesting is meddling in a federal crime. I'm gonna have to pass."

"Sure," she said, opening the car door. The interior light came on. There was the hint of an emotion in her eyes. What had it been? Hurt? Disappointment? With Jacqui, it was a kick to the gut. Before he could change his mind, she continued, "It really was nice meeting you. Thanks for the ride and getting my car towed."

"You're welcome," he called after her. Gavin wasn't sure if she heard. Jacqui had already closed the door and was walking to the stairs. He put the gearshift into reverse as his phone started to ring. The in-car audio flashed with caller ID. Ezra.

Ezra was one in a set of triplets, former military and Gavin's favorite sibling.

He backed out of the spot and answered the call. "Hey, bro. What's up?"

"I heard from Mom. She said you called the cops because you found a stranded motorist. Everything okay?"

Of course, Chief Lawson called Gavin's mother. But why hadn't she called Gavin directly? The fact that she reached out to Ezra instead stung. He pushed his hurt feelings aside. "It was some woman who'd been pushed off the road. I just dropped her off at her hotel. The tow truck will bring her car by later. No biggie."

"So, you're in town to work on a podcast?"

Here we go again. Gavin turned onto the main road. "I am."

"Brother, I gotta ask—why are you doing this? You're digging into a past that a lot of people want to keep buried."

"Is this about the drug smuggler that Caleb got out of jail? Ronald Spence."

"Among other things."

"Like what?"

"Like we are all trying to live our lives despite what Dad did all of those years ago. Why you want to find all the old garbage and show it to the world?"

"Maybe for me it's not old garbage. Maybe the question of why Dad did what he did is the first thing I ask myself in the morning. Maybe it's the question that wakes me up in the middle of the night. Listen, I want all of my siblings to be successful and happy—but maybe I'm sick of making concessions, since it's always me against the rest of you."

"That's not fair."

"Isn't it?" Gavin made a turn that took him out of town, into the mountains and toward his cabin.

"You're the one who comes to town for weeks and doesn't reach out to anyone, who misses Caleb's wedding, even. How're we supposed to feel?"

Okay, Ezra had a point. "I'm going to Caleb's tomorrow."

"Good. When're you going to stop by my house?

I met someone. Her name's Theresa Fitzgerald. She's great. She's got two daughters."

Gavin could hear the love and pride in his brother's voice. "You sound real happy. I'm glad."

"You could be a part of this, you know. We love you, man. We want you to be a part of the family."

"But only if I give up on my idea of Dad being the focus for my next podcast. Is that it?"

"No. We just want you here. That's all."

"Like I told Caleb, I'll think about changing my focus." He rubbed his forehead, fending off a headache. "Here's the problem, though. I need another topic—and fast."

"Sorry, I can't help you out with that." In the background, Gavin could hear high-pitched laughter.

"Is that them, Theresa's daughters?"

"It is. Movie night. Popcorn and something with a princess-pony."

"Go. Enjoy your night."

"You promise to stop by."

"I do," said Gavin before ending the call. "I'll see you soon."

Then, it was just him, the road and the endless night sky. As he drove, he realized that he could change his podcast—but only if he found another crime. Sure, people contacted him with ideas all the time. But to impress his sponsors, it'd have to be big.

Tapping his thumbs on the steering wheel, he continued to drive. Had he dismissed Jacqui's call for help too quickly? Certainly, horse thieves would make for an interesting and exciting episode. But if he offered now, would she still want his help?

Chapter Four

Jacqui always rented a suite at the Stay-A-While Inn when she worked in Blue Larkspur. Aside from it being close to the local office, it was like a small apartment. The living room was separated from a galley kitchen by a breakfast bar with seating for three. To the left was a bedroom and bathroom. In truth, her one-bedroom apartment in Denver wasn't much bigger.

Once in her suite, Jacqui changed into flannel sleep pants and a sweatshirt. She pulled a blanket off the bed and brought it to the sofa. Burrowing under the blankets, she tried to consider her next move. Now that she'd confirmed that the tip was valid, should she call law enforcement? And if she did, what agency should she contact? Fish and Wildlife? The FBI?

Her phone rang with an incoming video call from Steffanie. Jacqui swiped the call open.

"Hey." In March, Steffanie had her first child. Jacqui had to admit that motherhood agreed with her friend. She continued, "How's it going? Did you find out anything?"

"Turns out that the anonymous caller was right."

Jacqui spent a few minutes outlining everything she'd seen—including the injury on the horse's neck she'd noted, along with the car that pushed her off the road.

"Someone pushed you off the road?" Steffanie asked, her eyes wide. "You think that the two are connected?"

"I don't know what to think. But here's a bit of news that you'll find interesting. You won't believe who gave me a ride back to the hotel." Jacqui didn't wait for an answer. "Gavin Colton, the podcaster from *Crime Time*."

"No way. *The* Gavin Colton. What's he like?"

Now that was a loaded question. "First, his voice is perfection. Dark. Deep. Smoky."

"Hmm. Sounds nice. But what's he like. Looks. Personality. Did I mention looks? I need all the details."

"He is handsome. Brown hair. Eyes as blue as the ocean water. Looks fit. He's smart and notices everything—and I mean, everything."

"Sounds like someone might have a crush," Steffanie teased.

Did she have a crush? Okay, she'd admit to liking him, at least a little. "He found me on the side of the road, gave me a ride back to the hotel and called the police for me. What's not to like?"

"Hold on a minute." The camera's aspect changed as Steffanie set the phone on the side of her laptop. In the background, Jacqui could hear the clicking of fingertips on keys. "I'm looking him up right now. Oh my. He's more than handsome. That man is gorgeous."

"Yep, that's him."

She recalled a moment in the car when they seemed to connect.

"I hear something or read something, and I don't know," he'd said when Jacqui asked how he decided on which cases to cover for his podcast. Then, he'd said, *"My breath catches. My heart skips a beat. I can already imagine the first few lines of the script."*

In the moment, she imagined that she understood Gavin completely. *"Kinda sounds like falling in love. Except for the script part, I mean."*

He'd glanced at her while he drove. For the first time in forever, Jacqui felt as if she were understood as well. He said, *"You know, I've never thought of it that way— but you're right. It is."*

Steffanie's voice cut through Jacqui's memory. "And look at all of those models he dates."

Drawing her brows together, she asked, "All of those what?"

"The models. You mean to tell me that you haven't done an internet search on Gavin Colton yet?"

"Not yet. I have other things to worry about—like how to stop a pack of horse thieves." Yet, she rose from the sofa and found her laptop on the kitchen counter. After getting resettled on the sofa, she powered up the computer and entered Gavin's name into a search engine. The first few hits were about his show and then, there were all the tabloid stories. It seemed that Gavin liked his women tall, thin and glamorous. Suddenly, she felt defeated and exhausted. "Well, it does look like he dates a lot of models. Although, he's a celebrity in New York City, so whaddaya expect?"

"Are you okay?" Steffanie asked, her voice filled with concern.

"It's been a long day, is all. And I'm no closer to knowing what to do."

"Wait. I thought you were just going to Blue Larkspur to confirm that the call was real—nothing else."

"Yeah, but now that I'm here I should do something. Try to find out who these people are—or what they plan to do with the horses." Jacqui closed her laptop and picked up the phone. "The thing is, I don't know how."

"Exactly," said Steffanie. "That's because you aren't a cop. You know you have to turn this matter over to someone."

"Not Zeke," Jacqui said quickly.

"Fine, then. Someone else."

The thing was, Steffanie was right. As a federal employee, Jacqui knew that there were procedures to follow. Yet, she had a hard time letting go of the case. It was more than just letting Zeke know—and the fact that he'd take all the credit. If Jacqui wanted that promotion, she had to prove that she could solve problems. She made a decision. "I'll call the Bureau authorities on Monday. Until then, I'm going to stay in town and poke around. I'll see what I can learn."

"You what? No way."

Steffanie's words were interrupted by an incoming call. Jacqui checked the number. "What area code is nine-one-seven?"

"It's Manhattan, I think," said Steffanie. "Why?"

"Someone's calling me from that number." Jacqui froze. "Do you think it's him?"

"How'd he get your number?"

It was a good question. "I gave it to the police chief. Do you think Gavin memorized it?"

"There's only one way to find out. Bye, my friend."

Steffanie's face disappeared from the screen. The incoming call immediately came through her phone.

"Hello?"

"Is this Jacqui?"

"It is."

"Hi, this is Gavin. Um, Gavin Colton."

"Yeah—" she gave a small laugh "—I recognized your voice."

It was his turn to give a small laugh. "So, did your car show up yet?"

She hadn't expected the tow truck to deliver her car for another hour—maybe more. Was that the reason that Gavin was calling? "No," she said. "Not yet."

"That's too bad."

"It's not so bad if it shows up eventually."

"I guess you're right."

Sure, she hated awkward small talk as much as the next gal. But what did Gavin want? "Is there something I can help you with? Did I forget anything in your car?"

He paused. "Well, it's just what you said about your horse thieves and that you needed help."

"Right." And he'd said that he wouldn't get involved in a federal investigation. "I did."

"If you still want help," Gavin began, "I'm offering."

She stared at the phone and gaped. Was he joking? "That'd be great. But why the change of heart?"

"Well, I do have one ask. You have to let me use whatever we find in an upcoming episode of my podcast."

Would that be allowed? Then again, if she wasn't willing to call the police now, did she have any other choices? "Agreed—so long as I can remain anonymous for the podcast."

"The way I look at it—whoever called you is the key to finding out whatever is happening. Can you send me the voice mail you received?"

Jacqui couldn't argue with his logic, that's for sure. She found the message and sent it in a text. "You get it?"

"Got it. Anything else? Even something small might be a clue."

There was. "When I was on the range, I noticed that one of the horses had a wound to his neck consistent with a lasso."

"Both seem pretty solid." He paused. "Is there anything else you can tell me? Any other clue?"

"I think that the horses spend a lot of time where I found them. I noticed a small stream—and around here, a water source is rare."

"Water source," Gavin said, repeating her words. "Anything else? Even if you think it's small, it might be big."

"No," Jacqui said, thinking of her time on the range. "Nothing else, except…"

"Except what?"

"I'm not sure if it's even connected, but I found a half-full bag of loose tobacco." What was the brand name? She rose from the sofa and found her jacket. She unzipped a pocket and removed the red package. "Royal Moravian. The bag looks new—not like it'd been out in the elements for long. And I'm not sure if it was my imagination or not—but I might've smelled some cigarette smoke on the breeze."

"I'll get to work on what you've given me," Gavin said. "We'll meet up in the morning. I'll come to get you at eight o'clock."

"Eight, it is," she said, before ending the call.

Jacqui couldn't help it. She was excited to see Gavin again. True, he dated svelte supermodels—and she was neither svelte nor a supermodel. But after the fiasco with Zeke, Jacqui really didn't want a new romance. Which made Gavin perfect, because you couldn't really blame a girl for just looking.

THE SUN HAD yet to rise. Despite being in Colorado, Gavin kept himself on East Coast time—two hours earlier than the Mountain Time Zone—and he always woke before daybreak.

For Gavin, there was something therapeutic about a day yet to be born. Maybe it went back to his very loud and chaotic childhood home. As a kid, the only time he could find any peace was before the sun had risen.

He was back in the cabin and settled once more in his makeshift office. A pad of paper sat in front of him, and he held a pen. He'd made a list of everything he knew about Jacqui's case.

The anonymous call.

The mark to the horse's neck.

The pouch of tobacco, along with the scent of cigarette smoke.

The car being forced from the road.

In total, it wasn't a lot. But it was enough to get started.

To Gavin, it seemed like the tobacco came from a specialty store—not something that was available at every gas station in the country. After powering up his laptop, he searched the brand name and the city.

"Bingo. Only one store in the entire county." He scribbled the address for The House of Smoke on the pad of paper, although Gavin was familiar with the shops on Main Street. The store opened at 9:00 a.m., and it worked perfectly with the day's timeline. Hopefully, by noon, Gavin would know if there was enough material for an entire show.

Yet was there a story that stole his breath? Was there something in this tale that he could love? Pressing his pen into the paper, he tried to think of an introduction.

Where would the story begin? With the anonymous phone call made to the Bureau of Land Management? Would he start with a history of the wild mustangs? No, the story would start the moment he saw Jacqui on the side of the road. The words came to him, but he needed to capture them with his voice—not a pen.

Slipping on his headphones, he hit record and began to speak. "The road was dark and narrow. I hadn't seen another person for days, so I was shocked when I noted the car perched precariously on the side of a hill. But when I saw her walking on the side of the road, I knew she might be dangerous... But there was no way I could keep going. I had to stop."

It'd draw listeners into the episode, he knew that.

But Gavin wasn't sure that the introduction would make the final cut.

He set the headphones aside and saved his recording. Rising from the desk, he moved to the kitchen and poured himself a cup of coffee. He held the steaming mug and watched the sun break over the horizon. The light reflected off the still waters, and to Gavin, it looked like there were two worlds, stacked atop one another.

As the sky, the mountains and the trees came into full Technicolor glory, he couldn't help himself. He wondered what Jacqui would think about the cabin, the coffee, the lake.

While taking a swig of his coffee, he checked the time: 7:10 a.m.

As a kid, Ezra had always been the last to get out of bed. But Gavin bet that years in the military had changed his brother's habit of sleeping in. He wandered inside and found his phone sitting on a wooden table. After pulling up Ezra's name from his contact list, Gavin placed the call.

It rang five times before being picked up by voice mail. "This is Ezra. Leave a message."

He wasn't sure if he should be disappointed or relieved. Hanging up, without leaving a voice mail, he tossed his phone back to the table. As he turned for the porch, cup in hand, the phone began to trill.

He swiped open the call and turned on the speaker function. "Hey. Thanks for calling me back."

"Sorry I didn't pick up at first. It took a second to get to my phone. It's busy around here right now." In the background, Gavin heard the high-pitched laughing of children, along with a woman's voice. She gave admonitions to eat breakfast before the TV could be turned on.

Taking a slug of coffee, Gavin wasn't sure how he felt that his favorite brother had finally settled down. Gavin couldn't imagine trading his life for chaotic mornings filled with giggling kids and cartoons. But still, his chest was tight with an emotion. It absolutely wasn't jealousy—but he felt something. Longing, maybe?

He cleared his throat. "I didn't mean to interrupt the morning routine."

"It's easier to get two kids fed than twelve," said Ezra with a small laugh.

"I bet," said Gavin, suddenly not sure what else to say.

Ezra paused a beat. "I didn't ask last night, but where are you staying?"

"I rented a cabin near a small lake."

"Why there and not with Mom? She'd love the company, you know?"

Gavin refused to be guilted into staying with their mother. As much as he loved Isa Colton, he was an adult and needed his own space. What's more, his brother knew as much. That was one of the reasons he hadn't come home for Caleb's wedding—he just didn't want to deal with the onslaught of sibling attention. Although he did regret missing out—just a bit.

After a moment, his brother asked, "So, what can I do for you?"

"I need some help in the way of equipment to do outdoor surveillance." Gavin began to list all the specifications. If someone was trying to steal the mustangs, then they'd need video surveillance. What had started as an academic exercise last night with Jacqui's questions was now a reality. "I need it to record, even at night. And there's no power source around, so it'll have to have a long battery—or maybe even solar. You have anything like that?"

"I do, but…" Ezra sighed. "We gotta talk before I go helping you."

"Then talk."

Ezra said nothing.

Gavin shook his head. He knew better than to ask his family for anything. "I can hear a lot in your silence. What's the problem? I can pay a rental fee, if that's what you're worried about."

"It's not the money, man. It's never the money. But what're you doing? You want me to help you profit off our father's mistakes? I get that what Dad did is scandalous, truly. I bet it'd even make a good podcast. But you're a Colton. He's still your father. We're still your family. What you're doing, well." He sighed. "It's just not right."

"Are you done?" Gavin didn't bother to keep the snark from his voice. "First of all, I have the same right as you and everyone else to come to terms with what Dad did in my own way."

That seemed to take some of the fight out of Ezra. "I'm not saying that you don't."

"And second, this has nothing to do with Dad." Gavin continued before his older brother got to say anything else, "I'm working on a different story."

"Oh really? What's it about?"

"I'm in the beginning phases of the investigation. But if I'm right, then it's horse thieves."

"Horse thieves? Around here?" All of Ezra's enmity seemed vanished. Gavin's shoulders relaxed. "No kidding."

"No kidding at all. It looks like someone is trying to round up the local herd of wild mustangs. Who and why? That's what I plan to find out."

"And that's why you need all of the equipment, right?"

"Right." But there was more. "Someone forced a federal employee off the road yesterday. It might not even be connected, but it might be a warning."

"Is this the same person you helped last night?"

"It is."

"That's bold. Did the employee get a license plate? A make or model of the car?"

"Nope," said Gavin simply. "The car was running without lights."

Ezra cursed under his breath. "I can set you up, but it might take a little while."

"Define a little while."

"If you come by later this morning, I'll have what you need."

"Thanks, man." Gavin took a sip of coffee. Yet, he didn't need any caffeine. The excitement of the hunt buzzed through his system. "I'll see you soon."

"You got it. And, Gavin?" Ezra continued.

"Yeah?"

"It's good to have you home, brother."

Gavin smiled and shook his head. Maybe being home wasn't that bad. "Thanks, man. I'll see you soon."

Was it good to be home? Gavin wasn't sure how he

felt to be back in Blue Larkspur. His blood hummed—as it always did—with the excitement of a new story. Sure, it meant ditching his original idea. If he gave up now, he'd never explore all the crimes his father committed while a judge.

Yet, that might be for the best. Gavin wasn't close to any of his siblings. It's not that any of them were bad people. It's just that growing up in the Colton house was like being raised on a roller coaster. Nothing but going up, down and sideways—always at 100 miles per hour. As a young man, he couldn't wait to get the hell out of Blue Larkspur and find a place where he could think.

All the same, he didn't like being crosswise with his entire family. More than once, Jacqui had said that Gavin had been her lifesaver. Even though she didn't know, she was a lifesaver to him as well. As it turned out, the story of the horse thieves might be the key to reconciling with his family.

Chapter Five

Henry Rollins felt the headache before he even opened his eyes. The sound of voices drove into his ears like ice picks. He pried one eye open—his vision was blurry. Yet, he saw enough to know that he'd fallen asleep on the sofa again. The voices came from chipper newscasters on the TV he'd left on all night.

He sat up. The throbbing turned into the pounding of a hammer inside his skull. A wave of nausea rolled up from his gut. Henry gagged back the puke before he retched on the floor. He drew in a deep breath and looked around. An empty fifth of whiskey lay on the coffee table. There was also a cereal bowl with a crust of milk on the bottom. A bottle of beer with a swallow left. He grabbed the bottle and took a drink.

Sure, it was warm and flat. Yet, the single drink settled his stomach and took the edge off his headache. He reached for the remote and changed the channel on the TV to an all-sports network. An announcer was discussing the Colorado Mustangs' chance in the upcoming Sunday afternoon game. Henry's pulse spiked. He had $200 in cash. If he hit it big, he could really score. Then, he could make enough to get out of debt, move out of this crappy place, leave Blue Larkspur and start over.

But first, he had to deal with Silas Dunn.

His whole body still ached from the beating that he'd taken. All he could hope for now was that Dunn would be too busy to bother with Henry. Or follow up on the plan to steal a herd of horses from the range.

His phone pinged with an incoming text. He lifted it from the table. The message was from Dunn. Henry read the single word and felt his heart quit beating.

Update?

Henry reached for the whiskey. Not only was it empty—the bottle was bone-dry. "Dammit."

How was he supposed to deal without the benefit of a stiff drink?

FRIDAY AFTERNOON, DUNN sent Henry on a reconnaissance mission of sorts. He was to find out the number of animals in the herd and their exact location. He'd done both and even practiced lassoing a stallion to see if he could. He did.

Henry typed out a message.

37 horses on the range. My skills are still there. I'm ready whenever you get the buyers.

The last bit was a lie. He wasn't ready. How the hell was he supposed to lasso thirty-seven horses by himself? He'd have to call in a few friends…

But more than the logistics, things were about to get a whole lot more complicated. He'd been watching the horses when Jacqui Reyes, the woman from the Bureau of Land Management, showed up.

It wasn't supposed to be just her. She was supposed to call the FBI or at least, the local police. If law enforcement had gotten involved, Silas Dunn would have no choice but to back down.

But it hadn't worked that way.

Jacqui got all squirrelly and left quick.

In the moment, he'd been so worried she'd seen him that he'd forced her car from the road. Really, it'd been a simple reaction—part fear, part rage. In the glaring light of the morning, Henry had to wonder, had it been a good idea?

His finger hovered above his phone, and he hit the send icon. Henry rose from the sofa and his head began to pound. He walked stiffly to the kitchen and pulled open the refrigerator's door. Ketchup. Mustard. Old bread. Two eggs in an open carton. Nothing else.

Likewise, the cupboards were almost bare. What's worse, there was definitely no booze in the house.

He needed to make a run to the liquor store—that was for sure. Until then, he could cook up the eggs and kill the headache with a smoke. Last night, he'd flung his jacket across the kitchen table. Now, it lay atop a pile of unpaid bills. Patting down his pockets, he found a sheaf of rolling papers.

Yet, where was his pouch of tobacco? He checked the pockets again. Henry shoved his hands into each set of pockets on his pants.

Nothing.

Returning to the small living room, he pulled the cushions from the sofa.

Nope.

Not in his pockets. Not in the house.

Had he run out?

Henry brought back the last few minutes of his time on the range. He'd just rolled a cigarette when he saw a cloud of dust coming up the road. He barely had time to hide his car and himself before the government lady showed up.

His phone pinged again. Henry read the message from Dunn.

Any signs that the feds are keeping an eye on the herd?

Fingers trembling, he typed out his reply. It was an absolute lie, but what else was he supposed to say—unless he wanted another butt-kicking? And out of all the things in the world Henry wanted, another butt-kicking was last on the list.

No signs of the feds.

His hands still shook after tossing his phone onto the low coffee table. He tried to tell himself that the shakes came from last night's bender. Even in his heart and mind, Henry knew it wasn't true.

Had he really dropped his tobacco on the range? He drew in a deep breath and tried to figure out the odds that someone would actually find the bag. What would it be? One hundred to one? Maybe even higher. And then, the person who found the tobacco would have to be suspicious. And then, that same person would have to link the substance to the horses and the horses to Henry. What were those odds?

He sure as hell didn't know, but they weren't good.

He lay back on the sofa and tried to relax. But he was still tense, and what's more, he knew why. He'd just lied to Silas Dunn, a singularly dangerous man. And if that lie were ever exposed?

Well, there'd be deadly consequences.

JACQUI STOOD IN the bathroom of her suite and looked in a mirror that hung over the sink and vanity. At thirty-seven years old, she had to admit that she liked what she saw. Sure, there were a few wrinkles around her eyes, her mouth and on her forehead. But didn't that mean she'd seen a lot, smiled more and cared enough to think things through?

Fluffing her dark hair, she pivoted to the left and right. For the day, she wore a white T-shirt, her running jacket and jeans. It was a simple outfit, yet this pair of jeans really did make her rear look amazing. She smiled.

As she examined her reflection, Jacqui remembered all the pictures she'd seen online of Gavin with a bevy of models. Even if she were in the market for a boyfriend, which she was not, she'd never be the kind of woman who attracted a guy like Gavin Colton. She needed to turn off her libido and focus on finding out the truth. Who had called to warn her about the horse thieves?

Yet, it didn't mean that she couldn't look nice. Turning off the light, she wandered to the bed and found a cross-body bag. She had her phone, credit card, room key, car keys—all she needed for the day. A pair of sunglasses sat next to the bag, and she hooked them to the neck of her shirt.

Her phone pinged with an incoming text.

It was Gavin. Just seeing his name made her smile.

I'm in the parking lot.

Smile still on her lips, she replied, Be right down.

Bring the tobacco with you.

The red pouch sat on the kitchen counter. She picked it up as she passed. Got it.

Glancing one last time in the mirror that hung on the back of the door, she stepped out into the bright morning light. The sky was blue—without a cloud in it. Gavin sat on the hood of his luxury coupe, a travel mug of coffee in hand. He was parked next to her car. The sun turned his brown hair a shade of dark copper. He wore a dark green Henley and jeans. From where she stood, Jacqui could see a V of flesh exposed at his neck and her heart raced.

So much for turning off her libido.

He looked her way and smiled. Jacqui's chest grew warm. She lifted her hand in a slight wave. "Good morning."

"I hope so," he called back.

She took the walkway to the middle of the building and then came down the stairwell. As she approached Gavin, he stood. His shoulders were broad. The Henley accentuated the muscles in his arms and chest. His legs were long. In short, Gavin was physically perfect.

"Looks like the police chief made good on his promise to deliver your car."

"He did." Jacqui rubbed a scuff on the rear quarter panel where the other vehicle had made contact. "I'm just lucky that the damage is all superficial."

"That you are."

"And here's the tobacco." She held up the bag.

He took it from her and his fingers brushed the back of her hand. An electric charge danced across her skin. Had Gavin felt the connection, too?

She looked at him from under her lashes.

He watched her with those bright blue eyes of his. "Thanks," he murmured, his voice deep and sexy.

Gavin opened the door. "Your carriage awaits, milady."

True, she knew she was a capable woman. It was also true that Gavin was being a bit silly. But it was undoubtedly true as well that she appreciated the small act of chivalry—and the silliness.

"Why, thank you, kind sir." She gave a shallow curtsey before slipping into the passenger seat.

Gavin held on to the door and said, "I have a plan for the day. First, I found out that Royal Moravian—the brand of tobacco you found on the range—is only sold in one store in the entire county—here in town, actually."

It was an interesting fact. And yet… "How does that help us?"

"From what I saw on the internet, it looks like the tobacco is sold at a specialty store. Places like that tend to know their customers. If we're lucky, we'll come away with some names. One of those people might be the same person who dropped the tobacco, lassoed the horse and even drove you off the road."

"Makes sense. And then?"

"Later this morning, we can get some surveillance equipment. If the horse thieves come back, hopefully we'll have some video."

She hated to be so practical, but her budget was next to nothing. "How much will all this equipment cost?"

"I have a connection," he said with a wry smile that left Jacqui's toes tingling.

"Oh?"

Gavin bent down to look her in the eye. "It should be free. And if it's not, I'll cover the expenses."

"Really?"

"Really." He gave her that smile again.

Biting her lip, she looked away.

The engine purred to life. "Ready?"

She nodded. "Sure. But…" Okay, yeah, she knew that she was being irrational. It's just that…well, Jacqui couldn't even explain how she felt to herself, much less to Gavin. Still, she said, "This is my case. Those horses are my responsibility." She paused as he backed out of the parking place and drove slowly through the parking lot. "I can't trust someone else to do my job."

Gavin nodded. "I get it."

From behind her sunglasses, she watched Gavin as he drove. She'd been wrong to see him as merely handsome. Rough stubble covered his cheeks and chin. His hair was wavy and thick. Was she really staring? She dropped her gaze.

"I get it," he repeated. "I'll even share a little secret I've learned while doing my podcast."

"A secret. Sounds exciting."

He shrugged. "What I've learned over the years is that people fall into three categories."

Jacqui wasn't sure where the conversation was going, but she was fascinated by the way Gavin's mind worked. "Only three?"

"Let me rephrase." He cleared his throat. "There are three types of people when it comes to helping with investigations."

"What are they?"

"First, a lot of people are simply happy to be helpful. Second, a lot more want to help because they like the idea of being involved in something that might give them a few minutes of fame."

Nodding her head, Jacqui considered his words. "Makes sense, but what about the third group?"

"Those are actually the best at leading to the truth— and they're not helpful at all."

"Okay, you lost me. How can someone help you find the truth, but not want to help at all?"

"Because." He looked her way. Their gazes met and held. "It means that they have something to hide. It also means that I'm on the right track."

Jacqui folded her arms over her chest to stop from

shivering. The prudent thing would be to call the police now. Yet, she didn't. "Sounds dangerous."

"Sometimes," he said as he drove. "But right now, I'm just praying that we find someone helpful."

"I'll pray that we find a fan of your podcast," she said, teasing him a little.

It was then Gavin's turn to tease her in return. "Last night someone mentioned that I was the most famous podcaster on the internet. In fact, they'd been listening to my latest episode when I met them."

"That was embarrassing," she mumbled. "Am I ever going to live down my fangirl moment?"

Gavin placed his fingertips on the back of her hand. "Hey, it was sweet. And honestly, I was more flattered than you were excited."

His fingers rested on her flesh, and Jacqui's skin warmed with his touch. Her pulse raced, and she longed to wind her fingers through his. But to what end? Any relationship would go nowhere—and what's more, Jacqui had only given herself the weekend to discover what was really happening on the range. After that, she'd have to turn over whatever she found to the police and her superiors with the Department of the Interior. To continue unauthorized surveillance would jeopardize more than her career. Sure, Jacqui wanted to save the horses, but she didn't want to end up in jail.

She moved her hand from the center console and let his rest by her lap. Picking up the thread of conversation, she said, "That's actually nice of you to say."

He shrugged, unaware of the emotional war that raged in Jacqui's head—and heart.

"So, do you have any other life advice to give?"

"Life is too short to not eat the food you want. Or just sit and enjoy the view. But it's definitely too short to not tell the people you care about how you feel." He tapped his finger on the steering wheel. "That's what I've learned so far—and that you can basically do all of your wash on the cold setting."

She chuckled. Gavin was entertaining in person. No wonder she liked his podcast. "I'll remember what you said."

"About the laundry?" he joked.

"About being present."

They pulled onto Main Street.

"The tobacco shop is about half of a block that way," said Gavin as he pointed. "You ready?"

Was she? "If you are."

"All right, then." He parked the car in a space right in front of The House of Smoke. With the push of a button, Gavin turned off the car's ignition. From the center console, he removed the pouch of tobacco. He shoved the bag into the pocket of his jeans. "Let's go."

Jacqui opened her door and stepped into the morning. Already the air had started to warm, and she knew that it was going to be another beautiful late summer day in Colorado. She should be content, and yet…

"Wait."

Gavin stood on the sidewalk and pivoted to face Jacqui. He drew his brows together. "Yeah?"

Her heart pounded against her ribs. Jacqui had to admit a single truth. She wasn't comfortable with all the subterfuge. Government regulations. Rules. Laws—

that neither bent nor broke. That's where she lived her life. Then again, she was the one who'd reached out to Gavin for help. She was also the one who refused to call the police—or even her supervisor. Besides, this was still the weekend, and she was just gathering information on her own time.

"What's our plan?" she asked. Suddenly, Jacqui was too warm, and she slipped out of her jacket. "What am I supposed to do—beyond pray that the people are helpful?"

Gavin gave her the smile that sent her pulse galloping along again. "Do you trust me?"

Did she? "Sure. I mean, I'm here, so I must."

"Then come on." He tilted his head toward the tobacco store. "Let's go."

Jacqui rolled back her shoulders and tied her jacket around her waist. Using a tone that was filled with confidence that she didn't feel, she repeated, "Let's go."

Chapter Six

The House of Smoke sat between a florist shop and a bar. Jacqui pushed open the door and crossed the threshold. Gavin followed. The richly sweet aroma of fresh tobacco filled the air. One wall held a glass case that was filled with pipes of all varieties. Small wooden barrels sat on their sides in a crosshatch of shelves. A paper tag was affixed to the lid of each barrel. Names and descriptions appeared on each label. Firebawl—a spicy and tangy smoke. Or Blue Moon—mellow with floral notes.

A man stood behind the counter and smiled. "Morning, folks. What can I help you with?"

"Hey, my man," said Gavin, his tone overly amiable. Jacqui couldn't help but wonder if the friendly tone was an act. Was it all part of getting the guy to cooperate? "My name's Gavin Colton. I have a podcast."

"No crap. Are you *really* Gavin Colton?"

"You've heard of me?" said Gavin, seemingly taken aback. It left Jacqui wondering if that was part of the act, too.

"Of course I've heard of you and *Crime Time*. Man, your podcast is the best."

"Thanks," said Gavin. "Sincerely. That means a lot to me." He turned to Jacqui. "This is my colleague, Jacqui Reyes," he said, not giving away too much.

"Nice to meet you," said the clerk with a nod. "I'm T.J."

"Nice to meet you, too, T.J." Had Gavin been right about people being helpful? It seemed like he had been. Now, Jacqui could only hope that they'd learn something useful.

"Since you already know about me, I don't have to tell you anything new. But I do need some information, and maybe you can help me out."

"Anything you need," said T.J.

Gavin removed the bag of Royal Moravian from his pocket and set it on the counter. "What can you tell me about this brand of tobacco?"

The clerk glanced at the pouch. "We carry it here, but it's kind of expensive—as far as specialty tobacco goes."

"So, if it's pricey, how well does it sell?"

T.J. paused before answering. "We have a few customers who buy Royal Moravian, but not many."

Was it Jacqui's imagination, or had the young man's demeanor changed?

Gavin continued, "This was found on some federal land. You know who might've dropped this pouch?"

"No." T.J. shook his head forcefully—maybe a little too energetically if he were being honest. "None at all."

Gavin asked, "Is there anything you can tell me about the folks who buy this brand?"

T.J. stepped back from the counter and licked his lips. His gaze darted to the door and then, to Gavin. Taking a step back, the clerk said, "I'm not really sure that I can say a lot about our customers. They have a right to privacy, you know?"

Holding up his hands in surrender, Gavin continued, "I don't want to put you in a bad place with either your boss or the people who shop at your store. Also, I really can't say much about why we're asking you questions. But you do know what kind of podcast I produce, right?"

"Of course," said T.J. with a snort.

"So, you can guess why we're interested in who this tobacco might have belonged to, right?"

"I know." Sweat damped T.J.'s chest. The fabric of his T-shirt clung to his lanky frame. "I can't help you, man. I like your podcast—but really, I can't. If you want to buy something, let me know. Otherwise." He inclined his head toward the door. "You know."

"All right, man. Thanks for your time." Gavin removed his wallet from the back pocket of his jeans. He took out a business card and held it out. "This is my cell number. Call if you think of something."

The clerk's hands hung at his sides. He wasn't going to take Gavin's card, and they all knew it. Placing the card on the counter, he tapped it once. "Have a nice day."

T.J. said nothing as Jacqui and Gavin left.

On the sidewalk, Gavin walked back to his car and

wordlessly unlocked the doors. They both slipped into the sleek sports car, and Gavin drove slowly past the tobacco shop's large window. T.J. stood at the door and watched as the car passed.

Finally, Jacqui spoke. "I'd say that out of the three buckets you like to put people in for wanting to help, T.J. goes into the unhelpful bucket."

"I'd agree," said Gavin.

She paused. "I think he knows who the tobacco belongs to. And what's more, he's spooked."

He gave a terse nod. "I'd agree with you, again."

"So, what do we do now?"

Gavin turned left and then right, saying nothing.

"You never answered my question. Where are we going?"

He circled the block, parking near the intersection with Main Street. "I wanted T.J. to see us leave, because if I'm right—if we're both right—he's going to make a call."

All the puzzle pieces clicked into place. "And we're going to what? Watch the tobacco shop from down the street?"

"Exactly." Gavin reached into the small space behind the seats and withdrew a ball cap and a jean jacket. "It's not the best disguise." He held out the hat to Jacqui. "But it works."

After winding her hair into a bun, she pulled the hat onto the top of her head. With a wink, she asked, "Do I look like a different person?"

"You look great." He opened the door and stepped from the car.

Jacqui followed. A block from the smoke shop, a bistro had tables set out on the sidewalk.

"How's this look?" Gavin asked, pulling out a chair from the table.

It was a far cry from how Zeke always acted. He was always the first person to push through a door. During the time they dated, he had never asked what Jacqui thought or how she felt. Maybe the signs that her ex-boyfriend was only interested in himself were always there—it's just that Jacqui had refused to see them.

Was Gavin different? Or was she just fooling herself? Yet, her heartbeat raced at his simple and chivalrous gesture.

And honestly, it was the perfect Saturday morning for grabbing coffee at a quaint restaurant with a handsome man. It would have been easy for Jacqui to imagine that they were doing something other than working.

But they weren't.

As she sat at the table, adrenaline surged through her system, leaving Jacqui jittery.

The last thing she wanted to do was sit around.

A server, with two menus and two glasses of water, approached the table. "Morning, folks. What can I get for you?"

"I'll take a coffee," said Gavin. Then to Jacqui, he asked, "Do you want one, too?"

More caffeine was the last thing she needed. "How about an herbal tea. Do you have chamomile?"

"Honey and lemon?" the server asked, setting down the waters.

"Please," said Jacqui.

"And can you bring those in to-go cups?"

Jacqui had seen enough cop shows and movies to guess why Gavin wanted the drinks for takeout. A person never knew how long they'd get to stay in one place while working on a case.

"Sure thing," said the server.

"You never answered my question," Jacqui said, once they were alone. "What now?"

"Well, this is the boring part of any investigation. Now, we wait."

"What're we waiting for?"

Gavin rotated the glass on the table and gave a small smile. "I wish I could give you a definite answer, but I can't. All I can say, is that we'll know what we're looking for when we see it."

Jacqui nodded slowly and scanned Main Street. The businesses were just starting to open. Across the road, a woman wheeled a rack filled with clothes from her store to the sidewalk. Atop the rack was a sign: Final Clearance.

At a bakery, a man in a white apron set a flag in a flagpole. It read *Open*, but the *O* was shaped like a donut or maybe a bagel—Jacqui couldn't tell. She heard the whine of an engine and turned just as a car came around the corner.

Her pulse stuttered to a stop. The sedan was black. The windows were tinted. There was a scrape on the front quarter panel—the same kind a driver would get in forcing someone from the road. Her hands went cold, yet she began to sweat.

"Gavin," she said, her voice barely above a whisper. "I think that's the car from last night."

HENRY PARKED IN front of his favorite tobacco shop. His phone was wedged into the cup holder, and the screen glowed with an incoming call a second before it began to ring.

Caller ID read: The House of Smoke.

He glanced through the windshield. T.J., the clerk, stood behind the counter with a phone to his ear. Sure, Henry could ignore the phone and just talk to T.J. in person, but he swiped the call open.

"I'm parked outside the store, you know."

Inside, T.J. spun around to look out of the window. He waved at Henry. "Come in. Some people were looking for you earlier."

Henry's empty stomach roiled. Was it Silas Dunn? Or had someone else who was looking to collect on a different debt stopped by the store? He glanced out the window. The street was empty, save for a family looking into the window of a toy store. "People?" And then, "Never mind. I'll be right there."

Turning off the engine, he pocketed the keys and jogged to the store. With every step, Henry felt eyes on the back of his neck. T.J. looked up as he opened the door. Slipping inside, Henry pulled the door closed. "Hey, man."

"Jeez, who worked you over?"

Henry had almost gotten used to the fact that his lips were swollen, one eye was black and there was a cut that ran from his cheek to his chin. Still, he must look bad. "I'm fine."

"You sure? You don't look fine."

The last thing Henry wanted to do was talk about the beating that he'd taken. Turning the sign from Open to Closed, he asked, "You said someone was asking about me. What's up?"

"You can't do that," T.J. protested. "I'll get fired if you close the store."

"It'll just be for a minute, so we don't get interrupted," said Henry, looking over his shoulder. "Who were they? What'd they want?"

"Well, I'm not exactly sure what they wanted. But they had a pouch of that tobacco you like. They said it was found out on some federal land."

Henry cursed. So that *was* where he lost his stash. How in the hell had they found him so quickly? "What else did they want? Who were they?"

"They were looking into some kind of crime, I think."

"A crime?" That made no sense. "What kind of crime?"

"Dunno," said T.J. "They didn't say."

"Were they cops or something?"

"Naw, not cops. It was that podcaster Gavin Colton and his colleague. A woman named Jacqui Reyes—a pretty thing with dark hair."

Jacqui Reyes. Now, that was a name he knew well. She'd hired him—and a bunch of other cowboys—during the last wild mustang roundup. "Who in the hell is

Gavin Colton?" Henry asked, although the name Colton was familiar enough in Blue Larkspur.

"You mean to tell me that you've never heard of Gavin Colton and his podcast? *Crime Time?*"

"Never," said Henry. The sick feeling in his stomach returned. So help him God, he refused to retch on the floor.

T.J. continued, "You don't know what you're missing, man. *Crime Time* is the best. Abso-freaking-lutely the best." He paused and fished a business card from underneath the counter. Using the tip of his finger, he pushed it toward Henry. It was a simple card—white, with black lettering. There was also a phone number and nothing else. "You can call him, if you want."

Calling some podcaster was the last thing that Henry wanted to do. "What'd you say about me?" he asked, his voice a growl.

"Nothing, man." T.J. held up his hands in surrender. "I said we can't give out information about our customers is all."

"Seems innocent enough," he said. But was it? Still, the knots in his gut loosened a bit. "Did you say anything else? Anything at all?"

"Nothing." T.J. paused a beat. "I think that you should call him. Maybe there's a reward for whatever you saw."

"I didn't see nothing." His crappy day had just gotten a whole lot worse. Not only had forcing Jacqui from the road failed to get the police involved, she'd somehow enlisted the help of a podcaster. It meant that Henry had to get rid of them both, but how?

As GAVIN WATCHED the street, he mentally wrote the script for his next episode.

It didn't take long for a black sedan to show up at the tobacco shop. A single male, Caucasian, had exited the car and gone into the store. He had yet to emerge. In the short time he was on the street, I didn't get a good look at the guy—other than to see a man in a flannel shirt, jeans and a cowboy hat. But, when he came out, I planned to be ready.

Honestly, Gavin was never one for deception. He reported on crimes—he didn't solve them. Yet, he'd spent enough time with cops in both New York and Chicago to have an idea of how to run a surveillance. He balanced his phone against a glass of water.

"You think that's the car?" Gavin asked Jacqui, focusing the camera on The House of Smoke. "Is that our guy?"

She glanced over her shoulder before turning back to the table. "It was dark, so I'm not one hundred percent positive. But yeah, I think so."

After removing her sunglasses, she used the reflective front window of the bistro to watch the street. "When it passed, I saw a scrape to the bumper. Can you see any damage?"

Of course, if this was the car that forced her from the road, there'd be some damage to the fender. He glanced at the picture in the camera. "Nothing that I can tell."

"The door's opening," she said, her voice a low purr.

He ignored the fact that his palms were damp, and his throat was dry, and that Jacqui's voice seemed to dance across his skin. Hitting the record icon on his phone, he sat back and tried not to stare at either his phone or the store. It was important to look casual, even if his pulse raced until his heartbeat echoed in his ears. The store door was halfway open. The glass pane caught the sun and reflected light on the sidewalk.

"Come on," he urged a shadowy figure who stood just inside. "Come on."

A tall man with a thin ponytail exited. He wore a cowboy hat that he pulled lower over his face. Chin down, he unlocked the door of the dark sedan. He slipped into the driver's seat and shut the door, the tinted windows hiding him from view. The car backed out of the parking space and turned away from where Gavin sat. At the next intersection, the sedan turned left and disappeared for good.

He reached for the phone. "We got him on video, but will it be enough?"

Jacqui exhaled. "It has to be," she said, scooting her metal chair until she was next to him.

"I love your enthusiasm," he said, pulling up the video. "Ready?"

She gave a quick nod but said nothing.

Gavin hit the play arrow and the thirty-second clip began. He watched the scene once, twice. After seeing the video for a third time, Gavin tossed his phone on the table and cursed.

"We didn't get a clear image of his face," said Jacqui, giving voice to Gavin's frustration. "It's almost like he knew that we were watching."

Did the guy really know that Gavin and Jacqui had been down the street? He didn't think so. Would they be able to get security footage from the store? Gavin knew that plan was a nonstarter. T.J. would never cooperate... "The guy's careful, that's for sure."

Jacqui picked up the phone and watched the video once again. "He is and he isn't."

"That sounds pretty cryptic." Gavin leaned closer so he could see the screen. His elbow brushed against Jacqui's wrist. Elbows and wrists—not exactly the sexiest of anatomy. Yet, his entire arm warmed with the touch. Shifting in his seat, he broke contact. He'd wasted too much time in Blue Larkspur already. If he was going to have a new subject for his show, he had to focus. "Let's see what you found."

She let the video run until the final seconds. She hit the stop button. "See that." She pointed at the phone. "We have a clear view of the back of his car."

"And the license plate," Gavin added. But really, they didn't. The small rectangle of metal was nothing more than a white shape on the car's rear bumper. He took the phone, careful not to touch Jacqui again. Who knew what kind of feelings he might catch?

"Let me see if I can get a better image." He took a screen shot and expanded the picture. "Well, there's something." And *something* was the perfect way to describe the fuzzy numbers and letters on the license plate.

"From the colors, it looks like the tags were issued in Colorado at least." Jacqui removed the baseball cap and shook out her long hair. "But that doesn't really help us much."

"I know someone who can take a closer look at this." After removing his wallet, Gavin placed several bills on the table. It was enough for the drinks and a generous tip.

"Who's that?"

"My brothers." He stood, and Jacqui did as well. Together, they walked toward his car.

"Brothers?" she echoed. "As in plural?" Jacqui asked as he unlocked the doors with the fob.

"Actually, there are twelve of us Colton kids."

She stared at him for a moment before shaking her head. "You have eleven siblings? But I have to ask— how do you stay sane?"

He had to chuckle. "Sometimes I don't."

"I bet," she said with a chuckle of her own.

Gavin paused. He could tell her more—tell her about what their father had done all those years ago. Or how his mother had been heartbroken after his father's death—and that as a child, Gavin had felt all but forgotten. Or that his brothers and sisters worked diligently to clean up their father's mess and rehabilitate the family name, but when Gavin wanted to examine the crimes, he was reviled. It was all there on the tip of his tongue.

Then again, what would Jacqui think if he dumped all of this in her lap?

Honestly, he thought she might understand, or at least empathize.

Gavin started to speak, but in that moment, he lost his nerve.

Clearing his throat, he tried again. "You'll get to meet one of my brothers and then you can judge for yourself."

Chapter Seven

Ezra lived in a three-bedroom house with his new love, Theresa, and her daughters.

Gavin parked his car next to the sidewalk. Two pink bikes sat next to the front door. A dog stood behind the storm door and barked at their arrival.

Jacqui unlatched her seat belt. "Nice place."

"Yeah," said Gavin, uncertain. How had his former military brother been domesticated so quickly and so completely? It was a mystery to Gavin. "Ezra met a lady with a couple of kids."

"She nice?"

He unlatched his own seat belt. "I'm not sure, but we're about to find out."

A little girl—brunette with pigtails—had joined the dog at the door.

The girl watched as Gavin and Jacqui approached. As he got closer, Gavin realized that she still wore her pajamas, but had added a pair of fairy wings. She held a pink wand with a giant plastic gem on top. The dog continued to bark.

"Hi," said Jacqui. "Is your mom home?"

The girl nodded, saying nothing.

Jacqui tried again. "Can you get Ezra and tell him that his brother Gavin is at the door?"

The girl peered up at him. "You're Uncle Gavin?"

Uncle Gavin? Surprisingly, he liked the sound of that. "Uh, yeah. I guess I am."

She smiled and Gavin's heart melted a little. "Nice to meet you. You stay right there, and I'll be back." She ran off, her gauze wings fluttering. "Mommy!" the girl called. "Mommy, Uncle Gavin's at the door with his wife."

A dark-haired woman came from the back of the house, wiping her hands on a kitchen towel. She wore a pair of sweatpants and a T-shirt. Her hair sat atop her head in a loose bun. "What're you talking about, Claire? Uncle Gavin? His wife?" The woman's gaze stopped on Gavin and Jacqui, who were still standing at the door. She tucked a stray lock of hair behind her ear. "Oh. Hi. You must be Gavin Colton, Ezra's brother."

"I am. And you're Theresa. Ezra told me all about you." What was he supposed to say about Jacqui? Obviously, they weren't married. Had the child seen something in the way they interacted? Or was it just a juvenile assumption that two adults who were together were also involved romantically? For a split second, he didn't hate the prospect of someone like Jacqui being in his life. Shifting his weight from one foot to the other, he added, "And this is Jacqui Reyes. She's a colleague—not my wife."

"Hi to you both." After pulling the door open, she said, "Come in, please. Your brother had to go to the office, but he should be back in a bit. Can I get you coffee? Tea? Have you had breakfast?"

She led them to a bright kitchen. Another girl, almost a carbon copy of the first, sat with a fork in her hand, a plate of pancakes in front of her. She looked up from her food.

"Sweetie, this is your Uncle Gavin."

What was he supposed to do now? Gavin had never been around kids much. Did he shake her hand? Hug her? For some reason he remembered the toy store on Main Street and regretted not bringing a gift.

Jacqui stepped forward. "Those pancakes look yummy. I love pancakes—especially if there's chocolate chips in them."

"I've never had chocolate chip pancakes."

"They're the best. I'm Jacqui, by the way."

The little girl looked to her mother. Obviously, she'd been trained about stranger danger. And hadn't he heard something about their grandparents trying to kidnap them? "You know how to introduce yourself. Go on," said Theresa.

"I'm Neve." She shoveled a bite of pancake into her mouth.

"Nice to meet you," said Jacqui.

"Nice to meet you, too," said the child around her food.

"So, the two of you work together?" Theresa began. "Are you a podcaster, too?"

"Actually, I work for the Bureau of Land Management. Gavin is helping me figure out a bit of a mystery."

"You'll find out soon enough that there's always

something happening with the Colton clan. So, I'm sure you're in good hands."

Gavin slipped onto a barstool at the breakfast table, thankful that Jacqui was able to carry the conversation for the two of them.

"What do you do for the Bureau of Land Management?"

"I'm a wildlife biologist," she said.

"No way," said Neve. "That's so neat. I want to be a wildlife biologist, too."

"I thought you wanted to be an astronaut."

"I want to do both. I'll be a wildlife biologist in space." She shoved a big piece of pancake into her mouth.

The front door opened and closed with a bang. "Hey, babe." Gavin would recognize Ezra's voice anywhere. "You see that sleek car at the curb. Any idea if one of our neighbors got a new ride?"

His favorite brother entered the kitchen, a large cardboard box in his arms. He saw Gavin and stopped short. Despite the fact that he'd left the army, Ezra had kept his light brown hair cut short. He wore a blue T-shirt and jeans.

Suddenly, Gavin was a child again and trying to get his older brothers to let him play baseball with the big kids. His pulse pounded in his ears and his throat was dry. "Hey, man." He cleared his throat. "Good to see you."

Ezra set the box on the breakfast bar and kissed the top of Neve's head in one motion. He opened his arms to Gavin. "It's always great to see you. Bring it in for a hug."

Gavin wasn't a big fan of hugs either. But it beat his brother's ire. He stood and let Ezra slip an arm over his shoulder. Patting his back, his older brother said, "It's been too long."

Was Ezra sore that Gavin hadn't come to town for Caleb's wedding? Honestly, he wouldn't blame his brother if he was. Maybe he shouldn't have used work as an excuse to avoid the family event. Then again, it was too late to make a different choice. "Looks like you've made a nice life for yourself."

"No complaints. That's for sure." He held out his hand to Jacqui. "Ezra Colton, nice to meet you."

"Jacqui Reyes. Same."

"Jacqui is a wildlife biologist, and she works with Uncle Gavin," Neve announced.

Yeah, he definitely liked being Uncle Gavin. The notion surprised him. He wiped a hand down his face to hide his smile.

"That so?" asked Ezra. Then to Gavin, "When you called earlier you said you were working on something new."

Gavin paused. "Is there someplace we can talk?"

"Sure. All of this stuff is for you." Ezra picked up the box and tilted his head to the left. "My office is this way."

Gavin followed his older brother, Jacqui at his side. She was close enough to touch if he just reached out.

Is that what he wanted?

Actually, it was, he realized.

But he had to ask himself—what then?

Gavin had come back to the one place he never wanted to be—his hometown. And getting involved with someone from Colorado was the last thing he wanted. Balling his hand into a fist, he veered to the side and created more space between them.

"In here." Ezra opened the door with the toe of his shoe. "This is my home office."

In Gavin's estimation, the home office was like any other. A desk. Chair. Computer. Cabinet. Bookshelf. Yet, there were differences as well. Like, a locked safe. There was also an extra monitor on the desk that flashed through several different views of the street and around the property.

"Looks like you take security pretty seriously," said Gavin, gesturing to the monitor.

Ezra set the box on the desk with a *thunk*. "We had problems with the girls' grandparents. They were very much survivalists and one day, they took Neve and Claire."

"That's awful," Jacqui breathed.

"It was. I mean, we got them back safe and all. It's just things like that will stick with a child. Anyway, having the extra security makes both the girls and Theresa feel better. Hell, it makes *me* feel better."

"What happened to their grandparents?" Jacqui asked.

Gavin had to admit, she had a way with people. She paid attention. And what's more, she genuinely seemed to care.

"They're in custody. Mandatory psych admission.

Hopefully, they get some help while incarcerated. I'll never trust them to be around Claire or Neve, but there is the chance that they might get supervised visitation at their institution. If it's judged safe. They are family, so you know, one day maybe the girls will want to have a relationship with them."

"You're a good dad," said Gavin, seeing his big brother in a new light. Was it possible for him to have a new and better relationship with Ezra as well?

"I try to be a good dad, at least." Ezra lifted the lid from the box. "Now, let me show you all of the goodies that I was able to pull together for you."

"Before you show us all your techy toys, there's something I want you to see." Gavin took his phone from his pocket and pulled up the screenshot. "Is there any way for you to find out who owns this car?"

Ezra moved the box from the desk to the floor and took a seat in front of his computer. "First, we have to get that picture in a higher resolution. Can I see your phone?"

Gavin handed it over and waited as Ezra emailed himself the picture.

"Higher resolution?" Jacqui asked. "Is that possible?"

"Sometimes," said Ezra, bringing up the picture on a computer monitor. "Sometimes not. I have a program that'll figure it out for me." He entered several keystrokes. A thin line ran through the fuzzy image from top to bottom.

He stared at the screen, the episode script writing itself in his mind.

After each pass, the image became sharper. But would it be enough?

"The plates are from Colorado," said Jacqui as the image became clear enough to see a color pattern. "We were right about that, at least."

Pointing to the computer, Gavin said, "Looks like the first letter is a *G* or maybe a *C*. Definitely followed by an *L*."

"The final numbers are one-seven-seven," said Ezra. "I think it's enough for me to get an owner for the car."

"You can do that?" Jacqui asked. "Is it legal?"

"My business subscribes to a database where I can get ownership information from license plates." Ezra booted up his second computer and opened a program. "What were those plates again?"

Gavin read off a series of letters and numbers. His brother typed them into a search engine. It took only seconds for a hit. "Henry Rollins," said Gavin, reading the screen over Ezra's shoulder. He glanced at Jacqui. "The name sound familiar to you?"

She shook her head slowly. "I don't think so."

"We should see what the internet has to say about Mr. Rollins," said Ezra, while opening a new tab.

There were several hits for Henry Rollins. Most of them were from small-claims court, where he'd been sued for nonpayment. Gavin said, "Looks like he has a lot of financial issues."

"Yeah, but what does that have to do with the wild mustangs?" Jacqui asked.

It was a reasonable question.

Ezra added three words to his internet search. "Wild.

Mustangs. Colorado. The horses, I will add, are a twist I wasn't anticipating."

That combination brought up a notable hit. It was an article from the local paper on the roundup from two years prior. There, on the front page, was a picture of Jacqui along with a caption: Wildlife biologist from the Bureau of Land Management discusses how roundup makes for a healthier ecosystem.

"Henry Rollins had something to do with that last roundup?" Jacqui asked, her voice filled with incredulity.

"Let's see where he is in the article." Ezra searched the newspaper's site and found a black-and-white picture of a man on the back of a horse. The caption read: Cowboys, like Henry Rollins, round up wild mustangs. The horses are then sold to buyers around the country.

"Are you sure you don't know Henry?" Gavin asked.

"Positive," said Jacqui. "I hate to say it, but the roundup is a big operation. I was in charge, sure. But I didn't know every single person who worked for me. The cowboys, especially. The government contracts with a local operation, and the operation provides the ranch hands."

Gavin had a lot of questions. Was Henry Rollins the person who called Jacqui at her office? Had he forced her off the road? Both? Neither? Either way, Gavin needed to speak to the man. "Can you get me an address where the plates are registered?"

"Sure," said Ezra. He toggled the mouse. A printer in the corner began to whir as it slowly spit out a sheet of paper. "This is all the information I can get without going into the office."

Gavin scanned the page. There was a name and an address for a small town west of Blue Larkspur. "We can start by checking out this place." He folded the page and slipped it into his pocket. "Thanks, man. I owe you one."

"You can't leave yet." Ezra rose from his seat. "I collected all my techy gadgets for you." After picking up the box from the floor, he set it back on the desk. "The least you can do is hang out while I play show-and-tell."

Sincerely, he had missed his brother's sense of humor. Even if he *hadn't* missed feeling like the odd one out in the Colton family.

"What've you got?" Jacqui asked, stepping forward. Gavin admired the way she moved. Her motions were slow and languid, like a cat waking up from a nap.

"Since we have an address for that car, I have a tracking device." Ezra removed a metal box that was the size and shape of a cell phone. He pressed a button on the side twice and a light glowed green. "It has a battery life of forty-eight hours. And this—" he tilted the device to show the opposite side "—is a panic button. One click." He hit the button. "And I'll know." The screen on his computer changed to a map with a blinking red dot. "The back is magnetized so it'll stick to anything metal."

"Is tracking someone legal?" Jacqui asked.

Sure, Gavin wanted a story for his listeners. He just didn't want to break the law—or worse, go to jail.

"It depends," said Ezra, setting the tracker on his desk. "On if you get caught—or not."

"I'm not sure if I love that answer," said Gavin.

"Me either," said Jacqui.

"I'll give you the tracker and you can make up your own mind." He picked up Gavin's phone from where it sat on Ezra's desk. "I'll download the app to your cell. Then, you can see everything in real time." He handed the phone back to Gavin. "All set.

"And these are for surveillance of the range." Ezra removed a small lens from the box. It was attached via a cord to a black plastic box the size of a deck of cards. "Remote camera. Battery life, two weeks. And this," he said, removing a hunk of what appeared to be sandstone, "is made out of plastic."

"Let me see," said Gavin, reaching for the rock. "I'll be damned." Not only did it look completely realistic, but the bottom was hollow. There was a dime-sized hole for the lens.

"I have four cameras, along with their batteries. There're four decoy stones in here as well so that you can leave it all outside. Here's the deal, there's no way to remotely access this setup. You need the camera physically to review what it captures, but this is best for what you want."

"Thanks, man. I owe you." His chest was tight with gratitude. "And actually, what *do* I owe you? I told you that I'd pay."

"And I told you that Coltons stick together. You don't owe me a thing."

He wanted to argue but stopped as the security monitor winked to life. A car pulled up at the curb and parked behind Gavin's. Even with a grainy picture, he recognized the driver. It was his eldest sister. "Morgan," he whispered.

Ezra glanced at the screen. "Looks like it." And then, "You two gonna be okay?"

Gavin shrugged. "Honestly, I'm not sure. Aside from you and Caleb, I haven't spoken to anyone all that recently."

He gave a grunting laugh. "What? You just thought that you'd sneak into town and not see anyone in the family?"

The criticism stung and he snapped back, "It's not like anyone ever misses me."

"You know, sometimes you really can be a smug brat."

"Besides, I told Caleb that I'd stop by tonight for dinner," he said, his voice rising alongside his temper. "He said that Rachel would be there, at least. So, you don't need to lecture me on being a good brother."

"Maybe," said Jacqui, her voice small, "I should wait out in the car."

"I'll come with you," said Gavin, ready to leave his brother's house. He'd been wrong to come back to Blue Larkspur. Wrong to think that the past was behind any of them. Wrong to think that his old wounds would ever heal. He turned for the door.

"Hey, man," said Ezra.

He stopped and turned around. "What?"

His brother held the box. "You forgot something."

Gavin paused and reached for the tech. It was heavier

than he expected. "Thanks." He waited a beat. "You'll tell Theresa thanks for me, right? It was nice meeting her, and those two girls are great."

"You can tell her yourself and get to know the girls and Theresa more, if you want. You're always welcome here, you know."

Gavin shrugged. He didn't agree with his brother about him being welcome. Then again, there was no use in arguing. "Thanks for the gear. We gotta get going."

Ezra led them down the hallway and pulled the door open. "Keep the tech as long as you need." He held up a hand. "And don't offer to pay me again. Despite what you say, we are family."

Gavin almost smiled, but his big sister—Morgan, Caleb's twin—was coming up the walk. Her dark hair was perfectly cut and cascaded over her shoulders in waves. She was dressed casually, in a floral dress and coordinating cardigan. But on her, it looked chic and polished—like always. She made eye contact with Gavin and her sunny smile was replaced by a stormy frown.

Folding her arms, she stopped on the walk. "I heard you'd come back to town. And I don't even get a freaking phone call?"

"Great to see you, too," said Gavin, his voice dripping with sarcasm.

"Morgan, it's a wonder why he doesn't call with a greeting like that," Ezra cut in.

She rolled her eyes. "Of course you'd take his side." For the first time she seemed to notice Jacqui, who hung back near the door. His sister exhaled, and some of her rancor disappeared. "Honestly, it's nice to see you. It's been too long." She opened her arms to Gavin for a hug.

He shifted the box to his side and reached out for a one-armed embrace. "Good to see you, too." He awkwardly patted his sister's back before stepping away.

"I heard that you're working on a podcast about Dad. Is that true?"

Sure, she and Caleb were all about cleaning up the Colton name. It's just that *he* had a right to their father's life, same as the rest of his siblings. He had a right to understand the past that had shaped not only his family's dynamic. His father's behavior had set the trajectory for his kids' lives. Yet did it matter anymore?

He'd chosen a different story to tell, and another fight changed nothing. "Actually, I'm working with Jacqui Reyes on a different project." He stepped to the side and nodded toward Jacqui. "She works for the Bureau of Land Management."

Morgan stepped forward. "Nice to meet you," she said, as the two women shook hands.

"Nice to meet you, too," said Jacqui. Sure, she'd smiled at his sister. But she'd also glanced at Gavin and folded her arms across her chest.

Was it Gavin's imagination, or had this whole episode left Jacqui uncomfortable? And that brought up another question. What did she think of his large and messy family? For the most part, Gavin didn't give a crap what others thought of him—or his work. But for some reason, Jacqui's opinion mattered.

Chapter Eight

Jacqui sat in the passenger seat as Gavin drove. They'd entered the address for Henry Rollins's house into his GPS, and the town of Blue Larkspur disappeared into their rearview mirror.

"What's the plan?" she asked. "Are you going to try and interview Henry?"

Gavin shook his head. "I have a different idea."

"Oh yeah, what's that?"

"I want to know where Henry is going—who he's meeting with."

"So, you want to use the tracker?"

He shrugged.

Sure, Jacqui wanted to find out what was happening on the range. But Ezra had made it pretty clear that placing a device on a car wasn't exactly legal. She supposed that now was the time to ask herself a single question. What was she willing to do to discover what was happening on the range? Or maybe it was something different. Was she tired of working hard, following all the rules, and yet never getting ahead? "We can at least drive by his house, right? That's not illegal."

"No." The car slowed as they approached the entrance to a housing development. "It's not."

Two sandstone pillars stood on opposite sides of the road. Black lettering had been chiseled into the stone.

"'Town Square Villas,'" she read out loud. "Sounds swanky."

Gavin lifted his brow. "They were, but that was years ago."

The small houses were all in need of new paint now. Weeds grew through cracks in the sidewalk and choked the decorative stonework that served as front yards. Jacqui nodded slowly. "Definitely looks like it's seen better days."

Turn left here. The mechanized voice of the navigation system read off the directions. It didn't take long for Jacqui to figure out two things. First, the development was set up on a grid. It made driving through the neighborhood simple. Second, each street was named after a tropical island. Saint Croix. Jamaica. Antigua. Barbados.

Your destination is on the right. Gavin slowed as they drove by a bungalow with gray siding that at one time might've been white.

Jacqui looked at the street sign. "Cuba Court." She gave a short laugh.

"What's so funny?" Gavin asked, easing the car around the corner.

"My parents emigrated from Cuba when they were teenagers."

"Maybe it'll be lucky for us, then," he said.

Cuba hadn't been a lucky place for her parents. True,

her family faced their own challenges in America. Her parents arrived in Miami with nothing but a desire to work hard. No money. Hell, they didn't even speak much English. But if they'd been able to change their fate, then Jacqui could, too. She said, "Maybe."

She saw it in the driveway from half of a block away. "Is that it?" Leaning forward, her heart started to hammer against her ribs.

"Sit back," Gavin instructed, giving her shoulder a little push.

Jacqui leaned back into the seat, yet her spine was still rigid.

"Look at the plates as I drive but try not to stare. Read them off to me."

Jacqui didn't ask how she was supposed to look, read, and still not stare. Still, she did it.

"We found him," said Gavin. His bright smile turned Jacqui's middle to jelly.

Or maybe it was what she was about to say next that left her stomach trembling. "How are we supposed to get the tracker on his car?"

"So, we're going to do this?"

"What'd your brother say—it's not illegal if we don't get caught?" Was she really ready to break the law? Yeah, Jacqui was ready to take a risk. "Besides, we need to find out what's going on."

Gavin drove to the end of the street and parked next to a playground. "There's a few problems we're going to have."

"Only a few?" she joked.

He gave a small laugh. "First, is getting the device on the car without anyone noticing."

"That's going to be hard in the middle of the day. Harder still, in the middle of a neighborhood."

"True," Gavin said. "And we definitely can't let the guy see what we're doing."

"Do we come back later? Like at night, or something?"

"I hate the idea of waiting," Gavin began.

Jacqui did, too, but said nothing.

"I have an idea." He reached past Jacqui and opened the glove box, pulling out a paper map. "I'm going to go to his front door and ask him for directions. That way, he's distracted. And it's got to be me. This guy has seen you before."

It made sense and Jacqui nodded. "And then, what?"

Gavin took the tracker from a box in the back. "Can you place this under the rear bumper?"

Jacqui swallowed. Could she? Maybe she should be asking a different question—did she have a choice? "Sure," she said, her voice filled with more confidence than she felt.

"Click this twice to turn it on," said Gavin, pressing a button on the side of the unit.

"Press the button twice," she repeated.

Gavin held the slim metal device in his palm. Jacqui took the tracker; its back was magnetized and would hold to anything metal. If everything went well, she'd only need a few seconds to get it placed. But would she really get so lucky?

"I'll go first," Gavin said, turning his car around in

the middle of the quiet street. "And park behind his car. That way, he won't be able to see you from the door. What's more, I will block you from the road."

It made sense. "Are you sure you haven't done this sort of thing before?"

He smiled. "Not this exactly…" Gavin pulled onto the narrow driveway and put his car in park. "When you hear him answer the door, you'll have to move."

"Don't worry," she said, "I'll move."

"I'm going to leave the driver's door open. That way, no sound will give you away."

If Jacqui hadn't been so nervous, she would've been impressed by the way Gavin's mind worked. They had a plan to plant the tracker. Her throat was dry, but she swallowed.

He reached for her hand and squeezed her finger-tips. She looked at their joined hands and breath caught in her chest. His touch felt so right and dangerous all at the same time. Yet, Jacqui refused to be distracted by a man—especially when it came to doing her job—and let her fingers slip from Gavin's grasp. "Let's do this, then."

He gave her one more small smile and opened the car door. "We've got this," he said, and then, he was gone.

She scooted into the driver's seat and strained to hear over the engine's purr.

A chime of a doorbell.

Nothing.

The rapping of knuckles on a wooden door.

Another knock, louder this time.

The creak of hinges that needed greased, and then a rough voice. "Yeah?"

"Hey, man," said Gavin. "I hate to bother you, but I've gotten turned around. My aunt lives on Cayman Pathways and I can't find it. You mind helping me out?"

It was her cue to move. Jacqui slid from the car and crouched low as she moved between the grille of Gavin's ride and the dark sedan's rear. Dropping to her knees, she reached under the bumper.

Damn. It was polycarbonate of some kind—and definitely not metal.

She scooted farther under the auto. The muffler was metal—she could feel the tracker's magnet pull in her hand. But the exhaust was sure to get hot. How much heat could the device handle? It was a little too late to be asking that question—especially since Gavin wouldn't have much time at the door. She pressed the side button twice—just like Gavin instructed—and let the tracker connect with the muffler. She gave it a tug. The device didn't want to move.

Good enough. She scooted out from beneath the car just as Gavin strode into view. Wordlessly, Jacqui scrambled into the driver's seat and then clambered over to the passenger side. She dropped low into the seat in case Rollins was looking out his front window as Gavin drove away.

Gavin put the car in reverse and backed down the driveway.

"You're safe now," he said, maneuvering around a corner.

Jacqui exhaled, blowing a wayward strand of hair

from her face. Sitting up in the seat, she drew a deep breath. "That was intense. Is your job always like this?"

"Almost never," he said, answering her question. "But you got the tracker on the car? You turned it on?"

She nodded. "It's on the muffler."

"Great." His phone was wedged into the center console. Gavin picked it up and handed it to Jacqui. "Open the app and let's make sure that it works."

She did as he asked and stared at the screen for a moment, not believing what she saw. "Off line," she said, reading the app's notification. "That's impossible. I hit the button twice—just like Ezra said."

It was then that she realized their mistake.

Gavin must've realized it, too. He cursed. "Aw. Damn."

"But because you pushed the button once already..."

He picked up where she left off, "And then you pushed the button twice more..."

"We turned off the device." Jacqui wasn't sure if she should laugh or cry. "What do we do now? We can't go back."

"Not right now, that's for sure. Once it's dark, we'll have another chance."

Jacqui didn't like the newest wrinkle in their plan— but she was out of options and the clock was ticking. If she couldn't find evidence about who wanted to take the wild mustangs from the range, would the herd survive?

HENRY HAD MADE some foolish choices in his life. Yet, it did not mean that he was a fool. Moreover, he was a betting man. And he had to wonder at the odds that someone randomly needed directions and decided to stop at his house.

He couldn't guess at the odds, but he knew that it would be a crap wager to place.

Patting down his pockets, he found the card that T.J. had forced him to take. He read it once again: *Crime Time*, Gavin Colton, Journalist and Podcaster. There was also a phone number. After grabbing his phone from the table, he did some background research on the man in question.

It didn't take long to find a picture of the host, Gavin Colton. Without question, it was the same man who'd been standing at his door only moments before. It was the same person who'd discovered Henry through the tobacco shop.

What did Colton know?

Henry glanced at the card. He could call the number and tell the guy everything—just like T.J. suggested. The notion left him lighter, like he'd just set down a heavy rock that'd been strapped to his back for months.

Hell, Henry had forgotten what it was like to live without the burden of fear and regret. Quickly, he typed in the number and his finger hovered over the call icon. A bead of sweat clung to his brow. He wiped it away with his wrist.

The phone began to ring with a shrill jangle. He jumped at the sound and glanced at the screen. Bile rose in the back of his throat and he swallowed it down. Caller ID read: Silas Dunn.

The ringing continued.

Stopped.

Started once again.

"Dammit," he muttered, before swiping the call open.

"What the hell is the matter with you? You think I got all day to wait around for you to answer?" the loan shark asked.

"No, I… I…" he stammered.

"I… I… I…" Silas repeated with a mean laugh. "I didn't know you was a stutterer."

"I'm not," said Henry. His old friend, rage, took root in his chest. Yet, he couldn't direct any of his anger at the loan shark. He decided to lie. "I was takin' a crap is all, and you interrupted."

"You aren't sitting on the toilet right now, are you? Because that would make me sick."

"No, I'm not." Henry pinched the bridge of his nose. How had he gotten tangled up with the likes of Dunn? Trying to win more to pay off gambling losses had become a terrible cycle. It sucked Henry into the cyclone of financial destruction. At the time, Dunn offered calm. What Henry should've guessed, but didn't, was that Silas stood in the eye of the storm. "What can I do for you?"

"We're getting those horses tonight."

"Tonight?" His heart skipped a beat. "Are you sure that's best?"

Silas had already hung up. He looked at the phone. Gavin Colton's contact information was still on the screen. He deleted it and tucked the phone into his pocket.

Henry was in too deep to ask for help now.

He had no choice but to do what he was told. Because he still wasn't a fool—there was more at stake than just financial ruin. It was his life as well.

THE ENGINE REVVED as Gavin's car climbed the mountain road. The pavement followed the terrain, switching back and forth. He hadn't seen a car for miles. And honestly, he loved the feeling of power—like harnessing a mechanized beast—that came with driving on the open road. Ahead was a hairpin turn and he dropped his foot on the brake as he steered.

Everything considered, he was enjoying the drive far too much. And it wasn't just that he was pushing his car—and his driving abilities—to the limits. He loved having Jacqui at his side. They shared a love of adventure, that was obvious. But there was more that drew him to her. Being with Jacqui meant that Gavin never felt like he was alone.

He glanced in her direction. The sun shone through the windshield, lighting her dark brown hair on fire. Her cheeks were flushed, and the corners of her mouth were turned up in a small smile. It looked like she enjoyed the exhilaration and freedom that came from the open road as much as Gavin.

They crested the top of the hill, and a single road ran over top the plateau.

"There's a turnoff ahead." Jacqui shifted in her seat, leaning toward Gavin. The neck of her T-shirt gaped at the front, giving him a perfect view of her cleavage. He wasn't a creep—he wouldn't stare down her top. But it was impossible to miss the curve of her breasts beneath her shirt. She continued, oblivious to his physical reaction, "It's on the left."

"I figured." Gavin forced his eyes back on the road.

"I guess that taking a right would cause problems."

"You can say that again."

To their left were mountains. To the right was a steep cliff that dropped off into the valley below.

"See it up there?" Jacqui pointed and moved closer to Gavin's seat.

He let off the accelerator and the car slowed. Ahead and on the left, a dirt track led into the rocky wilderness. Either side of the road was marked with metal fencing that enclosed part of the range and a sign that read: Property of the Department of the Interior, Managed by the Bureau of Land Management, No Trespassing.

Gavin slowed even further as he made the turn. His car rumbled off the pavement and onto the narrow dirt road. His sleek European coupe was made for highway driving in the Alps—not off-roading in Western Colorado. Still, he had faith that his car could handle the track. "How bad is the road?" he asked, raising his voice to be heard above the grinding of tires on loose gravel.

"It's really well maintained. The ruts aren't too bad, so your undercarriage won't get damaged."

Gavin relaxed a little. "Good to know. I'd hate for us to get stuck out here—that's all." That was almost a lie. Sure, being stuck in the middle of nowhere came with its own problems. But would it really be that bad to be lost with Jacqui?

"Especially since you have dinner at your brother's house later," she said. "What was his name? Caleb?"

"I'm not sure that I'll go. After all, we have to fix that tracker…"

Jacqui shrugged. "What goes on between you and your siblings isn't really my business, you know?"

Gavin knew that he should let the conversation end. The problem was, he couldn't.

In that moment, Gavin realized an important truth. He *wanted* to tell someone about his past. He wanted to explain to another person what it was like to grow up as the forgotten Colton. What's more, he wanted that person to be Jacqui Reyes.

"There are a lot of dynamics in my family," he began.

"I understand. There are lots of dynamics in every family," said Jacqui. "But honestly, you don't owe me an explanation. I won't judge you—or them. I promise."

Sure, she'd given him a pass and he need not say anything. But the urge to speak was strong. He'd spent his whole life telling stories about other people. Had it all been to avoid saying anything about himself?

"My father used to be a judge," Gavin began. "He was well-known in town. Everyone liked and respected him. My parents had lots of friends. My older siblings went to nice schools, and everybody liked them because they were Judge Colton's kids…" He let his words trail off. Maybe he'd be a different person if he'd lived Caleb's and Morgan's lives. Or even Ezra and the rest of the triplets to a certain degree.

Jacqui sat in the seat next to him and said nothing. Yet, she watched him as he spoke. He looked in her direction. Their gazes met and held. He turned his eyes back to the winding dirt road.

"When I was only a few years old, my father was accused of sending people to jail for cash. What's worse, the accusations were true. He ruined a lot of people's lives by doing what he did. When his crimes came to light, the coward wound up dying in a car accident, leaving all of us to live with his legacy." Gavin's hands were shaking, and he gripped the steering wheel tighter. He continued, "By that time, my mom had a dozen of us. The older kids had led a good life until then and could handle the blow. There are a lot of twins and triplets in our family—and as you can imagine, they all have a strong bond."

"And you?" Jacqui asked. "Are you a twin, or a triplet?"

"Me? I'm not the only single birth but I'm the forgotten child."

Chapter Nine

"I'm sure your mother loves you…" Jacqui began.

Gavin stopped her with a shake of his head. "You ever see the movie about the kid who gets left home during the holidays? His family goes to Europe and he's asleep in the basement or something?"

"Yeah," she said, her tone hesitant. Gavin knew that Jacqui could guess where his story was going.

"I was about four or five years old the day that my mom planned to take us all to Glenwood Springs. We were supposed to swim at the hot springs and have lunch."

"Oh, no."

"Oh, yeah. They made it halfway to Glenwood before she ever realized that I wasn't in the car."

"I'm so sorry. You must've been terrified." She rested her hand on his arm. Most of the time, Gavin didn't want sympathy. But from Jacqui it was different.

"It was one of my first memories." His voice didn't hold a hint of emotion, but his eyes burned. "There I was, alone in the house. Barely old enough to go to the bathroom by myself. Definitely not old enough to cook.

I used safety scissors to cut open a box of cereal and ate it dry." He gave a wry laugh. "Other boxes of cereal in the pantry were already opened, but I grabbed the sugary one. I guess I was already a bit of a rebel."

Jacqui's hand still rested on his arm. She gave a quick squeeze. "There's a turnoff about one hundred yards ahead. You'll want to park your car, and then we can walk." She let her hand slip from his arm, but her fingers still rested on the center console.

The pressure to tell the rest of his story built in his chest—a great bubble, ready to burst free. It was like his tale could only be told in the small confines of his car. Once he got out, his resolve would vanish. "As I sat on the kitchen floor and ate the cereal, I couldn't help but wonder—why me? What had I done that caused my mom to leave me behind? Why was I the one that nobody loved?" Gavin's voice caught on the last word. He cleared his throat. "I know my mother loves me. I know she was under a tremendous amount of stress. I know that leaving me was an accident and an oversight. In fact, the moment she realized what'd happened, she called Chief Lawson. He came to the house and made me pancakes. We hung out until the family got back." He saw the turnoff and pulled his car onto another dirt road, narrower than the last, and filled with ruts and rocks. His sports car, with its low profile, would never make the climb.

Gavin braked. His fingers grazed the leather-covered gearshift, yet he didn't shift into park. There was more about that day he wanted to share. "My mother was a mess when she came home." After everything, it

seemed like he still had a need to defend her honor—
even if he was the one who'd been wronged. Gavin's
gaze was locked onto his fingertips. He traced the
stitching at the seams of the knob. "She truly was upset
with what had happened."

He paused. There was more to the story, but was he
willing to share the rest of it? The events of that day
were decades old. Still, they'd created a painful wound
that continued to be reopened. He began to speak, surprised by his own voice—especially since he hadn't
decided to *say* anything.

"But Morgan was mad. She was mad that the outing
had been ruined—like I'd hidden or something and that
it was somehow my fault. She was mad that I'd eaten
the sugary cereal. I think she was mad that Mom was
simply paying attention to me." The unforgotten resent-
ment bubbled in his gut, filling his mouth with the sour
taste of indignation. He gave a wry laugh.

He shoved the gearshift into park and turned off
the ignition. Without the rumbling engine, the silence
was total. In the quiet, Gavin couldn't help but hear his
own worries. Had he said too much? How was Jacqui
going to respond?

Then there was another question—one he was unwilling, or maybe it was afraid, to ask. What did Gavin
actually want from Jacqui?

He continued to trace the stitching on the gearshift
with his thumb. "Say something."

"I'm sorry that you had to live through that moment—that morning. I'm sorry that it left you mis-

trustful of your mother and has led to a tempestuous relationship with your sister."

He looked up at her. The sun shone on her from behind, leaving her features in the shadow and surrounding her with a halo of gold. It left Gavin blinded, dazzled, and he dropped his gaze. Yet some of the anger that stayed with him always now melted away.

"Thanks," he mumbled. And then, "That was just the first time of many that I was forgotten. Overlooked." He shrugged. "I'd like to say I got used to it…"

"Sounds like a death by a thousand cuts. Small injuries that have added up over the years." It was her turn to pause. "Not that being forgotten, or unseen, is a small injury. You're right to be upset. It's just…" Jacqui placed her hand on his. Her touch was warm and inviting. "It's just…" she repeated. And then, "Never mind."

Her palm began to slip away. He reached out and grabbed her fingertips with his own. "What if I don't want to never mind?"

She drew in a breath, a whisper of wind inside the car. "Forgiveness isn't about the other person, necessarily. It's about being able to let go of past hurts."

He'd heard that line—or something like it—before. Over the years, there'd been therapists. And ex-girlfriends. In fact, Gavin had an ex-girlfriend who'd *been* a therapist. "Don't worry, people have told me all of that before. Let go. Move on from the past. It's the toxicity of what happened years ago that's eating at you now."

Jacqui stroked the back of his hand with her thumb. The friction created a charge of electricity. It seeped into his skin, and his blood began to buzz. "That's not exactly what I'm saying." She ran her teeth over her bottom lip. He was mesmerized by her mouth. Her teeth. Her lips. He really wanted to know what she would say next.

"Yes?" he prompted.

"I think you need to confront what happened, sure. But you also need to make peace with what kind of relationship you can have with your family now."

"You saw my sister. What did you think of Morgan?"

"I wasn't around her long enough to pass judgment."

"That was a careful answer," he said, making light of the serious conversation.

"I appreciate that you recognize the needle I'm trying to thread."

All of a sudden, the car was too small. The sun was too bright, and the interior was stifling. He had to get outside. He needed to suck down fresh air like drinking from a fire hose. Sweat streamed down the back of his neck. He reached for the door's handle. "You ready?"

"Wait."

His hand still rested on the gearshift and her hand still rested on his. She gave his finger a squeeze. "If you didn't want to spend time with your family? Or, if you don't want to make peace with your past, why did you come back to Blue Larkspur?"

Ah. Now that was the real question. Gavin thought of one hundred different answers, yet he knew that none of them were true. At last, he said, "I don't know. It's just…" He stopped, unable to find the right words. Sure, he knew what he'd set out to accomplish, but Gavin felt as if he'd achieved even more by talking to Jacqui. What was it about her?

In truth, he knew.

With her, he felt seen, heard and understood—even if he didn't exactly understand himself. "Well, now you know all about my nutty family and why they drive me, well, nuts."

"For the record, I don't think that you're nuts."

He laughed. "That makes one of us, then."

She laughed as well. "Thanks for sharing."

He nodded but had nothing to add.

She said, "From here, it's a bit of a hike—a mile or so."

After opening the door, Gavin stepped from the car. A tough hike would do to help clear his mind. Then again, he had a lot to consider. Like, what did he want from his family?

HENRY ALREADY HATED HIMSELF. Leaning on the hood of his car, he flicked his lighter, then blew out the flame. Flick. Light. Extinguish. Again and again. He'd parked on the ridge overlooking the field where he'd tracked the horses. The morning sun shone on the mustangs' coats, and their flanks shimmered with reflected light.

Flick. Light. Extinguish.

Flick. Light. Extinguish.

Mesmerized by the dancing flames, Henry pondered the power of fire. It brought warmth, light, the ability to cook meat and boil water. In short, it *was* life. All the same, an inferno brought nothing other than a horrible death and complete destruction.

The profound thoughts pounded against the inside of his skull, and Henry reached into his pocket for his pouch of tobacco. Empty.

"Dammit." The word disappeared as it rolled out across the empty plain. In all the excitement at The House of Smoke—what with T.J. giving him Gavin Colton's business card—he'd forgotten to replace his tobacco. The headache turned from a pounding to a stabbing pain between his eyes.

Henry pinched the bridge of his nose and breathed. The sharpest edges of his headache smoothed out. He looked across the field and knew what he had to do next.

How had his love for these majestic creatures led him to be an instrument of their ruin? Then again, he knew.

He'd reached out to Jacqui Reyes in the hopes that she'd get in touch with the FBI. Or at least the local police. Instead, she'd come alone. He'd tried to scare her into calling the cops by pushing her from the road. Instead of being smart enough to get the authorities involved—making it impossible for Silas to steal an entire herd—she'd joined forces with a podcaster.

Who the hell does that?

Maybe he should have been more specific in his message. Or maybe, he should've called the cops himself. Or maybe he never should've taken the money from Dunn. Or maybe there were one hundred other *maybes* that could keep him awake at night. But now, none of that mattered. Jacqui and Gavin had found him. Soon, Silas would know what Henry had done.

He had to save the horses, and he only knew one way. He flicked his lighter to life once more. Cupping his hand over the flame, he bent down to a nearby tumble-weed. Touching the fire to the dry brush, he waited a minute until the whole thing was alight. Then, Henry kicked the ball of fire and watched as it rolled toward a clump of grass. The grass smoldered and a tendril of smoke rose in the air.

Sure, he was destroying the very land where the wild mustangs roamed. But the horses had their instincts that would keep them alive. They'd leave this high plain and find somewhere new to graze. In a few years, this plateau would recover.

But nothing short of the herd being gone would stop Silas Dunn.

He watched as a spark jumped from the clump of grass to a spindly juniper tree.

From there, who knew where the fire would go next?

Turning, he walked back to his car and slid into the driver's seat. He stepped on the gas, kicking up a rooster tail of dust and blocking his view of what he'd left behind.

THE GRAVITY OF what Gavin had shared wasn't lost on Jacqui. Sure, she didn't know him well, or really, at all. Still, he'd rarely spoken so openly about his family in the admittedly short time they'd known one another.

Honestly, she was touched that he'd taken her into his confidence.

And it left her with an interesting question. What should she do or say next?

The bright Colorado sun hung in a sky of brilliant blue. The temperature in Blue Larkspur had been warm, but on the mountaintop the air was crisp. Folding her arms across her chest, Jacqui trudged up the dirt road. It wasn't just the chill she was trying to avoid, but her feelings as well.

In Gavin, she saw a man worth saving. A person who needed understanding and care.

Then again, hadn't she seen the same in her ex-boyfriend at the beginning? And hadn't he tried to destroy her career?

Maybe she should be asking a different question. Was Jacqui always drawn to men who needed fixing? And if she was, then what did that say about her?

He walked just a few steps ahead of her. A backpack, filled with the cameras and camouflage, hung from one shoulder.

With each step, her boots crunched into the loose stone. As the climb grew steeper, her breaths came in short gasps. Other than that, there was no other sound. Jacqui had been quiet for too long. She needed to break the silence with something, but what?

Wheezing, she asked, "You okay with this hike?"

"I am." Gavin barely seemed to be out of breath. "And you asked me that already."

Had she? Damn. He was right. "Just checking." A stitch pulled at her side, and she drew a long breath in through her nose. The pain lessened. She walked on, trying to find the right words. They never came but she spoke anyway. "About what you said in the car," she began.

"Yeah, about that…"

Walking up the hill, she waited for Gavin to complete his thought.

He didn't.

"Thanks for what you told me." Her words felt like the right segue that was also a good combination of personal, honest, and yet vague enough to be universal. She paused, just in case he wanted to add anything.

He didn't.

"To start with, I really didn't judge any reaction you had to your family. I'm adult enough to know that we all have a past. Me. You. Your sister. Ezra. And even without you sharing your story, I'd know there was a story."

"Thanks," he said, giving his wry laugh.

Jacqui was starting to pick up on his signals. Like, she knew what he said was important. But what he left unsaid was supreme. She also knew he used his sardonic laugh—a glib mannerism—to gloss over a deep hurt. It was like a dirty bandage over a festering wound. He continued, "Then again, everyone has a story. Right?"

"Right."

Jacqui pressed her hands into the small of her back, bracing herself as the pitch of the hill increased. Was she supposed to do more? Say more? Before she could speak, Gavin asked, "What about you? What's your story?"

"Me? I'm the exception to the rule. I don't have one."

He gave his wry laugh again. "I don't believe that for a minute. You said your parents emigrated from Cuba. When? Why?"

It wasn't exactly Jacqui's story, but it was part of her foundation. Besides, she'd told the tale of her parents coming to America hundreds of times in her life. "My parents were young when they came to the United States. Not much more than kids. Both sets of grandparents had stayed in Castro's Cuba and hoped that the political upheaval would die down."

"And it didn't," said Gavin.

Jacqui rocked her hand from side to side. "Kinda. The food shortages that followed became untenable. You know Miami is only ninety miles from Havana. People all over the island were building rafts and setting sail. Several families from one village decided to make a run—or rather, a swim for the US." She paused and drew several deep breaths. "During the crossing, my parents clung to each other and really, they've never let go since."

"See. That's a nice story."

Was he joking? With Gavin, it was hard to tell. That was another thing she learned about him—everything was tinged with humor. Still, she said, "It is."

"And what about you?"

"What about me?"

"What's your story?"

"My dad worked as a mechanic until he retired. My mom started off as a housekeeper at a local motel. She worked her way up the ranks to being the housekeeping supervisor. Then, she was promoted to a front desk manager. By the time she retired, she'd been the manager for almost a decade."

"Your parents sound amazing. Smart. Hardworking. Fearless."

"They are pretty amazing," she agreed.

"But what about you?"

The top of the hill was less than one hundred yards away. Jacqui's legs ached. Her back was sore. Her lungs burned with each breath. Yet, she'd made it to the top of the ridge. "What about me? I've told you all about my job. Oh, I live in Denver and have a fifty-gallon aquarium with tropical fish."

"No boyfriend?"

"Not in the fish tank, no."

Gavin laughed at her joke. "Seriously, you already said that you aren't married. Are you dating anyone?"

"Are you trying to ask me out?" Jacqui was partly teasing, partly curious.

"Trying to gauge your story, is all."

Was she disappointed by his answer? "There's nobody in my life at the moment, if that's what you're asking."

At the top of the hill, she reached over her head and laced her fingers together. Bending at the waist from side to side in the Standing Side Bend pose. "I do yoga every morning, but I think I need to add some cardio. That hill kicked my butt. Look at you, you aren't even sweating." Pressing her hands together, she inhaled. After diving into a forward bend, Jacqui let the weight of her head and chest stretch the back of her body. "What's worse, I live in Colorado and should be used to the elevation. You're in Manhattan and that's at sea level."

Gavin pulled his damp shirt from his chest. "I'm sweating, but I run every morning."

Slowly, Jacqui rolled up her spine to standing. "Figures."

"Maybe I should take you for a run and then you can show me some yoga poses to do after."

Was he flirting with her? Or just being friendly?

Jacqui gave him her brightest smile. "Anytime."

Gavin moved toward Jacqui. He was so close that she could touch him—if she wanted. Was that what she wanted? Did she want to touch Gavin? To kiss him? To taste and explore him? Did Jacqui want to be kissed, tasted and explored in return?

She moved forward, erasing the space between them.

He stood without moving, allowing her to set the parameters of their exchange. Yet, at the base of his throat, Gavin's pulse raced. She lifted her hand to his face and placed her palm on his cheek. As she brushed her lips against his, she told herself that it was just a kiss. Even as he set her body on fire.

Chapter Ten

Gavin's pulse thundered in his ears, turning him deaf to every sound beyond his own racing heart and Jacqui's breath. Her lips were soft, but he wanted more. His fingers itched with the need to touch her.

Then, he heard it—a rustling sound in the bushes, the snapping of a twig underfoot—and his blood froze in his veins.

Gripping Jacqui's wrist, Gavin pulled her behind him—standing between her and whatever was in the bushes. He slipped the backpack, heavy with gear, off his shoulder and held it with one hand. If an assailant got too close, Gavin could strike them with the bag. It wasn't much of a weapon, but it was all he had.

"Hey, man," he called out. "Who's there? Come out slowly and you won't have to get hurt."

The rustling stopped.

"Come out."

Nothing.

Gravel on the ground began to shake a minute before a tremor ran up through the soles of Gavin's shoes. As if a hundred people began to run, the thunder of footfalls on the ground filled the quiet morning. "What in the hell is that?" he asked, as a cloud of dust rose in the distance.

Jacqui gripped his shoulder. "It's one of the mustangs." Her mouth was pressed to his ear so he could hear her over the drumbeat of horse hooves. "C'mon."

She laced her fingers through his and pulled him toward the sound. The trail through the brush was easy to follow. The horses had cut a swath through it. In the distance, Gavin caught a glimpse of a jet-black mustang. Its nostrils flared, and the powerful muscles of its legs flexed as it raced across the rocky ground.

"Jeez," he said, breathing hard as he slowed to a trot. "We'll never catch that horse. Did you see him? He was like a thundercloud coming to life." Gavin wiped his brow with the hem of his shirt. "Amazing. Just amazing."

Jacqui stood at his side. "Amazing," she echoed. "When I was here yesterday evening, the whole herd was grazing in a valley that's just beyond that ridge." She pointed to the left. "What I don't get is why he's all the way out here."

"That's not typical for horses?" Gavin supposed that he'd have to do a little research on equine behavior for the podcast.

Jacqui shook her head. "I don't know what made him scatter…" Her words trailed off as her gaze traveled to the ridgeline.

"What is it?" Gavin asked.

Jacqui lifted her hand. "Do you smell that?"

Gavin sniffed the air. Juniper. Pine. Dirt. Sweat. "What am I supposed to smell?"

"Is that smoke?"

He inhaled again, deeper this time. His heart ceased to beat. Faint, but unmistakable, the scent of smoke filled the air. "It is." He scanned the horizon. There was nothing but blue sky and mountain ranges for miles. "Where's it coming from?"

"I think it's close," Jacqui began. Then she saw it—a black cloud of smoke rising from the other side of the ridge.

"There." He pointed.

"The horses," she said, as she began to sprint toward the smoke.

"Wait," he cried out. "Jacqui, stop." As far as Gavin was concerned, there were many bad reasons to run into a fire. Danger. Destruction. Death. But none of them mattered and what's more, Jacqui wasn't interested in anything he had to say. It meant only one thing: he had to follow.

As he sprinted after her, his lungs filled with acrid smoke. Jacqui disappeared over the lip of the ridge. Gavin came up behind quickly and his gut dropped to his shoes. Several small fires burned in the valley below.

The mustangs whinnied and pawed the ground, terrified by the smoke and the fire.

True, the grazing horses had cropped most of the vegetation, but there was still plenty that could burn. Jacqui was running toward the closest fire—a clump of grass that was engulfed in flames. She kicked dirt on it, the cloud of dust choking out the blaze. Then, she stamped on the embers.

It was obvious that Jacqui planned to fight the fire single-handedly. And a big part of him admired her bravery. Then again, there was another part of him that feared her bravado would lead to her destruction. The plain was a bowl, set into the mountaintop. The fire was spreading fast—and by going down the slope, they could get trapped.

Gavin would have preferred more time to think, to plan, to come up with a strategy. The thing was, every second counted. He moved toward a bush that smoldered, stripping out of his jacket as he ran. Gavin slapped the flames with it. Fire leaped up, almost as if it were fighting back. His pulse spiked. He searched the valley for Jacqui. She was only a few dozen yards away, stomping on a new fire.

If they had to, could they escape?

He scanned the valley and quickly found a clear path to the ridge. They were okay, at least for now. Turning back to a fiery branch, Gavin slapped it with the jacket. The wood broke and the limb fell to the ground. He kicked dirt over the flames and stomped on it until there was nothing left but ash.

He moved to the next fire—a tumbleweed. Gavin slapped it with his backpack and the spindly plant burst into a hundred pieces. Bits of fire flew everywhere.

"Dammit." He cursed as sparks landed in the middle of a patch of dried grass. He crushed them with the toe of his shoe before they even had a chance to catch.

Gavin wiped sweat from his brow and scanned the

horizon. All the little fires seemed contained. Jacqui stood at the top of the ridge, shading her eyes with her hand. "What's it look like from up there?" he called out. "Is it clear?"

"I don't see any more fires if that's what you're asking. But there's something I found."

Gavin trudged toward Jacqui. The stench of smoke and soot clung to his clothes. He slipped his arm into his jacket. Pain engulfed his wrist and he pulled his arm loose. A burn—a red welt—circled his arm. When had that happened? He climbed the hill. "You okay?"

"Yeah," she said. "But my coat's ruined." She held up her jacket. It was blackened at the edges, and a hole had burned through one of the sleeves.

"Here." He held out his own coat. "You can wear mine."

She reached for his offered jacket and stopped. "You're hurt. Why didn't you say something?"

"It's nothing. A bit of a burn."

"A bit?" she echoed. "It's already blistered. We have to get some ointment and a bandage on that wound before it gets infected."

"I have a first aid kit in the car, but this can wait until we get back." Carefully, he shoved the sleeve of his shirt higher up on his forearm to avoid touching his wound. "What'd you want to show me?"

"This."

It took Gavin a second to realize that Jacqui was pointing with her foot. He knelt on the ground and examined the dirt. "Tire tracks?"

"And they're fresh, too."

"How do you figure?"

"They're pristine and we have a bit of a breeze. Tracks like this couldn't last for very long with the wind."

Gavin made a note of her words. *"Tracks like this couldn't last for very long with the wind."* That'd make it into the podcast, sure. The dirt was silty. "So, what does that mean? This fire wasn't an accident?"

"I don't think so," she replied.

They didn't have evidence, but his gut told him that she was right. "For now, let's assume that's the case. Who started the fire? And why?"

Jacqui lifted her eyebrow. "I have a guess."

"Henry Rollins." Gavin's pulse raced. The burn to his arm throbbed with each beat of his heart. Still, they had intel to collect. "For now, let's plant these cameras. Then we stick to our plan and revisit Henry's house after dark. That tracker needs to be enabled."

"Agreed."

He slid the backpack from his shoulder. The fabric grazed his wrist. Like a white-hot bolt of lightning shot through his arm, his wrist felt as if it were being burned all over again. Gavin grimaced with the pain.

Jacqui was at his side. "You okay? Of course you aren't okay. Let me take that from you."

She reached for his bag. Her fingertips grazed the back of his hand. Her touch was cool and soothing. The place where her fingers rested on his flesh warmed. An electric current ran up his arm. Had she felt the reaction, too?

Gavin's gaze met hers. Jacqui's eyes were wide. Her

mouth was moist. He moved toward her, just a fraction of an inch. She didn't retreat. He moved closer and closer still.

There was nothing to stop him from kissing Jacqui now. He placed his hand on her waist and gently pulled her to him. "I've wanted to do this since the first moment I saw you."

"Do what?" she asked, being coy.

"Kiss you," he whispered.

"What's stopping you, from doing it again, then?"

"I'm wondering if you want to kiss me, too."

Jacqui said nothing and placed her mouth on his.

Everything in Gavin's world melted away. The scent of smoke, which lingered on the breeze, no longer irritated his lungs. The burn on his wrist no longer hurt. The fact that his family drove him over the edge no longer bothered him.

For now, the woman in his arms was all that mattered.

JACQUI LEANED INTO the kiss. Her breasts were pressed against Gavin's chest. Her thighs were wrapped around his legs. Her fingers were tangled in his hair. And his tongue was in her mouth. Her heart raced and her skin tingled with his touch. And still, she wanted—no, *needed*—for him to be closer.

Maybe all the emotions that swirled and churned in her chest had been brought up during the fire. Or perhaps Jacqui had risked more in this single morning than she had in her entire life.

Whatever the reason, she didn't want to play it safe any longer.

Then again, hadn't she learned her lesson about trying to mix work and romance? "I…" She pushed lightly on his chest, creating space between them. "I don't know what came over me." No, that wasn't true. She knew what she'd done and why. Jacqui shook her head. "Actually, I've wondered what it would be like to kiss you from the moment I met you, too. And since the last kiss was interrupted."

He gave her that smile and her heartbeat raced.

"Well," she amended, "once I got over the fact that you're you and all. Still, I shouldn't have let my heart rule my head."

"Your heart?" he echoed.

Her heart wasn't the exact part of her anatomy that had been doing all the thinking. "You know what I mean."

Taking another step back, Jacqui scrubbed her hands over her face. It did no good. Her pulse still raced with his touch, and her lips still tingled with his kisses. What's worse, she wanted both again.

What was he thinking? What did he want? If he tried to kiss her again, would she have the fortitude to walk away? She thought not.

Jacqui took another step back. "We should probably plant those cameras and then get back to the car." She paused as a new thought came to her. "How's your wrist?"

Gavin examined his arm. "You know, it's burned and hurts like hell."

A pang of guilt shot through her chest. If it wasn't for her, Gavin wouldn't have gotten injured. Then again, if it wasn't for him, then the entire range would be in flames by now. Holding out her hand, she offered, "I can plant the cameras."

Careful to avoid his wound, Gavin swung the bag off his back. "I'm hurt but I can still help. Besides, we'll get done faster if we work together." He set the pack at his feet and opened a zippered pocket. Gavin removed a small camera connected to a black battery by a thick cord. Next, he removed a brown resin rock. True, it didn't match the landscape exactly, but it was close enough to escape all but the closest scrutiny.

"Here you go."

She took the offered device. "Thanks. Now, where do we put these?"

"The rock can hide the camera, but the battery needs light to work." Shielding his eyes with his hand, he scanned the range. "How about we put one up there." He pointed to a spot where several boulders leaned into each other. "Put it on the top and then, nobody will see the battery, unless they're up that high."

"Good plan." She scrambled to the top of the rock pile, set the device to record and then played back several seconds. The picture captured was a wide view of the entire valley. She called out to him, "How's this?"

Gavin stood next to the base of a charred juniper. He glanced in her direction and gave her a wide smile along with a cheesy thumbs-up. "Looks good."

She slid down the rock face. She turned to check her work. From the ground, the camouflaged rock blended in with the boulders perfectly. Gavin held two cameras—one in each hand. Dusting off the seat of her pants, Jacqui ambled toward him.

As she approached, he spoke. "If we call this the center line of the valley, we need to cover the western and eastern edges as well."

Jacqui took both cameras. "I'll go west, you go east."

"That's a solid plan, but how are you going to carry the cameras and the camouflage rocks?"

She saw the dilemma. With both hands full, how was she supposed to carry the fake stones as well? Lifting her elbows like chicken wings, she said. "Tuck the rocks in here. I can walk a few hundred yards with them tucked under my arms."

Gavin gave a quiet chuckle, and Jacqui could well imagine that she looked silly—maybe even foolish.

Then again, she wasn't always polished and poised. Did it bother her that Gavin had noticed? Maybe *bother* was too big a word. Still, her cheeks stung like she'd been slapped.

"What's so funny?" she asked, her voice full of defiance.

"You."

"What's so funny about me?"

"Well, it's not funny really. Still, you are one of the most resourceful people I've ever met. There's not a challenge you can't overcome, is there?"

Her neck and shoulders relaxed from tension that she'd been holding for a lifetime. "That's the nicest thing anyone's ever said to me."

"Really?" He held two of the fake stones. "You ready for these?"

It seemed as if the moment had passed. Yet, for the first time in a while, Jacqui Reyes felt understood and appreciated.

HENRY STOPPED AT a Quickie-Mart near his housing development for a six-pack of beer and a pack of smokes. Sure, he liked to roll his own cigarettes, but after starting the fire, his nerves were fried.

He approached the register. The cashier was a kid with brown hair the same shade as his Quickie-Mart T-shirt. "What happened to you?" he asked. "You get beat up or something?"

Henry pulled the brim of his hat lower over his eyes. "Or something," he said, placing his purchases and a twenty-dollar bill on the counter.

"You want a bag for that?" The teen behind the counter made change. He slid the bills and coins toward Henry.

Henry planned to pop the top on his beer as soon as he got behind the wheel of his car. Hell, if it went well, he'd be good and buzzed before he even got home— and that was only a few blocks away. "I don't need no bag." He tucked the cans under his arm and unwrapped the cellophane from the package of cigarettes. "You got any matches?"

The cashier slipped a cardboard square across the counter. "That's fifty cents."

On a day that was already lousy, that fact rankled

Henry. "When did people start charging for matches?" he snapped.

The kid shrugged and pulled two quarters out of the pile of change.

Henry grabbed his money and the matches. He shoved both into his pocket, leaving the cigarette wrapper on the counter. Without another word, he walked from the store and kept his eyes on the dirty concrete sidewalk. He couldn't—or rather, wouldn't—look up. He knew what he'd see. By now, the fire would be unstoppable. Black clouds of smoke would be rolling off the mountain, like a fog off the sea.

Yet, the horses would know enough to scatter. Soon, they'd find another place to graze. In a year or two, the grasses would be growing again. The wild mustangs would return. But before that happened, Silas would have to abandon his plan to round up the entire herd.

Still walking, Henry tapped out a smoke. He caught the tip between his lips and stuffed the rest of the pack into the breast pocket of his shirt. He struck one of the matches and held the tip to the cigarette. Once the tobacco caught, he drew in a deep breath. As the nicotine buzzed through his system, Henry found the courage to look at the mountain. His blood turned cold in his veins at the sight.

There was no smoke. There was no fire. How had his plan gone so wrong?

Chapter Eleven

With all the cameras planted around the valley, there was nothing more for Gavin and Jacqui to accomplish. They returned by the rutted road to Gavin's car at the foot of the hill. When they'd left for the range, he'd tucked his keys into a side pocket on the leg of his pants. He didn't need to get them out to open the door or start the engine.

It was a small miracle because with the burn to his wrist, he'd never be able to reach for the keys. He pushed a button on the passenger handle to disengage the locks.

Jacqui opened her own door. "Where's your first aid kit?"

Gavin recalled the small plastic envelope with bandages and ointment that was part of a thank-you gift for his expensive purchase from the auto dealership. "It's in the glove box."

She bent at the waist to get into the coupe, and the sight of her pert rear left him hungry with want. How had he become so muddled by lust in just a few short hours? What was it about Jacqui Reyes? He dropped his gaze as she backed out of the car and stood straight.

"Here it is." She held up the envelope and examined the contents through the clear plastic. "There's not much, but we can get you patched up a little bit, at least." After opening the flap, she dumped the contents onto the hood of the car. Four plastic bandages. Three rubbing alcohol wipes in foil packets. Antibiotic ointment in a tube the size of a baby's thumb.

Without a word, Jacqui opened one of the alcohol wipes and cleaned her hands. Next, she opened the ointment and placed a generous daub on her finger. "Let me see your wrist."

Dutifully, he held out his arm. She touched her finger to the burn and a spike of pain shot through his wrist. He grimaced.

"Sorry," she said, smoothing the ointment on his wound. "I know this must hurt."

It did—and at the same time, it didn't. Gavin would admit, if only to himself, that Jacqui's touch had a healing effect. Of course, he knew that she wasn't magical. Yet to be cared for by another was somehow medicinal. Therapeutic. Soothing. Lately, he hadn't needed anyone's touch for anything beyond momentary pleasure. But that wasn't always true. There had been a few women over the years who he had cared for—maybe even loved. When those relationships didn't work out, had he turned off his emotions?

"It's better," he said. "Really."

She wiped her fingertips on the used alcohol pad. "Now, let's get a bandage on that arm." She sifted through the bandages from the first aid kit. Before Jacqui said a word, he knew there were going to be problems.

The edge of the wrappers was brown and brittle with age. "You think those'll work?" he asked, his tone dubious.

"We can hope." Jacqui opened one of the bandages and the paper backing fluttered away from an adhesive side that no longer had any sticking power. She lifted her eyebrows and sighed. "I can drive us back to town. I don't want you to accidentally bump that arm of yours. We can stop at a store and get a proper med kit. I'll get you patched up. Then, you'll be on your way to healed in no time."

Memories of his childhood home filled his mind, and for some reason, he wanted to see his mom. It was a visit that he'd avoided since returning to Blue Larkspur.

Why did he want to go now?

Was it because Jacqui's touch had reminded him what it was like to be cared for?

Or had sharing the story of the day he'd been forgotten dredged up long-ignored emotions? And now, Gavin was ready to examine what had been festering in his soul for decades?

Or maybe the draw to go home wasn't as complicated as any of that. Maybe it was simply that he wanted his mom to meet Jacqui.

"I know somewhere else that we can go. It's not too far from here," said Gavin, speaking before he'd even made up his mind.

"Oh yeah?" she asked while tucking all the debris into the plastic envelope. "Where's that?"

Gavin exhaled. "Home," he said, the word sticking in his throat. He coughed and tried again. "We're going to go to my home."

To say that Gavin's sports car drove like a dream wouldn't quite be true. Jacqui never had dreams that were as exhilarating as steering the sleek auto as it hugged the pavement with each bend in the road.

"You have a hell of a car," she said, unable to keep from smiling as she spoke. She wanted to ask how much a European coupe with a rocket engine cost. Then again, she figured it was more than she could afford on a government salary.

"Thanks. I don't get a chance to drive it much—with living in a city and all." He pointed to the windshield. "You'll want to turn left at this next intersection." A decorative sign sat on each side of the road. Green Valley.

"Go to the end of the road and take another left."

Jacqui followed Gavin's directions. True, she'd lived in Colorado for years. And sure, she'd seen lots of developments like Green Valley in that time. It was made up of large houses that sat on massive lots. It was also true that in Miami, where Jacqui lived as a kid, there was wealth and opulence beyond belief. Yet, she never quite got over places like this.

"Now take a right. Two-zero-one Richland Avenue. It has a circular drive. You'll see it."

Jacqui counted off the house numbers on mailboxes

as they passed. Finally, 201 Richland. There was a security gate with a keypad. Gavin entered the code. The Colton family home was large and rambling, even by the standards of the neighborhood. "Looks like a nice place to grow up," she said, pulling onto the driveway.

Parked in front of the door was a police cruiser.

Gavin tensed as he leaned forward in the seat. She could tell that he was worried. And his concern left her worried, too. The car lurched to a stop.

She looked at Gavin. He stared back at her. His eyes were wide.

"Everything okay with your mom?" Of course, he wouldn't know the answer, but still she had to ask.

"I'm not sure." After unlatching his seat belt, he opened the door. Sliding out of the car, Gavin slammed the door shut and jogged toward the house.

With the press of a button, Jacqui stilled the engine. She followed Gavin up a short flight of steps. He didn't bother with knocking and pushed the front door open.

"Mom?" Gavin called out. His voice was full of concern. "Mom? Where are you?"

"Gavin?" a woman's voice answered. "Gavin, good Lord. Is that you?"

An older woman with shoulder-length blond hair wandered from the back of the house. She wore a white linen shirt and jeans. No shoes. Even though Gavin had dark hair and deep blue eyes, Jacqui could tell that this woman was his mother.

"Hey, Mom. There's a police car outside. Are you okay?"

"Oh sure, honey." A tall man with gray hair and a

Blue Larkspur police uniform came from the back of the house. Mrs. Colton turned to the man and gave him an indulgent smile. "Theodore stopped by to check on me." She patted the back of the man's hand in a friendly gesture. The older gentleman's face filled with a look of longing so intense that the emotion reverberated in Jacqui's chest. Mrs. Colton continued, "He's always such a good friend to stop by and make sure that I'm all right."

From where she stood, Jacqui could see two things very clearly. Gavin's mom was fond of the police chief. And for his part, the police chief was madly in love with Gavin's mother. Had Gavin noticed?

The older man stepped forward with his hand outstretched. Jacqui took it and shook. "Theodore Lawson," he said, introducing himself. "Pleasure to meet you."

Gavin added, "Theo, this is Jacqui Reyes. She's the stranded motorist whose car you had picked up last night."

The law enforcement officer's eyes got wide. "So that was you."

"Yes, sir," she said, remembering her manners. The handshake ended. "And thanks for getting my car out of that ditch."

"Best I can tell, your car was more than in a ditch. It was nose down on the side of a hill." He paused. "How'd it end up there, anyway?"

Did Jacqui want to bring the police into the investigation now?

Honestly, it seemed like a natural time to report what had been happening on the range to the cops. And Theodore Lawson wasn't just any cop either—he was the chief of police. For a moment, she saw the ease in passing on the burden to the older gentleman and then being able to walk away with a clear conscience. But would her conscience be clear? "It was an aggressive driver," she said without deciding. Then again, her words were decision enough. "He came up behind me and tapped my bumper. I just lost control." She shrugged and sighed to show her exasperation.

"Good thing that it was just a few scrapes to your car and nothing else. Those mountain roads are dangerous."

"Don't I know it," she said. The flow of the conversation seemed to ebb, and it was then that she noted the tension—like an odor—in the air. Jacqui looked around the entryway of the pleasant house and asked herself two important questions. Was it a mistake to come with Gavin to his family's home? And how had she allowed herself to get drawn so deeply into his life—and his past?

True, the house was grand, but not very well kept. The walls were covered in scuff marks and faded paint. The tile work on the floor was chipped and cracked. The finish on the doorknob had been rubbed off.

Was Gavin's family like their house? It wasn't until you got up close that you could see the truth—flaws and all. Then again, wasn't everything like that?

"So—" Gavin's mother drew out the word "—you're a friend of my son's?"

Maybe Jacqui hadn't remembered her manners as well as she thought. Holding out her hand for a shake, she said, "Jacqui Reyes. Nice to meet you. Your son saved me last night, and he's trying to help me with my work today." Then again, they'd come to Gavin's childhood home for a reason. She added, "He got burned and thought you could help him out with some first aid supplies."

"Burned?" Mrs. Colton drew her brows together and stepped toward Gavin. "Burned where?"

"On my arm." Holding up his wrist, he continued, "It's okay. I just need a bandage or something. We could've run to the store. I'm not sure why I bothered you with this..."

"Can I see?" Mrs. Colton asked, stepping closer.

Gavin hesitated a moment before extending his arm. "It's nothing. Honestly."

Sunlight streamed in from tall windows, and the burn to Gavin's wrist looked worse than it had on the range. Was it a trick of the light? Or was the injury getting worse?

"That doesn't look like nothing," said Mrs. Colton with a tsk. "Come with me. I'll get you patched up."

She made her way through the house to a spacious kitchen. A patio sat outside the back door and overlooked the red rocks of the surrounding mountains. The vista stole Jacqui's breath. "Wow," she whispered.

"Nice, huh?" said Theo. A coffee cup sat on the counter. He picked it up and took a swig. "You can lose a day in this room just watching the sun move across the rocks."

"Make yourself comfortable." Gavin's mom pointed to a kitchen island that was lined with stools. Gavin slid into a chair and Jacqui scooted onto the seat next to him. "I'm Isadora Colton, by the way. Call me Isa. You met Theodore, but I saw my baby's arm and forgot to introduce myself properly."

Jacqui said, "It's nice to meet you."

"It's nice to meet you, too." She turned to the cabinets that lined the wall. "Now where is my medicine kit?" She opened a cabinet. A drawer. Another cabinet. On her fourth try she stopped. "Ah, there it is."

Returning to the island, she held a black tackle box with a red cross emblazoned on the top. She set it on the counter and flipped the latch to open the lid. "Now how'd you get burned?"

"By a fire," said Gavin.

Isa said, "That's my Gavin—a man of few words. It's a wonder that he makes a living telling stories for as little as he likes to talk." While speaking, she removed a tube of antibiotic ointment, a sterile gauze pad and a roll of surgical tape from the kit. "Have you ever heard of his podcast? That's what they call it, right? A podcast?"

"Podcast. That's what they call it," said Gavin.

"I don't even know how you make enough money to cover any bills—much less pay for those fancy apartments of yours," Isa continued. "Chicago and Manhattan."

Jacqui found herself trying to gauge the emotions in the room. Gavin truly cared for his mother—that much was evident in his alarm over seeing a police car in the driveway. Isa cared for her son as well. Once she knew he was hurt, she focused only on tending to the wound. Yet, there was more.

Was the tension from earlier still hanging in the air? Definitely.

It was obvious there were decades-old dynamics with his siblings. Arguments that were never resolved. Insults that were never forgiven. But was that dynamic true for Gavin and his mother?

Her chest tightened as she realized that Gavin really was struggling with his own family. What he needed was an ally. Could Jacqui be that person?

She cleared her throat. "You asked if I ever heard of Gavin's podcast. I have. In fact, I'm a huge fan. Like you heard, an aggressive driver pushed me from the road last night. I didn't have any cell phone coverage, so I started walking. While I was walking, I was listening to *Crime Time*. Then he stopped to help, and I recognized him from his voice."

"Big fan?" Isa lifted her brows. "That's impressive."

Was Gavin's mother downplaying his success? "He's actually one of the most popular podcasters in the country. Millions of people listen to his episodes every week."

"Millions?" Isa swayed a bit where she stood. "My, I don't think I realized…" Her words trailed off as she arranged her first aid items into a row.

Jacqui pressed on. "You're the mother of a famous man. Someone who brings a unique perspective to the lives of people all over the world. More than that, he's the kind of guy who'd give a ride to a stranger and make sure that she got to safety. You have a lot to be proud of in your son."

"Of course I'm proud of him." His mother's cheeks

reddened, and Jacqui wondered if she'd pushed too hard. Isa stepped toward Gavin. "Now let me see that burn of yours."

Jacqui supposed that she'd said more than enough. She slipped from the barstool and wandered to the doors to the patio. Theodore Lawson followed and stood by her side.

"You want to step outside and get a better look?" The police chief glanced over his shoulder. Jacqui followed his gaze. Isa and Gavin stood next to each other at the counter; their heads were bent together. The coloring between mother and son didn't match. Yet, there was something that made the pair a matched set.

"I'd love to get a bit of air," she said.

Theodore opened the door, and Jacqui stepped onto the brick patio. The noontime air was warm, yet in the distance she could see the swaths of gold on the nearby mountains. This time each year, forests of aspen trees changed to their fall splendor. For a moment, she drank in her surroundings.

Theodore stood silently at her side.

After a moment, she spoke. "I think I overstepped with what I said. Gavin's mom didn't seem happy with me."

"Isa is really a kind person. Maybe you overstepped a bit." He sighed. "She's always had a bit of a blind spot where his brilliance is concerned. Besides," Theodore continued, "she'll admire you for standing up for Gavin."

Jacqui had about a million questions about the Colton family. After all, she'd seen two of them today already.

Yet, there was really only one thing that she wanted to know. "Why the blind spot, do you think?"

Theodore Lawson cleared his throat. "To be honest, I don't know. Could be that she has all those kids and life's been hard—plain and simple. It could be that Gavin reminds her of her deceased husband. Honestly, Isa loved him something fierce. Still, Ben Colton was a brilliant but flawed man."

"You think that she's afraid of Gavin being 'flawed.'" Jacqui hooked air quotes around the word. "Like his father?"

"It's just a theory."

The police chief was an easy person to talk to and be around. What's more, she had a feeling that Theodore knew more about the family than they knew about themselves. The question was, what did she need to know?

A knot of protectiveness was stuck in her middle. "Gavin told me about the time his mom left him at home." She paused waiting to see if the police chief would add anything to the conversation. He didn't. Jacqui continued, "He said that they'd gone to Glenwood Springs for the day but he was left behind. Said that you were the one who came by the house and stayed with him until his mom got home."

Staring off into the distance, Theodore rubbed the back of his neck and sighed. "He was such a little guy when it happened. I'm surprised he remembers it at all."

"He said it was one of his first memories," Jacqui offered.

"That'd be traumatic."

She nodded, not sure what else she needed to add.

"Well." A circular patio table surrounded by chairs sat in the shade of the porch's overhang. Theodore dropped into one of those chairs. "Some days I think that I'm too old for all of this."

"Too old for what? Your job?" Jacqui asked, taking a seat next to him. "Can you retire? How old are you? Sixty-eight years old?"

"You're a sweet girl, but I'll be eighty-two on my next birthday."

She gaped. "No kidding?"

Theodore shook his head. "No kidding."

"You look great."

"I feel tired."

"Me too and I'm only thirty-seven years old."

He laughed. "You're just a baby. The tiredness is worse. But to answer your question, I could retire. Could've retired years ago, in fact."

"Why don't you, then? You know, retire?"

Theodore shrugged. "I don't know. What would I do with myself?"

Sure, she understood that it was a question he never intended for Jacqui to answer. And yet she said, "You could start by telling Isa how you really feel about her."

It was the police chief's turn to gape at Jacqui. "Excuse me?"

"I know I'm an outsider here. I also know that the polite thing is to ignore what I saw. And I even understand that people—like you—may think it's rude to point out the obvious. But…" She sighed. "Life is too short to not eat the food you want. Or just sit and enjoy the view. But it's definitely too short to not tell the people you care about how you feel."

"I'll think on what you said." He paused a beat. "That's pretty good advice for someone so young. Where'd you get your wisdom?"

Jacqui smiled and shook her head. "Would you believe me if I told you that it was Gavin?"

"Actually, I would." He inclined his head toward the patio doors and the house beyond. "But what I do want to know is what's going on in there right now."

Chapter Twelve

Gavin sat at the island bisecting the kitchen. It was the same space he'd occupied for his entire childhood. A dozen years earlier, all the kids chipped in to pay for a kitchen renovation. The cabinets were clean and bright. There were more windows in the room than when he was a kid.

"The upgrades still look good," he said, the words sounding lame—even to him.

"You like it? It is sunnier in the kitchen than it was before." She opened the bandage's paper packaging. "How long have you been in town? How long are you planning to stay?"

The questions were simple enough. Yet Gavin felt as though he were stepping into a minefield in trying to answer. "I've been staying at a fishing cabin for a few weeks. I'm not sure how long I'll stay in Blue Larkspur. It depends on how long it takes to wrap up my newest series."

"The one you're doing about your father." It wasn't exactly a question or a statement. Yet, from his mom's tone, Gavin understood her words to be a challenge.

He said nothing. After taking a pair of scissors from a drawer, she cut four strips of surgical tape. "Caleb told me."

"I bet he did," Gavin grumbled. "Did he mention that my story concept has changed?"

"Changed? To what?"

The last thing he wanted was for Theodore Lawson to get involved in the case and shut down the story. Could Gavin trust his own mother to keep his confidence? "I'm not at liberty to discuss it right now."

She nodded as if his explanation was enough. "So, you never did say how you got burned."

"Yes, I did," he quipped. "Fire."

"Always a smart comment with you, isn't it?" His mother gave an exasperated sigh. "I don't want to quarrel, Gavin. Honestly. I'm just concerned. I'm your mother. Isn't being worried about you allowed?"

Leave it to his mother to guilt him into feeling like a heel. Then again, hadn't he come to her house for this exact moment? He could do without the snarky back and forth, of course. But hadn't he wanted some care and attention? And if that was so, why wouldn't Gavin just accept it?

"A fire started nearby where the wild mustangs have been grazing. It was spreading fast. There wasn't any time to call in the fire department—not that we had cell service. So, Jacqui and I put out the blaze." He regarded the wound to his arm. It was still angry and red. He wondered if it was going to leave a scar. At least he'd have a story to tell. "I guess I'm just lucky this is the worst thing that happened to me."

"You're both lucky." His mom opened the tube of ointment and then washed her hands. Using a tea towel to dry her fingers, she continued, "You couldn't call the fire department?"

It was a reasonable question. Yet, in the asking of something Gavin already told his mom, he felt the sting of skepticism—or worse, that she hadn't been paying attention at all. Why had he come home? But more than that, why had he even returned to Blue Larkspur? Being around his family filled him with the same angst he felt as a teenager.

"We didn't exactly have cell coverage," he repeated, his tone peevish. "Like I said already..."

"Well, of course not..." she began.

Gavin wasn't done, though. "Besides, what were we supposed to do? Watch the mountain burn while we waited for someone to show up?"

"No, I wouldn't think that you would." His mom placed a daub of ointment next to the burn and smoothed it over the blister. "It's just that what you did was dangerous. And even knowing that you were in danger. Well, it scares me." She swallowed and looked up, meeting Gavin's gaze. "I do love you. I hope you know that."

Did she love him? Maybe that was part of the problem. Did Gavin believe his mother when she spoke those words? "I know," he said dutifully. "I know."

"This past year has been busy. It seems like most of your brothers and sisters have found someone to love." Was his mom going to give him a hard time about the lack of a lasting romance in his life? It seemed so. Gavin gritted his teeth and said nothing. She placed the gauze bandage over his arm. "It's been making me think about things. About the past."

"Oh? Like what?"

Isa busied herself affixing surgical tape, seeming to not have heard his question at all. After an uncomfortable pause, she spoke. "There was a day, a long time ago, and something happened. You were so young, I'm not sure if you remembered. But…" She lost the thread of whatever she planned to say.

His heartbeat hammered in his chest. The rush of his pulse resonated as a throbbing to the wound on his arm. "But…" he coaxed.

"Well, I don't want to upset you if you don't remember."

"Try me."

After shoving the tape and ointment back into the first aid kit, his mom shook her head. "I don't know."

Gavin's jaw tightened again. This time, his teeth began to ache. "Try me," he said again. "After all, I am an adult—not a child."

"Well." His mother placed the first aid kit into a drawer and wiped down the counter with her bare palm. "There was one day when we all planned to go to Glenwood Springs. I packed everyone into the van. I mean, there are twelve of you. Anyway, I'm not sure what happened—even to this day, I don't know." She grabbed the tea towel she'd used earlier and wiped down the counter again. "We were about an hour outside of town, when I realized that there were only eleven of you in the car." She dabbed at the corner of her eyes with the towel. When she spoke again, her voice was hoarse with emotion. "Somehow, you were left behind. Back in those days, not everyone had a cell phone. I certainly didn't. I could barely afford to feed you all."

Gavin's chest was tight. "Mom, you don't have to," he said, reaching for her hand. "If it helps you at all, I do remember that day. I survived. I'm here."

"No, I need to say it—especially since you remember what happened. I found a phone booth and called Theodore. He came to the house and stayed with you until I got home. Driving back to Blue Larkspur was the worst hour of my life. It was also the lowest point for me as a parent." She drew in a deep breath. "I'm sorry. Forgive me?"

Could he do that? Was all he ever needed an acknowledgment and an apology? He drew in a breath, his lungs expanding. As he exhaled, tension slipped from his shoulders. The bright kitchen seemed to glow with reflected sunlight. "Yeah, Mom. I forgive you."

Isa gave him a watery smile. "Thanks, Gavin. And you know, I am proud of you. What you do is exciting—even if I don't quite understand everything about your job."

Gavin gave a small laugh. "Thanks. I'd offer to explain everything to you…"

She held up her hands in surrender. "I'm a graphic artist. If you ever want to collaborate on a new logo or a cover for a series, let me know. Otherwise, I'll just be your proud mom."

"Sounds fair." It was like a band of tension had always been drawn tight across his chest. Yet, in talking with his mother, it had loosened. Was this what it was like to be happy—or at least, content?

His gaze was drawn to the back doors and the patio beyond. Jacqui sat at a table with Chief Lawson. Finally, he'd found a place with his mother where they could both be comfortable—and truly, it felt great.

Yet, all he wanted now was to be with Jacqui again. The question was, did she feel the same?

THE DOOR LEADING from the house to the patio opened with a squeak. Jacqui turned at the sound. Gavin stepped out of the house, and her pulse jumped. Her palms grew damp. Just seeing him stirred up something primal that dated to a time when people relied on instinct alone.

She fidgeted in her seat as adrenaline surged through her system. But why? Were her instincts telling Jacqui that Gavin was dangerous?

She regarded him as he slowly approached. His fingers were tucked into the front pockets of his jeans. The sleeves of his Henley were pulled up almost to his elbows, and the cords of muscles in his arms were exposed. A large white bandage covered the burn on his wrist.

He drew closer and the buzzing of adrenaline left her breathless. Jacqui could no longer deny the truth. She was unquestionably drawn to Gavin Colton.

"Hey," she said simply.

He leaned a shoulder on the side of the house. "I know we have more work to do, but my mom offered to make us lunch. I'm fine taking a break for now, but only if you are."

She didn't know what time it was. Yet, at the mention of food, her stomach contracted painfully. "Lunch would be good." She checked her phone: 12:32 p.m. *Actually, lunch would be great.* "How's your arm?"

"Better." Gavin slipped into the seat between Jacqui and Theodore.

"Mom medicine is magical, am I right?" the police chief said.

Gavin gave a short laugh. "Something like that."

Theodore rose slowly to his feet. "I'll see if Isa needs help in the kitchen. Either of you want something to drink? A soda? Sun tea?"

"Tea is fine with me," said Gavin.

"Make that two."

"Be right back." The police chief ambled across the patio and disappeared into the house.

Once the door was closed, Jacqui turned to Gavin. "He seems nice."

"You say anything to him?"

"About the horses? Or the fact that we think the fire was set on purpose?" She shook her head. "Not a word."

Gavin stretched his legs out in front of him. "You can if you want, you know. After everything that's happened, talking to the police makes sense."

Was Jacqui ready to give up on the rogue investigation? "If I talk to Chief Lawson, you won't have a topic for your next podcast."

He shrugged. "I'd find something else to produce. I always do."

"Sounds like you're pretty resilient."

"Sometimes."

"What about now?" She tilted her head toward the house. "How'd it go with your mom? Seems like it was a little tense in there."

"It was." He looked out across the yard and to the mountains beyond. "My mom apologized." His voice was so low that Jacqui wasn't sure if she heard him right.

"She what? She told you she was sorry for that day you got forgotten?"

He nodded.

"How'd that happen? Did you finally bring it up?"

"Maybe I should have a long time ago, but no. Mom said that most of my siblings are finding love or some stuff like that. Then with everyone having a future, she's been examining the past. Forgetting to take me with her was one of the lowest points of her parenting—or so she said."

"So she said?" Jacqui echoed. "You don't believe her? I'd say leaving a child behind is a pretty low mark."

Gavin scrubbed his face with his hands. "Actually—" he blew out the one word with his breath "—I do believe that my mom is very sorry for what happened. I think she'd been so ashamed that she never mentioned it to me or talked about it again. I think that she hoped I didn't remember—and then, it was like the incident never happened at all. The thing is, it's always been a stain on our relationship. Now that she's owned what she's done, I feel like some of that stain has washed away. But can I let go of the past?"

"I'm sure you can," she said. "With time, at least."

"And what about me? I was more than a little diffi-cult as a kid—mostly because I was angry. But there was more. I thought I got to misbehave for being over-looked." He cursed under his breath. "Do I apologize to her?"

Jacqui wasn't sure if Gavin wanted an answer or not. Still, she said, "I'm not going to say that your relation-ship will be fixed overnight. I do think that asking for and giving forgiveness is a good place to start."

GAVIN CONSIDERED WHAT Jacqui had said. Honestly, her words made sense. "Forgiveness," he repeated.

All the same, Gavin had lived his whole life with the pain and burden of abandonment. It colored the world he saw. It drove him forward in life, always forcing him to be better and take another risk.

Without his anger and angst, who was he?

Or maybe he should ask a different question. If he forgave his mother—and himself—who would he be-come?

He glanced at Jacqui. God, she was pretty. And smart. And brave. And kind. "Thanks for..." He paused, not sure exactly what he wanted to say. He shook his head. "For a guy who tells stories for a living, you'd think I'd be better at speaking my mind."

She gave a small smile. "You're welcome. And you don't have to say any more."

Her hand rested on the table. Gavin placed his own hand next to hers. Her fingertips were close enough to touch. Did he dare to reach out?

The door to the house opened. Chief Lawson wore a blue-and-white-striped apron over his uniform. He also carried a large plastic tray by a set of handles.

"I've been recruited to run the grill."

He set the tray on the table. A plate of raw chicken breasts sat in the middle of it, surrounded by various seasonings and sauces in bottles. Two glasses of tea were tucked into the corner.

"Here are your drinks." Theo took both glasses of tea from the tray. After setting one in front of Gavin, the older man handed the other to Jacqui. "Here you go. Gavin, your mom is making pasta salad in the kitchen. She'll be out in a minute."

Glass in hand, Jacqui rose from her seat. "I'll see if Isa needs help in the kitchen."

Gavin stood as well. "Then I suppose that leaves me helping you with the grill, Theo."

He watched her through the windows, until even her shadowy form disappeared. His chest filled with an emotion he dared not examine too closely. Yet, Gavin saw potential for his future. He saw a life that he never dreamed of living. The question was, did he have the courage to claim what he wanted?

Theodore stood next to a large gas grill. "Hey, Gavin. You ready to get started?"

"Yes," he said, before dragging his gaze away. "I am ready."

It DIDN'T TAKE Jacqui long to find Isa in the kitchen. The older woman had several vegetables lined up alongside a wooden cutting board and a knife. On the stove, a pot of water was just starting to steam and boil.

Gavin's mom looked up as Jacqui crossed the threshold. "Hello, dear. Is there something you need?"

"Actually, I'm here to see if there's anything I can do for you."

"Care to dice for the pasta salad?"

"I'd love to." Jacqui moved to the cutting board and selected a sweet green pepper. With the knife, she divided it in half. After scooping out the pith and the seeds, she began to cut it into strips. How often had she stood in her parents' kitchen and helped slice peppers? It was too many to count—and the action was familiar as coming home.

"So." Isa emptied a box of macaroni elbows into the pot of boiling water. "You and Gavin just met last night?"

"I was lucky that he drove by when he did." She made a face. "Who knows what would've happened if I'd been stranded on that road for too long."

"You are lucky." Using a long wooden spoon, Isa stirred the pasta as the water bubbled. "And you're working together now."

Was it a question or a comment? Jacqui couldn't tell. She began, "I work for the Bureau of Land Management. Part of my job is to monitor the local herd of wild mustangs." From there, she decided to be vague and avoid any questions that she never intended to answer. "Gavin thought that my job was interesting and that he could make an episode or two for his podcast.

Me? I'm always happy to get some press for conservation efforts and the horses."

"But I thought Gavin's podcast focused on true crimes. Certainly, there's no crime happening on the range. Or is there? Does that have to do with the fire?"

So much for being vague and avoiding unanswerable questions.

"The fire was on the range, but we have no idea how it started." Jacqui cut the pepper into cubes and shoved them all to the side with the flat of her knife.

"You two need to be careful. I don't want to see either of you hurt—or worse."

"Yes, ma'am." She reached for a red pepper. "This one, too?"

"Please," said Isa.

Jacqui sliced the next pepper in half.

Isa took a package of romaine hearts from the refrigerator and set them on the counter. "I'm happy to see my son with a friend, though. Even if you're a new friend."

Was Isa criticizing Gavin again? Sure, her own parents wanted her to succeed. But more important—they wanted her to be happy. What did Gavin's mom want for him?

"I'm sure Gavin has lots of friends," said Jacqui, slicing the pepper into strips.

Isa rinsed the lettuce and set it on a paper towel to dry. "I have no doubt that Gavin has a great deal of notoriety. He's always been able to capture the spotlight. More than that, he excels at everything he does. He always got the lead in school plays when he was younger. In high school, he was the star of whatever team he joined. Then, he went to college and became editor of the university's paper. Everyone admires Gavin. But fans and friends aren't the same thing, are they?"

"No, they aren't." The exchange left Jacqui wondering how she would describe her relationship with Gavin. Certainly, she was a fan of his podcast, but there was more. They were working together, but were they a team? They'd kissed, but they were hardly lovers—or even romantically involved. She liked spending time with him. Did that make them friends?

"Your son is an easy guy to admire."

"Thank you. He is."

Jacqui had chopped up the second pepper without thought. "Now what?"

"We drain the pasta." Isa pointed to the stove. "Then, I'll teach you how to make my world-famous pasta salad."

"World-famous, eh?"

"Well, my family really likes the recipe. I'll make enough to bring some over to Caleb's tonight." Isa removed the pot of water from the stove's heat. "And you'll be coming too, right?"

"It's a family function," Jacqui began. "I really don't want to intrude."

"You're welcome, and besides with my son…" Isa placed a metal strainer in the sink and shook her head. "Well, never mind."

Jacqui had a feeling that she should leave well enough alone. Yet, where Gavin was concerned, she was always interested. "No, what?"

"Well, I have a feeling that unless you come over,

we won't see much of Gavin." Dumping the steaming pasta into the strainer, she continued, "You might've noticed but Gavin doesn't like to be around family all of the time—or most of the time. Or maybe it's any-time." Isa ran cool water over the steaming pasta. As the faucet ran, she glanced over her shoulder and looked at Jacqui. "You seem to have softened some of the rough edges for him." She turned off the water.

"I'm not sure about that," Jacqui began. "After all, we've only known each other for a day. It's been less than a day, really."

"He seems comfortable with you, is all I'm say-ing." With her back to Jacqui, she continued to speak. "Gavin's childhood was chaotic. I'm not sure I was the best mother to him. No." She gave one fierce shake of her head. "I've decided to embrace the future and that means being honest about the past. I was heartbroken when Gavin was young. I didn't give him the love and attention he deserved. I might be able to make up ex-cuses now, but really, he deserved better. I'd like to make a new start with Gavin. It's just that I don't know how."

She searched for something to say. Nothing helpful came to her. Until now, she'd only been worried about Gavin. But Jacqui could clearly see that Isa had been struggling all along. In truth, she was *still* struggling. Her heart ached for the woman.

"Anyhoo, I'm glad that he stopped by today. I'm glad he brought you with him. I rarely meet anyone from Gavin's life." Isa transferred the pasta to a large bowl. "You got those diced peppers for me?"

Jacqui lifted the cutting board. "Right here."

Using the flat side of a knife, Gavin's mom scraped the vegetables into the bowl. "I won't pester you about stopping by for dinner at Caleb and Nadine's anymore, I promise. But you are welcome to join us."

"I'll think about it," said Jacqui, not wanting to commit to anything. Then again, Gavin was helping Jacqui with the mystery on the range. She owed him a lot. Should she help him reconnect?

She thought about how her family—focused, opinionated, loyal to a fault—was the foundation of her life. Without her parents, who would she have become? Without a home base, would she be forced to wander?

During these last few minutes, Jacqui felt as if she'd come to understand Gavin a little bit better. What's more, she vowed to help him in any way she could. "You know," she said, "I don't have any plans this evening. If Gavin's agreeable, I'd love to meet more of the family and stop by."

Chapter Thirteen

The sun dipped below the mountain peaks to the west, turning the sky pink, gold and coral. Without the sun, the air cooled, leaving Jacqui chilled and wishing that her jacket hadn't been ruined in the fire. It was the only coat she'd brought with her. What's more, she hadn't made time to purchase a new one.

After having lunch with Gavin, Isa and the police chief, Jacqui had gone back to the hotel to shower and change. She now wore a long-sleeved T-shirt in olive green and khaki pants. Her hair was loose around her shoulders. She'd taken time to refresh her makeup as well.

For his part, Gavin wore a flannel shirt over his Henley.

"From what I gather, everyone in the family is going to be here tonight," said Gavin as they drove. "Like I said, there are twelve of us, so don't freak out. Caleb is the oldest brother and Morgan's twin. They're both attorneys. This summer, Caleb got married. My sister-in-law's name is Nadine. According to Caleb, she's an artist and I'll like her."

"What do you mean by that?" She glanced at Gavin. "*You'll like her.* Are you telling me that you've never met your sister-in-law? What about at the wedding?"

Gavin looked in her direction. "Didn't go."

Okay, Jacqui wanted to ask about a million different questions. But mostly, she wanted to know, "Why not?"

"My production schedule really was packed." He let out a long breath. "Honestly, I could've made it work—if I'd wanted."

"But you didn't?"

He shook his head. "With my family, I feel like I'm taking fire from all sides. And there's never anyone to watch my back—until I met you, that is." He gave her that wry smile that left her toes tingling. "Thanks for coming with me. If I didn't have you here, I might have bailed."

It was exactly what his mother predicted. Still, Jacqui knew enough to keep her mouth shut.

"Looks like everyone's here."

"We can leave if you want."

He put the gearshift into park and turned off the ignition with the push of a button. "No. Showing up was hard enough. I don't want to slink away with my tail between my legs. Besides, we can't stay late. We still have to find Henry's car and enable the tracking device."

Jacqui knew that she'd been thrust into the middle of a family dynamic she didn't completely understand. Then again, maybe she didn't need to. Maybe all she needed was to be a good friend to Gavin. "Should we have a sign or a code word or something that means get me the hell outta here?"

Sitting back in his seat, he laughed.

She liked the sound. She liked to see him smile and be happy. What's more, she liked that she'd been able to bring him some joy. Her cheeks grew warm, and she looked out the side window. Gavin's reflection was caught in the darkened glass. He regarded her with his dark eyes.

"A code word?" he repeated. "Like what?"

Jacqui hadn't gotten that far in her plans. "Something that wouldn't be said in a typical conversation, but we could work it in." She turned to look at him. Her heart skipped a beat. By now, she should've expected the jolt she got every time she looked at Gavin. But it always felt like the first time she'd ever laid eyes on him.

Still, his question about the code word hung in the space between them.

"I dunno." The code word had to be simple. "Maybe we can ask, what's the weather like tomorrow?"

"This is Western Colorado. It's always sunny." He winked to show that he was teasing. "But I like your idea. If things get awkward, I'll ask about the weather and then, you'll make an excuse to leave. Right?"

"Right."

"All right, then." He opened the door. "Let's go."

As they walked up the driveway, Jacqui's pulse began to race. Was it the brisk pace they'd taken on the incline? Or was she actually nervous to meet more of Gavin's family?

Before she could decide, the door opened. Morgan stood on the threshold. She wore a silk tank in deep burgundy and a formfitting black skirt. She held a stemless wineglass filled with rose-colored liquid. A wide smile had spread across her face. "Gavin. Jacqui. I'm glad to see you both." She backed into the door, pushing it open farther. "Come in. Come in." She pointed as she spoke. "Food and drinks are in the kitchen. It's back that way. Mom said that you helped with the pasta salad. She must like you—she doesn't share that recipe with anyone."

"I'm flattered," said Jacqui.

"You should be." Morgan had to raise her voice to be heard over the din of a dozen different conversations happening at once.

The house was filled with light, noise and people. She leaned in close to Gavin. "Are you related to all of these people?"

"Relatives? These are all my siblings. I told you there were a lot of us." He waved to a man with dark blond hair. "That's Dom. He's one of the triplets. And the guy beside him is Oliver, the third triplet." Oliver was tall—like his brothers, with light blond hair and deep blue eyes. "Those two go with Ezra—the brother you met this morning."

"Hey, man. You showed up. Good to see you." Oliver stepped forward and slapped Gavin on the shoulder. "You haven't me Hilary yet, have you?" He pointed to a blonde woman who was obviously pregnant. She held a bottle of water and stood next to Isa.

From across the room, Hilary must've heard her name. She lifted her fingers and gave a small wave. Yet, Jacqui noticed the look that filled Oliver's eyes. It was love, plain and simple. What would it feel like to have a man gaze at her that way?

Jacqui couldn't help but smile. She gave Hilary a small wave in return.

Oliver then turned to Jacqui. He offered his hand to shake. "You must be Jacqui. Nice to meet you. I heard all about you."

"All about me?"

"Well, from Ezra and my mom."

She swallowed.

"Don't worry, they said good things."

"I'm glad to hear it."

"What's the old saying?" Gavin asked. She could tell from his tone that he was about to make a joke. "Telephone. Tell a friend. Tell a Colton."

Dom stepped forward. To Jacqui, he said, "It's nice to meet you. My fiancée, Sami, will be here soon."

She looked around the house, packed with people, and wondered what it would be like to be a part of a large clan like the Coltons.

Wow. That was a lot of musing for one night.

First, she was thinking about loving looks and now, belonging to the family? Jacqui had to get a grip on her imagination.

"Nice to meet you," she said to Dom, offering him her palm for a handshake.

"Nice to meet you, too. Let's get back to your work," Dom said. "Ezra also said that he's been monitoring the tracking device he gave you, but it hasn't been activated yet."

Gavin glanced over his shoulder. Jacqui's gaze followed. Nobody was standing nearby. "Let's take this conversation outside."

"Sure thing," said Dom. "This way."

He led them through the kitchen and grabbed four bottles of beer as he passed a cooler. They exited through a set of sliding glass doors that led to a patio. It overlooked the river and had an outdoor seating arrangement. They all took seats. Oliver handed out the bottles of beer, giving one to Jacqui first.

"So." Oliver twisted the cap off and took a long slug. "What happened to the tracker?"

Gavin glanced at Jacqui. "Operator error, I guess you'd say." He continued, telling them how he'd knocked on Henry's door to distract their prime suspect. He concluded with, "We got the tracker on the car. We just have to go back and turn the damned thing on."

"What you did today was bold. Too bad it didn't work. Then again, an op like that in the daytime has to be done fast." Dom took a sip of beer. "You got a plan?"

"Besides going back tonight and turning on the tracker, you mean?" Jacqui asked. She had yet to open her own drink and rubbed the cold bottle between her palms.

For a moment, nobody said a word. They all understood the situation—and it was bleak. Gavin and Jacqui had one chance to track Henry Rollins—and they'd messed up.

Now, only a single question remained: What could they do to fix their mistake?

THE COOL NIGHT air was refreshing after the heat of the day. The lower temperature outside soothed his burn.

But there was more.

Was he really so relaxed around his family?

Sure, Gavin had always been close to this particular set of brothers. But the conversation with his mom had lifted a weight from his soul. Beyond that, there was Jacqui.

She was at ease with the Coltons, and somehow, having her with him allowed Gavin to connect. Reaching for his beer, he took a drink. He tried not to wonder about if he'd continue to get along with his family once his investigation into the horse thieves was over—or not.

Horse thieves.

Gavin returned his attention to the whole reason Jacqui was in his life to begin with. The tracker had been placed on Henry's car. Now, it had to be turned on. But how? "You guys are the experts here," he said, looking at his two brothers. "What do you suggest?"

"You really don't have a choice besides turning on the tracker in the middle of the night," said Dom.

The patio door opened. Ezra stepped outside. "Hey, how come nobody told me the real party was out here?"

"We were just talking about the tracker Gavin and Jacqui tried to plant this morning. It needs to be powered up. That's why there's no signal," said Dom.

Ezra rubbed his hands together. "An ops meeting. I love it." Pulling a lounge chair next to the table, he took a seat. "Hey, did anyone think to bring a beer for me?"

Jacqui handed over her bottle. "Here you go."

"Thanks." After accepting the beer, Ezra twisted off the cap and took a long drink. "So, what're we talking about? Do we have a plan?"

"Not much of one," said Jacqui. "But we're getting there."

Gavin wondered about Jacqui giving away her drink. Was she just being polite? Or did she not drink alcohol at all? Or was she simply not a fan of beer? Not that it mattered. In fact, Gavin never took a sip of booze, unless he was in a social setting.

It did bring up the fact that there was so much about her that he didn't know. He drew in a deep breath as he realized something else. Gavin had come to rely on Jacqui. Hell, he brought her with him as a buffer for his difficult family. Was it wise to rely on someone he didn't know well?

She continued, talking to his brothers. "When Gavin said it was operator error on our part—he was being polite. It was me, and I'm sorry."

Then again, how could he not like her? How could he keep himself from being drawn to a woman who was so genuine and honest? Gavin cleared his throat. "It was both of us. Not enough communication, but still—we need a plan."

"First, you can't go back to the subject's neighborhood in that luxury car of yours. Especially since you have out of state license plates. You'll stick out like a sore thumb."

What Oliver said made sense. "We can't take Jacqui's car either. We think that the subject forced her from the road yesterday."

"You can borrow my truck," Ezra offered. "Or I can do you one better. One of us can take care of the tracker for you."

Gavin was used to working alone. True, Jacqui was his partner. And it was also true that he liked having her at his side. But did he really want to work with an entire team? Especially a team that was made up of his family members, to boot?

"I'll take the offer to borrow your truck," said Gavin. "Thanks, man."

"No, thank you," said Ezra, taking a swallow of beer. "We're trading cars. So that means I get to drive that sweet ride of yours." He reached into his pocket and pulled out a set of car keys.

Gavin gave a chuckle and reached for his own fob. He held it on his palm as Ezra replaced one set with the other. "Okay, so we have a vehicle that will blend in. What else?"

"You need to blend in, too. As in you should dress in black," said Dom. "Or dark blue, at least."

"I have some darker clothes back at the hotel," said Jacqui. "If you don't mind taking me back, I can change after the party."

"Sure thing," said Gavin.

"What about you?" his brother Ezra asked. "You got something dark to wear?"

"Not with me. And I'm staying up at a fishing cabin. Getting there and back will take over ninety minutes."

Oliver said, "That brings up something else, brother. Why aren't you staying with Mom?"

Gavin's face warmed as his temper began to rise.

Honestly, he was just starting to think that his brothers were decent guys. "Is this an ops meeting, or pile on Gavin time?"

"Whoa. Whoa. Whoa." Oliver held up his hands in surrender. "I didn't mean anything by asking. I was just wondering is all..."

"Would any of you want to stay with mom if you didn't have to?" He glanced at each of his brothers. To their credit, none of them looked away but neither did they answer his question. "Mom is our mom. But I'm also a grown man, the same as all of you. I don't want to move back to my childhood home, especially since I'm in Blue Larkspur to work."

"Like I said, I didn't mean anything," Oliver grumbled.

Had Gavin overreacted? He felt Jacqui's gaze but lacked the courage to look in her direction. He didn't want to see the disappointment in her eyes. Gavin reached for his beer and took a swallow. "Don't worry about it, man. Water under the bridge, as they say."

Ezra cleared his throat. "I have a dark jacket in my truck. It's yours to borrow—if you want. That'll take care of your clothes."

"Thanks. I appreciate it."

"No problem. What're families for, am I right?"

Gavin sat back in his seat and took another drink of beer. Light and laughter from inside spilled out onto the darkened patio. In that moment, he had to admit a single fact. Gavin had no idea what families were for, or even what they were supposed to be. The triplets had each other. They were so close that they'd gone into business together. His eldest two siblings worked together as well. The rest of the crew was pretty close, literally and geographically.

Not for the first time, he felt as if their father's death had been a horrible accident for the entire family. It was akin to a plane crashing in the ocean. It's just that each of his siblings had made it to the safety of an island that was out on the water. And Gavin? Well, he was floating on the vast ocean all alone.

His entire life, he'd always thought it was just bad luck that separated Gavin from his family. Yet, what if that wasn't right. What if it was Gavin who had chosen to be removed?

That brought up another set of questions. And for those, Gavin didn't have any answers. Did he have the strength to swim for his family? And if he did, would they help to pull him ashore?

THE DOOR LEADING to the house opened. Gavin's younger sister Alexa stepped into the night. She held a bottle of beer by the neck. "Gavin. Buddy." She gave him a wide smile and opened her arms for a hug.

Rising from his chair, he moved to his sister and wrapped her in an embrace. "Hey. It's good to see you." As he hugged her, Gavin admitted that it really was good to be home. Turning back to the table, he nodded toward Jacqui. "Alexa, I'd like you to meet my friend and colleague Jacqui. Jacqui, this is one of my little sisters, Alexa."

Alexa gave a wave. "Nice to meet you. And any friend of Gavin's is always welcome."

"Thanks." Jacqui's cheeks reddened in a blush and Gavin's pulse spiked. "Everyone in your family certainly has been welcoming."

Dom pulled up another chair. "Have a seat."

Everyone scooted closer together to make a space for Alexa. Gavin returned to his own place next to Jacqui's. His knee rested against her thigh. The contact sent a shock wave up his leg. Had she felt it, too? Or did she think he wasn't respecting her boundaries?

Glancing at Jacqui, he tried to read her reaction.

Her gaze met his. She ran her teeth over her bottom lip. The gesture was sexy. Gavin couldn't help it. His mind filled with thoughts of Jacqui. His lips on hers. His mouth on her neck, her chest. His tongue on her breasts. His dick twitched. Shifting in his seat, he moved his knee and broke the connection. No point in torturing himself with wanting someone he'd never have.

Dom spoke. "Tell us, sis. How's work?"

"Of course you'd be the one to ask." Alexa took a sip from her beer. "He's technically still a federal agent, but he's on his way out sometime down the road. A new path."

"I'm just making conversation," said Dom. "But since you brought it up, I am interested in what's happening with the Spence investigation."

Alexa brushed a whisp of blond bangs from her forehead. "Spence is definitely a priority for all federal law enforcement, as you know, that's for sure." Leaning back in her seat, she sighed. "We have intel that suggests Spence is building a coalition of drug dealers. I know *you* know some of this, Dom, especially after your recent undercover work. But what I've told everybody stays at this table. It's all very top secret stuff."

"We won't say a word," Oliver vowed.

"Before you make that promise, there's more." Alexa took a long drink of beer. Leaning forward, she set the bottle on the table. "Spence is out for blood." She looked around the table, directing her gaze at each of the brothers in turn. "*Our* blood. Just look at what happened to Clay Houseman."

"Crap," Gavin said. "What's that mean?"

"It means we gotta watch our backs. And we gotta watch out for each other," said Dom. "Anything less, and one of us could end up dead."

For a moment, nobody spoke. Maybe Gavin should be staying at his mother's house. At least he could provide some kind of security.

Ezra lifted his beer in a mock salute. "Well, on that happy note." He finished the last swallow from the bottle. "I'm going to get another drink."

"Not if you're driving my car, you won't." Gavin took the empty beer from his brother's hand and stood. "Anyone else need something? A water, maybe?"

"I'll take a water," Ezra grumbled.

"Me, too," said Jacqui. "Thanks."

He opened the door, stepped into the house and made his way to the kitchen. Morgan stood at the counter, refilling her glass of wine. She looked up as he entered.

"You know what Caleb does with the empties?" He held up the bottles of beer.

She pointed. "In the sink for now."

Several empty drink containers were already lined

up in the sink. He added his two with the rest. "One more question. Does Caleb have bottled water?"

Morgan took a sip of her wine before setting her glass on the counter. "There's a cooler over there." She pointed to the far wall.

Gavin lifted the lid. It was filled with ice along with different beverages. He grabbed a bottle of water for both Ezra and Jacqui before letting the lid shut. "Thanks a ton," he said and walked toward the door.

"Hey, Gavin, you got a second?"

Did he? He wasn't in the mood to be lectured about the podcast—even though he'd changed the focus. Or maybe that was the wrong attitude. Wasn't Gavin trying his best to appreciate his family—Morgan included?

He set the bottles on the counter. "Sure, I've got a minute."

"It's about what I said earlier…"

His shoulder blades pinched together with tension. He'd been a fool to think that he could get along with Morgan. "What about it?"

"I was too harsh." She picked up her glass and took a drink. "I'm sorry."

His sister didn't look drunk. But was the wine making her amiable? "I appreciate your apology, but it's not necessary." And maybe it wasn't. "I get that Spence is a dangerous guy and me asking questions could cause problems that none of us want."

Morgan nodded slowly. "For the record, I get you wanting to understand Dad. I was a good bit older than you when he died. I still don't know why he did what he did." She let out a loud exhale. "If you ever want to talk. Ask questions. Whatever. I'm here."

Gavin's throat was thick with emotion. "Thanks." The one word came out as a croak. He coughed into his shoulder. "I appreciate it."

She nodded.

They stood in the kitchen and said nothing. For the first time in a long while, the silence wasn't filled with hostility but something else. What was it? Acceptance? Appreciation? Both?

"Well." He picked up the bottles of water from the counter. "I better…" He nodded toward the door.

"You going back outside?"

"I am. You want to come, too?"

Morgan rolled her eyes. "To hang out with our newly attached brothers? No way."

Hadn't Theresa been welcoming and kind to Gavin this morning? "What's the matter with the triplets having someone in their lives?"

"It's not just them. It's almost everyone. Caleb. Naomi. Rachel. Even Gideon." She took a swallow of wine. "Can you believe that Gideon finally found someone?"

"Are you drunk?"

She ignored his question. "Pretty soon, it's just going to be me and you who are single." She took another sip. "Unless you end up with your colleague."

"You are drunk." He placed a kiss on top of her head. "And I'm going back outside."

"I'm not drunk. I'm just being honest."

Gavin retraced his steps to the patio. Morgan had

been right. So many of their siblings were falling in love. Obviously, all the new couples got under Morgan's skin. His gaze was drawn to Jacqui, and he had to wonder—was being in love a bad thing?

Jacqui had to admit it. She'd enjoyed her evening with the Colton clan. They were a boisterous family, but there were lots of smiles and laughs to go along with all the noise. As the evening wound down, Jacqui's limbs and eyes grew heavy. She was ready for bed, but the night was far from over.

Caleb and his wife, Nadine, walked Gavin and Jacqui to the front door as everyone said good-night. "I'm glad that you both stopped by tonight." Nadine, a slim brunette in a long and flowing skirt in a patchwork pattern, placed a quick kiss on Gavin's cheek.

Caleb shook Gavin's hand. "Thanks for coming by tonight, little brother." Caleb was tall, with dark brown hair and brown eyes. A lock of hair fell on his forehead, and he shoved it back. "It's been good to see you."

Gavin said, "It's good to be seen."

"Really?" Caleb asked. "I thought you hated stuff like this."

Jacqui could feel more than see Gavin stiffen. "Well, tonight was nice."

After spending several hours with Gavin and his family, Jacqui had come to understand a few things. For the Coltons, Gavin was the puzzle piece that didn't quite fit.

Why?

Well, she didn't truly understand the reason. Maybe

it was that Isa was too busy for Gavin, and the rest of the family assumed that he was disposable, even without ever saying it aloud. Or maybe, it didn't truly matter.

Whatever the reason, Gavin was forever frustrated that he didn't fit either.

For tonight, at least, Jacqui was determined that Gavin would have someone on his side. She reached for his hand.

"Hopefully, there are more nice evenings for the whole family."

Nadine pulled Jacqui in for a quick hug. "I don't know what you two and the triplets were talking about earlier, but I hope that you both take care."

"Will do." Jacqui gave Nadine's shoulders a squeeze.

Then, with Gavin's hand still in hers, they stepped out into the night. The borrowed pickup truck was parked behind Gavin's car. He unlocked the doors to his brother's truck. Jacqui let her hand slip from his as she walked to the passenger side. Without him at her side, the cool night air seeped into her skin. Quelling a shiver, she pulled open the door to the truck. A black jacket sat on the seat. Lifting it up she said, "I found your nighttime attire."

Gavin took the offered jacket. He slipped it on and pulled the zipper closed. "How's that?"

Sure, she was standing only feet away from Gavin. And they were on a well-lit driveway. All the same, he did blend in better with the darkness.

"Not bad," she said. "It's a little thing that makes a lot of difference."

"Surprised?" He held out his arms, as if examining himself.

"Honestly? Yeah. Now, all I need is my own invisibility coat."

Gavin made his way to the driver's door, slipped behind the wheel of the truck and closed his door. "Let's run by your hotel and then…" He let out a long exhale. "We'll go back to Henry's house and get the tracker powered up."

Jacqui got into the passenger seat and closed her own door. "Let's go."

The drive to Jacqui's long-term-stay hotel passed in silence. She struggled with what—if anything—to say about his family. First, she thought they were overall well-intentioned people. Second, she felt his strain and wanted him to understand…well, understand what?

That she was on his side?

Jacqui and Gavin might be friendly, but they were hardly friends.

What's more, she only had one more day in Blue Larkspur. By tomorrow evening, Jacqui and Gavin would either know what was happening on the range, or she'd have no choice but to turn the case over to law enforcement. With the clock ticking, they didn't have much time together. And when Monday morning came around? Jacqui would be heading back to Denver. Gavin would be, well, she didn't know that either. And because there was a lot that she didn't know, Jacqui kept her mouth shut.

As Gavin maneuvered the big truck into the parking lot, the silence was too much. "You know," she began,

"I don't think that your family is all that bad. But I can see where some of what they say is hurtful." She paused, reminding herself that it wasn't her job to fix either Gavin or his family dynamic.

Putting the gearshift into park, he turned to Jacqui. "Thanks for having my back. I don't usually have an ally at family gatherings."

Not for the first time, Jacqui's heart ached for Gavin. Sure, she remembered Steffanie's warning about getting involved. But that was the thing: Jacqui was already a part of the situation, whether she wanted to be there—or not.

She laid her palm on his arm. "It'll be okay. Maybe not today or tomorrow, but I think you'll eventually work it all out."

He reached for her hand, winding his fingers through hers. "Thanks. I'm glad that I ran into you—well, it would've been bad if I had run into you. But…"

She laughed. "I get it." She paused a beat. "I guess I should, you know, go up and change."

"Yeah," he said. "I guess you should."

There were no other sounds beyond the rumbling of the engine and the whisper of Jacqui's breath as it mingled with Gavin's.

She knew that this was one of those rare moments in life where there were two clear paths for her to follow. Did she want to take the safe path, where she kept her wits and her professionalism? Or was she drawn to follow Gavin and see where the second one led?

Gavin shifted in his seat, moving closer.

Jacqui needed only to lean toward him. She could

erase the distance that kept them apart and kiss him again. What's more, she could invite him up to her room. But was that what she wanted? Maybe? Maybe not?

The thing was, she didn't know.

Well, if she didn't know—then, the answer was no.

Sliding back, she let her fingertips slip from his arm. "You'll wait for me? I promise to be quick."

Jacqui didn't wait to see what Gavin might say—or do. She opened her door and hopped down from the truck. She strode up the exterior stairs. The night air cooled the fever that burned every time she touched Gavin. Or looked at Gavin. Or heard Gavin's voice.

Maybe it would be better if Jacqui did call the police. That way, she could leave Blue Larkspur with her heart intact.

Fishing through her bag, she found the room keycard. Card in hand, she held it to the door and stopped. It was then that she noticed, the door and jamb didn't meet. Her mind went back to this same spot hours earlier, as she left for the day. Jacqui recalled the feeling of her palm on the handle as she pulled the door closed. Then, the pressure on the door as she made sure that the automatic lock was engaged.

Staring at the seam between the door and the wall, fear gripped her throat in its icy hand. Someone had been in her room. But why?

Chapter Fourteen

Gavin couldn't help himself. He watched Jacqui as she walked to her room. The curve of her hips. The sway of her rear. The way her shirt hugged her breasts. And the way the overhead light gleamed on her hair. Sitting back in his seat, he tried to drag his gaze away, but it was no use.

Sure, Gavin had desired women before in his life. He'd felt the bone-deep ache that could only be satisfied one way. But with Jacqui it was different. He didn't just want to fall into bed with her—although he imagined that the sex would be great. It was just...

Jacqui stood in front of the door to her room. Of course, it was odd that she stood there. But there was more. His heartbeat raced and he turned off the ignition. In the days and weeks that followed, Gavin tried to decide what alerted him first. Had he noticed that Jacqui's shoulders were tense? Had her spine suddenly gone rigid? Or from the parking lot, could he see that there was something amiss with the door?

He was out of the truck and racing toward the stairs before he realized that he'd even moved. Sprinting onto the second-floor walkway, he called out, "What's wrong?"

She was trembling. "My door's open. I'm positive that I closed it when I left." She swallowed. "That means someone's been in my room."

Gavin's heart stilled for a beat as a thousand different possibilities came to him at once. Each was worse than the one before. A gunman, lying in wait. A group of thugs, ready to beat Jacqui into submission. But as his mind raced through each calamity, he knew something else. "This is a hotel. Housekeeping has a key to your room. Maintenance. The management."

She drew in a shaking breath. "Yeah, of course." Jacqui let out a slow exhale. "You're right. It could be anyone—and not in a bad way either." She paused. Inhale. Exhale. Her trembling stopped. "I mean, you are right. It's just after everything..." She shrugged.

He reached for her shoulder and gave a squeeze. "After everything that's happened, you have a right to be spooked." He pushed aside all thoughts of lone gunmen or groups of thugs. "Let me check for you. Once you see that everything's okay, you'll feel better. Hell—" he let his hand slip from her shoulder "—we'll both feel better."

Jacqui folded her arms across her chest. "Sure. Thanks."

Gavin walked to the room, already mentally narrating his search like it was a podcast episode.

There was just a sliver of darkness that told that the door wasn't latched. But what was inside? We had yet to find out.

The tension was high. It was as palpable as electricity—the same as the moment before a lightning strike. For his podcast, this would be the perfect place for a commercial break. There was no way that people would quit listening now. His heart pounded against his chest. Drawing in a sharp breath, he pushed the door open—not sure what would follow, but he was ready for anything.

Light from the walkway and the parking lot spilled across the floor. Despite the darkness, he could clearly see the room beyond. His pulse began to race. "Holy crap."

"What is it?" Jacqui peered over his shoulder and into the room. "What the f—"

All the cabinets in the kitchen were open. Cushions from the sofa had been tossed across the room. A lamp, now broken, had been knocked off a table.

From where he stood, Gavin could see part of the bedroom. The covers, torn from the mattress, were strewn across the floor.

"I don't know what happened, but this definitely wasn't maintenance."

"You think?" asked Jacqui, a bite to her words. She pushed past Gavin and flipped on the light. "My room's been wrecked. Who'd do this? And why?"

"I think we know who." Gavin followed her into the room and slipped the phone from his pocket. He pulled up a contact number and placed a call. "As to why? Hell if I know, but this is too personal. We gotta get the police involved now."

"What? No. What about the horses? What about your podcast?"

The phone began to ring, and Gavin utilized the speaker function. "What about you? This is the second time in two days that you've been threatened."

Jacqui opened her mouth but whatever she was about to say was stopped by the voice of Chief Lawson. "Gavin? That you?"

"Hey, sorry for calling so late, but I'm at the Stay-A-While Inn by the airport and there's been an incident."

"Incident? What kind?"

"Someone broke into Jacqui Reyes's room."

Lawson paused. "Your new friend? The one who got pushed off the road. And then just happened to find a wildfire? That Jacqui Reyes?"

Gavin knew where the conversation was going. "That's the one."

Lawson said, "I'm on my way. But these incidents aren't random bad luck."

"There's nothing going on," Gavin insisted, interrupting.

"There is," Lawson said, his voice steady. "And when I get to the hotel, you're going to explain."

Jacqui shook her head and mouthed *No*.

Sure, he understood that she had a passion for the wild mustangs, but more was at stake than just someone planning to steal some horses. Obviously, someone was targeting Jacqui. To Lawson he said, "Just come. We can talk when you get here."

"Don't touch anything in the room. I'm on my way."

He hung up the phone and exhaled. For Gavin, this

was a game of cat and mouse. The only problem was—who was the predator and who was the prey?

Jacqui understood why Gavin called the police. But it was impossible to tamp down her frustration. "You didn't have to do that, you know."

"Do what?" Was he really going to be obtuse?

"Call the cops." She didn't want the police involved. Besides, would she even be a priority at all? "Whoever did this isn't here anymore." She scanned the suite. It looked like all her clothes were strewn across the bedroom. Her laptop lay on the floor. "And it doesn't even look like they took anything."

"You know why I called Theo," said Gavin.

And she did. Some of her anger slipped away. "Someone forced me from the road. Someone started a fire on the range. Now, someone's broken into my room." She paused a beat. "Sure, this is a mess. Is that really a crime if nothing was stolen?"

"This isn't a game." He reached for her shoulders and gave a quick squeeze. "You could end up getting hurt next time—or worse."

Jacqui wanted to lean into Gavin, to feel his embrace. She stayed rooted in her spot. "You don't know that there'll be a next time…"

"I do." He bent at the knees a little until his gaze met hers. "And you do, too."

Dammit, he was right again. "So, what do I do now?"

"You have to tell Lawson everything. There's no other way."

"Everything?" she echoed. Jacqui hated the idea of asking for help. Or worse yet, giving up.

"Listen, I trust Lawson. You can, too. I know this isn't how you hoped things would go…"

Before she could come up with an argument, the *whoop-whoop* of a police siren came from the parking lot.

"Sounds like Lawson's here." Gavin's hands slipped from her shoulders. Suddenly, she was cold. "Will you be okay by yourself for a sec?"

Folding her arms across her chest, she nodded. "I'm fine."

Gavin slipped out of the room.

Finally, she was alone. Jacqui couldn't help but ask herself a single question. *Would* she be fine? A cold sweat gathered at the nape of her neck. It was more than a petty crime of someone breaking into her room. It was a violation. It was humiliating. Then again, she supposed that was the whole point. Or was there more?

The door was still open. She watched Gavin. Standing at the edge of railing, he waved to the parking lot. He stepped back into the room and said, "Lawson's on his way."

Jacqui nodded. A moment later, the police chief pushed the door open. Theo Lawson no longer wore his uniform. He'd donned a pair of jeans and a sweatshirt.

The older man whistled through his teeth. "Someone did a number on this place. I know something's going on—none of this is random—so don't tell me different. But I gotta ask—who'd you piss off, Jacqui? Is there an old lover who lives in Blue Larkspur?"

"No."

"Who, then?"

"It's my job."

"With the Bureau of Land Management?" the police chief asked. It was impossible to miss the incredulity in his tone.

She said, "I got an anonymous call yesterday saying that someone was going to take wild mustangs off the range. I came here to investigate. I saw markings on the neck of a horse consistent with a lasso."

"So, you think this tip is legit?" asked Lawson.

"With all of this—" Gavin swept his arm to the side, taking in the wreck that was her hotel suite "—I'd say that the tip is legit. What's more, whoever is after these horses, well, it's become personal."

Lawson ran a hand down his face smothering either a yawn or a sigh—Jacqui couldn't decide. "And how're you involved, Gavin?"

"I asked him to help," said Jacqui. It might not have been the absolute truth, but it was close enough. "He has experience with investigations because of his podcast. He knows the area. He has contacts to help with surveillance."

"I get all of that," the police chief drawled. "But I know the area pretty well, too. You could've called me."

Was this the moment that Jacqui had to admit she'd been a bit of a cowboy by not following the proper protocol? Or that if she discovered the identity of the horse thieves, she was all but guaranteed a promotion? She shrugged. "I thought we could handle this on our own."

"Well, here's what we're going to do." A pile of papers had been strewn across a stool at the breakfast bar. The police chief lifted them up and tapped the edges on the counter until the pages were neat. He held them out to Jacqui as he sat on the stool. "First, you can tell me what—if anything—you found out about these horse thieves. Then, I need you to look through this room and figure out if anything's been taken. I'll file a police report."

"And then what?" Gavin asked.

"I don't rightly know what happens then. Before I make that decision, you need to tell me everything."

Jacqui glanced at Gavin. He lifted his brows. She read the expression to mean *Go ahead and tell him.* Or maybe, *What choice do we have?*

Either way, Jacqui could feel the situation slipping from her grasp—like sand through her fingers. It left her to wonder, had she been in control at all?

GAVIN STOOD IN the middle of Jacqui's room and knew two things to be true. First, if he lost the chance to cover the case of the horse thieves, he'd have nothing for his show in November. It'd be two big strikes against him. There was fierce competition for lucrative sponsors. If Gavin couldn't come up with a new series, would he get another turn at bat?

But the second thing he knew to be true was so much more important. The violence against Jacqui had escalated. Unless the police got involved, things were going to get worse.

So, sure, he hated that Lawson was involved—which meant that Gavin wasn't. But there was no series that was more important than the life of another person, especially if that person happened to be Jacqui. The need to protect her was strong—like he'd donned a suit of armor and was ready to do battle.

Him? A knight in shining armor? The image both surprised and amused Gavin. Yet, he took a step closer to Jacqui ready to fight with anyone—even Lawson—on her account.

Lawson's words, *"I don't rightly know what happens then. Before I make that decision, you need to tell me everything,"* still hung in the air.

Jacqui asked, "What d'you want to know?"

"Start with the beginning."

She fished her phone from her bag and opened her voice mail app. "I got this on Friday morning." She played the anonymous voice mail.

Lawson drew his brows together. "Any idea who left that message?"

"Not at first," said Jacqui. "The contact and number didn't show up on caller ID. I didn't recognize the voice either."

"You said that you didn't know who called at first. Do you know now?"

Gavin picked up the story. "Jacqui found a package of tobacco on the range. Once she and I started working together, we followed up on the clue and came up with a name. Henry Rollins."

"You know him?" Lawson asked Jacqui.

"Not really, no."

Lawson said, "That's not an absolute *no*."

Her laptop lay on the floor. "I'm not sure of the rules here. Can I touch anything?" Were the thieves after information? "Like my computer?"

"Go ahead."

Gavin knew what Jacqui planned to do—show Lawson everything they had. She brought the laptop back to the breakfast bar and booted up the power. "At least this isn't broken," she said as the screen winked to life. She entered a few keystrokes and brought up an article about the roundup from two years before. "I was in charge of that roundup, but I didn't do the hiring." She scrolled through the article until she found the picture of Rollins. "We hire an agency, and they bring in their own people. I try to talk to everyone on the range, but I don't remember speaking to Rollins in particular."

"But he'd know you, correct?" Lawson asked.

Jacqui gave a noncommittal shrug. "It's a pretty safe assumption that he would."

"You think Rollins is the one who left you a message?" Lawson asked, pointing to the phone. Before anyone could answer, he asked another question. "But if he called to warn you about what was happening on the range, then why force you from the road? Or start a fire? Or tear up your room, but not take anything?"

They were all good questions. "I have no idea," said Gavin.

"It's just that one doesn't seem to fit with the other," said Lawson.

"Agreed," said Gavin.

"Agreed," Jacqui echoed.

"Let me get in touch with my office. It may take a little digging, but I'll get an address for this Henry Rollins and one of my officers will stop by for a chat."

"Actually," said Jacqui, "there's no need to dig. We have his address."

Lawson lifted his brow. "You do?" he asked, his tone skeptical. "How'd you get that?"

From the corner of her eye, she glanced at Gavin. "Umm…"

Honestly, Gavin knew that he and Jacqui should've had a chat about what they were going to tell Lawson—and what they weren't. "We had some help."

"Let me guess," said the police chief. "Your brothers and their new private security outfit."

"I mean, they are my brothers," said Gavin. "So what if I asked them for a little help?"

Sitting back in the chair, Lawson crossed his arms over his chest. "Spill," he said. "You have to tell me everything."

"Everything?" Jacqui squeaked.

Lawson nodded. "Start with this Rollins's address."

"He lives in Town Square Villas on Cuba Court." She gave him the house number.

"And…" Lawson continued.

Damn. Gavin hated to admit what they'd done. Still, he knew enough not to lie to the cop—especially since Lawson was one of the few people that he liked and trusted. Or maybe he owed it to Lawson to be honest because of that trust and fidelity. Gavin spent a few minutes telling Lawson about planting the tracker—and for the first time, he was glad that it wasn't activated. As it turned out, placing an active tracker on someone's car in Colorado was against the law. He also told Lawson about the cameras they'd left on the range.

"I don't want you to have any more contact with Henry Rollins—you both hear me?" Lawson used a tone that Gavin hadn't heard since he was in high school. "I will send an officer to have a chat with Rollins. I'll also instruct the officer to remove the device and return it to your brothers."

And speaking of high school, Gavin definitely felt like a kid again. "Yes, sir."

"Then in the morning, you both need to collect those cameras. I know that it's public land managed by the federal government. But consider this a criminal case—and my office is now in charge."

"Yes, sir," he said again.

He then took his phone out of his pocket and placed a call. Gavin could only hear Lawson's side of the conversation. Then again, it was enough.

"Stan, you still on patrol?" Pause. "Good, I need you to check out an address for me on Cuba Court. Speak to the resident there, a Mr. Henry Rollins. Let him know that he's under suspicion for reckless endangerment with a motor vehicle, breaking and entering, and arson. See what he has to say." Pause. "Then look under the rear bumper. You'll find a tracking device on the muffler. Remove it and set it on my desk." Another pause. "Thanks, Stan."

Lawson hung up the phone. "I'm getting too old for this crap." With a groan, he stood. "All right then, let's look around this room and see if anything is missing or damaged. If you find that anything has been taken or destroyed, I'll call in CSI and they can dust for prints. If not, I won't bother right now. This is a hotel room and certainly there's probably a dozen fingerprint sets all over."

It took Jacqui only a few minutes to find all her belongings. "Everything's here. Nothing's broken."

"You sure?" Lawson asked.

"Positive."

"All right then, I'm going to visit the hotel's office and see if they've got any video of the walkway outside of your room or the parking lot. Hopefully, whoever broke into your room was caught on tape."

"Hopefully," Jacqui echoed with a sigh.

It was easy for Gavin to see that she was more than tired; she was exhausted.

"You take care," said Lawson, gruff but compassionate. "We'll get this all sorted." He picked his way across the littered living room to the door. There, he stopped and turned around. "I want those cameras gone from the range in the morning—remember."

"Sure thing," said Gavin. Maybe he should go and get them now...

Lawson let himself out of the suite. Before he had a chance to pull the door closed, his phone began to ring. "Yeah, Stan. Go ahead."

He paused a beat and then cursed. "Stay where you are. I'll call you right back."

Lawson stepped back into the hotel room and closed the door. Gavin's pulse began to race. He didn't know what the police chief was about to say, but he did know that it was nothing good.

"That call was about Henry Rollins."

"Yes?" Jacqui took a step forward. "What's going on?"

"Well, he's not home. I'm going to have a unit sit at his house till he shows up. And I'll get an APB out on Rollins's car, but for now, we don't know where he went. For your safety, I'll have a unit sit in the parking lot and keep an eye on your room, too."

Jacqui blinked slowly, and Gavin imagined that she was taking in all the information. "You can't find Rollins? There'll be a police officer in the parking lot?" She hugged her arms across her chest.

"It's for your safety," said Lawson.

"I…" Her voice trembled. "You think he'll come back?"

Lawson said, "I don't think anything. I do know that we need to be prudent. But, just in case Rollins decides to show up, I want a police officer here."

"I don't know if I can stay. I mean, it's bad enough that he was in my room."

Lawson rocked his head from side to side, considering what Jacqui had said. "We can get you into another hotel—at least for the night."

"I suppose…"

"You can stay with me," Gavin blurted out before he'd really made up his mind about anything. But the minute he spoke, he knew it was the right decision. "I'm renting a cabin at Larkspur Lakes—and nobody knows where I'm staying, not even my mom. Besides, then you wouldn't be alone…"

Jacqui looked up at him. Her eyes bored a hole into his soul, and Gavin's pulse continued to race. It was then, as he gazed at her face, that he realized something else important, too. Sure, it was a good idea for Jacqui to get out of Blue Larkspur for the night. But there was more than that. He wanted to be the guy who protected her and helped to solve her problems.

In short, Gavin wanted her to be with him.

Chapter Fifteen

Jacqui's mouth went dry, and her pulse began to race. "Stay with you?" she echoed Gavin's words. "I can't…" she began. But why not? "I don't want to intrude."

"You aren't an intruder," he said, his voice smooth and silky. "Trust me. Besides, the cabin is away from everything. It's hard to find and it has a better security system than this place."

Sure, his cabin was remote. If she were with him, then she wouldn't be alone. It's just that they would be together—and alone.

She drew in a deep breath. "I shouldn't…"

"What Gavin said makes sense, but if you need to stay in Blue Larkspur, then we can get you set up at the Budget Motel down the street."

"The Budget Motel?" Gavin grimaced. "That place is the worst. The beds sag. The roof leaks. The pipes shudder whenever anyone flushes a toilet. Can't you get her into a nicer place?"

"I'd love to offer everyone a luxury suite at a golf club. But at the police department, we have this thing called a budget," Chief Lawson snapped.

Now she'd done it. By being stubborn, Jacqui had caused the one thing she wanted to avoid—a conflict. She held up her hands. "You know, I'll be okay for another night."

"Here?" Gavin asked. "Alone?"

She scanned the wrecked room. Could she stay here by herself? Or would every sound be an unseen intruder? She knew the answer. Her head ached just thinking of the insomnia hangover she'd have in the morning. Maybe she'd be better off with the leaky roof and noisy pipes.

Then again, those weren't her only choices. "If you're okay with me staying at your cabin…" Jacqui began.

"Of course, you're welcome." Was it her imagination, or was there a tinge of eagerness in Gavin's voice? He gave her shoulder a squeeze and let his hand slip away. "There's two bedrooms. Right now, one is set up as my studio, but it has the best view of the lake."

"Sounds like it's settled then." The police chief opened the door once more. "I'll let you know when we find Rollins. If anything else comes up, call me. I don't want either of you to think you can take on this Rollins character. Someone's going to get hurt—you hear?"

Jacqui took the chastisement as it was intended—a bit of tough love. "Thanks for everything."

The police chief left.

For a moment, she stood in the middle of the room. The dishes had been torn from the cabinets and flung onto the floor. Her clothes were scattered all over the room. It'd take an hour just to get everything put back together. By then, she'd be exhausted. She sighed.

"Just get what you need for the night," suggested Gavin. "You can take care of all of this in the morning."

Jacqui gave a quiet laugh. "You a mind reader or something? I was just thinking about this mess and how it needs to be cleaned up."

Gavin smiled and shook his head. "No psychic powers. It wasn't hard to guess what you're thinking."

Just looking at his smile left her warm. Her lips still tingled from their kiss. Did he know what she was thinking now? "Let me get a bag packed. It'll just be a minute."

Gavin picked up the sofa cushions from the floor and set them back on the couch. "I'll be here."

Jacqui went into the bedroom and shut the door. Leaning on the wall, she slowed her breathing and controlled her runaway pulse. It was time that Jacqui admitted it to herself—staying with Gavin Colton wasn't simply about the getting away from her hotel. Or even having another person around for protection.

She found her duffel in a corner and began picking up her clothes that littered the floor. As she stuffed them into the bag, she knew that going with Gavin could be a huge mistake. What if they kissed again? Would she be able to stop herself from going further a second time? Would she want to?

Then again, maybe she didn't have anything to worry about after all. Maybe he would be nothing more than hospitable and a gentleman.

Jacqui refilled her toiletry bag, safe in the knowledge that Gavin had made the moves on her once, but she knew that he wouldn't likely a second time. He'd be too focused on potential danger. She knew that she should be happy to have a good friend who'd offered her a safe place to stay. But what if she was done playing it safe and she wanted something more?

GAVIN DROVE HIS brother's truck to the cabin. The ride took them nearly an hour. During that time, Jacqui slept. He imagined that she needed the rest. The last twenty-four hours had been nothing if not traumatic for her. Yet, he found it hard to keep his eyes on the road.

The dashboard lights turned her complexion golden. He was captivated by the tilt of her chin. The curve of her neck. The way her long lashes kissed her cheeks. Or how her lips parted slightly in sleep and each exhalation came out as a soft sigh.

It was that little hiccup of breath that landed in his chest and sent his pulse racing. So help him God. Gavin couldn't keep from wondering what noises Jacqui made during an orgasm. Gripping the steering wheel tighter, he reminded himself that Jacqui staying the night at his cabin was for her safety. To ogle her now would make him a creep of the first order.

He turned off the main road and onto the dirt track that led to his cabin. The truck rumbled over a rut. Jostled in her seat, Jacqui woke. "Sorry," she said, reaching her arms overhead in a languid stretch. "I must've dozed off."

"It's not a problem. Besides, you needed the rest."

"I guess so."

Now what was he supposed to say? The truck's headlights cut through the darkness. A wall of trees lined both sides of the road, the branches reaching across overhead. As a kid, places like this seemed like magical portals that led to a different realm. Sure, he'd shared a lot with Jacqui. Still, he wasn't about to dive that deep into his past. "When I was growing up, I always thought this was a tunnel."

Leaning forward, she looked out of the window. The darkened glass reflected her form. Her breasts pressed against the thin fabric of her shirt. The collar was loose and gave a perfect glimpse of her cleavage—if he cared to look.

He kept his eyes fixed on the road.

But oh man, was he tempted to steal another glimpse.

"I guess you're right," she said, with a quick laugh.

His pulse spiked. Had she been reading his mind? Had something in his mannerisms given him away? "Right about what?"

She pointed toward the sky. "The trees do make a tunnel." She sat back in the seat and folded a leg under her rear. "It's kinda cozy, if you think about it."

Gavin pointed. "I'm just up here. Less than a quarter of a mile."

"I can see why you decided to stay all the way out here. It's peaceful."

"Wait till you see it in the daylight. At this time of the year, the aspens turn the mountains into a sea of gold. Perfect leaf peeping weather."

"You know, in all my time living in Colorado, I've never just been leaf peeping." She yawned. "I mean, I work all over the state. So, I've seen the trees change every year for a decade, but just to take a day and drive around or hike." She shook her head. "Never."

For years, the autumnal change brought tourists from around the world to Western Colorado. The aspens were the biggest draw. As a kid who grew up in the area, Gavin always assumed that fall was just as spectacular everywhere else. Like lots of beliefs from his childhood, he'd been wrong. "Never been leaf peeping," he echoed. Faking an exasperated sigh, he continued, "You'll have to remedy that one day. Hopefully soon."

As soon as he spoke the words, Gavin knew that he wanted to be the one to explore the changing seasons with Jacqui. Like everything, he wanted to see his old world with her new perspective.

The headlights swept over the turnoff for his cabin—just a little more than a wide spot in the dense woods with a reflective sign. "Cabin 12."

He turned onto an unreasonably narrow lane. Branches of the trees slapped at the wide-bodied truck. As they got closer to the lake, tendrils of fog clung to the ground. The A-frame cabin seemed to rise out of the mist.

"Oh," she breathed. "This place is about perfect."

"I'm glad you like it." He cleared his throat, dangerously close to saying more than he wanted. "I mean, I like it, too. But there's something you gotta see." Excitement bubbled up from his middle—a kid at Christmas ready to open his presents.

He pulled up next to the front door and put the gearshift into park. After killing the engine, there was nothing beyond the silence, the darkness and the night.

"See what?" Jacqui asked.

"Come with me." He opened the door and hopped down to the ground. She followed. He held out his hand and she slipped her fingers through his. The moment they touched, Gavin knew that offering his hand had been a mistake. It's not that he didn't want to touch Jacqui—he did. A lot. And that was, in fact, the problem.

He led her past the darkened cabin. "Careful," he warned. "The ground's uneven."

As if to prove his words, the ground sloped downward and Jacqui slid. She tightened her grip on his hand.

"You okay?" He stopped her with another arm on her elbow.

"I am. Thanks," she breathed. In the darkness, her coral lips turned to the shade of a deep red wine. He'd kissed her at noon. Would she taste any different at midnight? "Where are we going?"

"You'll see."

The lake's warm water mingled with the cool night air and the entire shore was obscured by fog. Gavin stopped where water lapped against the land. The opposite mountains were nothing more than shadows against the night. Like diamonds thrown across an ebony cloak, the sky was filled with a billion stars.

"Wow. Now this is beautiful." She squeezed his hand before letting her palm slip from his. A picnic table sat near the shore. She climbed up and set her feet on the bench. Leaning back, she let her long tresses flow over her shoulders. Gavin's fingers itched with the need to touch her hair and to find out if it felt as luxurious as it looked. He moved to the table and sat at her side. "Thanks for sharing this with me."

"You're welcome," he said. "But there's more."

"More?"

The fog rolled across the lake, dissipating with the movement. Then, it all but disappeared. The lake remained, an endless plain of black. But in those still waters were the sky and the mountains and the night.

"I can see why you like this place. It's almost, well…" She let the words trail off before shaking her head. "Well, it is beautiful."

"What were you going to say?"

She looked up at him, her brows drawn together. "What?"

"Just now, you said this place is beautiful, but you were going to say something else. What was it?"

Even in the darkness, he could see the color rise in her cheeks. "Oh, that."

"Yeah. That."

"I mean, this whole place, it's, well…" She paused again. "Magical. And I don't mean that in a hocus-pocus kind of way."

"I get it," he said quickly. Gavin didn't bother to add that he felt the same way, too. "You know when people use the phrase *my happy place*?" He pointed to the ground. "Well, for me—this is it."

"I can see why." Tilting her head up, she stared at the stars. "How'd you find this cabin? It's pretty remote."

"Back when I was a kid, this place was owned by my friend. We'd come up here for long weekends. Cross-country ski in the winter. Hike in the summer. Doug was an only child. So, it was just me, Doug and his folks." He gave a half smile and shook his head. "After meeting my family, you can see the appeal."

"I can."

She shivered.

"C'mon. Let's go inside. We can get a fire going and you can finally warm up."

"It's my thin Miami blood," she joked. "It doesn't matter how long I live in Colorado. I'm never warm in the winter."

"It's not even winter yet," said Gavin with a laugh.

"Tell that to this girl from South Florida."

He jumped to the ground. Jacqui stayed on the table. "You coming?"

She glanced at him before turning back to the water. "I dated a guy, Zeke, for three years. We broke up over the summer." Her words floated across the lake and disappeared into the waters. She looked up at him and gave Gavin a wistful smile. "I thought we were going to get married. After three years together, it's what you do. Right?"

"Everyone has their own path." If nothing else, his siblings were all proof that there was no single correct way to live a life—or to fall in love.

"He was wrong for me from the beginning. He always wanted to know where I was going. Who was I with. At first, I was flattered—here was this guy who was completely obsessed with me." She paused a beat. "In school, I was always the smart one. The science geek. Guys liked me, but only when they needed help with homework. I was never the cute one."

"I don't know, you look pretty cute to me."

He was rewarded by Jacqui giving him a small laugh. The sound reverberated in his chest. She sighed and he leaned in closer. "Another problem—we worked together. I kinda figured we could at least be professional after the breakup."

Gavin said, "Zeke figured differently."

She gave a snort. "That's an understatement. We worked on a water conservation project together. I was the team lead. Honestly, he wasn't bad. Until we submitted our report." Jacqui paused. "It was my responsibility to turn in the final draft. Zeke was the best writer on the team, and he offered to give the pages one last polish. It was a generous offer and I agreed."

"Let me guess. You somehow got written out of the report," said Gavin.

"It wasn't that bad, but he did make himself the team's leader."

"What a jerk."

Jacqui nodded. "That about sums up Zeke. But there's more."

"More?"

"When I got the call about the horses, I should've gone to Zeke. Blue Larkspur is his territory. But I was worried that there was nothing to the tip. Or if there was, then Zeke would manipulate the situation to make him look like a hero and me look like the loser who didn't do her job."

"From what you said, he might've."

She shrugged. "Yeah, but that's why I've been so stubborn about finding out what's happening on the range. I wanted ironclad evidence that *I* could take forward. And now, I really am the loser who can't do her job—and my ex wasn't even involved."

"You really shouldn't be so hard on yourself." Sure, Gavin's words were true. But there was more. Now he knew why Jacqui wanted to avoid any romantic entanglements. What's more, he didn't blame her.

"Anyway, you've been so honest." Jacqui rose from the picnic table. "I figured I owed you some honesty as well."

"You didn't owe me anything—but thanks."

"I should be thanking you." She turned to look back at the lake. He followed her gaze. There, in the glassy water, was the reflected sky and all those stars. "You were willing to help me find out what was happening to the horses. Too bad it didn't work out."

"Yeah," he echoed. "Too bad. In the morning, I'll collect all those cameras we planted."

"I guess we weren't too good at all of the cloak-and-dagger stuff." Jacqui shivered. "It was fun while it lasted."

"You had fun?"

"Well, except for my car getting forced into a ditch. Having someone break into my hotel room. Oh, and you getting burned—how's your arm, by the way?"

Gavin had almost forgotten about his injury. "I'll live."

"Glad to hear it. You know—" she turned to him and placed her palm on his chest "—you're a pretty good guy." Her touch sent a shock wave through his body. It's as if his whole life, he really had been floating alone on an endless ocean. And Jacqui's touch was the lifeboat.

He wanted to say something. To touch her. Hell, what he really wanted was to kiss her again. But that wouldn't do. Taking a step back, he cocked his head toward the cabin. "Let's get inside. Even for a Colorado boy like me, it's starting to get chilly."

"Yeah." She stepped back. "Of course." She turned toward the cabin. He was on her heels. What happened next? Gavin would never know. Maybe the soil was loose and gave way. Maybe it was the uneven ground? Or maybe it was just poor footing. Whatever the cause, Jacqui pitched back. Gavin didn't have time to think— only react. He grabbed her waist, keeping them both upright.

Her back pressed into his chest. His arms were around her middle. She was soft and warm and just holding her felt, well, it felt right. Inhaling deeply, he got drunk on her scent and the cool evening air. "You okay?" he asked, whispering his words into her hair.

"I'm fine," she whispered back. "Thanks to you."

"Anything hurt?"

"Gavin." She spun in his grasp to face him. Her pulse raced, thrumming at the base of her throat. "I…"

His gaze was locked on hers. And despite the majesty of the mountains at night, he could see nothing beyond Jacqui Reyes. "You what?" he asked.

Jacqui swallowed. "I'm fine." Her breath washed over his chest. "Better than fine, really."

Better than fine, eh? Was she flirting? His dick twitched.

"You gotta be honest with me. What is it that you want?"

She ran her fingers through his hair and pulled him closer. "You know, I was just asking myself that same question."

Chapter Sixteen

Dear God, Jacqui wondered, what was she doing? Certainly, she knew—she was standing by the lake, being more than a little suggestive with Gavin. But his question was still there, unanswered even by her. What did she want? For now, Jacqui was ready to live in the moment. She didn't want to be haunted by the past or worry about the future.

"Being in your arms is nice." Her heartbeat hammered against her chest. Was it wrong to enjoy a night with a handsome man who found her attractive and interesting? Obviously not. But Jacqui couldn't remember the last time she found herself to be either. "We can start there and see where it goes."

He gave her that sardonic smile, and her cheeks warmed. She bit her bottom lip. God, he was handsome. Could Jacqui just give in to her desires for one night? And what about tomorrow? And the day after that?

No. She stopped herself before the worrying got started.

"You sure?" Had he read a bit of hesitation in her expression?

And was she sure? Actually, Jacqui knew what she wanted: Gavin.

She brushed her lips against his. "I'm sure."

Gavin dipped his head and deepened the kiss. "Do you like this?"

"Yes," she said, sighing. He slipped his tongue into her mouth and Jacqui pulled him closer. For her, Gavin was a foreign land—one that she intended to explore and make her own, at least for the night.

The notion left her breathless. Is that what she wanted? To fall into bed with Gavin, with no concern for the consequences. Then again, it was a stupid question—if only because she knew the answer.

Jacqui had been drawn to Gavin from the first moment that they'd met.

Had she wanted him from the beginning?

Not exactly.

But now she wanted him with a desire so keen it was an ache in her middle.

She needed to touch him everywhere. Jacqui traced his strong arms and broad shoulders. She moved her hands over his well-defined pecs and abs. Dear God, he truly was perfection.

He groaned, dragging his kisses from her mouth to her neck to her chest. "Oh, Jacqui, you're so beautiful." He reached inside her shirt, his touch blazing a trail across her flesh. Through the thin fabric of her bra, he caressed her nipples—first one and then, the other. "What about this?" he asked, his words mingling with his kisses. "Do you like this?"

"Yes," she gasped, her desire growing. "Oh, yes."

He lowered his head as he lifted the hem of her shirt. The night air cooled her skin, yet she didn't care. Jacqui was burning with a need that only Gavin could fulfill.

He teased her nipples again, this time with his tongue through the fabric of her bra. She pressed herself into him and traced the muscles of his back.

His fingers skimmed the waistband of her jeans. Jacqui shuddered with unexplored passion. "Oh, Gavin," she groaned.

"Tell me." His voice was husky and hot on her skin. "Tell me what you want."

It was really the question Jacqui had been asking herself since she met Gavin. What did she want? For now, she knew only one thing.

"You," she said, placing her mouth on his. "Gavin, I want you. Here. Now."

"Here?" he echoed. "Now?"

She licked the side of his neck and nipped his earlobe with her teeth. "Yes," she whispered in his ear, her voice rough with desire.

Gavin kissed her hard. Grabbing her rear, he lifted Jacqui from her feet. She wrapped her legs around his middle. He was hard and fit between her thighs perfectly. Holding her to him, Gavin walked back to the table. He set her on the edge. Jacqui's clothes were too tight. She kicked off one shoe and worked her leg out of her pants. Gavin opened the fly of his jeans before removing a condom from his wallet that he always kept with him. After opening the package, he rolled the sheath down his length. Jacqui scooted to the edge of the table, ready and waiting.

He pulled her panties to the side. She wrapped her legs around his waist. Moving his hips forward, he entered her in one long stroke. She watched as his cock disappeared inside her. The image left her light-headed.

"Dammit, you are perfect, Jacqui. Absolutely perfect."

"Oh, Gavin." She was transfixed by their sex as Gavin moved inside her and back out. Watching the act was almost as erotic as the pleasure itself.

Reaching for his neck, she pulled him to her. The table rocked beneath them. Jacqui pressed her mouth to his and claimed another kiss. Gavin ground into her pelvis with his hips. She let out a whimper of delight.

"That? You like that? Hard. Deep."

"Yes. Yes. Yes."

Gavin growled and drove into her hard, fast.

Then she became a sum of her parts. Lips. Teeth. Tongues. Mouths. Bodies. Sweat. Mountains. Water. Eternity. Throwing her head back, she cried out with her climax as she shattered into a million pieces and floated into the sky. For a moment, Jacqui was one with the stars.

She settled into her body, her heartbeat racing. Gavin pumped into her harder. He cursed through gritted teeth as he came. He placed his lips on hers once again. This time, the kiss was languid. "That was fabulous," he said, slipping out of her. Gavin tucked himself into his jeans. "But we have to go inside now. I need to take care of the condom."

Jacqui shimmied back into her pants and slipped on her shoe. She stood. Her legs were weak, and she took a single wobbling step. Gavin reached for her elbow, keeping her upright. "You okay?" he asked. "I can carry you to the cabin."

Her pulse slowed, and she could finally hear her own thoughts. What had she done? "No, thanks." She slipped from his grasp. "I'm okay. I can walk."

"You sure?" he asked, his lips twitching into that smile she loved. "I don't mind."

Jacqui couldn't deny it. The desire to let Gavin hold her again was strong. What's more, she could never go back from being his lover. No way to forget how he tasted. Or how his hands felt on her breasts. Or how his breath washed over her shoulder, hot and ragged, as he came.

It was all too intimate for the short time that they'd known each other. Worse than that, she'd been nothing more than a horny fool to think that she wouldn't catch feelings after sex. Her fingers itched with the need to touch him and feel his hand on hers again.

At the same time, she wanted to get away. To hide.

But she couldn't. With her car at the hotel, she was stuck with Gavin for the night.

He asked again, "You sure that you are okay? I really can carry you to the cabin."

"No." She shook her head. "I'll be okay on my own."

The minute she spoke, she regretted what she'd said. Because in her words, Jacqui worried that she'd glimpsed her destiny.

GAVIN UNLOCKED THE door to the cabin, painfully aware of the leaking condom. He flipped a switch by the door.

The room erupted in light as several lamps turned on at the same time. "Make yourself comfortable." He waved a hand toward the living area. "I'll be right back."

Thank goodness a half bath was tucked behind the stairs. Had he really just made love to Jacqui Reyes on a picnic table by the lake? As he threw the used condom into the trash, he knew it was a stupid question to ask, even of himself.

True, he hadn't invited her to the cabin for seduction. Rather, she was here for her own safety. From the beginning, he'd known that she was different from the other women he usually dated—and honestly, it was a good thing.

Which meant what?

He washed his hands and exited the bathroom. Jacqui sat on the sofa and stared out of the large glass doors. He watched her for a moment before clearing his throat.

She looked up at him, her eyes wide. What was she thinking?

"Hey. You want something to drink? Beer? Wine?" Then he remembered that she hadn't had any alcohol at Caleb's place. "Water? A soda?"

"Water's fine," she said.

He grabbed two bottles from the fridge and walked back to the living room. "Here you go." He held out the water.

She took it—reaching for the cap. Was it his imagination, or had Jacqui tried hard to keep from touching his hand? He dropped into a chair. Now what?

The tension in the room was palpable, almost like a living and breathing entity.

Had Gavin ruined his budding friendship with Jacqui by taking her as his lover? Sure, the sex had been great. But at the moment, he was kind of low on friends.

He reached for her and she started.

"About what happened outside..." he began.

She squeezed his fingers before letting her hand slip from his grasp. "I usually don't do that, you know. Fall into bed with a guy after only knowing him for a few hours. Or perch myself on the side of a picnic table. Whatever. You know what I mean." She unscrewed the cap and took a long swallow of water.

"It wouldn't matter to me if you did. But I don't want this to be awkward between us."

"No, of course not. We're both adults." She tucked a lock of hair behind her ear. "I'm thirty-seven. And you're what, thirty-three? Thirty-four?"

Gavin opened the cap and lifted his own bottle to his mouth. "Try twenty-eight." He took a swallow of water.

"Twenty-eight?" She cursed under her breath before taking another drink. "Wow. Now, I'm a cradle-robber."

Yikes. He really didn't know what to do about their age difference. Yet, he had to do something to soothe her anxiety. "You know, it's not that big of a deal."

Her head snapped around. "Not a big deal?" She bit off each word as she spoke. "I get that you're famous. But me? Not so much."

"Whoa. Whoa. Whoa." Gavin held up his hands in surrender. "I meant that the difference in age wasn't that big of a deal. Not to me, at least."

She slumped into the couch. "Sorry about overreacting. I misunderstood." She paused. "And sorry about what I just said. It was rude of me."

"No worries," he said. But there was a lot to worry about. Namely that having sex with Jacqui had now ruined whatever connection they had created. He sighed, searching for something to do—or say—that could make things right. He had nothing. It was a hell of a way to be for a guy who made a living off his words.

Then again, it was easy to be honest with his listeners. When he was recording, it was just Gavin and the mic. He looked at his shoes. "I've enjoyed everything about meeting you, Jacqui. The past twenty-four hours have been..." He paused, trying to find a single word to encapsulate their day together. "Remarkable."

The sofa creaked as she shifted on her seat. "It has been quite the day."

At least her tone was softer than before. "And with what happened outside..." Gavin wasn't typically the shy type, but he imagined that Jacqui might be. "Well, I don't regret what happened. It's been a long time since I felt such a strong connection with another person. I just hope that you don't regret it either." He glanced up. She was watching him. For a moment, they regarded each other. The silence stretched out. "Aren't you going to say something?"

"My ass hurts."

Had he heard her right? "Your what?"

"I don't think I have a splinter in my butt or anything. But my rear is definitely raw from the picnic table."

He laughed. "Sorry. That's not funny." He paused

a beat. "Is it too soon for me to offer a kiss to make it better?"

She smirked. "It is kinda funny and it is too soon for that offer." She finished the final swallow of water. "But thanks."

It was late. Gavin was tired. He stood. "I can show you to the guest room upstairs."

"What about my bag?"

Oh yeah. Her stuff was still in the truck. "I'll get it. You can go up and get settled."

"Fair enough," said Jacqui. She set the water bottle on the table and stood as well.

"Up the stairs. Door at the end of the hall."

He waited as Jacqui disappeared up the stairs before heading out to the truck. The air was cold. Gavin exhaled, his breath freezing into a cloud. Hustling across the drive, he opened the side door. Jacqui's bag had been stowed next to the jump seat. He got it out, locked his brother's truck and hustled back to the cabin.

Damn. It was cold. He wondered if Blue Larkspur would see an early snow this year.

Back in the cabin, Gavin stood at the bottom of the stairwell. "I got your stuff," he called out. Lights were on in the second-floor hallway. He didn't hear a response. Maybe she hadn't heard him. He tried again. "I'll bring it upstairs in a second."

Still nothing.

He hoped that she wasn't the kind to give him the silent treatment. He hated that.

Bag still in hand, he flipped the lights off. He locked the door, making sure to engage the dead bolt as well.

Holding the bag in front of him, he walked up the narrow steps to the upper level. There were three rooms on the second floor: the master bedroom to the left, the bathroom to the right, the second bedroom, also to the right, at the end of the short hallway.

The bathroom door was shut. Inside, the light was on, and it spilled through the crack between door and jamb. Obviously, Jacqui was inside, which gave Gavin the chance to put her belongings in the guest room and get settled in for the night. "I'll put your stuff in your room," he said, speaking to her through the closed door. "If you need anything, just yell."

This time, he didn't wait for her answer.

At the end of the hall, he pushed the door open with the toe of his shoe.

He expected the room to be empty. But there she was, standing at the window. Her silhouette was a shadow against the darkness.

Sure, he'd been inside her. He'd felt her nails dig into his shoulders as she cried out with her orgasm. Yet, to see her standing there, just an ethereal form, was somehow more erotic.

Like a magnet to steel, he was drawn to her. He wanted to kiss her again. To touch her. To hold her once more.

Yet, she'd been clear about what she wanted—and didn't—from him.

He remained rooted in his spot.

Clearing his throat, he set the bag on the floor. "Sorry to interrupt. I thought you were in the bathroom. I should've knocked first."

"I was and then I came in here and saw this." She stepped back from the desk that he'd converted into a recording studio. "I still think it's cool—your podcast, I mean. Although, I'll never quite listen to it the same way from now on."

Gavin hated the idea of Jacqui being nothing more than a nameless and faceless listener. "The recording part isn't that complicated. I have this microphone, which is pretty high-grade, and record onto my computer." He came to stand beside her. Hitting the power button, he brought up his latest episode—the one about his father, which would never be produced. Then again, if he didn't have the horse thieves, what did he have? "I have a program that allows me to edit on my laptop, too." Gavin hit play. The moment his voice filled the room, he knew that he'd made a mistake.

"The road was dark and narrow. I hadn't seen another person for days, so I was shocked when I noted the car perched precariously on the side of a hill. But when I saw her walking on the side of the road, I knew she might be dangerous... But there was no way I could keep going. I had to stop."

He hit several keys at once. The sound stopped.

Jesus. Now what was he supposed to say? "Obviously, the script needs some work."

"Am I," she asked, "dangerous?"

"I was just trying to capture the moment I first saw you. I was in a lousy mood and there you were, ready to change my life."

She moved to the wall and flipped the switch, turning on a single floor lamp. "Be honest. Are you still trying to make me feel better for what happened outside? Me pushing you away?"

"Neither. Both. Hell, I don't know. It's just a stupid podcast, okay?" He gestured to her bag. "There's your stuff. I'll take you back to your car in the morning."

Gavin strode toward the door.

"Wait." Stepping toward him, she reached out for his arm.

He stopped. "Yeah?"

"Your introduction was nice, really. I'd keep listening to that episode."

"Yeah, well, I shouldn't have gotten testy with you. Sorry about that."

"Friends?" she offered.

At least it was something. "Of course we're friends."

"All right, then. Thanks for everything. You've been life changing, too."

He laughed. "To our grand adventure, right."

"Right."

"Well, good night."

"G'night." Jacqui let her hand slip from his wrist.

He stood on the threshold and waited a beat.

Would she say anything more? Should he?

Neither spoke.

Then again, their silence said volumes. With a final nod, Gavin walked into the hall. A hard knot dropped into his stomach that he recognized well. It was the feeling of regret. Without another word, he pulled the door closed.

Chapter Seventeen

Jacqui slept surprisingly well. She'd risen before sunrise and remade the small bed. As she smoothed out the blankets, she wondered if she owed her good night's sleep to the fabulous sex with Gavin.

The sounds of movement on the first floor were unmistakable. As was the rich aroma of coffee brewing. She realized that Gavin must be an early riser as well. Jacqui got dressed, putting on a long-sleeved T-shirt, jeans and her hiking boots. The casual wardrobe suited her life perfectly. And at the same time, it had become her uniform.

She couldn't help but think of the classic style of Isa. The chic Morgan. The bohemian Nadine. Maybe when she got back to Denver, Jacqui could go shopping for something new and fashionable. Or at least, a few things that weren't so utilitarian.

After tucking all her old clothes into her duffel bag, she pulled the zipper closed. She cast one last glance around the room, and pulled the door shut.

In the kitchen, Gavin stood at the sink. His back was to Jacqui. He wore a tight T-shirt that hugged the muscles in his back, and a pair of flannel pants. Which, though baggy, somehow accentuated his tight rear. Her mouth went dry as she recalled watching him enter her during their lovemaking. If she hadn't dismissed him, she could've spent the entire night in his bed.

As if her thoughts had become audible, Gavin looked up from the sink and smiled. "Morning."

Her cheeks grew warm. "Morning."

"Want some coffee?" He used a paring knife to point to a full pot.

Jacqui set her bag by the door. "Sure," she said, thankful for something to do besides ogle Gavin. A set of mugs sat on the counter. She filled them both.

"How do you take your coffee?"

"Black," he said.

She placed the mug near where he stood at the sink. "There you go."

"I don't have cream, but milk's in the fridge. The sugar is in the white dish by the stove."

Jacqui spooned sugar into her mug and stirred. "Whatcha making?"

"I'm not a great cook. Then again, living in New York and Chicago, you don't have to be. But I figured you'd want something to eat. I have some fruit salad and bagels."

"Sounds perfect." She slid into a chair at the table.

Gavin set down a bowl filled with sliced fruit, a plate of perfectly toasted bagels and a tub of cream cheese. He took a seat across from hers.

For a few minutes, they both helped themselves to food and said nothing. Sure, what happened between them last night was in the forefront of her mind. But it didn't mean it was the only thing that needed to be discussed. "Have you heard anything from Lawson?" she asked. "Did Henry Rollins ever show up?"

Gavin chewed on a bite of bagel before answering. "There were no messages when I got up this morning. I haven't called yet. Like Theo said last night, he's getting old. I figured I'd let him sleep for now. After I drop you off at your car, I'll go back to the range and collect the cameras. If I haven't heard from him by then, I'll call."

Jacqui speared a piece of apple with a fork and shoved it into her mouth. As she ate, she thought about just getting into her car and driving to Denver. She could disappear, like she'd never even been in Blue Larkspur at all. It would be the easiest and the best thing to do. And if that were true, then why did she say, "I'll go with you."

"Go with me where?"

"Back to the range. I want to see the herd one last time before I leave." Depending on what happened when she got back to work, it might be the last time she'd be allowed to see the herd at all.

"You don't have to—" Gavin began.

"I want to," she interrupted. "That is, if it's okay with you."

Gavin took a long swallow of coffee. For a moment, Jacqui was transfixed by the movement of his throat. "The two of us collecting the cameras together is fine with me." He stood. "Let me get dressed, and then I'll be ready."

Within minutes, her bag was tucked in Ezra's truck, and they were headed down the narrow dirt road. The sun crested over the mountain peaks, and before Jacqui knew it, they were passing the sign that read: Property of the Department of the Interior, Managed by the Bureau of Land Management, No Trespassing.

"The truck is better suited for these roads than my sports car," said Gavin, turning onto the narrow track that led up the hillside.

Had it been less than twenty-four hours since they'd been forced to abandon Gavin's car and trudge up to the range? "Seems like we've been at this for days." Soon, it would all be over.

Gavin parked on a bluff that overlooked the valley where the horses had been grazing. Jacqui sucked in a sharp breath as her heartbeat began to race. It wasn't what she saw that caused her pulse to spike—it was what was missing.

"Where are the horses?" She unbuckled her seat belt and opened the door.

"Wait a second," Gavin called after her.

Head pounding, face numb, she ran toward the grassy plain. "Where are the horses?" The dirt was chewed up with hoofprints and tire tracks. And then, she answered her own question. "My God, they've taken all thirty-seven."

Gavin was at her side. "We'll get this figured out."

"No," she said. Her chest was tight. "We won't. They're gone."

Crap. She'd messed up. If she hadn't flubbed the tracker, they'd know where Henry Rollins had gone. If she'd told the police before last night, Theodore Lawson would've had time to do more. Her eyes stung. "It's all my fault."

"We will get things figured out," Gavin said again.

"Are you serious? How?"

He pointed to a large outcropping. "We still have the cameras."

GAVIN SHADED HIS eyes and watched Jacqui clamber up the side of a boulder. In the distance, a hawk screeched. The wind blew and a dust devil swirled across the ground. Once she reached the top, he called out, "Is it still there?"

Jacqui picked up the camera and held it over her head. "It's here." She paused. "I'm going to toss it down. You okay to catch?"

"Sure can." He held out his hands and she threw the device to Gavin. If this had been football, it would have been a perfect pass. The camera was aimed at his chest, and he caught it easily. He smiled. They really did make a good team.

Jacqui descended from the large stones, sliding the last few feet. Dusting her hands on her thighs, she walked to where he stood. "Let's hope that this worked. If not, we got nothing."

Drawing a deep breath, Gavin flipped open the screen. A timer continued to run. Nineteen hours and forty-seven minutes. He exhaled. "We got them."

He rewound the video. The screen was filled with much of nothing beyond the sun rising in reverse and the night. And then at 3:00 a.m., all of that changed.

"Here it is."

From Gavin's estimation, it took over two hours to round up all the horses and force them into waiting trucks for transport. Even with the video playing at ten times the normal speed, and backward, he could see the animals rolling their eyes in terror. Large lights had been set up and made the range as bright as day. A dozen men kept the herd corralled. One by one, the animals were lassoed and pushed into waiting trailers. The last one to be caught was a black stallion. He stopped the video as anger sizzled in his veins. "The bastards."

Jacqui groaned. "I can't believe that they took them all in one night." She pressed a hand to her stomach. "I might get sick."

"I know how you feel," he said. Honestly, he did. The video left him slightly nauseated. Yet, he was also furious at whoever had stolen the horses. That fury filled him with a steely resolve. "Now's not the time to give up."

"I wish I had your confidence. This is a total disaster. Forget that I'll get fired. My job was to protect those horses. And because of me they've been taken to who knows where."

"That's not exactly true," said Gavin.

Jacqui narrowed her eyes. "What d'you mean?"

He started the video the moment before the convoy arrived and scanned the terrain. "They came from over there." He fast-forwarded to the moment that the last horse had been captured. At 5:08 a.m. the trucks left the range. "They went back the same way."

"Okay, so we do know which direction they were taken. How does that help us? We don't know their destination."

He handed the camera to Jacqui and removed the phone from his pocket. "It might not help us, but it'll help the police." He pulled up Lawson's contact information. After placing the call, he turned on the speaker function. A four-note tone filled the quiet morning. Damn. He should've known better. "No service up here."

"So, what do we do? Go back down the mountain and call the cops?" Jacqui chewed on her bottom lip.

Was she, like him, doing the math? It was almost 7:30 a.m. If the mustangs had been taken at roughly 5:10 a.m., then the horse thieves had a two-hour-and-twenty-minute head start. By the time they had cell service, another twenty minutes would have passed. How long would it take for Theo to get investigators back to the range? Another hour? Maybe, two?

"It'll take too long," she said. "We have to go after them."

Sure, Gavin knew that the chief had warned them about any continued involvement in the case. What's more, he knew why. Still, he agreed with Jacqui. "Come on," he said, holding his hand out to her. She slipped her palm into his. And honestly, Gavin felt like the strongest man in the world. "Let's go."

GAVIN DIDN'T HAVE any problems following the trail left by the horse thieves. Their heavy trucks and trailers, loaded down with the mustangs, mowed over small trees and bushes as they headed farther into the mountains.

"We're lucky," said Gavin.

Jacqui glanced at him from her side eye. "I assume that you're joking. What's the punch line?"

"No joke. The horse thieves didn't bother to cover their tracks. My guess as to why they weren't careful is they never thought anyone would try and follow them."

"That, and a convoy carrying more than three dozen animals would be pretty hard to hide."

"There's that, too," he agreed.

The engine whined as Gavin drove up the side of a hill. On the dashboard, the needle for the tachometer measured the engine's workload and climbed. The heat gauge rose. "C'mon," he urged the truck. "You can do it."

They crested the ridge and Gavin slammed on the brakes.

Jacqui braced her arms on the dashboard. "Everything okay?"

Everything was better than okay. "Look," he said, pointing to a narrow valley at the foot of the hill.

A paddock filled with horses sat next to a portable camper. It was the kind of RV that was hitched to the back of a pickup truck or large SUV. Yet, there were no vehicles to be seen.

"We found them," Jacqui said, her voice filled with relief. "Thank goodness."

Sure, Gavin had been expressly told by the police chief not to continue with the investigation. And yeah, that also meant that the episode on the horse thieves would never be aired. Yet, old habits die hard, and he mentally dictated the next segment of his episode.

Above the rumbling engine, the whinnying of dozens of horses could be heard. The early morning light reflected off the window.

It took Gavin a minute to realize what that meant. "Crap," he cursed and put the truck into reverse.

"What's wrong?" Jacqui asked, her voice now filled with alarm. "Where are you going? We just found the horses."

"We did." Looking over his shoulder as he drove, he came down the hill the same way he'd gone up. "We can see the trailer and the window."

Jacqui understood immediately. "And if we can see them, then they can see us."

Gavin put the gearshift into park. "That's exactly what I was thinking. Although I didn't *see* anyone."

"They wouldn't take all that effort to steal those horses just to leave them unguarded," she said.

Gavin nodded, but then he said, "Unless the thieves never thought they'd get found out and that it'd be safe to leave—at least for a little while."

It was Jacqui who spoke next. "What now? We should head back down the mountain until we have cell service. Then, we can call the cops, right?"

Of course that's what they should do. "Do me a favor, open the glove box."

Jacqui popped the latch and the door tumbled open. "What am I looking for?"

Gavin wasn't sure. "I just wonder what Ezra keeps in his car, that's all." He leaned across the center console.

Just being close to Jacqui brought up all the memories from their lovemaking last night. The way her breasts felt under his palm. The way she tasted. The way when Gavin held her in his arms, nothing else in the world mattered.

He pushed aside all those thoughts and turned his mind to what mattered now. The way he figured it, he only had a few minutes to find out everything he could about the horse thieves.

Inside the glove box, more than a dozen maps were secured with a rubber band. There was a stack of napkins, a reusable straw—who knew his brother was so environmentally conscious?—and, jackpot, a pair of binoculars. "These'll work."

He reached for the binoculars and shifted back onto his side of the truck. "I want to check out that compound," he said, planning as he spoke. "The more we know about who's there, the better our information for Theo. You stay here. Keep the engine running. Honk if you see anyone. And if they get too close—just go."

"If you think that you're going to leave me here while you do my job, think again." Jacqui unbuckled her seat belt before opening the passenger door.

If Gavin were honest, he wasn't surprised by her answer. Her commitment to her job and her independent spirit were two of the things he most admired about her. Still, he didn't want Jacqui anywhere close to danger. "You'll be safer here…" he began.

"Forget it." She jumped to the ground. "I'm in this up to my neck, same as you. I'm going to see this through." She turned toward the hill and began to climb.

For a moment, Gavin considered chasing after her and arguing. He knew that it'd do him no good. He turned off the engine and followed her up the hill. The climb was steep. The air was warm. Sweat dampened Gavin's back and chest.

Only feet away from the ridgeline, Jacqui stopped. "Should we stay low or something? We don't want anyone in that shack to see us, right?"

She was right. "Follow me."

He crouched behind a large rock. Jacqui pressed into his side. He ignored his thundering pulse and brought the binoculars to his eyes. Looking through the ocular, he adjusted the focus. He didn't see much more than he had before. The horses, their eyes wide, had been forced into a pen far too small for their number. There were no cars or trucks parked nearby. The travel trailer looked empty. "I don't think anyone's down there."

He passed the binoculars to Jacqui. She scanned the scene. "I think you're right."

"Why?" Gavin asked.

Jacqui lowered the binoculars and regarded him. "Why, what?"

"Why would someone do this? Why would they steal all of the horses?"

"If you had a buyer, an entire herd could add up to some real money."

Gavin shook his head. "So, that's what all of this is about? Cash?"

"I'm no expert, but isn't money what motivates most crimes?"

"I guess," he grumbled.

Jacqui peered over the top of the boulder again. "We should go down the mountain and call Theo, right?"

"We can do that, sure."

She turned to regard him. "I can tell from your tone. Something's on your mind."

"On my mind?" he said, echoing her words. Sure, she was right. And what's more, how had she gotten to know him so well? "It's just that I have a plan…"

JACQUI HAD TAKEN the chief's warning about not continuing their amateur investigation seriously. It's just that she couldn't argue with Gavin's reasoning. His plan: wait and watch the compound for a few minutes and make sure it really was empty. Then, explore the trailer and see if there was any evidence about who'd taken the wild mustangs—and why.

What made his plan all the more convincing was a simple fact. To contact the police, Gavin and Jacqui would also have to abandon the herd. By the time help arrived, there was no telling if the horses would still be here—or not.

It was much the same as her argument to follow the trail. So, after surveilling the valley for almost fifteen minutes, she was ready to see if the small trailer held any clues.

They climbed down from the hill. Outside the trailer, a generator sat on the ground and hummed. A cord led to an outlet, which she assumed powered the whole structure. In their pen, the horses neighed and whinnied as Jacqui and Gavin drew close. The air was thick with panic and fear. How had it come to this? Then again, she knew. "I should've called the police from the beginning."

"Now's not the time to second-guess yourself." Three metal steps led to the single door of the trailer. Gavin climbed the first two and paused. "Let's find out what we can and get out of here."

He pushed the door open with the toe of his shoe. The structure was a single room with metal walls and a metal floor. An old sofa that sagged in the middle sat along one wall. A card table with a camp stove was shoved into the corner. Several folding chairs surrounded the table.

In fact, the interior of the room was unremarkable—except for a desk that held a computer. The system was older, as far as tech went, with a large tower hard drive and a boxy monitor.

Okay, Jacqui had been able to tell from the outside that the trailer was small. What she hadn't known was how very much like a cell it would seem on the inside. Her skin turned clammy. She wanted to escape. But was she really willing to waste this opportunity?

"Let's see what's on this." He pointed to the computer.

"It might be password protected."

"Might be," Gavin agreed, as he slipped two chairs in front of the desk.

He hit the power button and the monitor winked to life. The screen was filled with a single field: password. "Dammit," Gavin cursed. "You're right. There's no way to guess what it might be."

In Jacqui's office, there were some computers that

several workers could access for a variety of reasons. Protocol insisted that the systems be password protected. To her it was a waste of time—especially since the login information had to be posted nearby. "Check under the keypad."

"The what?" he asked, but lifted it all the same.

There, taped to the desktop, was a slip of paper. SD421976.

Jacqui tapped the paper. "That's the password. Initials and date of birth."

Setting the keyboard back down, Gavin said, "Let's try it out."

Jacqui held her breath as he typed—not certain what she wanted. Sure, she wanted to find out who'd taken the horses, and why. But she was ready to get out of the trailer, get off the mountain and call the police.

Gavin hit enter, and a gray wheel began to slowly spin.

The screen blinked and one file appeared. It was conveniently labeled *Horses*.

After double-clicking the file, a list of thirty-seven documents appeared.

"There are thirty-seven in the herd. I bet each one of those—" she touched the screen, her claustrophobia all but forgotten "—is about a horse."

She waited as Gavin opened the first document. "You're right."

It was a listing of the gender, approximate age, markings, coloration and approximate price. Colt. Black-and-white. Two to four years old.

There was also the name and address of a buyer,

along with a broker. Jacqui pointed to the name. "I know him. He must've been the one who arranged the sales so quickly."

"Looks like we hit the jackpot," said Gavin.

"Can you email the folder?"

"Not without an internet connection."

"You wouldn't happen to have a flash drive on you?"

"Sorry," he said. "Fresh out."

They had to get the evidence. But how?

Jacqui slipped her phone from her pocket and snapped a picture of the first screen. "Now all we need to do is figure out who SD is." She checked the photo. It was grainy but legible. "Until then, let's get pictures of each document."

"I like the way you think." Gavin opened another document. It was the same as the previous one. Mare. Brown, white socks. Six to nine years old.

Jacqui snapped another picture.

Soon, they fell into a rhythm. Gavin opening the documents and Jacqui taking the photos. It took them less than fifteen minutes to get through the entire file.

She checked the final picture to make sure all the information was visible. "This helps a lot. It doesn't bring us any closer to finding out who stole the horses, or why."

Still, they had a lot to pass on.

Gavin closed all the documents and rose from his seat. "Let's get those pictures to the authorities. They'll be able to do more than we can."

He was right. Still, she stood in the small trailer and

hesitated. Was there more to be learned? Were they leaving clues behind?

Gavin opened the door. Sunlight streamed across the floor. He climbed down two steps before turning back to Jacqui. "You ready?"

Was she? She scanned the room. A small twinge pulled at the back of her neck. Jacqui tucked her phone back into her pocket, and she pulled the door closed behind her. "Let's get out of here."

They stepped outside. The paddock was less than a dozen yards away and snuffles from the horses filled the air. "We can let them go now, you know," said Gavin.

It was true, they could. The horses would stay as a herd and eventually find their way back to the range controlled by the Bureau of Land Management. "But won't the chief need them as evidence? Won't that make his case against the thieves airtight if the horses are here? Not so much if it's our word against..." She paused. Aside from Henry Rollins, they still didn't have a name. "Whoever stole them in the first place."

"You're right about that, sure. But aren't there more important things than just finding out who took the horses?"

Jacqui regarded the horses in the pen. She had a decision to make: What was best for the herd?

A cloud of dust rose from the east, and her heart ceased to beat. Then, she realized what had made her so nervous in the trailer. She'd heard the far-off sound of engines. Outside, the horses' neighing had masked the noise.

Gavin followed her gaze. "What's that?" His voice was full of alarm.

"It's the horse thieves," she said, breathless. "They're coming back."

Chapter Eighteen

Gavin grabbed Jacqui's hand.

He said the only thing that came to mind. "Run!"

They sprinted up the narrow valley and headed toward the hill. Getting over the lip of the ridge was the only way they'd escape. But could they climb to the top of the slope in time?

A gunshot rang out, the report echoing like thunder. A cloud of dust erupted several feet in front of Gavin as the bullet struck the ground. The horses began to whinny, spooked by the thunderclap of gunfire.

"Oh my God," she cried. "They're shooting at us. Who shoots first and asks questions later? What kind of people are these?"

"They're the bad kind." Gavin tried to run faster, pulling Jacqui with him. The peak of the hill loomed in the distance. It was less than a quarter mile, but to Gavin it might as well be on the far side of the moon. Still, he wasn't willing to give up. Not yet. "C'mon."

Another shot. This one closer.

Were these bullets just a warning? And what would happen if they kept running?

A third gunshot rang out. His calf felt like a hot steel blade had been driven through it. Then, his leg went numb. His foot quit working. Gavin crumpled to the ground.

Dust burned his eyes. Sand and grit filled his mouth. He felt the blood pumping out of the hole in his leg, hot on his skin, with each beat of his racing heart. His jeans were doused in gore. Jacqui slipped her arm under his shoulder and pulled him to standing.

Pressing her lips to his ear, she screamed to be heard over the sound of approaching vehicles. "We have to get out of here."

"Leave me," he said. "You go. Call for help."

"No way." She pulled him along. "You and I are in this together."

Sure, they were brave words. But this wasn't some adventure for two amateur sleuths. The consequences were now deadly serious. He needed Jacqui to save herself. But how? He could think of nothing beyond the fiery agony that filled his leg. "Please, Jacqui," he said, gritting his teeth against the pain. "Just go."

"I'm not leaving you. And you're wasting your breath in arguing."

They hobbled forward a few steps before a truck raced past. The tires kicked up a khaki-colored cloud of dirt. It swerved to a stop, blocking their path. As the dust settled, Gavin could see two men sitting in the cab. They were both big guys with thickly muscled biceps. The driver revved the engine.

Gavin understood the warning—*take another step and I'll run you over.*

Lifting one palm, Gavin surrendered. He held tight to Jacqui's shoulder with his other hand. Two more vehicles came up from the rear—a dark luxury SUV and Henry's dark sedan.

Without warning, he began to mentally narrate another podcast episode.

The pain in my leg could only be described as fiery, which was in absolute juxtaposition to the blood that ran down my leg and pooled my shoe. Dust coated everything. My skin. My lips. Jacqui's hair. As I stood there, holding her to me, I knew that I'd do anything to keep her safe. The question was, could I bluff my way out of this situation?

Dear God, what kind of person was he that he couldn't turn off his internal monologue?

Then again, maybe his monologue would be enough to save their hides.

The passenger door of the SUV opened and a short man with slicked-back dark hair and a golf shirt jumped to the ground. The two men in the truck exited as well.

If Henry Rollins drove his own car, he stayed behind the wheel.

As the shorter man approached, Gavin swallowed down all his shock and alarm. "What the hell, man. Who shot me?" He glared at the guy with the gun, pain turning his vision hazy.

The shooter glanced at the shorter guy for guidance.

"This here is what you call private property. That makes you two trespassers."

"It's not private property," said Jacqui, her words filled with resolve. "It's owned by the federal government."

The last thing he wanted was for her to tell the truth. He squeezed her shoulder a little to give her a hint that something was up. "This is public land, which means we have a right to be out here hiking. We heard the horses and came to see what was going on."

The shooter again looked at the shorter man. "Silas?"

Gavin would bet money that this was the broker of the stolen horses.

Silas asked, "Why was you running if this is all public land?"

"Why would you shoot?" Gavin asked. "You know, you'll be lucky if I don't sue. Let's go."

He hobbled around the grille of the truck, leaning heavily on Jacqui. Had they done it? Were they about to walk—correction, limp—away? Gavin wanted to smile but dared not.

"Stop them," said Silas.

There was no way that he could fight off the two thugs, especially since one of them was armed. Gavin froze. What was his next best play?

Too bad his inner narration had nothing to offer.

Rough hands pulled Jacqui away from Gavin.

"Hey," he protested, swiping through the air for her arm. From the moment he saw her on the road, Gavin knew it was his job to protect her. But he'd failed. The thought left him sick, as pain throbbed through his leg with each beat of his heart.

They were spun around and forced to face Silas. Thank goodness one of the goons had him by the arm. Without him, Gavin would've fallen over already.

Silas asked, "You didn't really think that I was going

to let you walk away, did you? Maybe my boys are a little trigger-happy, but the last thing I want is for you to go back to town and call the cops. Especially since I don't believe a word of your BS story about hiking. And yeah, this is federal land, but being here without authorization is against the law."

"What'd you want me to say?" he asked.

"Start by telling me the truth." Silas wore a large ring on his pinky. He spun the band as he spoke. "What're you doing out here?"

"So, I tell you the truth and you'll let us go?" Gavin asked, dubious.

"I think you're failing to understand your situation," said Silas, stepping closer to Gavin. The scent of pine-tinged cologne rolled off the guy in waves. "It doesn't matter what you say. You're not leaving this valley alive."

JACQUI'S MOUTH WENT DRY. She tried to breathe, but her chest was tight. Silas's words still hung in the air, not yet blown away by the breeze. *"You're not leaving this valley alive."*

They'd never outrun or overpower these men with their guns, never mind that Gavin had already taken a bullet to the leg. It meant that if she wanted to survive, she had to think. Plan. Act.

What they needed was help. But how could she get in touch with the police, when she couldn't even make a call?

Jacqui's eye was drawn to Henry Rollins's car. Her

mind was drawn back to yesterday morning in Ezra's home office.

From his box of tech, he'd just removed a device that was the size and shape of a cell phone.

Was the tracking device still on Henry's car? Could Jacqui get to it and turn on the panic button without Silas and his goons knowing?

Did she have any other option than to try?

Using an old trick taught to every child when the subject of stranger danger arose, Jacqui turned to the man who gripped her arm and drove the heel of her shoe into his crotch. With a groan, he dropped like a sack of potatoes. She sprinted toward the car, barely aware of the screams and orders for her to stop.

Dropping to her stomach, she commando crawled under the auto. The stench of motor oil and gasoline was strong. At least Henry had turned off his engine when he parked, or she'd be crawling through a fog of exhaust as well. The device was where Jacqui had placed it the day before. She reached for the tracker as the car door opened and a pair of worn boots dropped to the ground. She turned on the tracker, double clicking the power button. It emitted a green light.

"What the hell are you doing?" Henry asked, while dropping to his knee and peering under the car. Her heart sank as his gaze traveled to the device. What would he do? What would he say? Was her one gamble a bust?

He stared at her and said nothing. Then, Henry nodded.

Jacqui wanted to weep tears of gratitude, but she

didn't have the time. Sliding her finger to the emergency call button, she pressed down. A small red light blinked on. Her distress call was sent.

Jacqui had only an instant to celebrate before rough hands grabbed her ankles and began to pull. She slid across the rocky ground. She clawed at the dirt, the rocks—anything that would keep her under the car. It was no use. Whoever had her legs was strong.

"You think you're smart?" It was the man she'd kicked. He recovered enough to pull her out from under the sedan—but now, he was mad. He jerked her to her feet and slammed his fist into her stomach. The impact of the blow sent Jacqui tumbling back into the car. She fell face forward into the dirt, unable to breathe. "That's for kicking me in the balls, you little bitch."

She lay on the ground, gasping for air. Sure, she'd enabled the tracker and had sent an emergency call. But was it enough? Would Ezra see the distress signal before it was too late?

GAVIN AND JACQUI had been walked—or in his case, been dragged—back to the cramped trailer. They sat side by side on the small sofa. There was a lot for him to regret, but what good would it do?

His inner narrator assessed his situation.

Silas had two henchmen—muscle-bound men who said little. Henry Rollins was also in the trailer and he said nothing. Finally, up close to Henry, I was able to see details that I'd missed before. Like the fact that he had a black eye, a fat lip and several bruises to his face. There were also cuts on his hands. As Henry re-

garded the floor, and I regarded Henry, I couldn't help but wonder if he'd been beaten by these henchmen.

We were forced into the trailer. And with so many people in such a small space, the stench of body odor hung in the air. But I kept asking myself—what was going to happen next? Were Jacqui and I going to be questioned? Beaten, like Henry? Although, we both knew the outcome was going to be much worse.

Silas had already told us how this story was to end. To be honest, I didn't worry about myself as much. But Jacqui? Well, I'd do anything to keep her safe. Too bad that I was out of options.

Jacqui reached for Gavin's hand, twining her fingers through his. The pain in his leg seemed to lessen. The simple touch gave him the courage to speak up. "What d'you want from us?"

"I want to know who you are," said Silas. "And I want to know what you know."

"We're nobody," said Jacqui, bringing up his earlier lie. "And if you let us go now, we won't say a thing, not even about how Gavin got shot."

"Stand up," Silas ordered Jacqui. "Empty your pockets."

Folding her arms across her chest, she glared at the man. Silas flicked his fingers, and one of the goons pulled Jacqui to her feet. Roughly, he patted her down and removed her phone from her pocket. "This is all she's got."

Silas took the phone and held it out to Jacqui. "Enter the passcode."

She snorted. "Figure it out yourself."

Gavin was impressed with her bravado. Then again, it would do no good to antagonize a man like Silas. He held the phone in front of Jacqui's face. Her image had been programmed into her lock, and the phone opened. Silas began to scroll through the content of her cell. "No messages sent or received this morning. No calls. No emails." He gave a chuckle. "Not very popular, are you?"

"Why would I call anyone? We're just out…"

"Hiking, you told me," Silas said, as he continued to examine her phone.

Gavin silently prayed that he wouldn't think to look at the photo roll. His prayers went unanswered.

Silas said, "Well, looky here. What an interesting picture for a hiker to take." He held up the screen. It was a photograph of the computer screen along with the purchase order for one of the horses. "Why don't we start over? You tell me the truth about who you are and what you know. You do that, and I'll take it easy on you. *Bam. Bam.* One shot each to the back of your head. You keep lying and I'll let my associates kill you slow."

Silas's words sent a chill down Gavin's spine. It was more than the deadly threat; he knew the other man would make good on his promise.

"What's going on?" Silas placed the phone on the floor and smashed the screen with his heel.

Jacqui looked over her shoulder, her gaze connecting with Gavin's. In her expression he saw more than fear and dread—but regret as well. "I'm sorry," she said, her voice thick with emotion.

"You don't need to apologize to him. It's me who needs to hear what you have to say."

Jacqui said nothing and Gavin could only guess what she was thinking or feeling. The thing was, over the last two days, Gavin had come to care for Jacqui. He'd been stupid not to tell her last night after they made love.

But now? Would he ever get another chance?

"Don't say you weren't warned," said Silas, gesturing to one of the goons.

"No," Gavin roared. He struggled to stand, ready to fight for Jacqui with his last breath. "I won't let you hurt her."

Silas smiled. The expression left Gavin cold. "You got this all wrong. I'm not going to hurt her to get her to talk. It's you who's going to feel the pain."

The goon slammed his fist into Gavin's face. His head snapped back, and he lost his footing. He stumbled backward, landing on the sofa. His whole face throbbed. Blood filled his mouth and he spat red on the floor.

"Now, I'm gonna ask you again once more real nice like. Who are you?"

She cleared her throat. "My name is Jacqui Reyes. I work for the Bureau of Land Management as a wildlife biologist. Managing the wild mustangs is part of my job."

"And who's he? Your coworker?"

She glanced at Gavin again.

"You keep your eyes on me, you hear?" Silas said. "Make sure that Jacqui understands that she keeps her eyes on me."

One of the henchmen kicked Gavin. The blow landed

near where the bullet had torn through his leg. The pain was too intense for him to contain. Despite himself, he screamed.

"Your friend," said Silas. Gavin lay on the floor sweating. "What's his name? What's he do?"

"His name is Gavin Colton," said Jacqui. Her voice was small even in the cramped space. "He's a true crime podcaster."

"Gavin Colton," one of the thugs said. "No kidding. I love his show."

"Shut up, stupid," Silas snapped. "Now, I have to ask myself how'd a wildlife biologist and true crime podcaster become a team? And how'd the two of you end up here?"

"Don't say anything," Gavin gasped. "Don't say a word."

Silas cocked his head to the side. The thug-fan kicked Gavin in the middle. He retched on the floor. Certainly, he didn't want to die, especially since he had so much to live for. Now, his life wasn't just about fortune or fame. Gavin had just connected with his family. There was Jacqui—she was the best thing to happen to him in a long time. Yet, to have such an ignominious ending was something he couldn't bear.

"We haven't known each other long," Jacqui said. "In fact, we just met on Friday night."

"Go on," Silas urged.

"I came into town from Denver that evening and checked in on the herd. On the way off the mountain, a car forced me from the road. It was a hit-and-run. Anyway, Gavin found me a few minutes later. I was the one who asked him to help me figure out what was happening with the horses."

"Happening with the horses?" Silas repeated, his tone suspicious. "Why would you even think that something was wrong with the herd?"

"Umm…" Jacqui's voice trembled.

"Umm? Is that all you have to say to me? You answer all of my questions when I ask, understand?" Silas asked.

"Understood," she said, her voice quavering.

"All right, boys, make him hurt."

One of the henchmen pulled Gavin to his feet. The other punched him on the nose. Gavin felt the crunch of cartilage giving way. He was hit in the gut. On the chin. On the cheek. His ears began to buzz.

Yet, he could hear Jacqui's pleas. "Stop it! I'm begging you. I'll tell you anything, just stop hurting Gavin."

"That's enough," said Silas.

The thug let go of Gavin and he slumped to the floor. Every part of his body hurt, ached or throbbed. He wanted to go to sleep and pray that he was shot before he woke up. But he refused to pass out and leave Jacqui alone with a group of criminals.

"I got a call on Friday morning. Someone warned me that there were thieves coming after the herd. They didn't give a name and blocked their number, so I don't know who it was. That's when I decided to come here and see if the tip was real. Or not."

"You got that message?"

"It was on my phone. The one you trashed."

"Well," said Silas, his voice a slow drawl. "There's

really only one person who it might be, so I don't need that message anyway."

The entire time they'd been in the trailer, Henry had neither said nor done a thing. Yet, he pushed the door open and jumped to the ground. Through eyes that were almost swollen shut, Gavin watched as Henry ran. One of the thugs removed his firearm from a holster at his hip. He took his time getting Henry into his sights. He pulled the trigger. The gun's report echoed in the trailer as Henry fell to the ground.

"Go make sure he's dead," Silas ordered. "Then dig a hole big enough for three. We'll come back for these two and bury them all together. Let's go."

The door slammed shut and Jacqui dropped to Gavin's side.

"Oh my God, how are you?"

"I've been better," he said, trying to make a joke.

"I turned on the tracker," she said. For a moment, her words made no sense. Was Gavin so damaged physically that he was hallucinating?

"You what?"

"The tracker Ezra gave us. I turned it on. I also hit the panic button. That's why I ran to Henry's car."

"Did it work?" He pushed up to a sitting position. The effort left him breathless.

"To be honest, I don't know."

"Then there's only one thing left for us to do?"

"Oh yeah, what's that?"

"Pray."

Gavin understood a single and sad fact. If he'd ever been the church-going kind, he'd have prayed for someone like Jacqui to come into his life. But now, there was no hope for them to have a future together—or even a future at all.

Chapter Nineteen

Ezra picked up the plate. "There you go, Neve. My world-famous chocolate chip pancakes." He waited as the child took a bite. "What d'you think?"

She chewed for a moment and then, her eyes went wide. "They are good as Miss Jacqui said. Chocolate chip pancakes are my favorite, too."

His chest felt tight, but in a good way. "I'm glad that you like them."

Theresa stood at his side, a coffee cup in hand. "Thanks for making breakfast." She placed a kiss on his cheek.

Honestly, Ezra should be thanking her. He never thought that his life would include great kids and an amazing woman. He pulled her to him and placed his lips on hers. "Oh, babe, you are so welcome."

Claire fluttered into the kitchen, fairy wings already on her back. "Do I smell pancakes? I do. I do."

To Ezra, it was amazing that two siblings could have such different personalities. Then again, he was one of a dozen Colton kids—and no two of them were alike.

"How many pancakes do you want, Claire Bear?" he asked, reaching for an empty plate.

"Two," said Claire. "And then, can I eat in your office?"

That was one thing he'd learned over the past few months—kids really would say the darnedest things. "You want to eat in my office? Why?"

"I like watching the flashing light on your computer."

Ezra's pulse went sluggish. "The what?"

"There's a red light on your computer that just blinks and blinks and blinks. It's like a fairy light showing me where a fairy lives."

The only thing that would bring up a red dot on a map was the panic button on the tracker he'd given to Gavin and Jacqui. But the tracker still wasn't powered up. He'd checked first thing this morning. Which meant…what? Had someone turned it on? But that'd be impossible, right?

He handed the plate to Theresa. "Can you take care of this, babe?"

He didn't wait for her reply. Ezra rushed down the hall. At the threshold, he stopped. His slow pulse started to race. Claire had been right. A red light pulsated on his monitor.

Crossing the floor, he sat at his desk and studied the screen. The tracker was on federal land, near where the wild mustangs grazed.

What in the hell was going on?

Pulling the phone from his pocket, he placed a call.

It was answered after the third ring. "This is Gavin Colton. Leave me a message. I'll call you back."

"This is Ezra. The tracker and the panic button have been turned on. I need to know that you and Jacqui are safe. Call me back, brother."

He hung up the phone, not satisfied in the least. Pulling up his contact list again, he placed another call. This one was answered after the second ring. "Ezra," said Dom, his voice a sleepy drawl. "It's Sunday morning. What's going on?"

"Nothing good." A hard knot dropped into his gut. "We've got problems and I need your help."

WITHOUT HER PHONE, Jacqui lost track of time. Gavin was hurt badly. Bruises and cuts covered his face. His nose was broken, and she suspected that he had a concussion. There was also the gunshot wound to his leg, along with the loss of blood. She gave him what first aid she could with next to nothing on hand. She'd been resourceful enough to rip the sleeves from her shirt and make a tourniquet for his gunshot wound. She'd helped him get settled on the sofa. His head was in her lap, and she stroked his hair.

And still, she didn't know how long they had been locked in the trailer.

Was it minutes? Or hours?

Or maybe, she should be asking a different question. How long did it take to dig a grave for three? Whatever the time, they didn't have much longer. There was so much she wanted to say to Gavin. They'd only spent two days together. Yet, she'd loved and laughed more than she had for years.

"Hey, Jacqui?" Gavin's lips were swollen, and his speech was slurred.

"Yeah?"

"You know, this would've made a hell of a podcast."

Her eyes began to water. It was time that she was honest with herself. Even if she had enabled the tracker, help wasn't coming. "It'd be the best episode ever."

"You know, I'm glad we met."

Was he? A pang of guilt filled her chest. If she'd never asked him for help—or if she'd gone to the police at the beginning—they wouldn't be in trouble. Her throat closed around a hard kernel of regret. "I am so sorry…"

He shushed her. "Without you, I never would've made peace with my mom or my family. I got away from the mic and telling stories to actually live."

"Usually living doesn't include so much dying though, you know?"

"Well, there is that." He gave her his wry smile and then winced.

"You okay?"

"Aside from the fact that everything hurts I'm fine."

She laughed out loud.

"I love your smile," he said. Lifting his hand, he stroked the side of her face. "Jacqui, kiss me."

Desperate to remember this moment, she placed her lips on his. As she kissed him, Jacqui was sorry about just one thing. Why had she pushed Gavin away last night? Why hadn't she just let him love her, even if it was just for a few hours?

And now, there was nothing left for her to do.

No. She wouldn't just wait around to get murdered.

She broke away from him and looked around the room. There wasn't much. But they did have the kerosene stove, the old computer tower and the heavy monitor. None of them were the best of weapons, but she didn't have the luxury of being picky. "I have a plan," she said.

"A plan?" he echoed.

"Well, maybe not a plan but I refuse to give in without a fight. Can you stand?" Although if they were going to get away, then Gavin would have to be able to do more than get on his feet. He'd have to be able to run as well.

He sat up. "I can do it. Tell me what you need."

She stood, crossed the trailer and looked out of the single window. The two henchmen were still digging the hole.

Jacqui ripped a length of cord from the computer and handed it to Gavin. "When they open the door, I'm going to be waiting with this." She picked up the heavy metal stove. "I'll hit the guy on the head and then you tie him up."

"That's one bad guy down. What do we do with the other two?"

"We hope that our guy has a gun, then we can shoot our way out. We don't need to make it back to our truck. We just have to get to one of the three cars and then, if the keys are in the ignition, we can get away."

"There's a lot of *ifs*."

She looked back out the window. The hole was complete. The goons dragged Henry's body to the pit and threw him inside. They didn't have much time now. "You have any better ideas?"

He gave a quick shake of his head. "None. But what if your plan doesn't work?"

"Then we'll die anyway, but I refuse to go down without a fight."

She glanced out the window again, and her stomach dropped to her shoes. "One of them is coming."

"You ready?" she asked.

"No, but I don't have any choice."

Jacqui pressed her back against the wall. The stove was heavy and the muscles in her arms ached. The door opened and a figure stepped through. Jacqui aimed at the back of his head and marshaled all her strength. She swung the stove. The metal connected with flesh and bone with a hollow *thunk*. The man stumbled and fell backward and out of the door. He hit the ground and a pool of blood began to spread from the wound to his head.

Damn. He'd fallen the wrong way. What was she supposed to do now? Leave the trailer and search his pockets for a gun or car keys and hope that she picked the correct vehicle? Or did she stay in the safety of the trailer?

Before she could decide, Silas screamed, "What the f— Shoot her! Shoot her now!"

The other thug pulled a weapon from a shoulder holster. He aimed and fired. The bullet hit the cookstove and ricocheted through the wall at her side.

She'd been lucky once, but Jacqui didn't think that her luck would hold.

EVEN EZRA WAS impressed with how quickly a partnership formed to investigate the tracker's location. There was Ezra, Dom and, of course, Oliver. They were joined by Chief Lawson and several of his deputies. They'd cut across federal land and found his abandoned truck at the foot of a hill. On the other side was the tracker. Each man knew that what waited for them on the other side was deadly serious.

"I say we deploy drones," said Oliver. "That way we can get an idea of what's going on."

Before anyone could agree or disagree, the sound of a single gunshot rang out. Ezra didn't think; he just double-timed it up the hill. Everyone followed. From the ridgeline, it was easy to assess the situation. Nothing that he saw was good.

There was a pit with what Ezra assumed was a corpse in the bottom. One man lay on the ground at the bottom of the trailer's steps. A pool of blood turned the ground black.

Jacqui stood at the door to the trailer.

"Christ almighty, did she bring a cookstove to a gunfight?" Oliver asked.

Ezra would've found it funny but his brother was right. Another man had a gun drawn—and it was pointed directly at Jacqui.

JACQUI STARED AT the man with the gun. Her heartbeat hammered against her ribs. There was no other means of escape. No way to fight back. These were her last moments on earth, she knew. Looking over her shoulder, she watched Gavin. He'd faded out of consciousness again.

She'd lived more in the past two days than she had for the past few years combined. Too bad they didn't have more time together. If they did, she wondered what other adventures they would have taken—if they had the chance.

The sound of a gunshot echoed off the hills.

She braced for the impact. The pain.

It never came.

She watched the thug. He still held his weapon, but a trickle of blood leaked from his lips. A tiny dot of red stained the front of his shirt. The stain grew as the man's eyes went wide. He fell forward and landed on his face.

In the distance, Silas growled with rage and frustration.

Then, a new voice seemed to come from the heavens. "Put your hands in the air and keep them where they can be seen."

Jacqui dropped the stove and jumped to the ground. She looked onto the ridge. Half a dozen men aimed their guns at Silas. It took her only a minute to recognize Ezra, Dominic, Oliver and the police chief. Waving her arms, she ran to the base of the hill.

"It's Gavin," she yelled. "He's hurt and needs help."

A MEDEVAC HELICOPTER was called to pick up Gavin and take him to the local hospital. By the time the chopper lifted off, more than two dozen law enforcement officers were on the scene. Jacqui had told her story over and over, always including every detail.

Yet, she wanted nothing more than to go to the hospital to see Gavin.

She sat on the hood of a police cruiser and spoke to Chief Lawson. "Any idea when I can get out of here?"

Theodore shook his head. "No idea. I'd say you're going to be here for a while."

"A while?" Even she heard the disappointment and dismay in her tone.

"Jeremy Michaels is on his way. He wants you to brief him personally."

Jacqui would be lucky if she still had a job by the end of the day. "How's Gavin?"

"Last I heard, he made it to the hospital. His brothers are headed there now. If I get an update, I'll pass it along."

She nodded. "Thanks for everything."

Theo narrowed his eyes. "You know, you two are lucky to be alive. If you'd died out here, we'd never have found your bodies."

Her eyes started to burn. She blinked hard. "I don't know what to say…"

Shaking his head, he sighed. "I don't mean to be gruff—it's just that I've always looked out for Gavin. Now, I'm looking out for you, too." He paused. "Besides, you'll both get to be heroes for stopping the horse thieves."

Yeah, but at what cost? More even than her job was Gavin's well-being. There were the wounds she could see—but were there others that she couldn't? Would he be okay in the end? And would she ever see him again?

GAVIN WAS COLD. At the same time, it felt as if his body wasn't completely attached to his mind. He blinked and opened his eyes. His mother stood next to his bed and stroked the back of his hand.

"Where am I?" His throat was raw, and it hurt to speak.

"You're in the hospital. They took you in for emergency surgery to get the bullet out of your leg. Your nose is broken. You have a concussion and several bruised ribs. But considering everything, you're actually lucky."

It all came back to him. The beating delivered by Silas and his goons. What he didn't know was how he made it out alive. He looked around the room. "Where's Jacqui?"

"The last I heard from Theo is that she was speaking to her superiors about what happened. It sounds like a lot of evidence was recovered from that trailer."

Somewhere, in the fog of his mind, he knew that his mother had given him good news. But Gavin couldn't process what was being said.

And yet there was something important he needed to say. "Hey, Mom."

"Yeah, Gavin."

"When I was a kid, I was kind of a pain."

"Not really," said Isa.

"No really, I was. I was mad about how everything worked out for me. I'm sorry."

"You don't have to apologize," she said.

"I do." There was more that he needed to say to his mother, but he couldn't remember. Maybe if he closed his eyes it would come to him.

His mom pressed her lips to his forehead. "You rest. I'm going to the waiting room to let your brothers and sisters know that you're awake."

Well, he was awake now. Yet had he heard her correctly? Sure, Ezra would come to the hospital. Maybe Dom or Oliver. But who else would stop by? "My what? Who's here?"

"Your brothers and sisters," his mom repeated. "You know—all eleven of them."

"They're all here?"

"Of course, Gavin. Where else would they be?"

He wasn't sure.

"We Coltons stick together—whether you like it or not."

Now, that really was too much for him to comprehend at the moment. But as Gavin let his eyes close again, he smiled. Finally, he understood what it was to be a family and that he had a place where he belonged.

Epilogue

Gavin sat on the deck, a cup of coffee in hand, and watched the sky reflected in the water. It had only been a few days since he'd been shot, and he had a long recovery ahead of him. In spite of his injuries, the doctors didn't think it was necessary to keep him overnight, so he'd been discharged on Sunday evening.

After spending three nights at his mother's house, he'd had enough doting and care. After cajoling Ezra, Gavin had gotten a ride back to his cabin—and so far, he was okay.

Sure, he loved his family but he also needed his space.

He could hear the revving of an engine, along with the crunch of wheels on the gravel road for a full minute before the car came into view. He rose from his seat and held tight to the railing.

She parked her small sedan next to his sports car and turned off the engine. Jacqui opened the door, and the sight of her took away his breath.

"Hey, stranger," he called out.

"I'm heading back to Denver this morning. Still, I couldn't leave without stopping by to see how you're doing."

"You know, everything hurts but it's good to be alive." Was this going to be how it ended between them? A quick goodbye before she left his life as abruptly as she had entered. He hobbled across the patio. "You want me to make you a cup of coffee for the road?"

"Sure," she said, climbing the steps to the deck. "But on one condition—you let me make it."

"You don't like my coffee?"

"Your coffee's great. It's not that. You just look like you could use a little TLC."

He walked slowly into the cabin. "I've had nothing but TLC from my mom and my sisters for days. Trust me, I can do without any more." The short walk had stolen all his energy. He set his cup on the table before dropping onto the sofa. "But I will let you grab yourself some joe and stay for a visit."

Jacqui filled a mug and joined him in the living room. "I stopped by the hospital on Sunday night, but you'd already been discharged. Theo told me that you were at your mom's. I didn't want to intrude. Then, he mentioned that you were here and, well, I decided to stop by. I hope I'm not a bother."

"You? A bother? Never."

"Hope not." She took a sip. "So, how are you? Really?"

"Honestly?" he asked.

She nodded.

"Everything does hurt. I am so thankful to be alive."

He reached for her hand. "Thank you for keeping me alive—for fighting for both of us."

She twined her fingers through his. When had his hand become a perfect fit for hers? "I'm glad it all worked out—except for Henry. Turns out, he owed Silas Dunn—the turd in charge—several thousand dollars. Seems like Henry wanted to trade a horse or two for his debt. But Silas wanted them all."

"Why'd he call you?" Gavin asked.

"I can only guess, but I think that he wanted me to call the police."

"Why didn't he call them himself?"

Jacqui slid her hand from his and reached for her cup. She took another drink of coffee. "Your guess would be as good as mine. But the bottom line is that we'll never know." She paused. "Are you still going to do a podcast about the horse thieves?"

"I haven't decided yet. Would it bother you if I did?"

She set the cup on the table. "I think you should. The world would be fascinated by your story."

"It's our story, you know."

She gave a small laugh and shook her head. "Yeah, but you're the famous one." She rose from her seat. "I should go. It's a long drive back to Denver."

"Don't go," he said.

She stared at him for a minute. "I guess I can stay a little bit longer. Do you need me to help with anything?"

"There's a lot that I need from you," he said. Gavin hadn't thought any of this through, but as soon as he started speaking, he knew that it was right. "But mostly, I want to see where we can go together."

"What do you want? To try a long-distance relationship?"

Long distance. Gavin didn't like the sound of that. "I want to know how you like your eggs cooked. Or what your favorite movie is. Or book. Or song. Or if you cry during greeting card commercials. I want to go leaf peeping with you. And I will always give you my coat because you'll always be cold." He drew in a deep breath. "I don't want to put a name on my feelings for you, Jacqui—not just yet. But I know that I want you in my life and not at a distance."

"How many jobs are there in Manhattan, or Chicago, for wildlife biologists? There must be some, but can I get one?" She paused. "All the same, I'm not sure that I want to move." She paused again and reached for one of his hands. She linked her fingers through his and Gavin knew they fit together perfectly. "Is it crazy to be thinking of a commitment after only a few days?" She kissed the back of his hand. "I want to try, though. I want you. Is there some way we can make this work?"

"What if I moved to Colorado?" he asked.

"You'd do that for me?"

"I'd do anything for you, Jacqui. Just tell me that you want me."

She reached for his other hand and brushed her lips across his knuckles. "I do want you, Gavin Colton." Then, she pressed her lips on his. The kiss was glorious and yet, his mouth was still tender.

Had he winced?

She ended the embrace. "Wow. Everything on you is sore."

"It is. But there are some interesting parts that you can kiss and make better if you want…"

She glanced at him from the corner of her eye. "We do seem to have a knack for getting each other into trouble," she said.

"And keeping each other safe," he added. "There are a lot more adventures out there for the two of us, you know."

She nodded. "Let's do it. There's nobody else I want to be with on my next adventure than you."

He lifted his cup. "Let's make it official with a toast. To us. To adventures."

She touched the rim of her cup to his with a clink. "To the beginning," she said, "of our very own happily-ever-after."

"You know," said Gavin, "I couldn't have said it better myself."

* * * * *

COMING SOON!

We really hope you enjoyed reading this book.
If you're looking for more romance, be sure to
head to the shops when new books are
available on

Thursday 13th October

To see which titles are coming soon, please visit
millsandboon.co.uk/nextmonth

MILLS & BOON

THE HEART OF ROMANCE

A ROMANCE FOR EVERY READER

MODERN
Prepare to be swept off your feet by sophisticated, sexy and seductive heroes, in some of the world's most glamourous and romantic locations, where power and passion collide.

HISTORICAL
Escape with historical heroes from time gone by. Whether your passion is for wicked Regency Rakes, muscled Vikings or rugged Highlanders, awake the romance of the past.

MEDICAL
Set your pulse racing with dedicated, delectable doctors in the high-pressure world of medicine, where emotions run high and passion, comfort an love are the best medicine.

True Love
Celebrate true love with tender stories of heartfelt romance, from the rush of falling in love to the joy a new baby can bring, and a focus on th emotional heart of a relationship.

Desire
Indulge in secrets and scandal, intense drama and plenty of sizzling hot action with powerful and passionate heroes who have it all: wealth, statu good looks…everything but the right woman.

HEROES
Experience all the excitement of a gripping thriller, with an intense romance at its heart. Resourceful, true-to-life women and strong, fearless face danger and desire - a killer combination!

To see which titles are coming soon, please visit

millsandboon.co.uk/nextmonth

LET'S TALK
Romance

For exclusive extracts, competitions
and special offers, find us online:

Get in touch on 01413 063232

JOIN US ON SOCIAL MEDIA!

Stay up to date with our latest releases, author news and gossip, special offers and discounts, and all the behind-the-scenes action from Mills & Boon...

 @millsandboon

 @millsandboonuk

 facebook.com/millsandboon

 @millsandboonuk

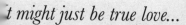

t might just be true love...

GET YOUR ROMANCE FIX!

Get the latest romance news,
exclusive author interviews, story
extracts and much more!

MILLS & BOON
Desire

Indulge in secrets and scandal, intense drama and plenty of sizzling hot action with powerful and passionate heroes who have it all: wealth, status, good looks…everything but the right woman.

MILLS & BOON
MEDICAL
Pulse-Racing Passion

Set your pulse racing with dedicated, delectable doctors in the high-pressure world of medicine, where emotions run high and passion, comfort and love are the best medicine.

MILLS & BOON
True Love
Romance from the Heart

Celebrate true love with tender stories of heartfelt romance, from the rush of falling in love to the joy a new baby can bring, and a focus on the emotional heart of a relationship.